The Humiliations of Pipi McGee

Beth Vrabel

RP|KIDS
PHILADELPHIA

To Collinsville Spoken Word, and to Emma, a poet it nourished.

Running Press Kids
Hachette Book Group
1290 Avenue of the Americas, New York, NY 10104
www.runningpress.com/rpkids
@RP_Kids

Printed in the United States of America

First Edition: September 2019

Published by Running Press Kids, an imprint of Perseus Books, LLC, a subsidiary of Hachette Book Group, Inc. The Running Press Kids name and logo is a trademark of the Hachette Book Group.

The Hachette Speakers Bureau provides a wide range of authors for speaking events. To find out more, go to www.hachettespeakersbureau.com or call (866) 376-6591.

The publisher is not responsible for websites (or their content) that are not owned by the publisher.

Print book cover and interior design by Frances J. Soo Ping Chow and Christopher Eads

Library of Congress Control Number: 2018945859

ISBNs: 978-0-7624-9339-5 (hardcover), 978-0-7624-9340-1 (ebook)

LSC-C

10 9 8 7 6 5 4 3 2 1

Chapter One

This year would be different.

I was sure of it.

"Welcome, students!" Principal Hendricks raised her arms in a cheer from her spot on the auditorium stage. Her red power suit gleamed in the spotlight. "We're so excited to have you back at Northbrook Middle School!"

Next to me, my best friend Tasha pretended to puke into her backpack.

"Stop it." I elbowed her. "This year is going to be different."

Tasha raised her eyebrow. She had the best you're-unbelievable look aside from my mom, whose facial expressions were expert level.

"I mean it, Tasha." I folded my hands on my lap and pasted a smile on my face, despite feeling Tasha's stare burn into me.

"You curled your hair, didn't you?" Tasha asked.

My shoulder-length brownish-blond hair was naturally wavy, but only parts of it. Most of it was stick straight. So, picture chunks of straight hair with random curlicues. Normally, I deal with it, shoving it back into a ponytail and moving on with my life. But this year was going to be different. This year, I'd do what Mom was always yakking about—*Take time with your appearance, Pipi. Make an effort.* I'd wake up fifteen minutes early every day and curl my hair so it'd all be bouncy and exciting, like my brand-new, different self.

Now both of Tasha's eyebrows were peaked. She pulled on one of my curls and then watched it bounce back. "Every year, you start off like an innocent little lamb thinking this time, everything's going to be so new and grand. Every year, I've got to come pry you out of the bathroom stall you're crying in by the end of September."

"That's not fair." I crossed my arms. "You know perfectly well that everything that has happened to me *was not my fault.*"

"Mm-hmm."

"Tasha!"

"*Pipi!*"

I glanced around, holding up my hands. "That's one of the things that's going to be different this year. I'm not going by Pipi anymore. I'm Penelope."

Tasha closed her eyes and shook her head. This time, I guess facial features weren't enough to convey her thoughts. "You're unbelievable."

"I've been Pipi McGee for four years—"

"Yep, ever since you—"

"Don't say it!" I put my hand over Tasha's mouth and she batted my arm away. Tasha crossed her own arms and stared at me. "Sorry," I mumbled. "But just, please. Don't say it. I mean it, this year's going to be different."

"Whatever." Tasha shifted in her seat and slipped earbuds into her ears. She thumbed at her audiobook app.

"That again?" I pointed to the picture of the book cover on the app. "Haven't you got the whole thing memorized?"

"'Course, I do." Tasha grinned. "But the final installment—*Crow Reaper: Reaping Death*—releases next week. Just enough time to listen to the first book."

I sighed.

Tasha shook her head, her long braids rustling against each other. "Uh-uh. No judgment, Pi—*Penelope*. You might be changing. I'm staying the same."

I glanced at Tasha, who closed her eyes as she listened, and I knew that wasn't exactly true. While each year I somehow managed to stay right where I was on the social hierarchy of Northbrook Middle School (the bottom rung)—always due to some unfortunate event *that was never my fault*—Tasha bumped up a few pegs.

That wasn't even true, really. She built her own ladder. Her ridiculously overachieving brain and athleticism put her in a league of coolness totally of her own, despite being totally obsessed—to the point of dress up—with a book series about a demon-hunting boy whose brother turned into a crow. And then there was the fact that she was gorgeous, tall and athletic with dark brown skin and eyes.

3

Principal Hendricks's smile seemed to stretch the auditorium. "As you know, this is my first year as principal of Northbrook Middle. As such, we're going to kick off things a little differently."

"Told you." I nudged Tasha, who just shook her head and bumped up the volume on her phone. My nose tickled, so I sat on my hands, keeping my smile firmly in place. I never touch my nose if I can help it. It's my least favorite feature. Plus, the whole first-grade thing . . .

My smile was smacked straight off my face when Frau Jacobs, the seventh-grade Intro to Languages teacher, shuffled forward and whispered in Principal Hendricks's ear.

Remember that part in *Harry Potter* where the old lady was actually a snake? Like the giant snake was just living inside the old lady's skin? I'm pretty sure J. K. Rowling must've met Frau Jacobs when she thought about that snake lady.

Frau Jacobs was about five feet, two inches tall, all sweet smiles and curly brown hair. She smelled like freshly baked cookies and clasped her hands together in delight while verbally carving your soul into confetti. Even though she was probably the same age as my dad, she looked like grandma material. Which, strictly speaking, also includes my dad.

Principal Hendricks's red lipsticked smile wavered a little at whatever Frau Jacobs whispered in her ear. Slowly, Frau Jacobs backed away and sat down, a satisfied little smile on her face.

"Yes, well, before I begin with what we're doing *differently* this year," (I didn't even bother to elbow Tasha this time) "the other teachers and I would like to remind you all about the dress code." A low rumbly groan rippled over the auditorium. Principal Hendricks held up her hand. I swallowed down the sour taste that flooded my mouth whenever I saw Frau Jacobs.

"Okay, girls. No exposed shoulders. No low-cut blouses. No tank tops. No leggings without a top that goes to mid-thigh. No shorts that are higher than finger length when your arms are by your side." Principal Hendricks rattled off the dress code like a grocery list. Behind her, Frau Jacobs cleared her throat. Principal Hendricks turned halfway toward her, listening to whatever she muttered, then turned back with a tight smile. "Frau Jacobs would like to add a few words."

My breath seeped out, and I fought the urge to cover my ears.

"Yes, *ladies*. As the famous soprano Frau Greta Mila von Nickel was fond of saying . . . well, I can't actually repeat it because even in German, an insult is an insult. But it comes down to this, ladies: each of us has an inner swine-dog that we must vanquish."

Principal Hendricks cleared her throat. Frau sighed and continued, "None of you are, of course, swine-dogs. It's an imperfect translation. In any case, remember you are here to learn. Not to be caught unawares at the distraction you are causing among others. I *will* dress-code you. I *do* expect you to be ready to learn at all times while you're here in this building, prepared and ready without excuse." I pulled up my knees and burrowed my head into them. Tasha, earbuds removed, stirred a little closer to me and hissed something under her breath about Frau shutting her pie hole.

Frau Jacobs smiled at all of us. "And, *gentlemen,* be clean and neat." She looked over the audience full of students, as though expecting applause.

Principal Hendricks stood back in front of the microphone as Frau Jacobs returned to her seat. "You likely don't remember that, at the beginning of kindergarten, you drew portraits of what you hoped your future selves would be, what you would look like at the end of middle school. Today, we're going to reveal those wonderful portraits and see how far you've come in seizing your dreams!"

Something cold crackled through my chest. My fingers stretched out and squeezed Tasha's knee.

She pulled out an earbud again. "What?"

"Bad," I muttered.

"How bad?" Tasha bit her lip. "Like, fourth-grade bad?"

I didn't answer.

Tasha's eyes turned to marbles. She looked toward Frau Jacobs, then back at me. "Pipi—is this *seventh-grade* bad?"

I didn't answer.

I didn't talk about seventh grade.

Ever.

My eyes darted around the room. No way could they show everyone's kindergarten portrait. There were, like, two hundred kids in my class. The lights dimmed and a screen lit up.

"No, no, no, no, *no*."

Tasha looked at the screen, her mouth stretching into a relieved smile. "Come on, Pipi. It can't be that bad. All of the drawings are goofy." Flashing across the screen were scribbly sketches of big bobblehead humanoids next to the artist's seventh-grade school picture. A few people laughed at Robert Andrew's portrait—a giant head with arms and legs stretching out of it.

Now, maybe most people don't remember their kindergarten self-portraits. Not me. How could I forget my first humiliation? Miss Simpson had held up my drawing in front of everyone, her face screwed up and red from holding in her laughter, as she told us to remember "sometimes the best thing to do when we make mistakes is to use an eraser or start over. *Don't* just keep going."

I bit my lip to keep from screaming. My eyes scoured the crowded auditorium. Maybe no one would be paying attention. No such luck. Everyone stared up at the screen with little grins. Each time a new portrait appeared, a little cooing sound would bubble up from spots in the crowd and everyone around that person would *ooh* and *aah*.

This was a disaster!

Three rows ahead of me, Ricky Salindo half twisted in his seat. When his eyes locked with mine, he quickly looked away. He remembered my kindergarten portrait, too.

I whimpered. Tasha elbowed me.

When I could be sure I could speak without screeching, I said, "There are two hundred kids in our grade. They won't get to everyone, right?"

Tasha shrugged. "Two hundred and nineteen kids. Pictures are up for about three seconds, so it'd take six hundred fifty-seven seconds to get through everyone, or roughly ten minutes. And probably ten percent of the student body moved here after kindergarten." My best friend has one of those super quick, bizarrely accurate math brains. I do not. "Oh!" she squealed. "It's me!"

Tasha's kindergarten portrait flashed on the screen. She had a red triangle dress, with brown arms and legs peeking out from the sides. Her hair was a lighter brown puff around her head. In careful writing, she had written her name, *Tasha Martins,* under her picture. She looked adorable and somehow exactly as I remembered her from when we first met, thanks to standing in alphabetical order in line for bathroom breaks. She had drawn herself holding a stack of books.

So cute. Alphabetical order. That meant I'd be—

It was worse than I remembered.

Let me set the scene, heading back in time eight years to tiny, poor Kindergarten Penelope dooming her future self.

Five-year-old Penelope sat at her table with colored pencils and crayons in a Tupperware container in front of her. She thought about her future self, what the Penelope of Eighth

Grade would be like. She drew a pink face and yellow hair. And then Miss Simpson said, "Now, class, think about what you really, really love in life. And then think about all the choices you'll get to make when you're a big thirteen- or fourteen-year-old middle schooler!"

What do I really love in life? Kindergarten Penelope really loved bacon.

Sweet, innocent Penelope was so proud of her drawing. Then Miss Simpson made her trying-not-to-laugh face. And she held up the drawing and everyone in the classroom laughed. Kara Samson said something about Penelope being a sillyhead.

Penelope stood up and screamed that she was *not* a sillyhead, and someday she *would* be bacon, and then Kara would be sorry.

Miss Simpson talked then about fantasy versus reality and that no one could grow up to be bacon. But she was wrong, Kindergarten Penelope vowed, and wrote in careful letters: *Penelope WILL be bacon.* And then Penelope screamed that she would be drippy and delicious one day, and kicked Miss Simpson's shin.

I remembered everyone's faces, all twisty and eyes squinty, their hands covering their mouths as they whispered and laughed. My own face had flushed so red I could see it flaming.

It looked like . . . well, it looked exactly like what was happening right now, this very second. Because it was happening all over again.

"No!" Tasha gasped as the portrait took shape on the screen. She wrapped her arm around my shoulder and squeezed. "Pipi. Pipi, why did you put boobs on the bacon?"

"Because it's older me," I whimpered and looked down at my still mostly flat chest.

I was too numb to react. Just stared at the screen, both reliving my first humiliation and then experiencing it fresh all over again.

Know how long it takes for the entire eighth grade to turn on a kid?

Three seconds.

First it was a buzz. Then a guffaw. Next laughter.

"It's Pipi McGee!" someone a few rows behind me called out.

"Sizzling hot!" shouted someone else.

Tasha jumped to her feet. "Shut it! Leave her alone!" Tasha pointed to Wade Michaels, a meathead jock who was laughing loudest. "Your drawing had ears bigger than your head, Meatlobe." Wade covered his ears with his hands and closed his mouth. Tasha jabbed a finger in nasty-laughing Patricia Reynolds's direction. "And, you! You didn't even draw a body, Patricia. You were just a blob girl. A *blob girl*." Patricia rolled her eyes but stopped laughing.

When I grow up I wanna be Bacon

Still standing, Tasha turned to me as the people around us finally quieted. "Don't listen to them, Pipi," she said. "Everyone loves bacon!"

"*Especially booby bacon,*" Wade called in a wheezy laugh. And the auditorium erupted again.

"It's fine," Tasha whispered as she sat back down. "I'm sure everyone will forget soon."

"*Booby bacon! Booby bacon! Booby bacon!*" the class chanted.

"It's okay," I whispered back. I grabbed my backpack and pulled it up my arm. "It's me. I'm a walking embarrassment."

"That's not true."

"It's like Kara Samson said last year. I'm a virus." I wiped at the pathetic wetness on my cheeks. "I'll be in my office. The third stall."

"Oh, Pipi," Tasha said. "It's not even September."

I shimmied past her, my head ducked low.

"Now, now," Principal Hendricks said from the front of the room as I exited, interrupting the slideshow. "Isn't it wonderful to see how far we've all come?"

"Booby bacon! Booby bacon! Booby bacon!" chanted the crowd, led once again by Kara Samson.

So much for this year being different.

Just like every other year, eighth grade was going to be an education in public humiliation.

Chapter Two

"I'm sure it wasn't *that* bad." Mom sat across from me at the kitchen island.

When I didn't answer, without looking she grabbed a brownie from the tray between us and shoved it into her mouth. Mom, a fitness instructor, almost never ate sugar. She only wore leggings that molded to her toned legs and tank tops that showed off the way her lean arms rippled with muscles. Her constant ready-to-go-for-a-run attire was in contrast to the way her dark brown hair with blond highlights was always styled perfectly and her makeup was always perfectly done.

Since opening her gym downtown, Mom said she had to protect her "brand" and "look the part." But every now and then she'd bake treats for special occasions—such as the first day of school—that weren't made from black beans and agave nectar. She always tried not to sample them and was usually pretty successful.

This time, as soon as the sugar hit her tongue, her fitness-instructor self turned into someone just interested in fittin' sugar into her mouth.

Alec, my stepdad, smiled at the back of Mom's head from where he leaned against the counter. Alec's always doing that, smiling at Mom like everything she does is wonderful, even shoving a brownie into her mouth. He saw me looking at him and winked. I tried to smile back, but it was wobbly. Then Alec wasn't smiling but looking at me with concern.

While Mom was all spandex and lipstick, Alec was suits and polish. He was about six feet tall, almost always either in a suit or a white button-down shirt. He worked as a financial adviser; that's how he and Mom met, back when she was finalizing details for opening her gym.

They were so in love it was disgusting.

Alec pushed off the counter and planted a kiss on the top of Mom's head. She handed him a brownie, and he shook his head. Mom shoved it into her own mouth without a second glance, then pushed the tray toward me.

It was kind of funny—Alec was pretty much the exact opposite of my dad, who was a soft, pale Irishman with thinning red hair and a potbelly, and who was more than ten years older than Mom. Meanwhile, Alec was a tall, broad black man with abs that rivalled Mom's. He was also about ten years *younger* than Mom, which was a topic she never wanted to discuss.

Speaking of my dad, he stretched out his hand to pat my arm. "Was it *that* bad, Penelope?" (Yeah, he was there, too. The divorce happened about five years ago, and honestly it wasn't all that traumatic. So much had been happening then at our house that Dad going from sleeping on the couch like he had since I could remember to sleeping in his own apartment didn't seem like a big deal. He and Mom might not have stayed *in* love, but they still loved each other and loved us. Dad even seemed to really like Alec; they played racquetball together in Mom's gym a couple afternoons a week.)

Dad was a newspaper reporter and had a way of asking questions that made you start blabbing even if you didn't want to. I nodded. "I think it ranks about third on The List."

"The List?" Alec asked.

"The List of Humiliations of Pipi McGee," supplied my older sister, Eliza. She placed a brownie on a little plate and handed it to Annie. "It's long and pathetic."

I nodded.

Annie glanced at Mom, who smiled, and then Annie dug in. Eliza's mouth set into a hard line at the silent exchange, but she didn't say anything.

I should probably explain this a little more before moving on with my story. Annie is actually Eliza's daughter—my sister had her when she was sixteen years old. It really messed Eliza up for a long time. Now, Annie was four and a half, and Eliza was a lot stronger as a person—she is about to graduate college (mostly through taking online courses at a local university) and has a job at a makeup shop next to Mom's gym. But for the first few years after Annie was born, Eliza was in pretty bad shape emotionally. Mom was the one who really took care of

Annie, getting up in the middle of the night to feed her, singing her silly songs, and teaching her how to use the bathroom. You know, mom stuff. Annie even calls Mom "MomMom" and Eliza, well, "Eliza," even though Eliza does most of the mom stuff now.

"Remember my humiliations when you have to do your self-portrait," I said to Annie.

"How was your first day of preschool?" Dad asked Annie to try to change the subject.

She shrugged. "We had to eat Joe's slop for lunch."

"Sloppy Joes," Eliza corrected. Annie sighed.

Annie was what a lot of people called an old soul. She had wide green eyes and my hair color, but hers was styled in a little pixie cut after an incident where she played barber in the bathroom with a pair of cuticle scissors. (Amazing how much damage cuticle scissors could do, especially if you cut your hair straight down the middle.) I had a pixie cut once, thanks to Vile Kara Samson, but Annie's hairstyle was much cuter. She had Eliza's perfect heart-shaped face. Picture a delicate angel—blue eyes, blond hair, pretty little nose, and dainty little features. That's Eliza. Like, *so* pretty that people bumped into each other on the street when she walked by, hoping she'd bless them with a smile or something. Or, at least, that's how she used to be. Now the first thing you'd see when Eliza walked by was her stop-sign scowl. Think, I don't know, of an avenging angel who might smite you for no reason at all.

Turning back to me, Alec said, "It can't be that bad, Pipi."

Dad turned to the side and raised his eyebrow. Mom eyed another brownie. "Come on!" Alec glanced at all of us.

"Pipi pees her pants," Annie said.

"That is *not* true!" I slammed my hands on the counter. "I *peed* my pants. Once." I looked to Alec. "That's the fourth-grade entry." His eyes widened and I knew he was doing the math, figuring out that fourth graders are at least nine years old and definitely shouldn't be peeing their pants. "And ever since, everyone—even my own *family*—has called me Pipi."

"It's catchy," Dad said. Eliza nodded.

I sighed.

"Okay," Alec said. "So, you had an accident in fourth grade and in kindergarten, you drew yourself as a breakfast meat—"

"With boobs," I added.

Alec continued, "How bad could the rest be?"

"Bad," Eliza said.

"Real bad," Mom added.

Alec crossed his arms. He and Mom had been married only a year, and apparently the courtship didn't include a rundown of her daughter's pathetic nature. Mom sighed. "It's like this: every year, something happens to Pipi. Something awful. And then that event is like the sun—everything else that happens to her that year revolves around the event."

Alec nodded. "Sounds a bit like a self-fulfilling prophecy. You think something bad will happen, so as soon as something bad happens, it becomes that thing."

I blinked at him.

"So, maybe," he continued, his eyes drifting toward Dad and back, "it's not that whatever happened is all that bad. You're just so prepped for it to be awful that no matter what it is, it's inflated to feel that much worse."

"Eh." Dad cleared his throat. I used to go with him on story assignments when I was a little kid. Reporters don't make a lot of money, and neither do fitness instructors, so I'd tag along if my grandparents couldn't watch me. This "eh" wasn't just a casual throat-clearing thing. This was a reporter tactic of Dad's. It was questioning someone's comment without straight-out casting doubt.

Sure enough, Dad pulled his reporter's notebook from his back pocket. "Let's go over the facts."

I grabbed the notebook and a pen from him and flipped to a blank page. I spoke as I wrote, "Kindergarten, drew myself as bacon with boobs, thanks to poor instructions from Miss Simpson."

"Another thing you'll notice," Eliza piped in, "is that it's never Pipi's fault, whatever happened. It's *always* someone else's."

I stuck my tongue out at her. Annie giggled.

"First grade." I scrawled a number one on the page and wrote *class picture* next to it. "My nose itched on the inside during the class picture. It was *just* an itch!" It itched again, just thinking about it, but I ignored it.

Mom was the one giggling now. She reached into a kitchen cabinet, way to the back, and pulled out a mug with my picture on it—one of those gifts you can order along with school pictures. And there I was, forever immortalized with my finger up my nose.

"Must've been quite an itch." Alec laughed. "Your finger's up to the knuckle."

My chin popped up. "Vile Kara Samson had a lot of hairspray in her hair. A lot. It irritated my nasal passage. Anyway, I was *not* a nose picker. I swear! But all of first grade, no one would invite me to sleep over or to play after school because I had 'boogie fingers.'" For months after that, I'd fall asleep rubbing my nose like I could somehow smudge it right off my face. Now, I never touched my nose if at all possible. It didn't help, of course, that my nose was long and wide.

I drew a number two for second grade. Next to it, I wrote *vomit-a-thon*. Eliza shuddered.

"Do I want to know?" asked Alec, reading the paper upside down.

"It was the second week of school. My allergies—again!—were bothering me on the bus. I coughed, and it led to a little throw-up. It wouldn't have been so bad if Sarah Trickle hadn't turned around to hand me a tissue. I sprayed her with Eggo."

"It was like dominos," said Dad, his mustache awfully twitchy for discussing something traumatic. "The bus driver called the office and said all the parents had to pick up their kids. Sarah Trickle must've let loose on the kid next to her. The next person puked on the person in front of him, on and on. Only one kid—Ricky Salindo—was vomitless. Steel stomach, that kid."

"And," I said, "every time Kara Samson so much as looked at me that year, she'd make gagging sounds. Like my face was a finger down her throat. She wasn't even on the bus! And since she's Vile Kara Samson that meant everyone else followed her lead. Can you imagine that? Everyone gagging when they see you? Even Sarah Trickle gagged around me."

Vile Kara Samson. Ugh. Picture a tall, curvy girl with long brown hair. A smile with full lips and perfectly straight white teeth. Blue eyes that always look mean, even while blinding a person with that perfect smile. The girl no one actually likes but whom everyone desperately wants to like them. She's paper-cut mean—leaving a sting that seems to go away, but brings tears to your eyes all over again as soon as it's reopened.

And joined at her hip was Sarah Trickle. Kara and Sarah, don't you just want to puke? (Don't—it has lifelong social ramifications.) They're cousins, and their moms are twins, so they practically are twins, too. But no one would mistake them as being identical. Sarah was everything Kara wasn't—quiet and kind, like a little doll with a tiny little smile. She wore her long red hair in braids down the sides. Everyone wanted to be Sarah nearly as much as they wanted Kara's approval. And Sarah was constantly trying to show that Kara wasn't as vile as she made everyone think. "She didn't mean it like that" and "She's just joking around" and "That's just Kara, just how she is" were phrases constantly dripping from Sarah's lips.

Mom pushed the brownie tray toward Annie and Eliza. "Well, when it comes to Sarah, it really wasn't her fault, lovey."

"Yeah," Dad said, "you should've seen her get off the bus. Head to toe covered in vomit. You really sprayed her."

Annie pushed the brownie tray back. "That's disgusting."

"Second grade also led to," I lowered my voice, "The Touch."

"The Touch?" Alec echoed.

Mom handed Annie a napkin. "Sort of like tag, but Pipi's always 'It.' If anyone touches her, they have to pass The Touch on to someone else."

Alec whistled low. "That's awful."

"Moving on. Third grade." I wrote *basketball mistake* next to the number.

Eliza snorted. "Pipi made the first basket of her entire life. For the wrong team."

"That's not *that* big of a deal," Alec mused.

I crossed my arms. "It was the boys versus girls match. Girls were ahead. *I'm* the reason they lost. Even the principal heckled me. I'm *still* picked last every gym class. Whenever someone makes a ridiculous sports mistake, it's called making a McGee. It was a big deal."

Alec grabbed a brownie.

Fourth grade. I wrote *peepee* beside it.

Mom patted my hand.

Without looking up, I said, "My zipper was stuck. And Kara Samson refused to get me help."

"For months, they called her PeePee McGee," Eliza added. "Now it's just Pipi."

"*Penelope.* This year, I'm going back to Penelope," I said. I wrote *Jackson Thorpe* on the paper next to the number five. My voice was super light as I said, "Some of the girls played a trick on me. I thought Jackson liked me. He didn't." I ran my hand along my neck, feeling how long my hair had grown since fifth grade. Dad sighed. His mouth was set in a line, but he didn't say anything. Alec didn't either. Mom muttered a nasty word under her breath.

"Sixth grade. Makeover issues," I mumbled.

Eliza laughed, and Mom stomped on her foot. To Alec, Mom said, "Turns out eyebrows take a long, long time to grow back."

"Eyebrow," I corrected as I wrote a seven on the next line.

Mom and Dad stiffened. Even Eliza didn't say a word.

Alec said, "Wh—"

"We don't talk about seventh grade," Mom cut him off.

Alec closed his mouth, realization dawning on him as he remembered. After a moment, he said, "But, Pipi, everyone has things like this happen to them. All of us have. I went to class once with two different shoes on, totally different pairs of sneaks. People busted me for weeks. But we move on."

"My list isn't like that," I insisted.

21

"The thing is," Dad said, still in his reporter's voice, "this is your last year in middle school. Next year, you'll be in high school. There are how many middle schools that funnel into that one building?"

"Five," I answered.

"Right, and each of those schools has about two to two hundred fifty kids. So *most* of the kids you're going to meet next year won't know Pipi McGee as the girl who picks her nose, pees her pants, pukes on her friends, and draws herself as bacon with . . . you know. You get a fresh start. A clean slate."

I slumped over in my seat with a groan. "No, instead I'll get . . . like . . ." I wish I could do math in my head like Tasha. Instead, I guesstimated. "A thousand people who can jump in on the fun of humiliating Pipi McGee."

"I'm sure it's not that bad," Alec muttered. Mom coughed on her bite of brownie.

"Someone tripped getting off the bus this morning," I said. "He recovered, straightened himself up, and said, 'Nearly pulled a McGee there.' My name is a synonym for doing ridiculous stuff. It's *that* bad." I swiped a fingerful of frosting from the pan and shoved it into my mouth in despair. "I'm going to be a laughingstock for the rest of my life."

Alec put his elbows on the counter next to Dad. "Or," he said slowly, "you can do things differently. Make a change."

Dad nodded. "This thing today that happened? That's, eh, not a *new* embarrassment. It's an old one you're just feeling again. So, nothing really happened this year, right?"

"Stop feeling sorry for yourself. If you don't like the way things are, change them," Eliza snapped. "Make it better."

Mom nodded.

"You guys act like changing is easy. That's not the way it works."

Everyone in the room except for Annie stood up. Each of them crossed their arms. Mom raised her eyebrow. "Look around, Pipi."

I scanned the kitchen. My plump dad was standing next to a much younger, much hotter stepdad in the same kitchen with Mom, who went from teaching classes at the YMCA to owning her own gym, across from my sister who had a baby at age sixteen and was soon going to be a college graduate. Okay, so maybe I wasn't going to get a lot of sympathy from this crowd on how hard it was to make some changes.

But the thing was, while their hurdles might have been a lot bigger than mine, that didn't mean mine weren't steep.

How do you stop being a joke? I was a literal joke in my school. Except for Tasha and maybe sometimes Ricky, no one saw *me* when they saw me. They saw Pipi McGee and waited for me to do something ridiculous so they could keep right on laughing. I didn't even know what I could be known for aside from a social virus.

I ripped out the sheet from the reporter's notebook, folded it in half, and put it in my pocket.

I paced around my bedroom, trying to get my thoughts to flow in a steady current instead of in thousands of ripples.

My room wasn't exactly a sanctuary for clear thinking. It used to be Eliza's, but after Annie was born, we switched bedrooms. While her room (now my room) was bigger, my old room had a door that opened to the smaller guest room. Mom had turned that smaller room into Annie's. When Eliza had this room, she had painted the ceiling a light blue and had darker blue walls. I added big white fluffy clouds across the ceiling when I moved in. Hanging down, attached by clear fishing line, were birds. My birds. I started making them in fifth grade, I think. I molded them with papier-mâché and painted them in super bright colors like teal, orange, and purple. Each one took a super long time to make, which is probably why I started doing it. When I'm making them, I'm not thinking about what everyone else is doing without me or saying about me.

Here's something no one knew: when you lifted the wings of each bird, no matter how small they were, you'd find a little compartment. I hid beads or pretty stones in there like a secret. I liked the idea that there was more to them than people thought.

Mom, Dad, and Alec were always on me to make the birds for art class. Alec even said he'd rent a stand at the arts festival for me to sell them, but I liked having my little flock around me. I was running out of ceiling space, though. Near the end of the first semester, Northbrook Middle School held a talent show. A little bit of me—small enough to fit into one of the bird's hidden compartments—thought about showing one of my creations at the show as my official talent.

Today, though, I ignored the birds, not even glancing at them as I closed the door to my room. People would only laugh at them so long as I was Pipi McGee, aka middle school laughingstock. I stopped in front of the giant corkboard over my desk. I ripped off the scraps of paper about last year's assignments, pictures of me and Tasha, and participation certificates from field day. Once everything was off the board, I reached into my pocket, smoothed out the sheet of paper, and tacked The List of Humiliations right in the center.

Dad was right. Alec was right. Mom was right. Even Eliza was right.

I picked up my phone. Tasha answered on the third ring. "What, your thumb's broken? Calls are for emergencies only.

I just got to the chapter where Finn realizes the truth about Maeve."

"This *is* an emergency!"

"Emergency like finding out your adopted mother is a witch?"

"This year's going to be different, Tasha."

"Yeah, yeah. You said that."

"I mean it. I have a plan. I mean, I've got the beginnings of a plan."

I heard a *whooshing* sound and knew Tasha was sitting up on her bed. "What kind of plan?"

"I'm going to right the wrongs of my early education. I'm going to set things right. When I enter high school next year, it will be with a clean slate. I, Pipi McGee, have a year of redemption ahead of me. No one is going to laugh at me. In fact, this year? *They*'re going to be the embarrassed ones."

Tasha breathed in and out deeply. "Maybe it's this book getting to me, but it sounds a little to me like you're talking about revenge."

"Redemption . . . revenge. I'll take what I can get. Are you in?"

"I'll be at your house in six and a half minutes."

"Are you quoting *The Count of Monte Cristo*?"

"No, Pipi. I'm quoting *my* favorite book. If you'd bother reading it, you'd know." Tasha sat up and crossed her arms. "Three years I tell you about this book and you have yet to even leaf through it. But, whatever. The point is, this isn't a plan. But maybe the plan is where Dantès lost his way, where he went full revenge instead of redemption. Maybe we should be looking for any opportunity and then take action instead of creating elaborate plots."

"So, it's not like I go in order, redeeming kindergarten, then first grade, then second—"

"Exactly!" Tasha bounced on the bed. "I'll be on the lookout, too. We'll cross-check. I'll hold you accountable and you'll seize any chance to leave the old whiny, sorry-for-herself Pipi behind."

I let the barb slip. "I take opportunities as they come. So long as one of them ends with Vile Kara Samson crying in a bathroom, it'll all be fine. Frau Jacobs, too. And Sarah Trickle, while we're at it."

Tasha's lips pressed together.

"What?" I said.

She shrugged and picked up the list where it lay between us. "Nothing." Tasha smoothed it on her knee. "I think this will work. Finn has to do this all the time in *Crow Reaper*. He prepares and puts himself out there, but he has to wait for the goblin he's hunting to make the first move. Then he cuts it down."

"Goblin? That could be a good Kara strategy. But are any of these goblins distractingly beautiful, super nice, and the girl everyone in the world wants to be?"

Tasha's eyes narrowed and the paper crumpled in her hand a little. "No. None of the goblins are Sarah Trickle. Because Sarah Trickle isn't a goblin. She's not even mean. She's freaking Mary Poppins, practically perfect in every way, and maybe, first opportunity you get, you should stop hating on the girl."

"She's Kara's best friend. That automatically makes her evil."

"You're *my* best friend. What does that make me?" Tasha snapped.

I blinked at her.

"Just because Kara and Sarah are friends doesn't mean they're the same. Besides, they're cousins. I wonder if they'd even *be* friends if they weren't family." Tasha sighed. "Is it possible your Sarah hatred is more because of Jackson Thorpe than Kara?"

I plucked the list from Tasha's hand and went to pin it back up on my corkboard. This wasn't the first time Tasha had tried to convince me that my hatred for Sarah Trickle was unwarranted. Someday she'd see. They'd all see. Sarah Trickle was also going down.

"Maybe I just want Little Miss Perfect to see the effects of her actions," I said, my voice so stiff and cold I sounded like Eliza. I even caught myself looking down my nose the way my sister often did. *"Maybe* I want Sarah Trickle to be the new Pipi McGee and *I'm* going to be the new Sarah Trickle. Ever think of that?"* And, as the new Sarah Trickle, *I'd* be the one Jackson Thorpe always seemed to revolve around.

Tasha stood, pushing her handbag up her shoulder. "Nah. I didn't think of that. I don't spend all my life thinking how badly I want to be someone—anyone—else. I happen to like being Tasha Martins. And I happen to like my best friend, Pipi, even if she can be an annoying brat more often than she isn't."

"Hey!" I said.

"Taking my opportunities when I see them." Tasha leaned against my desk next to the glass tank where Myrtle the Turtle peeked out at us.

Myrtle chewed a spinach leaf, her jaw working side to side like she was Tasha's backup, ready to start laying into me if Tasha let up. "If this is going to work, Pipi, you've got to stop feeling sorry for yourself all the freaking time."

Tasha jerked a thumb toward Myrtle, who snapped her head back into her shell. "You've got to put yourself out there. Get out of your own shell." She looked up at my birds. "Fly a little bit, maybe."

"You're really mixing up your metaphors." Now I was stuck thinking about a flying turtle bird and how I could create it. I shook my head. "But that whole put-yourself-out-there? It's

31

easy for you to say." Myrtle peeked out and moved backward toward the shelter of her water bowl.

"How do you figure that?" Tasha asked.

I crossed my arms. "Because you don't get scared. You just . . . I don't know. You just stand up for yourself. I don't do that. I don't know how."

Tasha's eyebrow popped up. "Easy? You think it isn't hard?" Her nostrils flared as she took a couple breaths. "You think I don't get scared? Don't have anything to lose?"

I swallowed. "Forget it, okay? Forget I said anything."

"No, I don't think I will." Tasha stood up straight.

"What's that supposed to mean?"

"How about *what I said*? I'm not forgetting about it. I don't *just stand up* for myself. I make myself stand." Tasha's eyes were slits. Her whole body tensed as she leaned toward me.

My heart hammered. I wanted to run, but this was my room and she was my best friend. "I don't know what I'm saying."

"So, think about it."

"That!" My hand jerked toward her. "Having something to say right away. *That* doesn't work for me. When I'm angry, when I'm embarrassed, I forget all my words," I finally managed. "When I'm upset, I sort of can't think of any words at all."

Tasha softened, her shoulders relaxing a little. "I know. But just grab the first ones that float in your head. Even if they're not the best words, they'll do. You just gotta stand up for yourself because, frankly, I'm tired of doing it for you."

I swallowed. Nodded. Standing up for me is sort of how Tasha and I became friends. I remembered in third grade, someone had pulled on one of her braids. Back then her hair reached the tips of her shoulders instead of flowing down her back to her waist the way it does now. This kid behind her had grabbed a braid and tugged.

That smile never left Tasha's face, even as her eyes narrowed. "Hands off my hair," she had said in a super calm, pleasant voice—the same one she would use to answer Ms. Fenton's math facts a couple minutes later. "Touch it again and I'll kick you in your privacy." The boy dropped the braid.

"Wow," I had whispered under my breath.

"What are you looking at?" Tasha asked, with that same eyebrow pop she was directing at me now.

"You. Being awesome," I had blurted.

"I didn't think you knew how to talk," the kid next to me said.

"'Course she can talk," Tasha snapped. "Mind your own business."

I had smiled. She had whispered, "It's really cool that you can talk." And we were friends. But that standing up for herself aspect never rubbed off on me. Time and time again, *she* was the one to tell people to knock it off when I was the one running to my official stall in the girls' bathroom.

Tasha sighed now and dropped her arms. "You know I love you. But, Pipi—"

"Penelope," I corrected.

She smiled. "*Penelope*. You want a fresh start? Want things to be different?" I nodded, feeling the corners of my eyes sting for no good reason. "Then *be* different. Take chances. Put yourself out there. Stop taking your cues from Myrtle."

"We've got this," I told Myrtle the next morning as I got ready for school. I caught myself rubbing my nose and shoved my hands into my pockets while I kept up the conversation with the turtle. Just because I wasn't going to be taking cues from Myrtle didn't mean we couldn't have a heart-to-heart once in a while. "We're not going to duck away from anyone or anything. We're going to find ways to redeem ourselves."

Myrtle dipped her cold-blooded face into her water bowl. Myrtle didn't care what I had to say. Myrtle didn't care about anything except being left alone. Like, if you walked by the aquarium while holding Myrtle, she'd press against your hands with her little legs as if she were trying to dig her way back to the glass enclosure.

I tossed in some carrot slivers and spinach leaves. "Starting today, we're open to opportunity, and the universe will provide."

Myrtle pooped a little in her water bowl.

"You're disgusting."

"Why are you talking to the reptile?" Annie asked. She only ever called Myrtle "the reptile." I'm not sure why.

"Why are you in my room?" I said instead of answering.

"Time to go." Annie was wearing a cardigan and holding her lunch box. Even though there was a day care at Mom's gym, Eliza had registered Annie to go to a preschool across town. It had "the rigor and expectations" Eliza said Annie needed, adding that the gym day care was too full of kids who spent the whole time they were in there pretending to be chickens and eating finger paint. If you asked me, Annie could use a little more time pretending to be a chicken and eating finger paint. Most of the time, it was hard to remember that she was a kid, because she was so serious. Even the little lunch box she had picked out looked more like a briefcase—black with a gray zipper—than something belonging to a four-year-old. I thought preschool for Annie should be about figuring out how to be a kid instead of acting like a mini adult, but no one asked me anything.

Annie stared up at the birds. She waved a little, with just her fingertips, then stared at me again.

I sighed, dumping Myrtle's water into the gravel around the dish and pouring in more water from the bottle beside my bed. I squirted antibacterial stuff on my hands and rubbed them together. "Fine."

Annie watched me with big hazel eyes while I shoved a book into my backpack and zipped it up. She cleared her throat. "MomMom says I shouldn't ask you why you drew yourself with bacon boobs."

"It's a long story," I said. "And it was an accident. And the boobs weren't bacon; *I* was the bacon. Besides, it happened a long time ago and no longer bothers me."

Annie blinked at me.

"I don't want to talk about it."

Annie nodded. "I don't like to talk about things, too."

"Like what?" I asked.

She blinked at me a couple more times. Then she sighed and said, "Mostly things I'm spying on, but also other stuff. Like that sometimes I can see my nose out of the corner of my eye when I'm trying to see something else, and then all I can do is see my nose and I can't stop. I see it right now, even though I'm looking at you."

This time I blinked at her.

"Girls!" Mom called. "We're going to be late!"

"And that we're all going to die someday," Annie added.

"Good talk, Annie."

Chapter Four

Tasha wasn't messing around with the whole universe-will-provide-when-you're-open-to-it concept.

During homeroom, the universe straight-up provided.

"All right, class," Mr. Harper called out shortly after the first bell. This in and of itself was unusual. Mr. Harper eased into the day, something we had all noticed last year when he taught seventh-grade social studies. Ricky was really the one who discovered a handy Mr. Harper hack—if you casually mentioned *The Great British Baking Show,* Mr. Harper's lesson would derail faster than a soufflé falls. The next hour would be devoted not to the Dust Bowl but instead to the harsh challenges of the Bread Bowl. It got to the point where even well-placed British slang meant we could all slouch back in our seats and grab our phones for some me-time before the next class.

Homeroom the day before had been mostly Mr. Harper telling us about the unappreciated art of biscuit towering, thanks to Ricky saying *cheerio* when Mr. Harper handed out a sheet of classroom expectations. And this was bloody convenient, as it gave me a moment to imagine snogging Jackson Thorpe.

Ah, Jackson Thorpe.

My deep, unrelenting love for Jackson Thorpe had begun at the tender age of eleven, when he stood beside the ladder as I climbed out of the swimming pool.

"Wow," he had said, his huge eyes the same blue as the overly chlorinated water. "Hope you're good."

That's how I chose to remember the interaction, anyway. (The actual rest of the sentence he had said was "at swimming so you can get away from Pipi's warm spot." The sentence, strictly speaking, had been directed to everyone *but* me. And everyone else had chanted *Pipi pee-peed in the pool.* Which I hadn't. Not that it mattered. No one would swim next to me the rest of the day, which meant just me and one other person in the far swim lane. It ended up being an okay day, I guess, all things considering.)

But, oh. Jackson Thorpe.

He sat on top of his desk now, his legs bent and feet on the seat. Five other guys, all of them basketball players like him, sat around his desk. Jackson's dark blond hair had been long and floppy last year. This year he was going for a close-cropped style. He had changed up his whole look, now that I made it past those blue eyes. He was wearing—I rubbed my eyes to make sure I was seeing real life—a black T-shirt. And black jeans. And black shoes. This was the dream outfit—the clothing he always wore in my dream sequence when he showed up on my front porch with a red rose and an overwhelming sense of guilt for the years he had spent laughing at me now that he suddenly realized I was actually his true love.

"Where's your jersey, man?" one of the basketball players asked.

They didn't know him like I knew him. No one did. No one else realized that Jackson reinvented himself every year. Last year, it was as a jock—soccer star, basketball star, baseball star. The year before that, in sixth grade, he was super into gaming, with a Minecraft shirt for every day of the week. By March, everyone who was anyone was playing on this elaborate server he had created to look exactly like the school. So, yeah, I was not part of the server, but I'm told there was a one-eyebrowed character who had a puddle of yellow around her. So, I guess I *was* sort of part of that experience.

This year, I guessed Jackson was still figuring stuff out. Whatever he ended up with would be incredible, I was sure of it.

The other guys were wearing their gold and navy basketball jerseys. "What do you mean you're not playing?" one of them said.

Jackson shrugged. "I'm not into it this year. I'm, I don't know, *evolving,* I guess. I spent a lot of time this summer thinking. You know, being philosphizable."

"Philosphizable?" one of the guys repeated. "You mean, philosophical?"

"Yeah. And *evolving.*"

"Evolving? What the—"

But then Jackson jumped to his feet and, in one fluid movement, pulled a notebook from the backpack leaning against the side of his desk. He flipped it open and slouched back against the desk with his feet crossed at the ankle.

"J. T.!" one of the other basketball players boomed. "What do you mean you're not playing?"

Jackson ignored him. Ignored everyone. Except for whoever just walked in. His eyes followed that person as she glided into the classroom.

Any guesses who?

Sarah Trickle. Perfect Sarah Trickle, with her perfect coppery red hair in two perfectly imperfect messy braids and her perfect little face with its perfect little freckles in perfect little constellations across her perfect tiny nose. Sarah Trickle was not even looking up from the tiny book in her tiny hands, with a perfect little smile as she read, not noticing how everyone in the entire classroom barely breathed as she moved past them in a perfect little vanilla-scented breeze. She was so cute, like a precious doll you'd cup in your hands and then put on a high shelf. I glanced down at my gnawed-on fingernails and my long legs bruised up from missing the pedal at Mom's spin class. I ran my hands across my hair; it felt like clumps of hay.

"What are you reading?" asked a girl named Patricia. She was always hanging around Vile Kara Samson and Sarah, like a sad little puppy hoping to be invited inside. Patricia yanked out her side pony and began whipping her hair into braids.

a steward of the community. This means volunteering. You and a partner will choose a place in which to volunteer throughout the first semester, so make sure you pick an organization that's important to you and one in which you feel you can make a difference." As he said this, Mr. Harper placed a slip of paper on each person's desk. Nope, that wasn't correct, I quickly realized. He put a slip of paper on each *girl's* desk. He glanced around when he got to Sarah's empty seat.

"She's in the bathroom," Jackson cut in.

Mr. Harper nodded, put down the paper, and continued. "By the time you finish high school, you'll be required to proactively help the community—see a need and fulfill it. That's a new requirement for your incoming freshman class. Think about joining—or even making—an organization or club that would enrich the school or wider community." He accidentally put two papers on my desk, so I handed one to Wade, sitting behind me, and motioned for him to pass it to Kara. "As an example, a group of new ninth graders created something called the Reckless Club, which focuses on ways to be inclusive."

Wade plucked the paper from my fingers and threw it onto Kara's desk. "You've got the Pipi Touch!" he shout-whispered.

I rolled my eyes.

Kara's mouth twisted as she picked up the paper. "Oh, grow up, Wade."

Wow, had Kara "Everybody Run, Pipi's Coming" Samson just stood up for me? Maybe some people can evolve. Maybe I wouldn't even need this whole redemption thing. I smiled at her in appreciation. But Kara didn't glance my way. The moment Wade turned back around, still with a cocky grin on his face, Kara pegged him on the shoulder. "Gotcha!" She laughed.

"No fair! No tag backs!" Wade groaned.

"Say it next time," Kara said.

I huffed out of my suddenly itchy nose and focused on Mr. Harper.

"When it's your turn to come up with a club, consider giving it a name that makes sense." Mr. Harper sighed. "Something direct."

"Oh," Ricky called out, his voice garbled by the muffin. "Like how *The Great British Baking Show* is just about British people baking."

Mr. Harper gasped. "It's about much more than that, Ricardo, which you'd understand if you watched. *And* I know you haven't because no one who has ever watched *The Great British Baking Show* would desecrate their bodies with a mass-produced lump of gluten disguised as a muffin." He shuddered and continued putting papers on girls' desks. "I'm passing out a list of places where you can volunteer," he said. "We've got exactly twelve boys and twelve girls in this class. How delightful! Girls, I've written the name of a boy who will be your partner on the page in front of you. Okay, *flip!*"

Universe! Tasha swore you'd provide. I'm counting on you! PROVIDE! I took a deep breath and flipped my paper, squishing shut my eyes and praying I'd see Jackson Thorpe's name across the top. Maybe I could make this Pipi Touch thing work to my advantage. He'd be my partner and we'd spend so much time together, he'd be forever Pipi Touch infected. We'd live alone on a little island, isolated but in love. We'd—

No such luck. *Ricky Salindo.* I sighed.

Ricky was nice and all—I'd known him since kindergarten, and he was one of the only people who had never ridiculed me. Even when he and Jackson were kind of friends, back in fifth grade during their gaming phase, Ricky never actually seemed to join in on the make-fun-of-Pipi train. They stopped being friends in seventh grade, though, when Jackson was going through his jock stage and picked up a bunch of new friends.

So, it wasn't a bummer that I was paired with Ricky. It was just a bummer that I wasn't paired with Jackson Thorpe. I knew down to my bones that he would someday realize I was the great love of his life.

I glanced over at Jackson Thorpe. He leaned a row over and snagged a sheet from Patricia's hands, trading it with the still unturned sheet on Sarah's desk.

"But . . ." Patricia muttered.

Jackson turned away from her as Sarah strode back into the room.

I walked slowly over to Ricky, plastering a smile on my face. "Looks like we're partners."

"Yep." He rolled up the wrapper to his muffin and tossed it into the bin a row of desks over. "Fight the enthusiasm."

"What?" I handed him the sheet, which included a list of places we could volunteer.

"Nothing," he muttered, but his ears were really red. "Okay, so, looks like we'll spend an hour every Tuesday and Thursday morning wherever we decide to go. Northbrook Retirement Home, the Met Food Pantry, Northbrook Primary Kindergarten—"

"Kindergarten!" I blurted, but it came out echoey. I looked around—Sarah and Jackson had both said kindergarten at the exact same time as me. *Thank you, Universe!*

That Thursday, Ricky sat next to me on the little bus heading to kindergarten. Mr. Harper arranged it so we could catch a ride on the kindergarten bus at the beginning of the day—which wasn't completely humiliating at all. Across from us was a little girl with thick, dark hair. She stared at us, barely even blinking, like Ricky and I were exotic animals in a traveling zoo exhibit.

"Just like old times," Ricky said. "Riding this bus, I mean. Only you're not wearing those little shoes with the buckles anymore."

The sun was streaming in the windows of the bus, making Ricky's black hair glow red along the edges. His smile was mostly just out of the corner of his mouth, and for a second he *did* look just like five-year-old Ricky. "You had on a Thor T-shirt," I said. "You wore it almost every day."

His smile stretched farther and he laughed, but mostly out of his nose, giving me a whiff of his peppermint gum. "Yeah. I was such a little weirdo."

I rolled my eyes. "I've got that department down, my friend."

Ricky shrugged. "All kindergarteners are weirdos." He gestured around the bus. We were in the second row. In front of us was a kid wearing a button-down shirt, his hair parted down the middle and slicked to the sides. The boy narrated everything the bus driver did as if he were a commentator in the Olympics watching an ice skater. "Now he's turning the wheel a *little* bit. Now his foot is pushing the pedal to the floor. The sun is shining in his eyes. He's muttering now for me to be quiet. Oh! Wow! Wheel's turning! Wheel's turning!"

"But some are more weirdo-ey than others." I laughed.

Ricky half smiled again, and his eyes narrowed. "Why did you want to volunteer in kindergarten so badly? I mean, you don't exactly look back fondly on that year."

I snorted. "I don't look back fondly on *any* year."

Ricky watched me, waiting for a longer answer. Should I tell him my plan? Tasha had said we were going to need to seize any opportunity. I had called her last night (despite her *why no text?* message). I told her how I was determined to scratch kindergarten off my list by the end of the day. To pull it off, Ricky could be useful.

"I just want . . ."

Ricky's eyebrows popped up.

". . . to make a difference," I finished. "To make sure no other little weirdo stays a weirdo beyond kindergarten."

"I dunno," Ricky said. "These guys seem to *like* being weirdos."

Narrator Kid raised his voice to be heard over the noise in the bus. "Now he's pushing forward the lever and we're braking, folks. We. Are. Braking."

"For now, maybe," I said as we gathered our backpacks and moved toward the aisle to exit the bus. Jackson Thorpe and Sarah Trickle were already by the school doors. Jackson had his hand on his chest and seemed to be reciting something—poetry, most likely—while little girls gathered around Sarah as if she were Snow White. "But, someday? They're going to want to be like those two."

Chapter Five

The first half of volunteering at the kindergarten was a blur—Miss Gonzalez, the teacher, put each of us in different positions around the room. Sarah had to get the kids out of their coats and show them how to hang the coats on their hooks. Jackson and Ricky were in charge of helping the kids do their "morning work" (today: coloring a picture of a tree). I was supposed to take lunch orders. This meant showing the kids pictures of different lunch options—ham sandwich, hamburger, or salad.

Miss Gonzalez told us that the first couple weeks of kindergarten were like herding kittens, but that the kids would get the hang of the system by the end of the month. She was optimistic, for sure, that Miss Gonzalez. Most of the kids couldn't even remember if they liked ham sandwiches.

A freakish number of them chose salad.

"Why would you pick a salad over a hamburger?" I asked one little girl. She had her hair in two pigtails and freckles covered her face.

She shrugged. "Croutons."

Behind her, three other kids in the salad line nodded solemnly.

"You're all choosing salad so you can eat the croutons?"

They nodded again. "And eat cheese," Pigtails said. "My sister is a second grader. She told us all about the croutons."

After the Pledge and a "meeting," during which three kids shared interesting facts about themselves (including that one of them has a dad whose breath smells like queso, leading to several minutes of excited exclamations of "queso breath!" "queso breath!"), Miss Gonzalez sent all of us out to a little courtyard "to burn off some energy."

"Aren't you coming?" Ricky asked Miss Gonzalez.

"No, I'm going to watch from the window." Then she muttered to us, "Tire them out. Please tire them out." I checked the clock. We had been there for only twenty-two minutes.

Remember the mission, I reminded myself as I surveyed the courtyard. *Redemption or revenge.* I sighed a little as I took in the scene. Already, in this first week of school, I could pinpoint who was the future Sarah Trickle. The little girl's hair was curled in long ringlets and her headband matched her tunic. Her running shoes had small bows that coordinated with her leggings. She looked like she had jumped out of an American Girl catalog as she stood in the middle of the playscape, laughing at something someone said. Five other little girls stood a distance back from her in a half circle. They also laughed, but mostly kept their eyes on the future Sarah Trickle, copying her pose when she bent at the waist and when she covered her mouth with her hands.

It was as easy to spot the future Jackson Thorpe. He was the stocky little boy with the spiky blond hair pumping his arms as he led the dozen or so kids chasing the actual Jackson Thorpe around the playscape. All of them wore athletic gear. All of them laughed like running was something enjoyable and like they barely noticed the attention they were getting, even as they wove directly between the girls.

And then there were the rest of the kids.

Somewhere among them was the future Pipi McGee, waiting for me to save her from her fate. Which one, which one?

I turned around and smacked straight into Pigtails.

"Do you have a dog?" she asked.

"What? Me? No. I, um, have a turtle, though,"

Pigtails's nose crinkled. "Someday I'm going to have a dog."

"Oh, yeah?" I asked. I spotted Ricky, sitting in the shade reading a thick book that was resting in his lap. Behind him, three kids stood in a strange, still formation. One had his foot sticking straight out, wobbling with a frozen smile on his face. Next to him, another boy stood with arms outstretched and stiff. A girl sat cross-legged on the ground between them, her eyes wide open as they glided side to side, making sure the other two weren't moving, either.

Ricky peeked up from his book and saw my confused face. "They're playing statue." He shrugged. "It's a game I made up with my little brothers and sister."

The foot-sticking-out kid fell to the side. "You lose, Marvin," Ricky said.

"Oh, come on!" Marvin pleaded. "Let me play again!"

"Oh, all right," Ricky said, the corner of his mouth twitching. "Just remember, no moving, no talking."

Marvin fell back into place.

I strode over to them, Pigtails shadowing me. "You're an evil genius," I told Ricky. "You know that, right?"

Ricky grinned, then looked back down at his book. "What are you looking for?" he asked as I scanned the playground again.

I chewed my lip. "You know, anyone who feels left out."

Ricky's mouth twitched. "What are you up to?"

"What do you mean?" I asked, keeping my voice light.

He folded over the corner of his page and closed the book. *Crow Reaper.*

"Hey, Tasha loves that book!" I said.

Ricky's forehead crinkled. "Yeah, I know. She recommended it."

I kept my eyes on the playground. Now the future Sarah Trickle was braiding the current Sarah Trickle's hair. Jackson and his crew ran circles around them.

"The stuff you were saying earlier," Ricky said, "about looking out for weirdos . . ."

Pigtails pulled on my shirt. "Someday I'm going to have a dog," she said again.

"Yeah, I know." I glanced back at Ricky, feeling my cheeks flame. "I think it'd be cool to find a kid like me, I guess. Impart some wisdom."

Ricky's shoulders shook as he kept in his laughter.

"What?" I stomped my foot.

"Your wisdom?"

"Shut up."

"It's going to be a great dog," Pigtails continued.

About two feet in front of us a little boy sat on a patch of blacktop—his chin resting on his palms—staring into space. *Was he the McGee?* Full of imagination, deep in thought, still waters running deep? I sat down next to him.

"What are you thinking about?" I asked.

The little boy shifted. Yellow sidewalk chalk on his fingers looked extra bright against his dark skin, especially when he smudged it across his cheek as he shrugged. "Legos, mostly."

"What about them?"

"Well, like, *why* are they Legos?" He blinked.

I blinked.

Okay, so maybe he's not my little McGee.

Pigtails slipped her hand into mine, making me jump. Her hand was hot and sticky, and I tried not to think about why that might be. Ricky leaned back on his elbows and smiled at the girl.

"What kind of dog?"

Pigtails turned back to Ricky. "A cute dog," she said. "Not an ugly dog with ugly little spots all over its ugly little body."

"What are you going to name your dog?" Ricky asked Pigtails.

"Spot, probably."

Ricky erupted in laughter so loud his statue kids toppled over behind him. "Looks like the future Pipi McGee found you."

Pigtails glowered at him, her mouth twisted and eyes narrowed. "What's that supposed to mean?" we said at the same time.

———

My moment had arrived!

Art class. When Miss Gonzalez called us back inside following recess in the courtyard, bins of crayons sat on all the tables and a sheet of white paper waited at each seat.

"Find a chair, children," she called. "We're going to kick off a Northbrook Primary tradition—creating self-portraits! What do you think self-portraits are?"

Lego Boy raised his hand. You would not be surprised by what he thought self-portraits might be.

"No, David," Miss Gonzalez responded. "Self-portraits are not Legos. Anyone else?"

A surprising number of students felt very confident about entirely guessing what self-portraits might be, including Pigtails, who said, kind of hopefully, that they were a type of cake. Finally, Miss Gonzalez explained that the kids would be drawing pictures of themselves. "Yes, your own selves."

All of the twenty-four kindergarteners looked down at their bodies in surprise. Two clapped. They were the future Sarah Trickle and Jackson Thorpe. Pigtails raised her hand.

"You will be drawing pictures of yourself when you are older, like our helpers today! Think about what you will look like and what you will be doing when you are big kids like they are.

"Yes, Piper?"

Ricky shot me a look. *Yeah, I know. Piper sounds a bit like Pipi.* I rolled my eyes and his shoulders shook.

"But what if you're not a kid when you're bigger?" Piper asked.

"We're just thinking about when you're an eighth grader—thirteen or fourteen years old, Piper. So, you *will* be a kid."

"No. By then, I'll be a unicorn."

The rest of the class laughed, some of them even pointing at Piper, whose face turned redder and redder. "I will!" she bellowed. "I will! I will! I will! And then I'll poke all of you with my—"

Piper

"Now, class!" Miss Gonzalez clapped her hands hard three times. Though it was just day three, the class knew to copy her claps and quiet down. "We do not laugh at each other in this room." She turned to Piper and quietly added, "Nor do we threaten to poke each other with one's unicorn horns."

"Horn," said Piper, crossing her arms, face still red.

"Excuse me?"

"Horn. Unicorns only have one horn. I'm going to poke them with my horn." Her eyes narrowed, and she glared around at each kid looking back at her. Quietly, she growled, *"Someday."*

"That's enough, Piper." Miss Gonzalez turned back to the class. "I want you to draw yourself as a human." She ignored Piper's groan and my slow clap. "And I want you to draw yourself *carefully* and *with detail*. That means choosing the right colors, taking your time to draw yourself very well, and *filling in* with color. No peek-a-boos of white spots in your drawing! We're going to work on this until snack time, so *stretch* out your work." Miss Gonzalez couldn't seem to get through a sentence without *emphasizing* a particular word.

"May we take the drawing home when we finish so our parents can see it?" Future Sarah Trickle asked while actual Sarah Trickle leaned down and whispered that she was so smart for using *may* instead of *can*. I rolled my eyes. Or at least, I would've, had I not noticed Piper doing the same thing.

"These are *very special* drawings," Miss Gonzalez said, "and will stay in our classroom in a *very special* binder for the remainder of the year. Your parents will be able to see them at parent-teacher conference in *November*. But they'll stay here in the *binder,* and then at the end of the school year, they'll be given to the guidance counselor, who will put them in your *permanent file*. But don't worry." She glanced toward Sarah,

Jackson, Ricky, and me and winked. "You will see them again."

My cheeks burned. *Mom and Dad had* seen *my Bacon Boob drawing and just left it there, in my* very special *permanent file without ripping it from the binder? How could they?*

Piper yanked on my hand. Her brown eyes were serious. "I'm going to add the horn somewhere no one will think to look."

And I'm going to erase it, Little McGee. I looked around the room. Lego Boy was already at his seat, sketching himself in little rectangles with knobs on the top of a rounded head. Narrator Boy from the bus drew himself with his head tilted like a hinge. Piper sank into the seat in front of me, plotting where to hide her horn. I'd fix them all, the moment I had a chance. I'd sneak into the binders, round out Lego Boy's body and erase his knobs. I'd straighten Narrator's head. And I'd eliminate Piper's horn, wherever she hid it.

I glanced over at Future Sarah Trickle, who drew herself in a lovely little dress with a big red bow in the middle of her hair. She carefully sketched out her face, fringing her eye with long eyelashes. Oops. She forgot to draw a second eye. I'd skip her binder.

Ricky elbowed my side. I hadn't even heard him move across the room. "What are you up to?"

"What are you talking about?" I asked, smoothing my hair with my hands.

"Creepy smile on your face, your head nodding like you're in the middle of a deep conversation. What are you plotting?"

"Why would I be plotting anything?"

Ricky raised an eyebrow. He was super good at that. "I don't know. You've been up to something today. Tasha even said something about it."

"Tasha?" I pulled my eyes away from Future Jackson Thorpe's paper, in which he was catching a football in the air, a huge smile stretching from ear to ear. Something about learning that Ricky and Tasha had been talking without me felt strange, like two pieces of bread calling themselves a sandwich without the peanut butter holding them together. I guess it was also kind of odd to think of yourself as peanut butter.

"Earth to Penelope!" Ricky said.

"You called me by my name," I said, surprise coloring my voice. My eyes locked with Ricky's. His eyebrow lowered and his face stilled, that sideways grin going soft for a moment.

He nodded. "Penelope," he said softly. "I like your name."

For some reason, my cheeks flushed. I nodded. "Me, too," I whispered.

"So . . ." Ricky said as I worked to get my face back into a neutral expression. Geez, how desperate was I to be a regular person if someone calling me by my actual name was enough to make my face practically explode into flames? "You're up to something . . ." Ricky prodded.

I bit my lip, eyes gliding around the room to make sure Jackson and Sarah weren't within earshot. I nodded. "I'm going to make up for everything."

"Everything?" Ricky asked.

"Yeah, everything that has happened to me. Before we get to high school, I'm going to redeem myself for all of my humiliations."

Ricky tilted his head, looking like Narrator Boy for a brief second.

"Things like the bacon drawing of myself," I whispered. "I'm going to redeem myself by making sure these twerps don't do the same stuff I did."

"And how are you going to do that?"

I fixed my gaze on a little pail of palm-sized erasers. "I'll do what I have to."

Ricky crossed his arms.

"What?" I asked. Miss Gonzalez glanced over at us and then gestured toward the kids. Ricky started to walk away, but I grabbed his arm. "What?" I asked again.

Still not looking at me, he said, "Do you remember kindergarten?"

"Of course, I remember kindergarten. Why do you think I'm here? This is where it all started, where everything began to fall apart."

He shook his head, his dark hair falling across his forehead. "Do you remember anything else about kindergarten?"

I shrugged, ignoring the urge to rub my nose. "I remember everyone laughing at me. I remember crying."

Ricky looked at me then.

"What?" I asked.

"Do you remember anything about anyone else?"

I shook my head, feeling like I was missing something important. "Like what?"

Ricky huffed from his nose. "Like Sarah?"

My turn to huff. "You mean like how everyone chased her around at recess and begged to go to her sleepovers and wormed their way into the seats next to her on the rug? Yeah, I remember."

"I was thinking more about how she cried under the table when we all had to count to one hundred. You marched up to the teacher and demanded to go next, even though you couldn't do it either."

"I could so!" I yelped.

Ricky laughed, all the stoniness falling from his face. "Yeah, you said, 'I count it *my* way. You count it yours.' First and only time Miss Simpson ever got mad."

"I forgot all about that." I laughed. "I was pretty fierce, wasn't I?"

"You scared me. But I dunno. She could have you beat." He pointed to Piper, who was drawing her picture so hard the pencil point broke. Ricky's chin jerked toward Jackson, who was posing with an imaginary football, acting like a model for Future Jackson Thorpe. "What about him? Remember when he thought he could fly?"

I gasped. "That's right! He jumped off the top of the monkey bars and got stitches on his chin."

"And Miss Simpson made him show everyone what happens when—"

"Kindergarteners don't think through their actions," we finished in unison.

"I forgot all about how she used to say that." I snorted. "It was so annoying."

"Yeah, I know," Ricky said, but I didn't know if he meant that he knew it had been annoying or that I had forgotten all about it.

A moment of quiet felt thick between us. "What about you?" I asked.

"What about me?" Ricky knelt down and helped Lego Boy sort through the bucket of skin color crayons for the perfect brown.

When he stood up, I asked again, "What did you do in kindergarten?"

He flashed a smile, gone as quickly as it had appeared. "I was with you. The whole time, Penelope. But you don't remember that, do you?"

I tried to nod or laugh or do anything with my face aside from showing my surprise but totally failed. Ricky huffed again. "All you remember is the drawing."

I sighed. "That's why I have to redeem myself. So I can move on."

"And then what?" Ricky asked.

"And then I can be myself!"

"And who's that?"

"I don't know."

Miss Gonzalez stood from where she was kneeling next to a student and narrowed her eyes at us. I plastered a smile on my face and replaced Piper's broken pencil with a new one. Slowly, Miss Gonzalez lowered herself down again.

Ricky looked at me, both eyebrows raised. I knew he was waiting for an answer.

"Maybe," I started, choosing my words carefully, "if none of the embarrassing things had happened to me, I'd be like her." I pointed to Sarah. "I mean, look at her!" Sarah glided around the classroom. The little kids' heads turned everywhere she went, watching her with huge smiles, like she was an angel or something. "What's so great about her aside from her never accidentally drawing herself as breakfast meat, throwing up all over everyone, peeing her pants, removing an eyebrow—"

"I get it. I get it!" Ricky cut in as Future Sarah Trickle brought her perfect little drawing to the front of the room and placed it on the table. First one done, but her drawing was completely perfect—she even caught the missing eye. The drawing showed a little girl with long brown hair, a triangle dress, sun shining with a big smile on its yellow face, green grass growing all around. "Sarah's like that drawing. So perfect it doesn't seem real."

"I know." I groaned.

"But, you?" He sort of laughed. He nodded toward Piper's drawing. It was full of stuff—rainbows and clouds and toys and a bicycle and something that kind of looked like a tree with marshmallow blossoms. In the middle stood a giant dog, totally brown without a single spot. On top of the dog's head was a teeny tiny little girl with a tiny horn sticking straight out of her stomach.

"You are like that," Ricky finished. "You're authentic. You're a spotless dog named Spot."

"Did you just call me a dog?"

Ricky sighed and went to help Lego Boy finish his drawing.

Chapter Six

"Tell me again," Tasha said, her elbows nearly touching mine as she leaned across the counter at Mom's gym. I was on the opposite side, sitting on a stool, making sure customers flashed their membership card as they streamed into the gym. You'd be shocked how many people tried to use other gym passes to get into Mom's gym. I kept telling Mom to invest in one of those scanners like they have at Starbucks, but she said I'm the only scanner she needs. In other words, the only one she doesn't have to pay.

I rolled my eyes at my best friend. "He was reading *Crow Reaper*."

Tasha squealed and clapped her hands, making her earrings swing. She was wearing some of my birds as earrings. I had given them to her for her birthday; they were super tiny blue parrots, like a bird we had seen at the zoo on a field trip. She had fastened them to giant hoops. I overheard someone asking her once where she got them, and Tasha just winked at me and said, "A local artist." I liked that she had called me an artist, but it kind of bothered me that she didn't say I made them, though

later she told me that was because I was so secretiv
art. (After kindergarten, who could blame me?)

"Ricky likes *CR*," Tasha whispered. "Who
thought!"

"Well, the books are pretty popular, aren't they?"

Tasha ignored me.

I glanced around for Mom. She was getting ready for her
next class—spin. It's where a bunch of people pedal superfast
for an hour while my mom yells at them at the top of her lungs.
Class starts off slow and easy. Then, *bam!* Mom hits you with
nineties music and screams at you to *move, move, move* like it's
the end of the world. I kept telling her to vary the music and
work with the giant projection screen—so many missed opportunities to show awesome backgrounds. I even took her through
a routine I made up myself, but she said she didn't want to mess
with the graphics. Everyone left class feeling endorphin-rushed
happy and so sweaty that I had to open the doors to the gym
for about fifteen minutes to get rid of the condensation and
funky odor.

Now Mom was standing by her main bike, flipping through
her phone, probably adding more boy band songs to her dated
soundtrack.

"*And,*" I added, now that I knew Mom wasn't in earshot, "I
made progress on The Plan."

"What?" asked Tasha, her thumbs brushing the blue bird
hanging from her ear.

"The Plan," I repeated. "In kindergarten volunteering. They just started making self-portraits and I'm going to make sure no one, you know . . ."

"Pulls a McGee?" Tasha finished.

I winced. "I wish people would stop calling it that."

"How are you going to do it?" asked Tasha, giving me her full attention at last.

"This one kid—Piper—she wants to be a unicorn when she grows up." I opened the drawer behind the desk and pulled out a couple strands of cherry licorice. Mom kept the sugar hidden, but not well hidden.

Tasha snagged her piece. "So, Piper drew herself with a horn?"

"A hidden horn," I said around a bite, "so Miss Gonzalez wouldn't see it. She put it coming out of her stomach."

"Aww! That's not so bad," Tasha said. "I bet it's kind of cute."

"It's adorable. Now. But I'm looking out for the kid." I leaned toward Tasha and lowered my voice as a group of gym-goers streamed in. "If she's following in my less-than-esteemed footsteps, who knows what damage her spike-belly could do by eighth grade?"

Tasha considered what I said. "So, you erase the horn and then scratch kindergarten off your list? Seems like a fair plan."

I nodded. "Yeah, technically, it'll be time to move on . . ."

"But?" Tasha prompted.

"But I'm going to keep an eye on this kid."

Tasha smiled. "You like her."

I nodded. "I do. I'm going to look out for her. Make sure she ends up with the right kind of friends. That sort of thing."

"Are you sure—" Tasha opened her mouth to say something more just as the door opened again, but then she quickly snapped it shut. Her eyes widened as she took in the newcomer's reflection in the mirror behind the desk. Her hand darted out and curled around my elbow. "Pipi—"

I looked up. All the sweetness from the candy left my mouth. My breath sucked inward as my lungs cowered. My heart, on the other hand, thrummed like it was the middle of Mom's spin class.

In front of me stood the reason I don't speak about seventh grade. Ever.

Frau Jacobs.

"Ah, Miss McGee." Frau Jacobs's thick lips pulled back in what was supposed to be, I think, a smile but which really looked like two slugs stretching out in the sun. White specks of spittle gathered at the corners of her mouth. "Whatever are you doing behind that desk?"

I stared at her, my heart slamming away in my chest. Its message was clear—*Get away! Get away!* But I couldn't, wouldn't, move. *We don't leave in the middle of the class* Frau's sugary sweet voice echoed in my head.

How could someone who looked so much like everyone's favorite grandma—spittle aside—actually be evil? A five-foot-two-inch-tall, sugar-smelling goblin. Frau Jacobs was decked out in what looked like kite material—super loose-fitting wind-breaker pants and jacket, all of it smattered in bright red and orange starbursts.

Frau Jacobs, who induced the nightmare of my seventh-grade year.

That year held the humiliation so huge that even I, some-one so used to humiliation my name is synonymous with it, can't even talk about it.

My face burned. My ears burned. My throat burned.

"Hel*lo*?" she said in the same sugary voice. "Miss McGee?"

Tasha elbowed me. "Her mom works here," my friend said. Where I was burning alive, Tasha had gone ice cold. Her glare should've frosted the air between us, turning our breath into puffs of white.

Frau's eyes slid to Tasha. "Are you in my German 1 class?"

Tasha crossed her arms. "No." It was a clipped word.

Frau's eyes widened. "Goodness," she said in her fake, sweet way. "I suppose I would've remembered you."

"I suppose you would've," Tasha snapped back.

Frau's smile stretched as she turned back to me. "I'm here to give spin a try. Melissa—why, she must be your mother—came to a faculty meeting last month to talk up the gym."

"Yeah," I mumbled as Frau Jacobs continued smiling at me, and I realized she wasn't going to move until I responded. "She was talking to the coaches about cross-training students."

"Well, I thought, why not give it a whirl, so to speak!" Frau Jacobs continued.

I didn't say anything. She blinked at me. "Which way is the class, Miss McGee?"

Tasha sighed when I didn't speak. She thumbed to the open gym behind her. "That way." She thrust a towel into Frau Jacobs's hands. "You're going to need this."

"Oh, goody!" she said.

I shuddered as Frau Jacobs passed.

"Did you hear?" Tasha asked in the silence that remained. "Frau Jacobs dress-coded Anika Patel yesterday."

"Anika?" I echoed. "But she never does anything wrong, ever!"

Tasha nodded. "She was wearing one of those shirts with shoulders cut out, you know?" She mimed cutting away at a triangle of fabric at the top of her arms. "The rest of it was a freaking turtleneck. Dress-coded for a *turtleneck*."

Something to know about Frau Jacobs, she had a particular idea about respect. As in, she demanded it from students while simultaneously ridiculing said students, making comments about how obsessed we were with social media and how we cared too much about what we looked like, and throwing out obscure questions regarding current events just so she could sigh heavily when Becky Sprenkle didn't know that the president had landed in London earlier that week. "Maybe if you spent less time worrying about your makeup, Becky . . ."

The biggest thing Frau went on and on about was our complete lack of self-respect as it pertained to dressing appropriately for school. She'd point out a girl's "so-called leggings or whatever they're supposed to be" and say how they should be treated like tights. The whole shoulder cut-out trend nearly threw her over the edge. She acted as if writing dress code violations was her civic duty or something. "Dress for the classroom," she would singsong to a girl before sending her to the office. "Not the playground. The *boys* have come here to learn, not to be distracted by your shoulders."

"Wow." I shook my head. "Did Anika have to go home?"

Tasha sighed. "No, she wore the Shirt of Shame."

I shuddered. The Shirt of Shame was this extra-large white T-shirt with Northbrook Middle School written in Sharpie across the front. Kids who violated dress code had to wear it all day if they didn't want their parents to be called. Poor Anika.

A retching sound rippled through the gym. Mom stood beside her bike, the one at the front of the room facing rows of others, spraying vomit across the floor.

Frau Jacobs turned toward me, slug smile still in place, as I rushed into the room to see what had happened to Mom, with Tasha close behind. "Looks like you aren't the only McGee lady who finds controlling bodily fluids difficult," Frau Jacobs said. She covered her mouth with her hand as Mom rocked back and let loose another torrent of puke. "I believe I'll skip this class after all."

Tasha stood beside me. She pointed toward the door. "Yeah, well."

Frau Jacobs sailed by us and I leaned into Tasha.

I pushed through the throngs of people rushing toward Mom. She knelt by her bike, a thin film of sweat beading along her forehead, mopping up the puke with one of the sweat rags. "What happened?"

"Bad cheese," she whispered. "I knew the cashew cheese couldn't—shouldn't—be a thing. But I let Alec talk me into it. Cashew and cheese have no business associating." Her face looked a little green in the fluorescent lights.

"Okay, everyone," I said. "Spin is canceled, but the open gym has lots of bikes!"

Mom moaned again as another cashew cheese wave caught up to her.

"Stop thinking about it." I knelt beside her, swiping another rag across the floor to clean up. Tasha lugged in the mop and bucket combo we kept in the closet. I usually helped mop up at the end of the day so we could get home faster, so Tasha knew where everything was kept.

"Thanks," I whispered to her as she quickly backed out of the room with her hand over her nose. Tasha was on the bus *that* day in second grade when I set off the vomit-a-thon. She has had a bit of a delicate stomach ever since.

"Did everyone leave? I could probably rally," Mom said.

"Yeah, everyone's gone."

"Oh, thank God." Mom flopped back on the floor. "Sorry," she muttered.

"Why don't you go home? I'll clean up. Spin was the last class of the day, anyway."

Mom ran her arm across her forehead. "That's probably a good idea. You've got everything covered here? I mean, Sasha is in the back leading an aerobics class if you need her. And Steve will be here in a half hour to take over at the front desk," Mom said.

I nodded. "Yeah, we've got it."

Mom squeezed my shoulder. "I know. You've been through so many spin classes, you could've just taken over."

"Only with better music and graphics."

Mom was just walking out the door a moment later, plastic grocery bag in hand just in case the cashew cheese struck again, when in walked Sarah Trickle, trailed by a half dozen girls, all of them on the Northbrook Middle School basketball team. Vile Kara Samson, of course, was the team's captain.

"Hi, Penelope!" Sarah said brightly. "Coach said we should start cross-training, so I was kind of hoping we could check out the spin class? I know we're late and all, so if we have to do it another time—"

Mom's face split into her business smile—the one she wore special for prospective clients. "Oh! Yes!" She glanced back at me with wide eyes.

For weeks, Mom had been trying to get an *in* with the

coaches at the middle school. She said it'd be the way to really secure the gym's position in town, if it was where local athletes went to train. And here they were, taking her up on it, just as she was leaving. *Why, Cashew Cheese? Why!*

Mom bit her lip, then turned back toward Sarah and the other girls. "In fact," Mom said, my day once more taking a turn for the worse, "my daughter has crafted a special class *just for* student athletes, with hip music and killer graphics."

"Oh, my stars," Tasha whispered under her breath. "Your mom just said the words *hip* and *killer*."

All of the basketball players turned to me. I spotted Kara laughing behind her hand as she leaned into another player. But, of course, Sarah wasn't laughing. Her perky little face brightened. "Oh, wow!" she said. "That sounds perfect!"

"I don't know," Kara said. "Which daughter?"

"Yep," Mom said, carefully not meeting my eyes and ignoring Kara entirely. "Just go on back into the main gym and find a bike. Pipi—*Penelope*—will be right in to get you started." The girls passed by and Mom called out, "And remember: we have meeting rooms here. You know, if you want a cool place to hang outside of school, you could make one of the meeting rooms your space for clubs or whatev."

Tasha mouthed *whatev* at me, and I internally groaned.

As the girls filed into the room, Mom clutched her stomach again. "Thanks a million, Pipi," she said and darted to the bathroom.

Kara narrowed her eyes as she passed me. "Ew," she muttered.

Sarah cocked her head at Kara. "It'll be fun," she said, and smiled at me.

I tried to smile back, but I'm not sure it actually worked. Tasha crossed her arms and gave Kara a stare down. Kara shifted so her back was slightly to Tasha, but I heard her whispering.

Great. Now I had to lead Vile Kara Samson and Sarah Trickle and the rest of the basketball team in spin. I curled my hands into fists to keep from rubbing my nose.

"It'll be fine," Tasha said. She grabbed her backpack and was about to head toward the door.

"Where are you going?" I held tightly to her arm.

She shrugged off my hand and smiled. "What could go wrong?"

"Don't you say that. Don't you ever say that to me."

Chapter Seven

Tasha texted me an hour later.

Then again twenty minutes after that.

Finally, she called. "Why don't you answer texts like a regular person?"

"Because I can't put into words what happened after you abandoned me." I plucked Myrtle out of the tank and flopped back on my bed, perching her on my chest.

"That bad?" Tasha whispered. "What happened?"

I considered my words, not sure how best to phrase it.

"Oh my stars," Tasha breathed. "You passed out, didn't you? You passed out and Sarah had to call an ambulance."

"No."

"Okay, good. That's good. So, a light fixture fell out of the ceiling, startled you, and you broke a leg or something?"

"Nope. Nothing broke."

Silence from Tasha.

"Oh *no*. You farted. You totally farted in the middle of teaching the class. Don't worry. We can handle this. Everyone farts. It's going to be okay."

"I didn't fart."

More silence. Then, "What exactly happened?"

"Honestly?" I rolled onto my belly, holding Myrtle, who tried to swim in midair. I put her on the bed in front of me and she burrowed under my pillow. Sometimes being around Myrtle made me more confident about my own social skills. "It was . . . kinda amazing."

Tasha sucked in her breath. "What?"

"For real." As shocked as I was to be saying that, it did sting a little to hear Tasha's surprise.

"You didn't McGee it at all?"

"Well—" I started.

"Lay it on me. I'm ready!" Tasha's voice was high.

"I was *about* to say that I really didn't. When we first started class, I set up the screen with the green field and soft, easy music. I heard muttering in the back from Kara." Tasha huffed from her nose but didn't interrupt. "She said, 'Yeah, sure. *She's* going to help us play basketball.'"

"That's cold," Tasha hissed.

"I know, right? Third grade could've happened to anyone."

Tasha was silent. Okay, so maybe not *everyone* would get the baskets mixed up and let down every girl in their grade. But still, that was a long time ago.

I continued. "But then Sarah said Kara didn't mean it, so . . ."

"So, Kara kept on being obnoxious, just quieter," Tasha finished.

"Right. And then the playlist got faster. I switched the scene to the woods and it slowly got shadowy—I used the dimmer remote Mom always ignores to actually make the room darker—and the music switched to super creepy, something's-following-you music. Maybe for a little bit, I was kind of showing off, going superfast, but then I kind of got lost in the show myself."

"The show?"

My cheeks burned even though I knew Tasha couldn't see me through the phone. "It's not really a show, but it kind of felt like it. And then we were through the woods and tearing through the city scenes, and the music was fast and loud, and then, before I knew it, we were back to the countryside scenes and class was over."

"And that's it?" Tasha asked.

"That's it. I mean, aside from Kara falling when she stopped off the bike." I snickered. "I had to stay pretty late to clean up all the sweat, too." I worked to keep my voice low key. "Because, the truth is, I *rocked* that class."

"Huh." Tasha went quiet.

"They all said they'd be back on Thursday. Even Kara."

"Won't your mom be better by then?"

"Yeah, I guess so." Mom still got a little pale anytime anyone said "cashew cheese," which coincidentally had become Annie's favorite words, but otherwise she seemed fine. "But Mom said I could lead it again if I wanted."

"Do you want to?" Tasha's voice sounded strange.

"I don't know. Maybe."

Tasha didn't say anything.

"Is everything okay?" I asked.

"Sorry," Tasha responded. "I'm just having a moment." She breathed out slowly into the phone. "Just imagine, if I were your mom, I'd be making a scrapbook page and labeling it, *The First Time Little Pipi Joined Something.*"

"Oh, shut up," I snapped. "It's not like I'm joining the team or anything. I'm just leading a spin class. And maybe . . ."

"Maybe what?" Tasha asked.

"I don't know." I picked up tiny pieces of spinach Myrtle must've missed when she was eating on my bed earlier. "The team needs a manager, I guess."

"OMG. You're the basketball team manager now?" she said. "I left you at the gym and you were one way, then I talk with you and suddenly you're, I don't know, different. Talking to Sarah Trickle. Being a spin instructor. Signing up to be a team manager. You know the girls' and boys' teams share a manager, right?"

"Yeah," I said, feeling my face flush even deeper. "I'm not for sure. I'm just thinking about it."

"*Jackson Thorpe!*" Tasha gasped.

"It'd work out in my plan, you know? The List. If I had more time around Kara and Jackson, I'd have more opportunities. Let the universe provide and all that."

"*Yeah!*" She whistled low. After a beat, she said, "Just don't . . ."

"Don't what?"

"Don't be yet another Sarah Trickle fangirl," Tasha said super soft.

"Weren't you the one who told me I shouldn't hate her so much? And you're the one making mental scrapbook pages for my being a joiner."

"Yeah." And finally, Tasha sounded like herself again—about to laugh but also ready to roll her eyes if necessary. "But that doesn't mean you have to go and be yet another one of her bffs."

"*You're* my best friend, Tasha," I said. "Even if I manage the basketball team. Which I'm not even sure I want to do."

"Cool. So, how's this going to factor in your plan for The List?"

"I don't know," I said, shrugging even though she couldn't see me. Myrtle peeked out from under my pillow. I sprinkled the spinach bits in front of her. "Just a few thoughts I've got swirling around."

I heard a *whoosh* through the phone as Tasha plopped onto her bed. "So," she said, "what was with Frau Jacobs coming to the gym?"

"I know, right? Hopefully it's a one-time thing and I won't see her again, ever. The one perk so far of being in eighth grade is no more Frau Jacobs."

You know that whole universe-will-provide philosophy?

Sometimes the universe can be such a jerk.

Because guess who I saw as soon as I got into homeroom the next day?

"Good morning, class," Frau Jacobs singsonged out from the front of the room, where she half sat, half leaned on the edge of Mr. Harper's desk. She waved her hands to greet us as if she were the conductor of an orchestra, clearly expecting us all to sing *good morning* back to her. But it was the beginning of the day, so I was the only one paying attention. And no way in the world was *I* going to wish Frau Jacobs good morning.

Frau Jacobs sighed heavily, throwing her arms and smacking them down on her thighs. She was wearing a long denim skirt and a bright yellow T-shirt, her school ID badge and a pen hanging from a purple crocheted cord around her neck—teacher-mourning-the-nineties attire. Sighing again, Frau Jacobs trudged over to the light switch by the entrance to the classroom, her plastic clogs slapping against the linoleum tiles louder than should've been possible. Thrusting her neck forward and shaking her head at us, she sighed again and flipped the lights on and off a few times. *"Hello."* She drawled out the word in the sudden silence.

"That's better." She straightened up and swung her fisted hand back and forth like some cheesy singer in a musical about to take off in a skip. She even had a bit of a bounce in her step as she made her way back to Mr. Harper's desk.

"Where's Mr. Harper?" Jackson called out from the middle in the room.

"I was about to get to that," Frau Jacobs answered with a tiny smile. It reminded me of those cartoons where a cat swallows a bird and is smiling but also keeping it inside its mouth.

"Will he be back tomorrow?" Kara asked.

Frau Jacobs cupped her hand to her ear and peered around the room in mock surprise. "Did I hear someone speak just now without raising her hand?"

Kara raised her hand. Frau Jacobs ignored her. Directing her attention to the rest of the class, she said, "Mr. Harper isn't going to be here for a while. He's taking a sabbatical."

"For real?" Ricky laughed under his breath, a grin stretching across his face. How could he be happy about this? "I can't believe it! He did it, didn't he?"

"What are you talking about?" Jackson asked Ricky.

Ricky spun in his seat to face Jackson. "He made it onto *America's Secret Bakers.*"

"The TV show? No way!" Jessica said.

Frau Jacobs clapped her hands, drawing the class's attention. "Yes, yes, Mr. Harper is seizing an opportunity to compete in reality television, something apparently worthy of a sabbatical, according to our esteemed new principal." Frau Jacobs's shoulders rose and fell in another dramatic sigh. "And so, while

Mr. Harper is off baking cupcakes or whatnot, I'll be taking over yet *another* class. This homeroom." Frau Jacobs smiled. "We will be kicking off each and every day together for the rest of the semester."

A hush fell over the room. A few kids, ones who were in seventh grade Intro to Languages with me, twisted in their seats to shoot me looks. I felt their eyes on me but kept my stare pointed down at my desktop.

Did you ever flip your eyelid inside out? Really, don't. It's incredibly gross. But for a while in second or third grade, there was this kid at the park who'd always flip his eyelids inside out and then chase girls around the playground with his arms outstretched like a zombie. In that moment, finding out I'd begin every single morning with Frau Jacobs for the rest of the semester, I felt like my entire body was flipped inside out like that. As if everything I worked so hard to keep inside—everything too tender for even air to touch—was flipped right out for everyone to see.

I sucked in my breath.

Whispers rattled around the classroom. Whispers about last year. Whispers about me. Someone laughed just behind me. They'd do that next year, too, and—just like how someone else said, "what?" and a new person filled him in on the story— the humiliations were going to follow me wherever I went.

I don't talk about seventh grade. Ever.

But for just a moment, I let myself remember.

The entire school staring at me, laughing at me. Frau standing in the middle of them all, wearing a smug little smile. The shame that nearly swallowed me whole—shame that kept me curled up in a ball on my bed, for the whole weekend after that day.

I shuddered and forced the memory away.

I was going to save others from going through what I had.

But I also was going to get my revenge.

I was *going* to see Kara and Frau Jacobs's faces dunked in shame.

And *I* would be the one standing in the middle this time, smiling.

Chapter Eight

"Pipi," Frau Jacobs said as I left homeroom. I was the last one out, after accidentally tipping my bag and spilling my pens across the floor—all things that happened because I was trying too hard to get away. "If you're always the last out the door, you won't have time to swing by the facilities between classes. Part of becoming a woman is managing one's own needs."

I zipped up my bag and passed her as I rushed out the door. No one had been in the classroom to hear, thankfully. When I got to algebra, Tasha already was there, sitting in her regular seat next to mine.

"Ugh! I heard Frau Jacobs is replacing Mr. Harper," she whispered as I took my seat. She pressed pause on her audiobook and slipped her earbuds out of her ears. "It's only homeroom. Just ignore her."

I nodded as I opened my textbook. I felt like everyone was watching me, but of course they weren't. Then I decided to risk a look around, just to be certain. Sure enough, someone was, in fact, staring my way. Ricky. Only he was actually watching Tasha.

Tasha had lunch on Tuesdays and Thursdays with the fantasy book club (she was president), so I was left on my own in the cafeteria. (She also had lunch with the track team on Fridays—she's the captain. Tasha said I could join them, but the few times I did, there was a weird silence whenever Tasha tried to bring me into the conversation.)

Usually I spent those days wandering around the school during lunch period, eating a granola bar or ducking into the art room if no one was there and working on my birds. But the art teacher had a sub today and the room was locked.

Since it was a beautiful, bright day, everyone was eating outside in the courtyard. All around me, people were laughing, huddled in groups around picnic tables, passing their cell phones around to show off pictures. Except for me. I found a little niche behind a row of bushes. There was a table on the other side without anyone at it, but I knew that was just a matter of time. Instead, I went to the far side of the bushes and sat down in the shade.

Honestly, I was happy to be alone. Whenever I asked Mom if I could be homeschooled (which was pretty much daily), she said, "No, Pipi. You'd never leave the house. You'd be up in your room talking to Myrtle all day." And she was right. Everyone else knew how to *be* around other people, while I was hiding behind the hedge so no one would talk to me. This, of course, was part of what tackling The List was supposed to change. But for now? For today? I was cool being in the shadow.

I popped in my earbuds and was listening to music that might work for spin class when I noticed how low my battery was. I turned off the music and was about to go inside until lunch was over when I heard a familiar name: Eliza. *Who was talking about my sister?*

I peeked through the hedge. There was Vile Kara Samson, Sarah Trickle, and Jackson Thorpe.

"I'm just saying," Kara spoke to Jackson, "it's pathetic. She was in my brother's grade. Max told me Eliza was such a snob, always acting like she was so much better than everyone." Kara raised her eyebrows. "Now look at her. Max's in college, in a frat, and Eliza McGee is shelling mascara with a kid who I hear is a total weirdo. Probably thanks to living with Pipi."

I sat down so hard my tailbone hit the flagstone. Fury roared through me. Talking about me was bad enough, but Eliza? *Annie?* Max Samson had asked Eliza out a half dozen times during her sophomore year. She always had said no. The only boy she ever dated was a senior, who never wanted anything to do with her—or Annie—after he found out she was pregnant. And I knew that a lot of people assumed Eliza was a snob, but I was there once when Max asked her out to the movies. She was so nice, thanking him but saying that she didn't want to lead him on. He had called her a name and stormed off.

Sarah murmured something too low for me to hear.

Kara sighed. "Whatever."

"Besides," Sarah said a little louder, "I heard Eliza was taking classes."

"Parenting ones, I hope." Kara laughed, not noticing that no one joined her. "Max said he heard the kid doesn't even call Eliza 'Mom.' That she thinks she's more of a sister. How messed up is that?"

I took a deep breath and peeked between the branches again.

Jackson was writing in a notebook, occasionally staring off into space. "She's still hot, too," he said. "I mean, her hair, it's golden as the sun. And her eyes, they're like blueberries in a . . . ah . . . spring horizon." He quickly scrawled more into the notebook. Kara shook her head and turned back to her sandwich.

"How long are you and Jackson going to stick with this whole poetry thing?"

"You don't stick with poetry," Jackson said. "It sticks with you." Again, he stared into the distance for a second, his mouth silently reforming the words he had just spoken, then he hunched back over the notebook.

"You know what Mr. Harper was saying about community service projects? That club he mentioned?" Sarah shrugged. "I really like the idea. Some schools even have these clubs—"

"You are *not* joining a poetry club. That is so dorky." I couldn't see it from the hedge, but I'm one hundred percent certain that she rolled her eyes. I heard her zipping her lunch bag. "I'll see you after school."

"Right." Sarah sighed.

Jackson closed his notebook. "Oh, is lunch over? I was so caught up in my poetry writing."

Sarah sighed again. "No, Kara's just headed to the bathroom."

"Hey," Jackson said, "what's wrong?" His voice was so gentle, I nearly swooned.

Sarah forced a smile. "It's just Kara. She was being . . . you know, Kara."

Jackson tossed his notebook into his backpack and tucked his pen behind his ear. That was his new look this year. "Sometimes I wonder why we're even friends with her."

Sarah's smile was less forced now. "She's my cousin. I *have* to be friends with her." She bit her lip, then said, "I shouldn't have said that."

Jackson laughed. "Secret's safe with me."

Sarah sighed. "Yeah, I know, but secrets are part of the problem."

Jackson moved closer to Sarah. "You know, not everything has to be a secret. That's up to you."

Sarah let out a big breath in a whoosh. "But it's not just that. It's mostly Kara; she's just a little much sometimes. Mom says it's just the way they are—she says even when she was a kid, she knew better than to cross Aunt Estelle. Max and Kara are just like her. *We don't back down* is like the family crest. Dad says they 'tell it like it is.'"

Jackson nodded. "How it is for them, maybe." His voice was lower, almost a growl, when he said, "I know about Max.

My dads told me to stay away from him. They heard about how he harassed a kid for being gay. Didn't he write a slur on his locker?"

"He scratched it into the metal. And I'm sure that's not the worst thing he did, though it was what he got caught doing." Sarah shuddered. "Yet he and Aunt Estelle act like *he* was the victim for getting suspended."

"That's really messed up." Jackson's hands curled into fists and he shook his head. "Kara better never say anything like that in front of me."

"She won't," Sarah said. "Not in front of you or me."

"Must be tough for Kara to live with someone like that," Jackson added.

"Yeah," Sarah said as she gathered up containers and shoved them back into her lunch bag. "That's why Kara spends so much time at our house. Mom says I'm a good influence, but sometimes . . ."

"Sometimes you want a break?"

"Maybe that's why the club thing I was telling you about is so appealing, you know?" Sarah said.

Jackson stood and held out his hand to help up Sarah. "Yeah, it'd really make a difference, I think. Pop says it'd be super brave."

A poetry club would be super brave? I guessed it'd be brave for Sarah to create something that didn't involve Kara, but Jackson seemed to be giving an awful lot of credit to Sarah.

After all, wouldn't *he* be making the club, too?

"Let's go," Sarah said instead of replying.

They finally left. I slowly got to my feet, feeling my back crack and wishing it were Vile Kara Samson's face. Whatever it took, I was going to make sure she paid for what she had done to me, and now for what she had said about Eliza and Annie.

Kindergarten volunteering days were the best part of the week (aside from the weekend when I didn't begin my day with Frau Jacobs). I focused my time on training Piper how *not* to be a future Pipi.

"Listen," I told Piper as she put the final flourishes on her self-portrait (now including a penciled-in dinosaur with spiky legs, and a house with a big smile and glasses), "these are going to be displayed on the first day of eighth grade. *Everyone* will see your drawing."

"I better add some purple, then." Piper sucked on her bottom lip as she swept purple across the sky.

I handed her an eraser. "How about we tone it down just a tad? Maybe get rid of your unicorn horn?"

Her crayon still pressed to the paper, she peered up at me. Her little forehead was puckered. "Why?"

Ricky was sitting across the table next to Narrator Boy ("Now I'm adding a red hat. Here's my red hat. Isn't it red? It's a hat."). He shot me a look. I ignored him.

"Well, because it's supposed to be how you're really going to look. You don't have a unicorn horn coming out of your belly."

"Yes, I do." Piper smiled and went back to her drawing. "You just can't see it."

I pressed the eraser into her hand. "Trust me."

Piper's forehead wrinkled again.

"I drew myself as something silly when I was in kindergarten. Know what happened when they showed my portrait this year? Everyone laughed at me. Everyone." I pointed to the eraser. "Do you want everyone to laugh at you?"

Piper shook her head, then she erased the spike. I pointed to the dinosaur. "This, too."

"*Pipi*," Ricky whispered.

I ignored him again, focusing on Piper.

Piper sucked on her bottom lip again, then erased the dinosaur.

"And that's why you should never try to shape your own eyebrows."

Piper ran a finger along her eyebrows, I think, to make sure she still had two.

"When you're older, I mean," I added. "Your eyebrows are perfect right now."

We were doing something Miss Gonzalez called Centers. All around the room were stations, including arts and crafts, play dough, play kitchen, and dress up. A half dozen girls circled around Sarah at the kitchen center, bringing her plastic ingredients. She stirred them in a big bowl.

"Why don't you play with those girls?" I said to Piper. "They look like they're having fun."

"All they want to do is play house. *Boring!* Who wants to pretend to make dinner?" She stuck out her tongue. "I want to be a dinosaur." She looked toward the girls and shrugged. "I guess I could pretend they're my dinner?"

"No!" I stopped her. "Listen, Piper. Remember, I'm trying to keep you from being laughed at and picked on." All morning, I had been imparting my wisdom to Piper, who finally seemed to get it. At least I thought so when I convinced her not to give herself bangs in the arts and crafts center, which had led to the disastrous makeover story. "Once a kid starts to be made fun of, it never stops. For all your life, these girls will say, 'Remember when Piper tried to eat us at school?' and you'll have to live with that forever."

"I'll be a dinosaur forever?" Piper bounced up and down. "Yay!"

I sighed. "No, you'll be picked on forever." My nose itched, like it needed me to remember the nose-picking incident of first grade. "Forever."

She stilled and rubbed at her eye.

"I'm just trying to save you, that's all. Try to be like the other girls a little. Maybe play a game with them?" I opened the

92

big cardboard box behind the little theater curtain set up at our center. It was filled with piles of clothes—dresses, hats, scarves. I pushed a frilly bonnet onto her head. "You love to pretend! Pretend you like to play dress up."

Piper rubbed at her eye again. "I'm all itchy."

"Maybe it's the dust from the clothes," I said, wrapping a scarf around her.

"No." Piper blinked a bunch of times. "My eye's all sticky, too."

I peered at her. Her right eye was a little goopy with light green stuff at the corners, and the white part of her eye was a little reddish. "Stop rubbing it," I said, "and I bet it'll be better. Now twirl."

Piper spun in a circle and laughed. I did, too, just a tad too loud. "You look gorgeous! Like a movie star!"

Future Sarah Trickle smiled over at us and nudged the girl beside her. Real Sarah Trickle said, "Would you like to go play dress up, too?"

The girls narrowed their eyes as if considering. This was Piper's chance to get in with the right crew!

"It's super itchy," Piper said, rubbing at her eye some more. I pulled her hands down from her face. "Maybe I should tell Miss Gonzalez," she said.

"No!" I whispered. "The girls are on their way over." I snagged the eye patch from the box. "Look! You're an awesome pirate princess!"

"I love pirates!" Future Sarah Trickle said. "I'll be a pirate, too!" She wrapped one of the scarves around her head.

I grinned at Piper. "*See?*" I whispered.

Piper nodded, a small smile tugging her face. "Do you want to use my eyepatch?" she asked.

Future Sarah Trickle said, "Are you sure?"

Piper nodded and pulled it off her face. "I'll just pretend to have one on." Piper's eye did look squished shut. Future Sarah Trickle immediately put on the eyepatch.

"I want to be a pirate, too!" cried another girl.

Future Sarah Trickle handed her the eyepatch as Piper danced around with a Beanie Babies parrot on her shoulder.

"Can I have the parrot?" Future Sarah Trickle asked Piper.

"No, I'm playing with it right now," Piper said.

"But I want to be a pirate!"

"You shouldn't have given up the eyepatch," Piper pointed out.

"I shared the eyepatch with Jessmarie. You should share the parrot." Future Sarah Trickle crossed her arms.

"When I'm done," Piper said. She made the parrot nod.

"That's not fair. We're all sharing." Future Sarah Trickle looked at Jessmarie, who super slowly pulled off the eyepatch and handed it to the next girl to strap on. After a few seconds, a third girl poked her on the shoulder and, still being watched by Future Sarah Trickle, she passed along the eyepatch. Future Sarah Trickle held out her hand for the parrot.

Piper took a half step backward, right onto my foot.

I nudged her forward. I whispered, "Remember, you want to be her friend."

Piper whispered back, much too loudly, "No, I *want* to play with the parrot."

I raised an eyebrow. Piper sighed and handed over the parrot. Future Sarah Trickle tucked it on her shoulder and pretended to feed it crackers.

"So, when do we loot?" Piper peered at the other stations.

"We're *nice* pirates," Future Sarah Trickle said. All of the other girls surged forward, holding hands and skipping in a circle with Future Sarah Trickle. Piper sighed again and joined the circle, looking a little cockeyed with her one puffy red eye.

And I could just see it, a flash of little Piper being older— my age—and part of that bigger circle. Someday she would look back on this moment and thank me, I thought, even though now Piper's one opened eye was locked on the parrot on Future Sarah Trickle's shoulder.

When I got home that afternoon, I drew a thick red line through *Kindergarten* on my list of humiliations. *Someday Piper will thank me,* I thought to myself again.

Then I walked over to Mom's gym as usual.

What was unusual was Mom's smile as I pushed through the door. "Your friends are waiting for you!"

Usually, Mom had on lots of waterproof makeup and her hair was slicked back into a smooth, high ponytail. Usually, she wore matching, high-end gym clothes, some sort of spandex in black and silver with bright turquoise or magenta accents. *Selling the dream* is how she phrased her attire. But today, her face was bare, her hair was in a topknot, and her clothes consisted of sweatpants with an elastic waist and one of Dad's old sweatshirts.

"Tasha and Ricky?" I asked.

"No, your basketball friends!"

Just then Vile Kara Samson walked out of the weight training room to fill her water bottle at the fountain beside the desk. She smirked at me.

Mom reached across the desk and squeezed my shoulder. "The team's using the gym for training. Thank you, Pipi. Seems they were pretty impressed after the spin class!" Her voice was soft with surprise. "I owe you. I'm still feeling under the weather from that . . ." She mouthed *cashew cheese.* "I had to cancel a couple classes this morning. But the whole team became members this afternoon! That's huge for the gym."

Mom's hand slid from my shoulder to cup my cheek. "They asked you to be one of the trainers, Pipi! Spin classes once a week."

"What?"

Mom patted my cheek and turned back to the computer.

Sure, I had a dozen or so playlists I had made just for spin. And, yes, I downloaded a lot of backgrounds for classes, too. But those were for fun, for when I had to kill time at the counter. And they were never made with the intention of spending any time with Vile Kara Samson. Suddenly being told I *had* to be the spin class leader made all excitement about *being* a spin class leader dissolve.

"Do I even get a say in this?" I asked Mom.

"I pay in art supplies," she answered.

So unfair! She knew I needed more paper and brushes.

Mom's fingers stopped typing on the keyboard. She looked up at me. "I'm counting on you, love. And Coach says the basketball team is, too."

I had another flash from *The Count of Monte Cristo*. Dantès was only able to enact his revenge once he was accepted into the powerful people's company.

"Fine," I grumped, even though I already was thinking of an awesome new playlist.

Chapter Nine

I took Annie to a park outside our neighborhood after dinner and was surprised to see Tasha sitting under a tree, listening to an audiobook. Tasha has dyslexia, so while she loves books, listening to them instead of reading them in print better suits how her brain works.

"Hey!" I said, plopping down next to her. "How are you?"

She shrugged and hit pause on the audiobook. She wasn't smiling. "I stopped by the gym after school today. Your mom told me you were with the rest of the basketball team." Tasha made the last two words way too high-pitched.

"Yeah, I guess it's kind of official. I'm the manager." I plucked at a few pieces of grass, keeping my eyes on Annie, who was sitting alone on the swings. "I'm helping with the training through spin classes and cardio drills. I've got to go to the games, too, to help keep score and stuff like that."

Kids were playing all around Annie, dragging trucks through the sand and darting between the slides and monkey bars in a game of tag. A little boy ran up and tagged Annie, but she ignored him and kept pushing herself on the swing. She was so different from me—I had always been alone and *wanted* to figure out how to join in. Annie only wanted to be left alone.

"So, will you, like, have practice all the time now?" Tasha had a large shopping bag with her and pulled it closer while she talked, bunching it up against her side. "Because usually we hang out after school."

Remember stone soup? That awful Girl Scouts soup that leaders made you try, even though it was made under false pretenses—the leaders asking each girl to bring a can of her favorite soup to a meeting, then mixing it all and heating it up? Remember how the different soups never quite meshed together, even though that was the whole point ("Everyone brings something new to the pot!"); it still tasted like a half dozen different soups in each bite? That's kind of how I felt—a mix of things that don't belong—as Tasha's question fell brick-heavy between us. Annoyed that *she* was annoyed about me being on the team. Defensive because she seemed to think it was such a bad idea— did she really think I couldn't do it? Angry that she wasn't happy for me. And something else, too. Something altogether new.

I was feeling a little, I don't know . . . it's just this was the first time *ever* that Tasha was the one left out. That I was a member of a team—I mean, technically I wasn't *on* the team, but I was part of the team—and she was the one who wasn't. Usually, I followed Tasha around, cheering her on. I was the one in the audience while she sang on stage during chorus. I was the one in the stands while she killed it during cross-country season.

I was the one looking basic in T-shirts and jeans while people snapped pictures of her decked out in Renaissance clothes during the Faires she dragged me to every single autumn (I always complained, but I secretly loved the Scotch eggs and the fake English accents). And I didn't mind any of those times on the sidelines—really, I didn't. Tasha stood out wherever we went because she was incredible, and I got to be her best friend. But this time? Maybe I was a little smug that I was the one able to say, "Sorry, I'm busy."

"I don't care that you're busy," Tasha snapped. "But it'd be nice to *know* before I headed over to the gym."

"I didn't know you were going to stop by, and Mom didn't tell me you were there."

"I was going to say hi but you were jumping rope with Sarah."

"Oh," I said, ignoring the way her voice pitched again when she said Sarah's name. "Yeah, Sarah Trickle's the team co-captain, so she was really showing me around a lot today."

"It looked more like you were showing *her* around."

"Well, it's Mom's gym, so maybe I was. We have actual practice in the gym on Thursday. I'm pretty nervous. I don't even know a lot of basketball rules. I'll spend most of the games on managing the buzzer and—"

"Why do you do that?" Tasha interrupted.

"Do what?" I blinked at her, but Tasha was squinting back at me like I was the one not making sense.

"Say her whole name. Every time you mention Sarah, it's with first and last names. You do it with Jackson, too. Why?" Tasha leaned back on her elbows as if I were about to deliver a huge explanation.

But my mind went blank.

Why did *I do that?* I shrugged.

"I mean, you talk to her now, right? And you volunteer with her in kindergarten. And you talk *about* her all the time."

"I do not!" I crossed my arms.

Tasha rolled her eyes and continued, "I think you're on a first-name basis. I mean, she doesn't go around calling you Pipi McGee."

"Penelope," I corrected. "She calls me Penelope."

Tasha's eyes narrowed. "Whatever. You're just so weird about her."

"I am not!" If my arms weren't already crossed, I would've done it now.

All that smugness I had been feeling? It completely evaporated. No longer were my feelings a soupy mix. They were straight-up, boiling hot embarrassment. In a small voice, I said the truth: "I can't just call her Sarah. She's Sarah Trickle. She's like, this entity. This huge embodiment of perfection, of everything I'm not. I can't just say Sarah because it'd be like saying I'm anywhere close to the same hemisphere as her."

"She's just a person," Tasha said, her voice gentle again. "Same as you. Same as me. If you're really going to do this List thing, if it's really about revenge or whatever, why are you try-ing to be like them?"

"I'm not!" I snapped. "I'm just . . . looking for an opportu-nity to make things better, okay? And part of it is figuring out how Sarah Trickle does everything right and all I do is muck everything up!"

"*Pipi,*" Tasha whispered.

"Penelope!" I yelped back.

Tasha shook her head again. I was getting a little sick of that. "You're my best friend, Pipi. And I want you to be happy, but I'm not sure if this whole thing is going to do that."

"You don't know what you're talking about." I threw my arms in the air. "I'm working on a plan. I scratched kinder-garten off my list today. Of course I'm happy!" I snapped. Mentioning kindergarten made me remember why I was here—to keep an eye on Annie. I scanned the playground for her; she was still sitting alone on the swings.

"The Piper kid? You got her to change her drawing?"

I nodded, forcing a smile on my face to prove my happiness. "That *and* I figured out a way to make her play with Future Sarah Trickle."

Tasha nodded. "Cool," she said. "You seem super happy about that."

"I am," I snapped.

"Obviously." Tasha pushed herself up from the ground. "I'll see you tomorrow." She slid the bag strap up her arm and placed an earbud into her ear. "Ricky and I are going to meet at the *library* after school, if you want to come."

"Sure," I said, then added, "unless I have practice."

"Right. Unless you have practice." Tasha waved over her shoulder. "Bye, Penelope."

As she walked away, I realized why she had put such a strange emphasis on library. Tomorrow was the *Crow Reaper* finale release day—something Tasha had talked about for months. The library was having a party to celebrate it, with *CR* trivia and free cookies. She was going to go over characters with me, help me figure out what to wear. That's probably why she had that big shopping bag with her, so we could work on my costume.

But since I wasn't around, it seemed she had made plans with Ricky instead.

Oh, hey there, left out feeling! Not nice to have you back again.

At lunch the next day, Tasha was hyped up about the book release. I had stayed up all night to craft a palm-sized crow for her. Tasha squealed when I gave it to her. She used a bobby pin to tie it to the pile of braids curling around the top of her head like a crown.

When Ricky walked by our table wearing a T-shirt with a giant black crow screen-printed across it, Tasha cheered.

"Oh," Ricky said, a half smile tugging at his face. "Seemed like a good day for this."

"It's *perfect*!" She pulled on his arm. "Sit down with us!" Ricky glanced around, nodding at me, then sat next to Tasha.

Tasha even wore makeup today—something she rarely did—her lipstick and eyeliner a bright turquoise blue. When I asked her about it, she said Eliza showed her how to do it.

"My sister? *That* Eliza?" I asked.

Tasha nodded, and just for a second that awkwardness snapped back in place between us. "Yep," she said. "I went into her shop after school yesterday."

"It's not really *her* shop," I muttered. "She just works there."

Eliza and I were never close—like when I was a newborn, Eliza would tell my parents to "leave the baby here" whenever we went to someone's house. But our relationship really twisted when she was pregnant with Annie. Eliza was so angry all the time then. She never wanted to leave the house. Anytime she saw me peeking at her belly, she'd snap at me. I get that it was a super tough time for her—I really do—but I was just a kid excited about a baby. Like this one time, I kept asking Mom questions about what the baby would look like, what she'd call us, where she'd sleep, where she'd be while we were at school or work. Eliza had stormed into the room and screamed, "Enough! Enough about the baby. All the time, all anyone wants to talk about is *the baby!*" And then she burst into tears and stomped to her room.

Mom said emotional swings were part of pregnancy, but Eliza's anger went a whole lot deeper than that. I felt singed every time I was around her. I guess I got used to avoiding her, even though I couldn't get enough of Annie.

Tasha raised an eyebrow. "Have you been in the shop lately?"

I shook my head. "I hate makeup."

Tasha shrugged. "Maybe you should stop by sometime."

"Are you saying I need makeup?" I leaned forward in my seat. "Don't you remember sixth grade?"

I shot a look at where Vile Kara Samson sat in the middle of the cafeteria.

At the beginning of sixth grade, Sarah and Kara had hosted a joint birthday party. Not only are they cousins, with their moms being twins (Delle and Estelle. Seriously.), but they also have birthdays two weeks apart. Every year, they had these huge birthday parties, with every girl in the class invited. Every year, the party was themed. In fifth grade, it was a circus theme, complete with cotton candy vendors, pony rides, and a giant trampoline.

The best part of every Kara-Sarah party were the gift bags. For the circus party, everyone left with little paper versions of the big top. When you tugged on the little red flag, the big top pulled back and glitter burst all around. That was the level of these parties.

It didn't even matter if Kara made your life miserable or Sarah was so perfect it made your teeth ache. Everyone was there. I never missed a party, either (except for first grade, when my invitation somehow never made it home—that was the year of the nose picking, remember?).

Well, sixth grade would be the last giant Kara-Sarah party. The theme was makeover. They brought in cosmetologists from the local beauty school and hair stylists from a salon. A dress company brought in gowns for the day so we could dress up. At the end, guests were handed our gift bags—zippered makeup pouches with our initials painted on them. It took Kara and Sarah forever to make sure everyone got the right bags. Kara smiled as she handed me mine. "Hope it helps," she said. Tasha and I compared bags on the way home.

We both had lipstick. Tiny tubes of mascara. Eye liner—hers in gray, mine in brown. Tasha's had a small pot of blush. I had something else. Wax, with "eyebrow shaping instructions inside" printed on the box. Tasha had snagged the box from me and pressed the button to lower the car window. "Your eyebrows are fine," she said, prepping to throw it back onto the Samsons' lawn.

I had plucked it back out of her hands. "It's no biggie," I said, shoving it back into the pouch.

It wasn't like I hadn't been aware that my eyebrows were growing in thick, straight lines. Wax, the little instructions read, was the best way to shape eyebrows. My eyebrows had never been shaped. They were shapeless streaks. *Eyebrows are essential to framing your face,* the instructions said. *Without properly shaped eyebrows, your face is never going to stand out.*

After my family went to bed that night, I had grabbed the box. Following the instructions, I carefully applied wax above and below my right eyebrow and pulled with just a little crying. Okay, a lot of crying. But the eyebrow did look much better. Just as carefully, I began applying to my left eyebrow, only to suddenly have to sneeze. I fought it, like I always fight touching my nose. But then, *achoo!* And, bam. Wax covered not just the top and bottom of my eyebrow, but my entire eyebrow. I jerked my hand away in horror, but some of the wax was on my finger, too, and soon I was holding my eyebrow in my hand. My whole eyebrow, there in my hand. I've sworn off makeup ever since (though I'm somewhat addicted to lip gloss)

I forced my mind back to the present, discussing makeup—or lack of makeup—at lunch.

Tasha took a bite of her sandwich, carefully so as not to smear the lipstick. She slowly chewed and then said, "I don't think that's what I said." She turned to Ricky. "Ricky, is that what I said? Did I tell Pipi to wear makeup?"

Ricky's eyes turned to circles. His mouth opened and closed a couple times. Finally, as if she hadn't asked him a question at all, he said, "Love the blue! It's just how I pictured Freya."

Tasha grinned. "Really? I have that spray stuff to dye my hair white in my bag—but my mom flipped when I asked her to help put it on this morning."

"Nah, I think it's perfect," Ricky said. "If you could breathe frost, it'd be more than perfect."

"Is Elsa in this book?" I asked.

Tasha's hand slammed the table. "Freya would eat Elsa for breakfast."

"*Slowly,*" Ricky said with a laugh. "She'd *slowly* eat Elsa for breakfast."

"Fine, I give. Who's Freya?" I asked, bracing myself for a half-hour explanation of some fairy character. That's what usually happened, anyway, if I expressed any interest in anything remotely *CR*. It was kind of boring, but it made Tasha happy *and* gave me time to think about the rest of my list. What was I going to tackle next?

Only, Ricky and Tasha exchanged a long look, small smiles on their faces. Finally, Ricky said, "Freya cannot be explained. You'd have to read the books to understand."

"That's right," said Tasha, taking another careful bite of her sandwich.

My nose tickled, probably stuck on that evil eyebrow-destroying sneeze memory. I ignored it. Finally, I couldn't resist. I cupped my hand over my nose and quick as I could, brushed it with my thumb.

Ricky watched me. Or rather, looked at my nose.

Oh, no! Had I knocked loose a booger or some? super quickly, I brushed at my itchy nose.

Ricky's eyes narrowed. Just as quick, he b.. nose. Was this a secret signal? *It's going to happen again! going to be known as Picker Penelope all over again!* I whapped at my nose.

Ricky mimicked the motion. "Did I get it?"

"Get what?" I could see my red cheeks blaring, my nose a huge white runway of shame in the middle. I ducked my head and rubbed at my giant nose with both hands.

"Weren't you motioning to me?" Ricky pointed to his nose.

"No! You were motioning to me!" I sat on my hands, traitor nose still itchy.

Tasha leaned back in her seat. "Pipi's weird about her nose."

"Oh," Ricky said. "Why would you be weird about a nose?"

Tasha glanced at me, then said, "She thinks it's too big or something, so she covers it up all the time. I think she'd go Voldemort if she could."

I threw a bunched-up napkin at her, which she dodged with a laugh. "Shut up."

Ricky shrugged. "Well, I think your nose is nice."

"It's enormous and takes up most of my face," I said. "I'm not *weird* about it. I just don't like drawing further attention to it."

"Like I was *saying*," Tasha said, "before I was rudely assaulted by your napkin. Go to Eliza's shop. I bet there are, like, contouring tricks if you're that bothered by it."

Traitor nose itched. "Contouring?"

Tasha shrugged. "If you don't like it, do something about it. I used to hate my mouth—"

"Your *mouth*?" Ricky interrupted. "Why would you hate your *mouth*?"

Tasha laughed, then Ricky shook his head like the idea didn't process. "Know what helped?" she said to me. "Makeup. Now my mouth is my favorite feature."

"Yeah, it's great," Ricky said.

Odd silence seeped around us.

"So, yeah, do something about it," Tasha continued. "Your nose, I mean. If you don't like it, do something about it."

Chapter Ten

The library was only three blocks from school, so it was easy to get to once classes let out. I knew better than to think Tasha would be waiting to walk with me. She'd be way too excited to get to the *CR* party. I had a notebook in my hand, ready to stop walking and scribble down thoughts if I came up with the next part of my plan.

I needed to do something bold. Something permanent. Something that would really prove to everyone that I, Penelope McGee, was different now.

As I walked, I wrote the same couple of words over and over, trying to figure out how to address them—*nose, vomit, basketball, peepee, Jackson Thorpe, eyebrow* (plus another word referencing the thing I refused to talk about from seventh grade). Okay, I could do this. My eyes went to Jackson's name. It wasn't exactly the first time I had written his name. Even thinking about it made my cheeks burn bright, remembering how Fifth-Grade Pipi had filled an entire notebook with his name. And, of course, one enormous *Penelope Claire Thorpe.* I held my current notebook against my chest in a moment of silence for poor Fifth-Grade Pipi.

The only real revenge for *that* humiliation would be to have Jackson fall in love with me. Of course, I wouldn't, upon confession of his undying love, rush away from him, laughing and pointing, the way he had done to me. We'd stay in love. Redemption *and* revenge, see?

I almost circled Jackson's name, making it the unofficial next target in tackling The List. But the chances of Jackson falling in love with me would be much greater once I lost the Pipi Touch forever.

I circled *nose. How could I redeem myself for being the nose picker of first grade?*

When I heard someone shout, "Hey!" I turned around thinking it'd be Tasha, even though I figured she'd already be at the library. Instead, it was Sarah Trickle.

I did that kind of backward glance to make sure she was actually waving at me before turning fully around. "Hey," I finally said back.

Sarah Trickle trotted up to me. "Are you going to the library?"

"Um, yeah," I said, pulling my backpack off one shoulder and swinging it to the front while we walked. I unzipped the bag, holding the notebook in one hand while I tried to make an opening wide enough to shove it inside.

Sarah plucked it from my fingers. "Let me help!" Her eyes widened when I snatched the notebook back out of her hands and shoved it into the bag.

"Sorry," I mumbled. "I don't like . . . I mean, that notebook is . . . I don't like people seeing it, I guess."

"Oh!" Sarah's smile stretched and her eyes seemed to glisten a little. "I know what's going on!"

"You do?"

Sarah clapped her hands together. "I have a notebook just like that—one that I don't let anyone see. You're writing poetry, aren't you?"

"Well, I wouldn't really call it—"

"No," she said and squeezed my shoulder. "It's cool! I understand." She stopped, still holding on to my shoulder, so I had to stop, too. Then she squeezed my other shoulder with her other hand. "I know, believe me, I know, how hard it is to say who you are, what you care about. But this shouldn't be." Her smile stretched, and her voice dipped secret soft. "I'm a poet, too."

"Actually . . ." I searched through responses, but somehow *No, it isn't a book of poetry. It's a list of humiliations and how to seek revenge* couldn't quite form in my mouth.

"That's been my big hang-up, too. When can you really say that you are something?" Sarah squeezed my shoulders again. "So, I'm just going to do it. Just call myself a poet."

"Uh, sure," I mumbled.

Sarah laughed. "Sorry, guess I'm a little intense. I'm just, I don't know, figuring myself out."

Now it was my turn to laugh. "You? What's there to figure out? Everyone loves *you*."

Sarah stopped again. Even though she wasn't holding my shoulders anymore, I paused, too. Her nose wrinkled up. Her perfect little nose. "What are you talking about?"

My wide, flat nose twitched. "Why the self-reflection? I mean, why would you change anything about yourself? Some of us"—I gestured down over my body—"have *years'* worth of events to figure out. *Tons* of things to change. Not you. Everyone wants to be you."

Sarah swallowed. She looked strangely hurt for someone who was just told she was perfect. "That's definitely not true."

"*Sure,*" I said.

The quiet between us was thicker than the humid late-summer air. Finally, she said, "We're not the only ones, either. Jackson's a poet, too."

I snorted. "Oh, yeah, I noticed that."

Her eyebrow (perfectly shaped, by the way) popped up in the air.

"I think I heard him say he's evolving, or something," I finished.

"Right." Sarah smiled. "He's been sharing a lot of his poetry with me." Under her breath, she added another *a lot.*

Seize opportunities! my brain screamed. I remembered what I had overheard at lunch—when Kara shut down Sarah's idea of a poetry club. Just me and Jackson. In a club. Together. (And, okay, fine. Sarah, too.) He'd be the first to see the bold new me, to notice how much *I* evolved this year. "If only there was, like, a place where we could meet. Us poets, I mean. A get-together or a . . ."

"A club!" Sarah bounced on her toes. "Yes! I know!" By now we were steps away from the library.

I shrugged. "My mom has space. In her gym. We could meet there."

Sarah stopped, standing stock still. "That could work! It'd just be the three of us—you, me, and Jackson—to start, but hopefully more people will join once they see us performing."

"Performing?" I felt a little like a parrot.

Sarah laughed. "A bunch of schools around us have Spoken Word Clubs. They go to performances and everything. I think we should start one. Get a head start on the community ser- vice thing Mr. Harper was saying we have to do in high school. It might even give us clues—you know—inspiration, for other clubs we might want to create. What do you think?"

"Absolutely!" I could probably figure out how to avoid actu- ally sharing and writing poetry. It wouldn't be too hard. "I don't know about me performing, but, yeah, absolutely."

"Yes!" Sarah jumped up and down. Before I knew it, her arms were around me in a quick hug. I gasped like she had squeezed out all my air, even though her hug was quick as a clap. *Sarah Trickle just hugged me and invited me to be in a secret club with Jackson Thorpe.*

She backed away and glanced around. Her forehead puck- ered. "Aunt Estelle's pulling into the parking lot now. Gotta go. But, um, one thing . . . it's kind of, you know, something we shouldn't tell . . ."

And here it was. The part where she remembered she was talking to Pipi McGee, the social virus. My face flamed as that empty feeling I had after the hug filled right to the brim with shame. "Don't worry," I said. "I won't tell anyone you talked to me."

"I knew you'd understand," she said, her eyes still on the parking lot. She turned suddenly so she was behind me. And, of course, since I'm enormous compared to her teeny tiny perfect little doll self, I entirely hid her. I glanced over my shoulder toward the parking lot. Vile Kara Samson was darting out of the library toward the car. "So just us, okay? And maybe we should meet, I don't know, fifteen minutes after spin?"

I gulped. "Why not make it twenty? That way no one will see you hanging out with me."

She flashed a quick smile. She actually *smiled* at that. "Perfect! I'll see you tomorrow, Penelope." She peeked over my shoulder, then grimaced, obviously trying to figure out how to get to the car without being spotted walking with me.

Luckily, that's when I noticed Ricky and Tasha standing in the grass by the front of the library. Ricky was spraying the white dye onto Tasha's braids. "My friends are over there," I said to Sarah. "See you around."

"Oh!" she said, and I tried not to notice how relieved she was that I wouldn't be trailing her to the parking lot.

Concentrate on being in the club. Concentrate on The List, I ordered myself as I trotted toward Tasha and Ricky. *Do* not *cry, Pipi McGee. Don't you dare cry.* So what if the nicest girl in the entire school would rather hide than be seen next to you? So freaking what? Tasha saw me lumbering toward her and her laugh choked off. Ricky took a half step back as I fell into Tasha's arms.

"Oh, no," she said, patting my head. "You okay?"

I nodded into her shoulder. One tear didn't listen and trickled down my cheek.

"Want to talk about it?" Tasha asked.

I shook my head. "Sorry," I said and brushed at my cheek with the back of my hand as I dropped my hug. "Guess I'm just overcome with excitement for *Crow Reaper.*"

Tasha laughed a little too loudly, but her eyes locked with mine. I nodded, letting her know I was okay.

"Sorry for the hug attack." I forced another laugh. "Poor Tasha. You've got so many years of the Pipi Touch, you'll never be free of me."

"Pipi Touch? Is that a thing again?"

"Did it ever stop?" I rolled my eyes.

"Nope, no way. No feeling sad on *CR* day!" Tasha tugged me forward. "Let's go! I've been trying to download the audiobook all morning, but I think the librarians must've embargoed the library copy or something until after the party."

The "party"—I knew from experience—was a bit of a

stretch. Tasha was the only *Crow Reaper*-obsessed person in Northbrook. At the last release, the librarians had a plate full of cookies and a half dozen copies of the book on a table in one of the rooms usually reserved for quiet study. (Know how I said everyone loves Sarah? Well, that's definitely true. But the adoration the library has for Tasha is something next level. The teen librarian has a framed picture of Tasha on her desk. For real.)

The party last year lasted only a few seconds for most people—just long enough to grab a cookie and say hi to Tasha. But the librarians had played the first chapter of the audiobook for Tasha and me in that little room. I had slipped earbuds into my ears and listened to music instead, but Tasha was so excited. Now, a couple people held open the library doors and gestured for her to come inside.

"The librarians said we couldn't start until you got here," one of them told Tasha with a whiny voice.

"Blame her," said Tasha, jerking a thumb my way. "It's her fault we're late."

"Wow," I said, "looks like even more people have read the books than last time."

Tasha rolled her eyes. "They're here for the cookies and you know it. But who cares. Right, Ricky?"

Ricky laughed. "Right! Just means we get to be first to find out about Death's secret purpose. And the catalyst."

"And meet the goblin king!" Tasha squealed.

"You guys are so weird," I said. They ignored me.

Inside the library, the books were in a pile. The cover image was of a little boy with an enormous shadowy crow stretching out behind him.

"*Whoa*," both Ricky and Tasha said at the same time, even though, of course, they'd seen the cover a million times before. I nabbed a cookie.

Ricky grabbed one, too, and Tasha looked around for the speaker. The librarian walked toward her with hands raised. "I know what you're going to ask: Where's the audio? Here's the thing—and I've been on the phone with the distributor all morning—it looks like this last book isn't on audio yet." Tasha gasped, but the librarian just continued: "We've got plenty of copies, as you can see. But you'll have to wait for the audio. Sorry, Tasha."

"But . . ."

"I'm sorry," she said again and then tried to corral the line of kids into an orderly cookie-grabbing procession.

I breathed out slowly. Tasha picked up a copy of the book and flipped to the first page. Her eyes filled with tears. "I wanted to stay up all night reading it," she said softly. Her eyes scanned the words and then she slammed it shut. The words jumble on her sometimes. When she's rushing—the way she would be to see what happened next in the story—they jumble even more. Tasha works with a vision itinerant at school to make her work accessible; it's not like she can't read. But audiobooks are kind of like her escape, a way that she can just fully enjoy the story without accommodating the way her brain works differently with dyslexia.

Ricky glanced at Tasha, then his eyes met mine. I pulled the book from her hands and opened it up again. I cleared my throat and began to read, walking slowly to a chair. Tasha paused for just a second and then followed me, wrapping her arm around my shoulder.

"What?" I said when I reached page two. "What? Who is Maeve?"

Ricky sighed and plucked the book from my hand. "Nope. No. You don't get to ask questions. Read the other books." He picked up where I had left off. I watched them for a minute, Tasha sitting with her knees drawn up, staring into space as Ricky read to her in a smooth, steady voice. He must've read a lot to his little brothers and sister because he did voices and everything.

I nabbed another cookie, gave Tasha a quick hug, and headed home.

After leaving the library, I went to Dad's condo complex, which was only a few blocks from my home. I knew *technically* both places were home, but Dad's place never really felt like it. I had never hung a poster on the walls of my so-called bedroom there, which was really just a walk-in closet with a bed and a tiny window. Don't get me wrong; it wasn't that I didn't feel welcome at

Dad's or that I loved him any less than Mom. It was just that the condo was so much *Dad's* place, whereas Mom's house was *our* house. When Dad and Mom were still married, he had a basement den full of newspapers he wanted to read but hadn't gotten around to, a record player for his Motown records, and a coffee pot always brewing in the corner. Dad's place now was like one giant basement den.

Dad was sitting in the middle of his lumpy couch with a slice of pizza in one hand and the remote in the other when I came in.

"Pipi!" he called when the door swung shut with a loud click. "Oh, man! Lost track of time!"

Dad had random hours at the newsroom—when news was breaking, he could work round-the-clock shifts. But newspapers weren't exactly rolling in cash lately, so he didn't get overtime. Instead, he banked up the hours so when it was slow at the paper, he wouldn't go into the office at all. Today must've been a slow day.

Actually, looking around, the week must've been slow. I could see drifts of dust swirling through the dim light that was seeping through the drawn curtains. The room smelled stale, like old pizza and newspaper. Which was because of all the old pizza and newspapers laying around.

"Dad, how old is that pizza?" I asked as he bit down. The cheese had congealed to plastic consistency.

"Pizza never goes bad," he said. But his jaw was working

IS THAT **MOOOLD??!**

awfully hard to yank the bite from the crust.

"I don't think that's actually true. When was the last time you had a vegetable?"

"It's got sauce!" Dad brushed crumbs from his stomach and groaned as I yanked back the curtains to let in more light. Surrounding Dad were coffee mugs and pizza boxes.

"What happened?"

Dad crossed his arms He was quiet for a moment, then tossed the slice into an open pizza box. Quickly, I snagged it and dumped the whole box in the trash can. "Kid died. Hit and run. Was on his bike. His father was right there. Couldn't stop it."

I blew out my breath in a puff and sat down next to Dad. He let his head fall on my shoulder. He might not have left the house for days, but he still smelled good—like deodorant and mint shampoo. "Driver's just a kid, too," Dad added. "Only seventeen. Charged with manslaughter."

I leaned into him a little more. I'd been toted around to crime scenes and house fires and accidents often enough as a reporter's kid to handle the facts. Whenever the news broke, Dad headed out and covered it—he marched right up to police officers or suspects or victims and asked them questions, his notebook a barrier between them. His face was always expressionless until he filed the story. Then? I glanced around the dark, dirty den. This.

He held on to things too long, from pizza to pain. His little condo was testimony to that. He still had boxes in the corners, labeled *yearbooks* and *college textbooks,* even though he had moved out of our house more than five years ago.

I knew the cycle—knew it was behind my parents' divorce— and also knew it was useless to try to reason him out of it. What he needed—what *I* needed, I reminded myself—was bold action. We were going to change our ways. Reinvent ourselves. And if copious amounts of bad eighties movies on TBS had taught me anything, it was that there was only one place where a teenage girl could reinvent herself. (Not sure about dads, but it was probably the same place.)

"Get ready," I told him. "We're going to the mall."

"Why in the world would we do that?" Dad moaned. "The mall? The mall full of people?"

"Yes, Dad!" I slapped his leg. "People! You need to be around people."

"The mall full of sound? Full of . . ." He spit oɪ   ə next word: "Lights?"

"Yes. Sound *and* lights!" I bounced next to him. "A new home store opened a couple weeks ago. We should get you some nice throw pillows. Maybe a salt lamp or something."

Dad muttered some words that would've made Mom's face go tomato red.

I grabbed Dad's chin, cupping it with my hands. His cheeks were bristly with whiskers. "Enough wallowing! We're changing. You and me."

"What are you talking about?" he asked, his squished-up face making me laugh.

"We're changing, Dad. We're going to face issues head-on. We're going to reinvent ourselves." While there was no way I'd go to Eliza's makeup shop—I could just picture her looking down her nose at me and laughing at any attempt I made to be beautiful—the mall was full of makeup shops. I couldn't stop thinking about Tasha's contouring comment. "You also haven't paid me allowance in six weeks," I reminded him. "Ready to go?"

Dad's face twisted but, still holding his cheeks, I made him nod.

Chapter Eleven

At the home store, I filled Dad's cart with sunny yellow pillows and a white slipcover for his couch.

"You can bleach it," I said when he groaned about the color. "Or even eat at a table." I let my eyes drift down his pizza-sauce smudged brown T-shirt, his brown khaki pants, and his old, beat-up brown leather shoes. "Everything on you is a shade of depressing. And it's worse in your apartment." I poked his chest. "Brown walls, brown carpet, brown curtains. Even your couch is brown. Reinvent yourself!"

"Why?" he grumped. "It's my favorite color."

"It's boring."

"It's me," he replied with a shrug.

I smiled. "Every single time I complain about being bored you tell me bored is another word for lazy." I added a fake aloe plant to the cart. "Besides, you're never going to have a date, like, ever, if you don't reinvent yourself."

Dad blinked at me a couple of times. Dad hadn't dated anyone since the divorce. Mom used to say that he was married to his work. And maybe in a lot of ways he was. But for just a moment, something flashed across his face. The expression—sad and, well, *lonely*—made tears pop in my eyes.

"Pillows are not the path to reinvention," he finally said. "And you can put a slipcover over it, but it's the same couch."

"Yes, but now it's going to be pretty." I directed the cart toward a stand of salt lamps.

Dad paused. He threw a gray blanket into the cart. "I'll sit on this," he said.

A half hour later, Dad handed me a folded-up pile of bills, mostly fives and ones. "Keep your phone on you and don't buy anything silly. Meet me in an hour."

"Where are you going?" I asked.

"First, I'm going to unload two hundred dollars' worth of pillows and a lamp I could lick into my car trunk, and then I'm going to get a haircut." He smiled.

"And a shave?" I suggested.

Dad nodded. "I've gotten boring, haven't I?"

I crossed my arms. "A bit."

He rubbed the back of his neck. He took a deep breath and I thought for a moment he was going to tell me something profound. Instead, he simply said, "Meet me here in an hour."

The walls of the makeup shop were all shiny black. So were the counters. A half dozen employees walked around with aprons full of makeup brushes. Mirrors hung everywhere. Every. Where. I had hoped there would be signs like those at grocery stores indicating the contouring pencils. No such luck.

There were buckets of eyeliners, though, in all different colors. Dozens of different shaded powders. Pot after pot after pot of eyeshadows. Foundations in a thousand shades and varieties. Probably a million types of face wash and curling irons. Soon I was in front of the store with only a half hour left.

A tall black woman with bright orange eyeshadow and teal eyeliner approached me. "May I help you?" She had a gold hoop in her nose with a thin gold chain that stretched to a diamond stud in her ear.

"How do I contour?" I blurted.

She laughed and ushered me toward a chair in front of a huge mirror rimmed with lights. "Have a seat, love." Once I settled, she asked, "Now, what makes you think you need to contour?"

I stared at my nose in the mirror. "I want my nose to be smaller."

She paused, her mouth pursed as she studied my face. "Your nose isn't your problem."

"It isn't?" My hands flew to my face. *What was my problem?*

"Nah. Your nose is fine. It's cute, even. The problem is you don't draw any attention to it."

"Why would I draw attention to my nose? I hate it." I frowned at my reflection, but she just smiled back.

"I used to think my ears were too big. Now, I draw a line"—she ran her finger along the chain from her nose to her ear—"right to my ears." It reminded me of that afternoon when Tasha told me she used to hate her mouth and that now it was her favorite feature. The lady shrugged, swiveling me around so my back was to the mirror. "When you hate something, it's all you think about. When you enhance it, you find its beauty." For a few moments, she dipped a cotton swab into different pots and then swiped it along my cheeks and eyelids. Then she swiveled me back. I blinked. And blinked again.

"I look exactly the same," I said.

She smiled even wider. "But now your face is moisturized." She leaned down so she was looking me straight in the eyes. "There's nothing wrong with your nose. Only thing wrong is what you think of it." She faced me toward the mirrors again. "Look at that face. *Really* look at it. Your nose is straight. Your pores are *tiny*. Your nose is . . . well, I'd say it's noble."

"Noble," I repeated. I looked. You know what? My nose *was* nice.

"Besides," she said as she crumpled up the cotton, "I'm not sending a kid home with a mountain of overpriced makeup she'd never remember how to use. My daughter, she's about your age. She told me this girl, she tried to give herself a makeover a couple years ago. One thing led to another, and then this kid suddenly had one eyebrow." The stylist threw back her head, guffawing. "Can you imagine? Like being in middle school isn't hard enough. Try going at it with one eyebrow!"

I closed my eyes. "Does your daughter go to Northbrook Middle?"

"How'd you know?" she said, wiping at the tears seeping out from the corners of her eyes.

"Just a guess," I murmured, eyes on the chain glinting from her nose in the Hollywood-style light shining from the mirror.

I met Dad at the mall entrance of the home store. His hair was crisp and swooping over his forehead, and his face was clean-shaven. Even better? He had shopping bags in his hand.

"New clothes?" I asked.

He waved them in my direction. "Following my kid's advice. Getting rid of the brown."

I peeked inside the bags. "Everything in here is black."

"Black is bold."

"Black is a start, Dad." I sucked on my bottom lip for a second. "Where are all your bags? All that back allowance should've burned a hole in your pocket."

"Well," I said, "speaking of being bold . . ."

"Uh-oh. Why do I think this is leading somewhere I don't want to go?"

"Can we swing by just one more shop?"

"*Pipi*." Dad groaned. "You had an hour! I'm going to break out in hives if I have to stay here any longer."

"I just need you to sign a permission form at this one place." I grabbed his elbow, leading him back into the mall despite his grimace of shopping-induced pain.

Finally, I got him to the piercing section of a trendy jewelry store. "You want your ears pierced? Aren't they already?" Dad asked.

I shook my head. "No. My nose."

Dad laughed. "Yeah. No."

"C'mon, Dad! Sometimes you have to love the thing you hate. I want to love my nose." He shook his head, as if trying to process my words, which, okay, fine, didn't make a lot of sense.

"There is no way in the world I am sending you back home to your mother with a pierced nose. No offense," he said, looking up at the piercing attendant, who had clearly practiced on himself quite a bit, judging from the hardware in his face.

The attendant shrugged and went back to cleaning the piercing equipment. "Truth is," the guy said, "nasal tissue closes a lot faster than ears. Safer, really."

"I'm calling your mother," said Dad, punching out the digits on his cell phone. I sat down in the piercing chair, and the attendant put a little blue dot on the side of my nose with a marker. He held up a mirror. "Here?"

"Perfect!" I said.

Dad held the phone to his ear. "Don't get too comfortable there."

I heard the ring the next aisle over. "Mom?" I called out.

My mom's face peeked out from behind a counter. "Pipi?" She stepped toward us, holding Annie's hand. "What's going on here?"

She looked at Dad. "Andy? You look . . . very nice."

Dad straightened. "You can tell the truth, Missy. I look hot."

Mom laughed. "It's just so odd that you're both here."

Annie tugged on Mom's hand. "Can I go home with them?"

"No," Mom said in her forced-brightness voice that she used just before snapping. "We're here to pick out a nice present for Tabitha's fifth birthday."

"But I don't like Tabitha. Can't I just give her gum?"

"No," Mom snapped. She took a deep breath. Her mouth was white. This was not the first time she had had this conversation with Annie. "We are not getting her gum. We are getting her something in this store." She blinked at me. "What's that dot on your nose?"

"Pipi wants to get her nose pierced," Dad blurted.

Mom's hands did this quick flap thing that always precedes her totally losing her cool. Annie tugged on her sleeve again. "Can I pierce Tabitha for her birthday?"

"No!" Mom snapped. "No. No one's getting pierced."

"Except for me." I stood up, so I could look Mom in the eye. "I love my nose, okay? I love my nose. It's big and wide and I've spent years—years—hating my nose. My noble nose. No more!" I stomped my foot. "No. More."

Mom's eyes went scary wide.

"Besides," I said, "Piercing Guy says it's no big deal. Tiny hole. Grows shut." My voice tapered off at the end.

"No big deal?" Mom's hands flapped again. "Fine." She sat in the chair. "Me first."

"What?" Dad, Annie, Piercing Guy, and I all said at once.

"I don't have the energy to discuss this with any of you." Mom's glare spun around to all of us, including Piercing Guy. "I'm too tired to think, much less argue, about why putting a metal rod through a perfectly good body part is a poor idea. No offense," she said to Piercing Guy, who just nodded and picked up the piercing needle. "I've thrown up every afternoon for the past two weeks just because of one disgusting piece of . . ." She shuddered, and Annie leaned in, whispering, *"Cashew cheese."* Mom turned a little green and clenched her fists.

"Every day?" Dad said. "For how long?"

"Like I said, two weeks," Mom said. "I'm bloated and tired and I just needed to pick up a tiara or a princess hat or something for a little *b-r-a-t* whom Annie doesn't even like for a party I don't even feel like taking her to, yet Eliza won't speak to me because I'm MomMom and she's Eliza. Then I come to this store and here you both are. Andy is getting to be the super cool makeover dad who takes his teen daughter for her nose piercing and buys her stuff at the mall, while I'm the heavy who has to say no. Well, not today, mister." She said all of this in a huge rush, none of us having a chance to say anything (except for Annie, who kept whispering *cashew cheese* over and over again).

"So . . ." Piercing Guy asked.

"Oh, my," Dad said, his eyes wide. "Tired? Sick? Bloated?"

"Yes!" Mom said. "Yes. So, pierce me. Pierce me!" Mom

just about snarled. "I don't have time to argue. I don't have the energy to argue. If one of us is getting pierced, we both are." She turned toward me. "If you think it's no big deal, then you won't have any issue seeing me go first, will you? Huh?" She looked at me, and I realized she actually wanted me to answer.

"Okay," I squeaked. Piercing Guy handed her the form and pen. She, still glaring at me, scrawled her name.

"So, same gold stud?" Piercing Guy asked. He put a little dot on her nose and held up the mirror.

"Well, Pipi?" she snarled.

"Um . . ."

Piercing Guy moved the needle toward Mom's nose.

Dad rushed forward. "I can't let you do this, Missy." He pulled her up and slipped into the chair. Piercing Guy dutifully put the dot on the side of his nose and held up the mirror. Dad nodded without looking.

"If anyone takes the shot, it's me. *Be bold,*" he shout-whispered in my direction.

"You guys are sending me really opposing messages," I said.

"No," said Mom, crossing her arms. "Andy, get out of the chair."

"I can't let you take a piercing in your condition," Dad said. He nodded to the Piercing Guy, his eye twitching. Piercing Guy nodded back.

"Andy!" Mom snapped. "What do you mean 'in my condition'?"

Dad arched an eyebrow at her. Her hand went to her stomach. She winced a little and then seemed to be counting something on her fingers.

"In her *what*?" I gasped.

"I'm pregnant," Mom said, her eyes huge.

"You never knew. Both times I had to point it out to you. We both had to point it out to Eliza." Dad laughed.

Mom is pregnant? What!

Piercing Guy leaned forward.

"Gah!" Dad screeched.

"*Cashew cheese,*" Annie whispered.

"Next," Piercing Guy called.

"That. Was. A. Bluff!" Dad cried. He jumped to his feet. His watery eyes spilled over. His hand touched his nose, where a gold bead now lived, embedded in his flesh. "I winked at you, man. I winked!"

"You sat down." Piercing Guy shrugged as he cleaned off the piercing needle with astringent wipes. "You sit down, you get pierced. Who's next?"

Annie jumped into the seat.

"No!" The three of us said, yanking her out.

Okay, so maybe it was wrong to take advantage of Mom's shock over her ex-husband figuring out she was pregnant before she did. And maybe I totally took advantage of Dad's shock at getting his nose pierced at fifty years old.

But I took Annie's place in the chair. "Me."

Mom's hand drifted to her stomach. Dad's drifted to his nose. Annie sighed.

My noble nose.

I sucked in my breath as Piercing Guy took aim.

A piercing was the perfect way to draw attention to what I used to hide.

But my dad was crying. A lot.

And getting pierced involved metal being forcibly shoved through my skin.

"Stop!" Dad and I said at the same time as Piercing Guy moved closer. Dad grabbed my arm. "If you still want your nose pierced, that's what you can have for your fourteenth birthday," Dad told me as Piercing Guy rolled his eyes. My birthday was three months away. But it still counted, I told myself, as enough to scratch first grade off The List.

Chapter Twelve

I stood in front of my corkboard, staring at The List.

Holding a red Sharpie, I slashed through first grade.

My eyes snagged on the other six items still on The List. I had a lot of work left to do; even so, I thought I'd feel . . . I didn't know. More accomplished. I'd see Piper in two days. Watching her play with all of her friends—that'd make me feel better. And until then I was going to pretend like my nose already was pierced. My noble nose.

A soft knock on the door scattered my thoughts. Mom peeked in, then swung the door wide open. I could hear Eliza reading a bedtime story to Annie down the hall.

"I just don't think a toad being a friend to a frog is interesting," Annie said.

"I love this story. We're reading it," Eliza replied over Annie's enormous sigh.

"Hey," Mom said. She closed the door behind her.

"Hey," I answered. I glanced down at her stomach.

"So . . . your dad is pretty observant," she said.

I opened my mouth to congratulate her on the baby, then

closed it again. I didn't know what I was feeling. Sure, I was happy for her and Alec—he was going to be an amazing dad. But also a little . . . not happy? Like, I got why she was with Alec and not my dad. I totally was on board with that. But them making a new family together? It felt weird. Really weird. Not to mention that this baby would be Annie's aunt, and Annie was only going to be five by the time it was born. And the biggest thing, the thing I definitely wanted to *not be thinking about* was that health class video we had to watch back in fifth grade.

"I know you have questions," Mom said. "This was just such a surprise. I'm a grandma! Alec and I weren't even—"

"No!" I blurted. "No, nope. No questions."

Mom laughed. "Okay. No questions. Let me just tell you the important details. I'm about two months along. We're due this summer, best I can figure. But I'm going to ask you not to say anything to Annie. I told Eliza a little bit ago, and she's going to decide when and how to let Annie know. I'm not talking about it publicly for another month or so, either."

"How did Eliza take the news?" I asked, remembering her cold tone while reading to Annie.

Mom sighed. "She'll be fine." Again, her hand flashed to her stomach. I studied her face and the line between her eyebrows that seemed carved into her face when she was worried.

"I'm happy for you, Mom," I said, and I meant it.

Mom's smile was radiant. "Really? Are you really okay with this?"

"A baby?" I answered. "How couldn't I be?"

Mom rushed over and gave me a hug. She ran her thumb along my nose. "Thank you," she whispered.

Love is so mysterious.

Take my parents, for instance. I knew they once had been in love. I had seen pictures of my dad with his arm slung around Mom's shoulders; Mom in her wedding dress, her face glowing and happy. But now? The idea of them kissing was just disgusting. And now Mom was with Alec; they were so easy and right for each other. Mom said she knew the moment she saw him that she was going to love him, and when they actually started dating, it just felt right. Like it was meant to be (like me and Jackson Thorpe).

But sometimes people fall for each other and it's like, *huh?*

Such as, I don't know, Ricky Salindo and Tasha Martins.

We were sitting together at lunch and Ricky was still reading that book aloud to Tasha. (Her usual book club meetings were canceled this week so that members could read the new release.) Ricky had a great voice and he got into the story so much that he made each character sound different. But this was the third book in a series—a series I still hadn't started to read—so I didn't know what was going on. And something about the little smile on Tasha's face made me feel like I was intruding. I could've sat with other friends, but . . . I didn't have other friends.

"Wait!" Tasha suddenly said, interrupting Ricky. "He's in love? With Priscilla?"

"I know, right?" Ricky said.

"Yeah," I said. "Wow!"

They both turned to look at me, Tasha's eyebrow high.

I shrugged. "Playing along."

Ricky smiled at me, his dimple flashing for a second, but Tasha focused back on Ricky. "I totally didn't see that coming!"

"I know what you mean," I said with a little more feeling that I probably should've. She turned back to me again.

I glared toward where Jackson trailed behind Sarah in the lunch line. Ricky followed my gaze. He made a snorty sound from his nose. Smile gone.

Tasha rolled her eyes "Don't you think it's time to give that up?"

"Give what up?" Ricky asked, his eyes darting between us.

"Nothing!" I snapped. Ricky ducked his head back to the book. "Look," I said to Tasha, "I am over it. I'm *totally* over it. But he's still on The List."

"The List?" Ricky repeated.

"My list of humiliations," I said.

Ricky's eyes met mine over the book. "Ah, The List. That's why we're volunteering in kindergarten, right?"

I nodded. Tasha, who was super blurty today, added, "And

it was back in kindergarten when Pipi decided Jackson Thorpe was the one for her."

I stuck my tongue out at her. "Not true. It was fifth grade."

"So, how do you redeem yourself for liking Jackson?" Ricky's face was behind the book again, which made it strangely easy to answer.

"I'm not redeeming myself for *liking* him," I said. "I'm redeeming myself for fifth grade."

Tasha's forehead wrinkled. "Which one was fifth grade?"

"You know . . . the notebook," I answered. Ricky shifted, lifting up the book to cover more of his face. "So, it's not that big of a deal really," I started to tell Ricky, my cheeks burning and nose itchy. Why had I even brought this up? "Kara told me she thought Jackson liked me."

"That was the height of the Pipi Touch movement," Tasha said to Ricky.

"Oh, yeah! Pipi Touch! I remember that!" A boy passing by us laughed and jabbed my shoulder, then poked the kid behind him. "Your hair's gonna fall out, man."

"I *cut it off!*" I stood and yelped. "My hair didn't *fall* out." But the boys had moved on by then. I sighed, watching the Pipi Touch spread around the cafeteria.

Ricky cleared his throat and then continued as if nothing

had happened. "Maybe I'm wrong, but I thought Jackson was, like, the one who came up with the Pipi Touch to begin with. Shouldn't *that* be why he's on your list?"

I lifted my chin. "No, he was the first to call me Pipi after the peepee accident of fourth grade. And who could really blame him? It's catchy."

Tasha nodded.

"The Touch thing happened before that, in first grade." I glanced at Ricky. "Nose picking," I reminded him. "Everyone just changed it from The Touch to the Pipi Touch after the peeing-my-pants thing in fourth grade."

Tasha squinted like she was solving a math problem in her head.

"I remember now! *Fifth grade* started with Kara." To Ricky, she said, "She messed with Pipi for weeks," Tasha said. "Told her Jackson only liked girls who wear white dresses." Tasha waved an arm toward me. "Guess who looked like a child bride for weeks?"

"You were there, Ricky," I said. "Remember? You, Kara, and I had lockers next to each other. You saw it all unfold." I was proud of how steady and nonchalant my voice stood.

Ricky shrugged, making Tasha laugh. "Pipi," she said, "it probably didn't make an impression on Ricky the way it did you. *I* barely remember it, and I was your best friend."

Tasha turned to Ricky. "Kara then told Pipi that Jackson loved short hair."

Ricky cleared his throat again. "Okay with you if I read ahead?"

Tasha gasped and tugged the book from his hands. Ricky's cheeks flushed.

"So, yeah, I chopped off my hair. *Not because of The Touch*," I snarled toward the boys' backs. They were still jabbing each other back and forth where they sat across the cafeteria.

"You cut off your hair because you thought Jackson liked you?" Ricky said.

"What?" I asked.

He and Tasha exchanged looks.

"You *believed* The Touch?" I yelped.

Ricky shook his head, but his ears were awfully red. "Nah, of course not. It's just, isn't that a little extreme? Cutting off all your hair like that?"

My hair had been so long I could sit on it, but I had convinced Mom that I had always wanted a pixie cut. By the end of the week, that's what I had.

"Your hair was so pretty, too," Ricky said. He ducked his head back into the book.

The silence around us felt as awkward as cotton stuck in my ears. Tasha crumpled up her napkin. "I wouldn't change anything about myself for a boy." I blinked at her. She was wearing blue lipstick. Again. "I happen to like this color," she snapped. Tasha can sometimes read my mind.

"What do you like about him?" Ricky asked. Tasha and

I exchanged a quick glance, then both cracked up. Ricky shrugged. "Well, I guess if you go for the popular, handsome, athletic type." He grinned, then went back to the book.

"What I don't get," Tasha said, "is what made you think he liked you?"

"Just Kara. She was pretty convincing." And I was pretty gullible. "Honestly, like you said, it was a long time ago. I barely remember it."

Tasha crossed her arms and stared at me, reading my mind again. Here's something true: most of the time when I say "honestly," I'm about to lie.

I remember every bit of what happened.

Of course, Jackson had never actually told me he liked me. A couple of times he had nodded as I passed him in the hall, and I knew it was a secret message because Kara had told me he was too shy to talk to me. Kara had been extra nice to me that year, laughing at anything remotely funny I said; complimenting my headband and then wearing one like it. I felt like that year, I was so different. I felt like at any time Kara would call me up on the phone and ask me to go over to her house for a sleepover. So, when Kara nudged me one day at our lockers, winked, and said, "I know someone who likes you!" of course I believed it.

She suddenly liked me. Didn't it make sense that Jackson would, too? I knew Kara and Sarah were always with Jackson, so naturally she'd be in a position to know if he liked someone.

And in fifth grade? That someone was *me*. I had somehow gotten cool without even realizing it.

I'd have to make the first move, she had said, because Jackson was, get this, shy. I couldn't believe it. We had so much in common!

Picture me, standing by my locker. Wearing a long white dress. Hair so short the stylist had used an electric razor on my neck. Bursting with excitement because Jackson's bus had been just in front of my bus, and we had walked together down the hall. (Sort of. I was mostly trailing behind Jackson, but every half step our legs were kind of next to each other. And he didn't quicken his steps to get away from me. Then Wade had bumped into me from behind and screamed, "It gave me the Pipi Touch." He had jabbed at Jackson. But *Jackson didn't scream,* and that had to mean true love, right? He just rolled his eyes and trotted ahead down the hall. He kept the Pipi Touch! He *obviously* loved me.)

I did what any reasonable eleven-year-old girl would do. I wrote his name over and over again in a little notebook I kept just for the purpose of writing his name. I loved writing his name moments after seeing him get off his bus. Ricky and I would be first to our lockers—his was on the right side of mine, Kara's to the left—and Ricky would talk and talk and talk about Minecraft while I wrote and wrote and wrote *Jackson Thorpe* in cursive. On this day, in honor of this miraculous event (*He kept the Pipi Touch!*), I added a giant *Penelope Claire Thorpe* with a super fancy swirl on the first *p*.

"What are you doing?" Kara had asked that day near my locker.

"Oh, nothing!" I said. She and Ricky peeked over my shoulder; I quickly slapped shut the notebook and threw it into my locker.

With a little smirk at Ricky, Kara leaned in. "So, the boy who loves you? He's getting super close to telling you he likes you," she said. Around her, a trio of girls I didn't really know laughed. "He's going to ask you to go out with him. Like, later today. He just told me."

Ricky rolled his eyes and slammed shut his locker. "Bye, Pipi," he said, but I kept my eyes on Kara. Around her the girls all nodded, eyes wide. Kara crossed her arms.

"Really?" I bounced a little, and then they did, too. But I had just seen Jackson heading to homeroom. I paused. "When did you talk with him?"

Kara rolled her eyes. "Earlier, okay? Trust me! Today's the day."

"Who said what?" someone asked. Sarah Trickle. Her locker was on the other side of Kara's.

I looked at poor Sarah, who had squandered her shot with Jackson. I remember feeling bad for her as I stood there, practically already the future Mrs. Jackson Thorpe. Kara's face flushed. "Nothing."

I blinked a little. Kara turned back to her locker and her eyes slid to mine. She rolled them and made a face, and I understood—even she occasionally got sick of perfect Sarah Trickle. Kara turned and skipped off toward class, but Sarah stayed, watching me. "What's going on?"

Well, the truth was about to be out, wasn't it? I lifted my chin. "Jackson Thorpe is going to tell me he likes me today."

The rest of the girls giggled and rushed back to Kara, whispering in her ear. I heard her squeal Jackson's name, and for a second, I panicked. Maybe I shouldn't have told Sarah? I mean, I figured he had been talking to Sarah as much as Kara and already knew, but maybe I should've just pretended not to know so that when Jackson told me, I could act surprised?

Kara whipped around, her mouth popped open like she was so excited for me. Then she collapsed in giggles, leaning into the other girls. I breathed out. Everyone was so happy for me and Jackson!

Sarah pinched her mouth shut. "I don't think that's true," Sarah said, her eyes downcast. "I don't think he likes you, Pipi." She said it like *she* felt sorry for *me*.

I lifted my chin and shrugged. She didn't have to believe it for it to be true.

"I mean, not that he wouldn't like you." She swallowed, her eyes still too wide, too sad looking. "It's just I don't think Jack—"

"Jack*son*," I interrupted, "likes lots of things you don't know about." I let my eyes drift over her pink and purple tie-dyed T-shirt and pink shorts. She didn't even know Jackson loved white. She grabbed her long ponytail in one hand and twisted it around her fist.

"Maybe," she said. "If he does like you, that's—"

I didn't even try to, but a *hmpf* noise leaked out of me at the word "if." She didn't think I was good enough for Jackson. Well, too bad. He liked *me*.

"It's just sometimes Kara thinks things are funny. You know, just a joke? But if you don't know her the way I know her, then . . ."

The bell rang, and I turned on my heel, striding away as fast as I could from the other girls.

Tasha had been waiting for me in second period. "Pipi, I heard Kara and some girls talking and—"

By then the teacher had called for attention, cutting off whatever Tasha was going to say. She looked worried, so I flashed her a smile and whispered, "I know. It's about me and Jackson, right?"

Tasha squinted at me over her shoulder. "And you're okay?"

"Of course, I am!" I laughed.

He was going to tell me he liked me. Soon. Kara told me and had let it slip to other people, too. My whole life was about to change. Tasha smiled at me, but it was the same sad sort of smile that Sarah had been sporting.

"Don't worry," I whispered.

Tasha cracked her knuckles and nodded. "We got this."

Which was a little strange, I guess. I mean, looking back,

it was pretty obvious, wasn't it? Anyone could've seen through Kara and what she was up to. Anyone with half a brain would've questioned a little bit before believing that someone like Jackson would like someone like me. Anyone else would've realized it had all been a lie, way before she wore the same white dress three days a week like some pathetic bride wannabe. Way before she chopped off her hair. Way before she filled a notebook with a boy's name.

They don't call it pulling a McGee for nothing.

I heard whispers all day, linking Jackson and my name. And I'd smile. *Smile.* Tasha told me all lunch that she thought I should go home. "Just tell the nurse you don't feel well."

But I didn't listen. I figured she didn't get it. "No!" I tried to explain. "This is great. Really. It's good stuff!"

Tasha said, "I think you really might be sick."

And I had laughed.

Kara had told me how shy my crush was, so I figured he wouldn't tell me he liked me until dismissal. The day passed in a blur. And then the bell rang. I walked slowly to my locker. I was picturing how my dress was billowing out around me and how I held my books in my hands, pretending they were a bouquet and the hall a church aisle. (Whatever. I watched a lot of soap operas with Mom.)

And there was Jackson, standing by my locker with Kara and a bunch of other kids, including the girls from that morning. His shoulders were shaking.

"Guys, stop!" he said, but I could hear the smile in his voice. Still, how awful that his so-called friends were picking on him when he was so nervous—so nervous, in fact, that he was shaking! I quickened my steps.

He turned then, a huge grin on his face. That's when I noticed my locker door was open. That's when my heart stopped thudding. It seemed to stop altogether. He was holding my notebook. The Jackson Thorpe notebook. It was open to the page with *Penelope Claire Thorpe* scrawled out in giant loopy letters.

Jackson Thorpe handed me the notebook, or at least he tried to. My arms didn't seem to be working, so it fell between us. He shrugged. "So, um, I don't like you. No offense or anything. I just don't like you. Like, at all."

He pushed his backpack up his arm. "Is it true what Kara said? The white dress thing? The hair?" He laughed, and everyone around joined in.

I blinked, but it must've taken an extra-long time for my eyes to open back up because when I did, Jackson's forehead was wrinkled. "I didn't know anything about what Kara did or the notebook thing." He shrugged. "But it was just a joke, right? Don't make it a big deal, okay?"

I nodded, and he bumped me on the shoulder with his fist. "Cool."

I saw him swipe at Wade as he walked away. "Oh, yeah! Pipi Touch!"

Kara had slowly twirled her locker combo. "You totally fell into that whole thing. Right, Ricky?"

Ricky, on the other side of my locker, had slammed shut his door and ran for his bus.

Kara's laughter had followed me out of the school that day. Or maybe it was hers and everyone else's.

I winced three years later, remembering.

"Barely remember it," I said again, even though by the time I went through the mental play-by-play of that particular humiliation, Ricky had finished reading the chapter and the bell was about to ring.

"But how do you redeem yourself for all of that?" Ricky said as if the conversation hadn't stopped at all.

"I'll figure it out," I said. *By making Jackson fall in love with me for real and possibly shaving Kara's head,* my mind supplied.

He swallowed. "Wouldn't the best thing be to get over it?"

Tasha snorted. "If you haven't noticed, Pipi doesn't exactly get over stuff."

"That's not fair!" I said. "That's the whole point of this List thing. To *get* over it."

Ricky opened his mouth, then closed it again.

Tasha said, "So, what's the plan?"

I shrugged, thinking about the poetry club thing. "I have a few ideas."

Kara grabbed her bags from the table and headed out of the cafeteria. She always was the first to leave lunch. Every girl in school knew she commandeered the girls' bathroom on the second floor for the last ten minutes after eating. Kara was nothing if not predictable. And vile.

As she left, Jackson and Sarah exchanged a glance. Then they both got up, too. Holy moly. They were walking toward me! My whole body spasmed.

Alert! Alert! Jackson is approaching! Alert!

Chapter Thirteen

As Jackson approached our table, Ricky scooted closer to Tasha and began reading aloud again. Tasha turned her back slightly away from him, but I knew both of them would be listening in on whatever Jackson had come over to say. Just in front of me, Jackson smiled and nodded. My heart did this strange little fluttery thing, like it expanded too big for a second, letting too much blood through, all of which immediately rushed to my face.

"Hey, Pipi," he said with a half smile, just big enough to show off his straight, perfect teeth.

"Heep," I said. I have no idea why. *What is wrong with you, Pipi?*

Jackson just kept on smiling as if I hadn't combined *hello* and *help* into one word. Then he shifted to the side a little and there was Sarah.

"Hi, Penelope!" she said.

Not trusting my blabber mouth, I just nodded.

"So, Sarah and me were talking," Jackson said. He glanced at Ricky, who was still reading the book to Tasha, then back at me. "Can you talk for a sec?"

"Yelp," I said. *Why? Why, Pipi?* Since there was only a minute left before class, I grabbed my stuff and followed them to the hallway.

"Sarah says you're into poetry, too. That's great," Jackson said. "I mean, we should all be, you know"—he stared off in the distance for a second—"braided into the community of those who speak their spirits."

Sarah stepped a little closer. "I was telling Jackson what you said about meeting at the gym." She pushed one of her braids off her shoulder. "There's an open mic thing in Collinsville in a couple weeks, and I thought it'd be really cool to go." She shifted a little, and her eyes darted down the hall to where Kara had gone. "The thing is, though, my poetry is kind of personal. . . ."

"The total baring of one's soul onto the page," Jackson cut in.

"Right," Sarah said, her mouth tightening a bit. "So, I'm trying to keep it kind of quiet, you know? Until I feel like I'm any good at it."

"Yeah, Sarah and me figured you'd be safe since no one really talks to you except Tasha and Ricky," Jackson said.

Sarah's face pinked. "I didn't say it like that. I mean, if your friends are into writing, then definitely invite them, but—"

"No, no," I said. "It's fine. I won't tell anyone. I promise." I was in a secret club! Hidden from Vile Kara Samson! "It's totally fine to meet at the gym."

Jackson put his hand across his heart and stared into the distance. "It'd be like . . . like homecoming after a swift river cuts—"

"So, I'll see you at training?" Sarah broke in, then darted away. I glanced behind me to see the bathroom door swinging open down the hall and Kara stepping out.

"—through the emptiness of our poetry-less souls," Jackson finished.

"What?" I stammered. "Oh, yeah. That's great."

"Just came up with it, just there," Jackson said. "The stanzas"—he popped his hands out like a fan—"they just come to me, you know?"

"That's great," I said. Again.

"So, what are your poems about? Mine are mostly, you know, about the futility of existence," Jackson said, walking down the hall next to me. *Jackson Thorpe was walking down the hall with me!* "Stuff like that."

"Oh, um, my poetry is really . . ." *Nonexistent. My poetry is nonexistent because I do not write poetry.* "Developing, I guess."

Jackson nodded. "Cool. I could really show you a lot about it. How to write and stuff."

"Right," I said, stopping by my English class door. "Tonight."

In the hall, a couple kids gaped. Jackson leaned forward. "But, um," he said, his voice low, "we've got to keep this club thing private, you know? For Sarah. She's trying, you know, to figure out how to do stuff on her own. So, let's keep it all secret."

"Yeah, totally," I said. "Totally. Definitely. Secret." But Jackson already was striding away down the hall.

"What were you doing talking to *her*?" Wade asked him.

Jackson just laughed and disappeared around the corner.

When my legs stopped acting like their bones had dissolved and agreed to carry me into the classroom, I spotted Tasha sitting on top of her desk. She hopped to her feet when I walked through the door.

"What was that about?" she asked, meeting me just inside the room. We got to choose our seats the first day of class, so her desk was in the row next to mine.

Kara pushed through behind me, rolling her eyes and saying, *"Excuse* me," as she shoved by.

I shrugged, trying to look casual. "Oh, nothing."

"It wasn't nothing," Tasha pressed. "Jackson and Sarah talking to you in private? What is up with that?"

Kara paused, her back stiffening. I bit my lip to keep from smiling and nodded toward Kara. Tasha glanced behind her, saw Kara, and her eyebrow raised to the roof. "I'm not going to get into it," I said. "It's kind of a secret. Just between us." Kara's head jerked to the side and I shifted my focus to Tasha. After a beat or two, Kara kept going to her seat.

"Pipi," Tasha whispered.

"It's all part of The List," I whispered back.

Tasha stared at me for a second. "Okay," she said. "Keep your secrets."

I glanced at Kara, who was now seated across the room, talking with a couple other basketball players in the class. I heard her complaining about having to go to the gym ("I mean, *Pipi's* mom owns it. Ew.") for training, but it didn't even bother me, knowing *she* was feeling left out.

"Look," I said as low as I could to Tasha. "You wouldn't like it anyway. We're sort of making a club."

"You don't think I want to be in a club with you?" Tasha crossed her arms. "I'm the queen of clubs."

"Not this kind of club. It's a writing club, a poetry thing." I slid into my seat and pulled out my English notebook. It took me a second to realize Tasha was still standing there next to my desk, staring at me. "What?"

Her mouth was set in a hard line. "And you thought I wouldn't want to be part of a writing club because?"

I looked around as if the words I needed would be scattered near me. "Well, you know," I said.

"I know *what*?" Tasha stared at me.

"The dyslexia thing," I said. "You wouldn't want to be in a writing club when you can't wri—" I bit off the rest of the word, realizing too late what I had been about to say. Tasha, judging from her gasp, realized it, too. "I don't mean that," I said, jumping back to my feet so we were eye to eye. "I didn't mean that. You know I didn't—"

Tasha took a step back, but her face was scary and still. "I don't know *what* you mean lately."

I grabbed her hand and squeezed it. Tasha blinked at me but didn't jerk her hand away. "It's all part of The List stuff. Please, just trust me."

After a long pause, Tasha nodded. "This stings, but I'm going to let it slide. I don't think you meant it the way it came out."

"I didn't! I'm a doofus," I said. "I should've thought—"

"You're not a doofus," Tasha answered. "Just don't forget who your real friends are."

"Friend," I corrected. "Singular, as in, just you."

Tasha smiled a little and swung our hands. Across the room, Kara snickered. "Ew!" she said. "They're holding hands."

Tasha whipped around. "Grow the heck up, Kara!" Only she didn't say heck. Thank goodness the English teacher was always late to class.

Unfortunately, someone else was in the hall. Frau Jacobs's face popped into the classroom. "Now, now, Tasha Martins. I thought that might be you. Inappropriate language!"

"Yeah, but she was being ridi—"

"Enough! You will not speak to me that way. I deserve *respect*!" Frau Jacobs slithered further into the room. Everything I ate for lunch tried to jump up into my throat at the sight of her.

Somehow, I found myself on my feet. "But you don't know—"

Frau Jacobs's face swiveled from Tasha to me. "Don't tell me what I do or do not know, Miss McGee. I doubt Miss Martins and I need insight from a person known to struggle with basic hygiene."

"Hey!" Tasha snapped. Kara cackled in the corner, and the rest of the class's noise was buzzing around me. Frau Jacobs's arms crossed her chest.

And me? I sat down, my arms at my sides, my back curled as I stared down at my lap. If I could've folded myself into origami, I would've. My body felt too big for the chair, too much and too disgusting and too embarrassing. I wanted to stand up for my friend, but who would listen to me? I was a joke, the fill-in for whenever anyone wanted a well-at-least-I'm-not-her moment. Or worse? I was a virus, apt to infect anyone by association or touch alone. It was just a comment from Frau Jacobs, right? And it wasn't like it was any worse than any of my other humiliations. This wouldn't even make The List. But it buckled me.

Kara laughed again from the corner, but she wasn't alone. Loads of other kids laughed along with her.

Frau Jacobs turned her attention back to Tasha. "Miss Martins, what is it that you're wearing?"

Everyone—including Tasha—looked down at her outfit. She was wearing a white and black striped T-shirt, with shiny black leggings and a denim jacket. Her T-shirt reached her hips in the front and flowed longer to mid-thigh in the back.

"Uh, clothing?" Tasha said.

Frau Jacobs huffed as though that were questionable. "Put your hands at your sides."

"Are you serious? You're *dress-coding* me?" Tasha said. "This isn't even your class!"

Just then the actual English teacher came in. Miss Miller was new—this was her first year teaching—and her eyes widened at Frau Jacobs and Tasha's standoff, but she didn't say anything, just strode quickly to her desk at the back of the room.

Tasha shook her head at Miss Miller's back, then sighed and put her hands at her sides. "See?" she said. "The back of my shirt goes well past my fingertips. Satisfied?"

Frau Jacobs shook her head. "The dress code calls for shirts to be longer than your fingertips when your hands are at your sides and to completely cover a girl's backside."

"It does," Tasha said.

"No," Frau Jacobs said. "The back does. The front does not."

"How is the front of my shirt supposed to cover my backside?"

Frau Jacobs smiled. "Go to the office, dear."

Vile Kara Samson snickered. Frau Jacobs turned to her and a thick eyebrow popped up. "Is that your shoulder, dear?" she asked. Kara rolled her eyes but pulled up the side of a cardigan that had fallen, exposing her shoulder.

"Perhaps you'd like to accompany Ms. Martins to the office?" Frau Jacobs continued in a sugary voice. "Unless, of course, you can maintain control of that sweater?"

A few of the kids who had been laughing at Tasha were now smirking at Kara.

Miss Miller cleared her throat. "We're covering important

themes today in this class. Items that will be on the next exam?"
It sounded like she was asking Frau Jacobs a question. I remembered that on the first day Miss Miller said what a thrill it had
been to start teaching in the same school she had attended as a
student. Chances were, Frau Jacobs had been one of *her* teachers. Miss Miller cleared her throat again. "I think we'll make an
exception today." She turned to Tasha and nodded. "So long as
Tasha remembers to dress more carefully in the future."

"I'm sure the other students in your classroom would pre-
fer to concentrate on the lecture you're about to give instead of
Miss Martins's attire," Frau Jacobs snapped.

"There is *nothing* wrong with my clothes! I bought these
with my grandmom." Tasha glanced around the classroom.
"You guys know this is ridiculous, right?" Several girls were
nodding their heads or tugging at their own T-shirts. A couple boys were openly grinning at each other, but many looked
annoyed. Kara crossed her arms and watched everything with
an eyebrow peaked. I squeezed my eyes shut when Tasha's head
swiveled in my direction.

Frau Jacobs sighed. "I don't make the rules, dear. Unlike
many teachers, however, I do enforce them."

Miss Miller's eyes narrowed a little at that. "Thank you for
your guidance on this issue, but I'll take it from here."

Frau Jacobs nodded, unfolded her arms, and slapped her
knees. "Alrighty then." Over her shoulder her eyes once again
swept down Tasha and she shook her head.

"Okay, class, let's continue," Miss Miller said, and for a moment the classroom was filled with the sounds of students grabbing notebooks and pencils.

"Are you okay?" I whispered to Tasha.

She nodded, but her chin wobbled.

Frau Jacobs would pay for this.

Maybe it was the pure rage for Frau Jacobs and Vile Kara Samson that pumped through me that afternoon, but spin class was so intense even Coach asked me to tone it down. "I want the girls to be able to walk!"

I skipped all the countryside scenes and had the team pumping through a cityscape I had downloaded. When Kara's pace slowed, I moved to half-standing and pumped even faster. Sarah kept up, her grin growing the faster I went. Afterward, I wasn't sure my legs would hold me when I slipped down from the bike, but when Kara collapsed in a puddle beside her bike I stalked out of that room.

Sarah told me Jackson would be coming to the gym a half hour after practice, so I grabbed a towel and headed to the showers. I was still in the stall toweling off when Kara and Sarah came in. They were wrapped up in arguing with each other and didn't know I was there.

"What do you mean your mom's picking you up? My mom is right here! She'll take us home," Kara said.

"Sorry," Sarah said. "I've got plans, okay?"

"What kind of plans?"

Sarah dampened a paper towel and squirted soap into it. She ran it along her arms and behind her neck. Kara handed her a clean gym towel to dry off. "I'm hanging out with Pipi," Sarah said.

"Gross," Kara said.

Honestly, I was so used to hearing Kara say mean stuff about me that it didn't even hurt anymore. Yep. Not at all. Not even a little.

"Stop it," Sarah said. "She's nice."

"She's disgusting. Remember when she threw up all over you? You had nightmares for weeks."

I was suddenly grateful for Annie's early years, when we'd all move silently throughout the house so as not to wake her. Without making a sound, I wrapped the towel around my dripping hair and pulled on the clean clothes I had kept in Mom's office. Maybe sweats and a T-shirt weren't the ideal outfit for making Jackson fall in love with me, but they were a better option than Sarah's sink shower.

"Is it for a project for class or something?" Kara asked. "I'm sure I could get you out of being PeePee's partner."

"No," Sarah answered. "And don't call her that."

Kara snickered.

Sarah sighed. "It's for . . . it doesn't have anything to do with you."

I peeked through the half-inch space around the shower

door. Kara tugged on Sarah's braid. "We're cousins *and* best friends. You can tell me anything."

Sarah splashed water on her face but didn't say anything.

"*Sarah.*" Kara stretched out the name. "Aunt Belle told Mom you've been secretive lately. She asked me to keep an eye on you."

Sarah locked eyes with Kara's in the mirror. "I do *not* need you to keep an eye on me, Kara. I don't need you to protect me anymore."

Kara huffed from her nose and shook her head. "Please, Sarah." Kara's eyes flipped to her own reflection. "Have you ever thought about what perfect little Sarah's life would be like if it weren't for me? *I'm* the one who strikes first. *I'm* the one who keeps your secrets. I swear, if you weren't my cousin, I could destroy you. Not that I would, of course." She smiled and kept her voice as pleasant as two moms discussing the weather. "The only thing keeping you from being exactly like PeePee McGee is me." Kara smoothed her hair back into a new ponytail and twisted her head from side to side. Then her eyes met Sarah's again. "Oh, hey. I just rhymed. Maybe I'm a poet, too. Maybe I should join your club."

Sarah's face had been bright red from the workout. Now it drained of all color.

Kara smiled at her. "Oh, you thought I didn't know about that little poetry thing you've got going on with Jackson? My mom thinks you've got a crush on him, that you've finally come to your senses."

Quietly, Sarah said, "That's not going to happen. Jackson knows I don't like him, and you do, too. We're just friends. I wish you'd—"

"Oh, I'm not like my mom. I don't think you're confused. But I do think you *need* to be smart. And smart people don't talk about things better left quiet. Just me and you. It was a risk to add Jackson, but that's where it should stop." Kara said. "It's like we're our own little club." She tugged on Sarah's braid. "Let's keep it that way. Trust me. Some things are better left unsaid."

She turned on her heel. "See you later, Sarah. Don't forget to wash off the Pipi Touch when you get home."

Sarah watched the door slam shut behind her cousin. She pulled in a deep breath, stared at herself in the mirror for the longest minute ever, and then left the bathroom. I sat there, wondering about what I had heard.

Chapter Fourteen

Mom gave us a small workout room at the gym for our poetry meeting. It was filled with exercise balls, so we perched on those while we talked. My mind whirled with what I had overheard in the bathroom—what was the secret Kara wanted Sarah to keep to just her, Sarah, and Jackson? Did Sarah really mean it when she said she didn't like Jackson *and* that Jackson knew it?—but Sarah didn't seem to notice; she was too focused on talking about the poetry club. Jackson bounced on an exercise ball, but I rolled mine against the wall, then leaned against it. A side benefit of leading a super intense workout: I was too beat to be hyped about being in a room with Jackson. I tried not to look directly at him too long in case doing so was like staring at the sun and I'd go blind. He, however, glanced only at Sarah.

Sarah meant business with this poetry club thing. "Okay, so I've been canvassing other schools in the area on what clubs they offer—most have poetry or creative writing clubs in high school, but almost none that are student-led in middle school. Kicking off new clubs this year could give us an edge in carrying them over to high school, making that service project a breeze." She opened her notebook, where she had written down details. "With poetry, starting a club in middle school will be an advantage when we go to open mics. Less competition. And we'll be a step ahead when we enter high school."

"Right," Jackson said.

"You were really serious about the open mic thing?" I asked.

Both of them looked at me. "Yeah, that's the ultimate goal, right?" Jackson said. "Any chance that we have to perform before the school talent show, the better."

"Talent show? Like in front of everyone?" I squirmed.

"There's an open mic in Collinsville," Sarah said. "It's held the first Tuesday of the month, but it's not until eight at night."

"Have you been to one?" Jackson asked. "What if they're weird about kids showing up?"

Sarah nodded. "I went the last couple months. Told Mom I was studying." Her face flushed. She took a deep breath and when she spoke it was in a gush. "The openness—the way everyone just spills their heart out there for everyone—it's amazing. Everyone just *listens* to everyone else. They cheer each other on, no one interrupting or changing what anyone says. Just a person and a microphone, and everyone else *listening* to hard stuff, stuff that others would rather ignore. It's—"

"Wait." I sat up super straight, my momentum sending the exercise ball shooting from behind me. "Isn't poetry, like, just *writing*? Why would we need a microphone?"

Sarah shrugged. "It depends on your style." She smiled

toward Jackson, who was muttering to himself across the room, chewing on his pencil, and then scratching out words in his notebook and writing down new ones. "His is, I guess, more traditional. Mine is way different."

I fought the grin tugging at my mouth. Jackson's mutterings had been about sunsets that shined as brightly as "tremendous basketballs in a sky filled with hope" and "golden opportunity as unchecked as the net during a game against the West York Raiders."

Sarah asked, "Is there Wi-Fi here?"

Soon I was watching the dozens of YouTube videos of spoken word poets Sarah pulled up on my phone. A lot of it I couldn't access because of Mom's filtering system on my phone, but what I could see was nothing like what I had thought of as poetry—it was raw and real. And the performers, standing up there in front of the mic? Maybe the poetry thing was getting to me, but it felt like they were grabbing their ribcages, ripping them open, and letting words fly out.

I could make Sarah and Jackson think I was all into poetry by nodding along with them when they talked about it, but no way could I fool *anyone* on stage. All other humiliations would pale next to being in front of a microphone and having *nothing* to say.

"I can't do this," I told Sarah. "I mean, listening to that? I don't have anything that makes me feel that much."

Sarah smiled. "I saw you writing in that notebook."

Jackson's head flipped up from his own writing at those words.

I sighed. "Not *that* notebook, Jackson." He nodded and went back to his writing.

Sarah's gaze on me didn't waver. "Anyone who writes with the intensity you had that day has a lot to say."

"Yeah, but nothing I'd want to share in front of an audience."

Something flickered across Sarah's face. "You might be surprised," she said. "After you think about it, I mean. A stage, a microphone. Everyone in the audience. You can say whatever you want, whatever you need, and they'll hear you. They'll have to hear you."

I looked at her, remembering the overheard fight with Kara in the locker room. Remembering all of the references to secrets. "Do you have a lot to say?" I asked. "I mean . . ."

Sarah glanced at Jackson, who was still muttering to himself, and then ducked her head. "I don't know that I have *a lot* to say, but . . ." She took a deep breath, then glanced up at me. Her cheeks had red circles in the middle. "Maybe what I want to say is hard to hear."

"Because it's sad?" I asked. An unwelcome rush of something—sympathy, I guess—gushed through me. For Sarah Stinking Trickle. This was totally *not* helpful to The Plan.

She shook her head. "No, hard to hear because no one . . . it kind of . . . needs a bigger . . ."

"What you need," said Jackson, his voice slicing through

Sarah's pause, "are more metaphors. That's key. The key that unlocks the heart." He mimed unlocking his heart. "Like this." He straightened his spine and threw out his right arm. In his left hand, he held his notebook. "I sat on a chair of air, a bubble of space encased in plastic." He stretched the word *plastic,* somehow making the first syllable rhyme with *space.*

I squinted at him. "But," I pointed out, "that's *not* a metaphor. You're literally sitting on a chair of air."

"Yes!" Jackson said, now thrusting his arm into the air. "You get it!"

"Yeah," Sarah said slowly. "I think I do. Like you're literally sitting on an inflatable chair, encased in plastic, but we're metaphorically sitting on past events—memories as light as air—that we've wrapped in something artificial to make solid beneath us."

Jackson's eyes widened. He nodded to himself. "Wow. Yeah. I mean, right. Exactly. That's exactly what I was thinking." He lowered his arms and wrote in the notebook. I heard his low mutterings, "*wrapped in something artificial. Make solid . . .*"

"Huh," I said. *Was that really what Jackson had meant?* "You're super good at this," I told her.

"Thanks," Jackson said. Sarah just smiled. "Don't worry," he added. "You'll get there. Just pay attention to what I do."

We left soon after that, when Mom said it was time to head home for dinner. Sarah texted me a list of other spoken word poets to check out.

Jackson texted me one of his poems. And then another. And another.

I had really thought texts from Jackson would be more thrilling.

Saturday morning, Eliza had to go to work, so Mom was going to drop off Annie at the birthday party. I was in my bedroom, finishing up another bird. This one was small, only about the size of my thumb. I had my iPad open to a page on mountain bluebirds and was using that as I added a final touch—a dark brown feather down its cobalt blue back. Already, I had tucked a shiny rhinestone in the secret compartment under its wing. Bluebirds are supposed to mean good luck and, from what I was overhearing between Eliza and Annie, Eliza could definitely use some bluebirds right about then.

She was trying to convince Annie to wear a headband to the party.

"Those are to keep hair out of people's eyes," Annie said. "My hair doesn't even reach my eyebrowns." When Annie stopped calling eyebrows eyebrowns, I'd wear all black and cry for days on end.

"But it looks pretty," Eliza said.

"Looks aren't important, Eliza," she said.

"Annie," Eliza said, "would you call me Mom? Or Mama?"

I peeked out of my bedroom and down the hall to where

they stood in the bathroom, silhouetted in light. Annie was standing, Eliza kneeling in front of her. Annie touched Eliza's cheek. "Is this because MomMom is having a new baby?"

Eliza shook her head. "No," she whispered. "It's because you're *my* baby."

Annie dropped her hand. She took such a deep breath that I saw her shoulders peak. Then she said, "I'll think about it if I don't have to wear the headband."

"That's called blackmail," Eliza said, "and it's not very nice."

"Neither are headbands."

"I thought you loved headbands," Eliza said. "Mom said you picked out a bunch of them as Tabitha's present!"

Annie shifted, hand on her hip. "Exactly."

Eliza laughed, a quick chuckle that soon was joined by Annie's giggle. "Okay, you don't have to wear the headband." She swept it off Annie's head and smoothed the hair back into place with her palm.

"Thank you, Eliza," Annie said.

Eliza sighed. "Have a good time at the party. Try to make some friends, okay?"

Annie skipped from the bathroom down the hall. She pushed open my bedroom door. "MomMom says you're supposed to come, too."

"What? Why?" I asked.

Annie put one hand at her side and gestured outward with her other hand, suddenly looking just like Mom. "'I don't know what Pipi's up to lately, but she's been secretive and moody. I'm going to get to the bottom of it.'"

"She said that to you?" I gasped. _____

"No," Annie said. "She said that to Alec. But I heard. And then Alec said . . ."—now Annie lowered her arms, stood up straight, and deepened her voice—"'You should spend some time with her. One on one.'" She crossed her arms. "And then MomMom said that she was going to come up with an excuse for you to come along today."

"You shouldn't spy on people, Annie."

"It's my job."

"Spying is definitely *not* your job."

"I'm training." Annie skipped down the rest of the hall. A few minutes later, Mom told me she needed my help running errands.

I grabbed the bluebird, made sure the brown paint had set, and shoved it in my pocket. A little luck wouldn't hurt me or Annie, either.

The birthday party was where every little squirt in town celebrated—P. Art Tee's Pizza.

It was a giant room with a million video games whirring and blaring, laser lights whipping around from the ceiling, a giant ball pit in the middle, ride-on animals stationed throughout, and buckets of popcorn and cotton candy next to slowly rotating pizzas on buffet tables along the sides. Amid all of it were a trillion small kids going absolutely bananas, running, jumping, screaming, laughing. A couple dozen parents sat at long tables along the sides with bouquets of balloons, piles of presents, and sheet cakes. The parents seemed to be in two factions—a group who followed kids around, snapping pictures, and a second that sat wincing and rubbing at their temples.

"So, okay," Mom said to Annie as we stood by the entrance. She had always been a wince-and-rub-temples P. Art Tee parent. "You just go straight through there and find Tabitha's table."

Annie clutched my arm with both hands. "You can't leave me here."

"Look how much fun everyone's having!" I said. Annie slowly raised a hand and pointed to a corner where a kid was puking into a trash can.

Mom glanced around. "Let's just find Tabitha's table, okay?"

Annie's grip on my arm didn't loosen. We walked past a half dozen party tables looking for Tabitha's party. "There she is!" Mom pointed across the cavernous room. I shifted Annie's grip from my arm to Mom's. A conga line of kids streamed between us.

"I'll wait here," I said, as more and more kids joined the conga line. Mom and Annie disappeared behind them. I sank onto an empty bench seat at one of the party tables. After a second, something poked me in the knee. I peeked under the table. Big brown eyes gazed back at me.

"Piper?" I asked.

The kindergartener was crouched under the table, blinking like an owl. "Hi," she said.

"What are you doing under there?"

Slowly Piper wormed out and sat across from me. She pulled a paper cup of Coke closer, wrapping her hand around it. She rested her chin on her other hand and then leveled me with a weary look. "It's like this, Pipi," she said. "I got the Pink Eye."

I squinted at her. "Your eyes look fine."

"No." She sighed. "I mean I had the Pink Eye." She shook her head, then took a swig of Coke. "And then so did everyone else."

"Everyone?"

"Remember the pirate dress up?" Piper said.

I squirmed. "Eyepatch?"

Piper sighed. She took another gulp of soda. "All the girls got crusty eyed. Thanks to me."

"That was a few days ago. They've all got to be better now, right?"

Piper shrugged. "I don't think so. No one's here. 'Cept you."

I looked down the long table, noticing the unicorn placemats and a unicorn cake. *Happy 5th Birthday Piper* was iced in pink and purple across the top of the cake. "It's your birthday?" I asked.

Piper scrunched her eyebrows together. "That's why you're here, right?"

"Oh," I said. "Uh, yeah. Of course. Happy birthday!" I gulped. "Who did you invite? I bet they're just running late."

Piper pushed away the cup. "The whole class. They were supposed to be here at one o'clock. What time is it now?"

I glanced at the wall clock. It was one thirty-seven. "Oh, just about that time."

"Mom said she's going to make sure they all didn't go to the other P. Art Tee's." Piper pointed to a woman standing by the entrance with a phone to her ear. I could just make out a loud, "It's Piper's birthday and no one is here. How could everyone in the class suddenly have plans? What do you mean your daughter *changed her mind*?"

Piper slouched in her seat, the fist holding up her face smooshing it. "They said they don't want to be friends with Pink Eye Piper."

"Who said that?" I asked, feeling the same cold rush as when I overheard someone talking about the Pipi Touch.

"Everyone," Piper said. "Guess they're not coming to my party. At least I'll get one present." She then looked at me straight on.

"Uh . . ." I glanced around. Mom headed in my direction with Annie wrapped around her leg.

Mom's face was red and her mouth set in a hard, white line as she hissed, "You have to stay at the party! Play with your friends!" Annie didn't say a word, just clung to Mom's leg like a spider monkey.

"Wait here a sec, okay, Piper?" I weaved through the crowd of kids to Mom and Annie. "Listen," I said to them, "I'm going to stay."

"What?" Mom and Annie said in unison.

"That little girl, Piper, she's one of the kindergarteners I volunteer with. No one came to her party."

Mom's face softened.

"And it's kind of my fault," I whispered, thinking about how I had ignored Piper's swollen eye.

"*Penelope!*" Mom's mouth was a white line again.

"I'm going to fix it!" I held out my hand to Annie. "Annie, do you want to meet my friend Piper?"

Annie stared at my hand a second, then glanced over her shoulder to where Tabitha's party was in full swing. I could tell who Tabitha was because she wore a giant fluffy tutu and a rhinestone crown. She was twirling, her mouth in a see-all-my-teeth smile. "Does Piper smile like this?" Annie bared her teeth.

"No," I said, "but she does think she's going to be a unicorn someday."

"Okay." Annie grabbed my hand and let me pull her to stand beside me.

Mom glanced from me to Annie and over our shoulders at Piper. "Can you at least get Annie to circle back to Tabitha at some point?"

I nodded. "Absolutely."

Mom patted Annie's head. "Okay. Guess I'll have to spend the afternoon alone." She rubbed at her temples as the P. Art Tee DJ pumped out another techno song. "See you ladies in two hours." She handed me a twenty-dollar bill and whistled as she walked away.

"I'm not going back to Tabitha," Annie said as soon as Mom was by the door. "I think she's a robot." She made the all-teeth smile face again. Tabitha rushed by in a crowd of other tutu-ed girls, making the same overly smiling face.

"I see what you mean," I said. "Listen," I said, kneeling next to Annie. "How about you just run over to Tabitha's table while no one's there, grab the present you brought, and sneak it back over to Piper? Then you'll *technically* have circled back, right?"

Annie nodded. *"Spy training,"* she whispered to herself. Then Annie darted ahead, ducking when she got to a video game machine, then dropping to all fours to crawl to Tabitha's table. Her little hand stretched up to the table, searching for the present she had brought and knocking it to the ground. Then she scurried back, clutching the gift, in the same secret agent style.

"You really have been training to be a spy," I told her.

"Mostly at home." Annie leaned toward me. "I've seen a lot."

I tried not to think about what that meant and concentrated on the fact that we were seriously low on party guests for Piper. I grabbed my phone, firing out a text. *SOS. Piper. At P. Art Tee's. No one came to her bday party. Can you come?*

Ricky wrote back in seconds. *Be there in five.*

It only took him four minutes to show up with a half dozen little kids. Three of them were literally hanging on to his legs the way Annie had been earlier with Mom. All of them had Ricky's thick, dark swoop of hair and huge brown eyes.

"You came!" I said.

"I have five little brothers and a sister, and this is an all-you-can-eat pizza buffet a block from our house." He shook one of the kids off his leg. The little boy fell back, laughed, and jump tackled his leg again. "I say P. Art Tee's and they assemble faster than the Avengers."

I filled in Ricky on what had happened. Then he rounded up his siblings. "Birthday party time, guys."

"Woot woot!" the six of them said together and marched forward like, well, the Avengers.

Two hours and four pizzas later, Piper was beaming. She bounced up and down, throwing invisible unicorn treats to Ricky's brothers and sister, who jumped to gobble them up. Even Annie joined in; I hadn't seen her smile so much ever. The cake was demolished, and though Ricky's siblings hadn't come with gifts, they did give her mountains of tickets they had won in the games, which she used to buy everyone whoopie cushions.

Annie handed Piper the gift she had bought for Tabitha, who didn't seem to notice that Annie was at a different party. Piper tore open the card first. Annie had made it herself. It was a robot

with a tutu. The gift was a bunch of headbands. Pipe[...]
all on at once, making Annie giggle.

"And, um, here," I said, not looking at anyone but Pip[...]
pulled the tiny bluebird out of my pocket. "This is for you."

Piper held out both hands and I placed the bird inside.
"*Whoa,*" Piper said, tilting her hands so she could see the bird.

"That's really cool," Ricky said.

"Pipi makes them," Annie said. "Her whole room is filled
with them. MomMom says it's so she won't feel so lonely, but
Eliza says it's creepy."

"Thanks, Annie," I muttered.

"*Spying,*" she whispered, her eyes wide.

"Did you really make that?" Ricky asked. He held out his
hand and Piper tipped the bird into it. He tilted it under the
light, checking out the little black beak and the lines on the
feathers. Those take forever. So does blending the blue to
the white so it overlays like separate feathers.

I shrugged, my cheeks burning. "It's just for fun."

"It's really amazing," he said.

Piper tapped his hand. "Sorry," Ricky said and gave the bird
back to Piper.

"It's for good luck," I told her.

"No," she corrected me. "It's for my birthday, silly goose!"

Piper's parents snapped dozens of pictures and thanked
us over and over again for coming to the party. Though Piper's
mom looked nothing like Eliza, they both had that same

xpression when they saw their daughters. I used to think it meant Eliza was worried Annie was going to mess up. But now, watching Piper and her mom, I realized I had it all wrong. She was worried she was going to mess up her daughter.

"I pushed her to have a party," Piper's mom told me. "She said no one would show up, but I made her invite everyone. If it weren't for you guys . . ."

Piper's dad rubbed her back and offered us more pizza. Ricky held his stomach. "Well, maybe just one more," he said and grabbed a slice.

After Piper's parents turned away, I whispered, "How can you eat this? The pizza tastes like a foot."

Ricky wiped at his mouth with a paper napkin. "Bad pizza is still pizza."

"You should meet my dad," I said. "Thanks again for coming."

Ricky shrugged. "I got out of a day of babysitting and scored free lunch. Plus, I got to hang out with Piper." He crumpled the napkin. "And you. You're not so bad."

"Oh, wow. Thanks." I picked up the napkin and threw it at his head. "You're just jealous I creamed you in Skee-Ball."

Ricky dodged the napkin and laughed. "I mean when you're not trying to exact revenge or being completely obsessed with bad things that have happened to you, you're fun to be around."

"Not you, too," I said, crossing my arms. "You sound like Tasha."

"You should listen to your friends," Ricky said.

I sucked in my breath. Did I have two friends—Tasha *and* Ricky? I pushed the thought away. "Listen, I'm trying to *stop* obsessing about The List. That's why I'm doing the whole thing."

Ricky crossed his hands behind his head. His voice was even and light. "Yeah, but what's it cost other people?"

"That's so not fair," I said, my heart thumping. "I didn't know Piper had pink eye."

Ricky grabbed one of his little brothers and swiped at his pizza-sauced face with a napkin. "Tell the others—five-minute warning." Then he turned back to me. "I wasn't talking about Piper."

"Who are you talking about?"

"I've got to go," he said. "Forget it, okay?"

"You told them five minutes. It hasn't even been thirty seconds."

Ricky stood. He smiled, but it looked more like a grimace. "This—" he glanced around the party table, covered in prizes and surrounded by all of the kids, with Piper and Annie right in the middle—"has been a lot of fun. Because it was *just* about having fun." He shrugged. "I get The List thing. I do. Just don't forget who your real friends are." He clapped his hands three times. "Salindos, assemble."

Ricky's siblings rushed toward him, the littlest three grabbing his legs. "Happy birthday, Piper," he said with a salute. "See you at school, Penelope."

Chapter Fifteen

Monday was an in-service day, so I didn't see Ricky again until we took the bus to kindergarten volunteering on Tuesday. On the way, Ricky and I shared pictures we had taken at Piper's party.

"Wow." I laughed. "I didn't think I could smile that big!"

"Who would've thought that the best party we'd go to this year would be for a kindergartener?" Ricky laughed.

"Wait," I said. "There've been parties?" I hadn't been going to parties. Was Ricky going to parties? Was Tasha? Were they going to parties *together*? Ricky laughed again.

Narrator Boy paused in describing the bus driver's expert handling of the right turn into the school parking lot and turned toward us. In a voice so loud it carried to the back of the bus, he said, "Eighth graders went to Pink Eye Piper's birthday party. They said it was the best birthday party. Now the eighth graders are nodding. Look at them nod!"

A little hand poked my shoulder from the back. "Did you really go to Piper's party?"

"Yep," I said.

"It was awesome, too," Ricky added. He held up his phone, showing a shot of all of us gathered around Piper as she blew out her candles.

"Did you get the Pink Eye?" another kid whispered.

"No." I scrunched my face and shook my head. "Of course not."

"Yeah," Ricky said. "Piper's super cool."

All the little kids said "ooohhh," their mouths forming perfect circles.

When we got to the school, Narrator Boy was the first one off the bus. Like a tiny town crier, he went into the classroom, telling everyone about the "big kids" who went to Piper's party.

"Look at this!" I tugged on Ricky's sleeve. "Everyone's talking about Piper, and not in a 'got the Pink Eye' sort of way. We did it!" I bounced. "She's super popular."

"Didn't you already cross kindergarten off your list?" Ricky asked.

"Yeah, but it's like we reversed the Pipi Touch for Piper." I pointed to the coat room, where a dozen kids surrounded Piper, asking her about her party.

"Is it true the big kids were there?" Future Sarah Trickle asked.

"Was it so much fun?" asked another kid.

"When will you have another?" asked a third.

Sarah and Jackson were already in the classroom. "What's going on?" Sarah asked.

I laughed. "We crashed Piper's party on Saturday."

"You guys were hanging out?" Sarah asked, surprised. *Yes, Sarah,* I answered in my head. *Sometimes I go to parties, too.* Mental me pushed away the whole *for a kindergartener* aspect.

"Yeah, for a while on Saturday," I said instead. Then, feeling babyish, I added, "It was just P. Art Tee's."

Sarah laughed. "Beats what I did—teaching Kara how to do laundry since her dad is traveling and Aunt Estelle doesn't know how, either."

Ricky nudged me with his elbow. "So, I was thinking I could totally win the next round of Skee-Ball. Want to bring Annie next Saturday to P. Art Tee's? Rematch with my little brothers and sister?"

"That sounds—"

"Pipi!" Jackson shouted from across the room. He trotted toward us. "I've been texting you all weekend." Miss Gonzalez pulled the lunch bucket cart down the aisle, and Jackson wedged between me and Ricky to let her by.

"Oh," I said, "yeah, I wanted to talk . . . um . . . in person." Truth was, Jackson had sent me a dozen poems over the past two days. They were long. Like maybe you'd fall asleep in the middle of dinner trying to read them. And I tried—honestly, I truly tried—to find the existential the-past-is-a-ball-of-air bit in lines like *the ball sliced through the air like a pizza cutter divides the pie,* but I just couldn't do it.

"So, what did you think?" Jackson asked.

"They were really, really great," I said. "I really like all the descriptions where you, um, described all the stuff."

Jackson grinned. He pushed his beautiful blond hair from his face. For years of my life, I dreamed that someday Jackson would call my name from across the room. That he would smile at me as he pushed hair from his face. That he would send me poetry was beyond any dream I could create. Except I didn't really think about the poetry itself—like that it would be boring.

"Thanks," he said. "What else?"

"Well, it was really deep."

"You didn't get them, did you?" Jackson said. He grinned again, temporarily blinding me.

I shook my head. "That doesn't mean they aren't—"

"It's cool," Jackson said. "I'll explain it all to you. Don't worry; you'll get poetry soon." He patted my head. My brain seemed to split into two pieces. One half screamed, *OMG! Jackson Thorpe touched me!* The other half whispered, *Did Jackson just* pat *me like a puppy?* I shushed both of them as Jackson continued. "Maybe you just need time to think about them. I'll check in with you later this week. You're going to be at the game Friday, right?"

"Right," I said. The first basketball scrimmages for both the girls' and boys' teams were right after school at the high school. As manager, I'd make sure the players had basketballs to practice with during halftimes, fill water bottles for players when they were called off the court, and pretend to be busy and important.

"Here," Jackson said and shoved a piece of paper into my hand. "I seriously *just* wrote this." He shook his head like he couldn't believe his own ability. "Read it. Think about it. Really *think*. Think about the concept of life as a continuation of fate's basketball, okay?" he said. "I'll see if you get it before the game."

"Right," I said again. Jackson kept on talking about his poetry, reading lines from memory and then explaining those lines. Again, split brain was sputtering at the same time. One half: *He wants to know what I think!* The other? *I like him more when he isn't talking.* "I've, um, gotta go. I've got to talk to someone."

I pushed past Jackson and ducked into the cloak room to find Piper. "Hey," I said as she pulled her lunch bag out of her little backpack. "Look who's so popular today!"

Piper crossed her arms. "Why is everyone talking to me?"

I grinned and knelt in front of her. "Because you're awesome. They all feel bad about not coming to your party." I squeezed her hand. "This is your chance, Piper! Your chance to be really popular."

"Why?" Piper asked.

I rocked back on my heels. "Well, because. They all want to be like you now. They all want to know what you think."

"Just because you guys came to my party?" she side-eyed the kid standing too close to where we talked.

I shrugged. "I guess so. Isn't it great?"

Piper shook her head.

"Sure, it is!" I laughed. "You've got so many friends now."

Piper's face brightened. "That's right! I do!"

"That's right!" I echoed.

"I've got Annie! And Tomas, and Henry, and . . ." Piper's voice trailed off. She glanced at Ricky. "What are their names?"

Ricky laughed. "I have trouble keeping track, too. Tomas, Henry, Martin, David, Raul, and Martha."

"Yeah!" Piper said. "They're all my friends. And so is Mr. Pickle the Bird." She reached into her pocket and pulled out the bluebird I had given her.

"Its name is Mr. Pickle?" I asked.

Piper's forehead wrinkled. "Of course, it is."

Miss Gonzalez called the class together for morning meeting. The kids gathered in a circle on the rug, most of them still peppering Piper with questions about her party. "You were all invited. If you wanted to know, you should've come!" she hissed.

Future Sarah Trickle squeezed in beside Piper. "I love your headbands."

Piper patted the four headbands on her head. "Thank you," she said. "My friend Annie gave them to me."

"You could share one with me," Future Sarah Trickle said.

"No, you'd get the Piper Pink Eye." Piper crossed her arms.

Future Sarah Trickle laughed. "You don't have that anymore!"

I'm not sure what Piper said next, but it sounded a lot like *"For now."* Future Sarah Trickle played with Piper's hair. Piper wiggled toward the girl next to her.

Narrator Boy whispered, "Everyone wants to be next to Piper. Piper is frowning. She is frowning. Her face is red. Red, red, red."

Miss Gonzalez clapped her hands four times fast then twice slow. The class automatically repeated the pattern. "You're all super excited to share this morning!" she exclaimed. "Who would like to share something exciting about their weekend first?"

Narrator Boy raised his hand. Miss Gonzalez nodded at him. "Yes?"

Narrator Boy stood. He straightened his shorts. "I took the city bus to the zoo. First the doors opened like this." He bent and straightened his arms a couple of times. "Then we got to our seats. The seats were brown. There was gum under my seat. I sat down. I buckled my seatbelt. Mama sat down. The seat made a sound like a fart. Mama buckled—"

"Perhaps," interrupted Miss Gonzalez, "you could skip ahead to the part where you're at the zoo?"

Narrator Boy nodded. He cleared his throat. "We got to the zoo. The bus driver said, 'We're at the zoo!' He pulled the brake. The bus stopped. The doors opened like this—"

"That sounds lovely," Miss Gonzalez said. "Thank you for sharing. Anyone else?"

More kids whispered Piper's name, but not about her. *To* her. I nudged Ricky. We were sitting at tables beside the rug. "She's like super popular now!" I whispered.

Ricky grimaced. "I think she's going to explode."

With each whisper, each time Future Sarah Trickle or any of Future Sarah Trickle's friends played with her hair or touched her crisscross-applesauced legs, the creases in Piper's forehead deepened. A low growl bubbled out of her.

"Piper?" Miss Gonzalez called. "Would you like to share? Many of your friends seem to be excited to hear something from you."

As though it were an invitation, a dozen or so kids erupted. "Piper had a big party! Big kids were there!"

"They were there!" another said, pointing to me and Ricky. "At P. Art Tee's!"

"P. Art Tee's! P. Art Tee's!" the class chanted.

Miss Gonzalez held up her hands. "Now, now!" she said as the class quieted down. "Piper? Anything you would like to share?"

Piper, her little hands in fists, shook off the girls playing with her hair and went to stand beside Miss Gonzalez's rocking chair.

"Thank you all for *not* coming to my party," she said.

"What?" Miss Gonzalez said as Ricky choked on a laugh.

"I invited all of you to my party and none of you came. I'm really happy about that because I don't like any of you. I don't like kindergarten. I only like P. Art Tee's. But if you see me there, don't talk to me." With that, Piper went back to her spot and sat down.

"Piper!" Miss Gonzalez said. "We do not speak to our friends that way."

"I didn't," Piper said, her eyes wide with surprise. "They're not my friends."

"Piper!" the teacher said again. "Apologize."

Piper, still looking confused, said, "I'm sorry for not liking any of you."

At school the next day, I spotted Ricky on the way to lunch. His shoulders immediately started shaking with laughter again. "'I'm sorry for not liking any of you.' That was epic!"

I fell in place walking with him to the cafeteria. Since it was Wednesday, I could sit with Tasha. "Yeah," I said, "but what about tomorrow? Those kids are never going to play with her again."

Ricky stopped in his tracks, making me stop, too. "Don't you get it, Pipi? She doesn't *want* to hang out with those kids. She doesn't care. It's awesome."

I guess because we stopped so suddenly, someone bumped into me from behind, knocking me to the side. The boy glanced at me, but it was like his eyes glazed over. He went on talking to his friend.

"Hey!" Ricky called to him.

"Ricky!" the boy said. "Did I knock you? Sorry, man."

"No, but you hit Penelope," Ricky said.

"Oh, yeah." He shrugged. Then, grinning, he knocked the kid beside him. "The Touch, man." The boy looked from Ricky to me and back. "Want to sit with us, Ricky? Room at our table."

"Nah, I'm good," Ricky said after a pause.

The boy's face scrunched up. "Seriously?" He glanced at me, then back at Ricky. "*Oh,*" he said super slowly. "You wanna sit with Tasha today?"

Ricky's jaw tightened, but before he could say anything, the boy said, "Cool. See you later."

Neither of us said anything else until we got to the table, where Tasha was waiting for us. I plopped into the seat across from her and put my head on my arms. Ricky sat next to Tasha and looked over my head across the cafeteria.

"Hey," Tasha said, not looking at either of us, her mouth set.

I raised my head, peeking at her. "What's up?"

Tasha shook her head, still not looking at either of us.

Something behind me distracted Tasha. I glanced at Ricky just in time to see him roll his eyes. I turned around to see Vile

Kara Samson standing in front of me with her arms crossed. Her usual table was missing Sarah and Jackson. I smirked, remembering. Sarah had said something about talking with the school secretary about starting official school clubs during lunch. I had said I wanted to have lunch with Tasha, and of course Jackson would've followed Sarah there.

Kara's breath came out in huffs through her nose, and, furious, she held herself still. Even so, her voice lilted, like mid-laugh, as she said (way too loudly for how close we were standing), "Is it true what I heard? That you and Ricky were hanging out at *P. Art Tee's* this weekend? For a birthday party?" She chuckled, but it sounded like gargling glass.

"So what?" I said. I had wanted it to come out angry, but it ended up being mumbly.

"So what?" she repeated, again in too high a voice. I glanced around. Just like I had thought, dozens of people were no longer chewing or talking but were watching our table. "Seriously? Are you, like, five or something?"

A couple people laughed, and Kara dropped her arms. Her mean smile seemed more genuine now. In a sing-song voice she added, "Did you jump in the ball pit, Pipi? Did you play with all the other kindergarteners?"

"Lay off, Kara," Ricky said. I looked over my shoulder at him. Just like Kara, his voice—casual and bored—didn't match his demeanor, which was still and angry. His eyes were narrowed and his hand curled into a fist next to his lunch bag.

And me? For just a second, I felt pathetic. Like such a pathetic baby. Who *did* go to P. Art Tee's anymore? But then I remembered Piper, how we had turned her party around. And we *did* have fun.

Kara watched me, her upper lip twitching and eyebrows raised, like she was waiting for me to bolt or cry or crumble.

Instead, I straightened my shoulders. I smiled over my shoulder at Ricky and then back at Kara. "Yeah, actually. It was awesome."

She blinked a few times.

To Ricky, I continued, "I had no idea I was a Skee-Ball wizard."

Ricky's shoulders rolled back. "Whatever. I let you win."

"Sure, you did." I laughed. "Just like I let you win at *Pac-Man*."

Ricky grinned. "You'll see. Next time, you're going down."

Kara's mouth hung open a little. "Next time? You're both so boring."

"Oh, Kara, don't be sad," I said. "I'm sure whatever you did over the weekend was super cool. What was it? Oh, yeah. Figuring out the laundry machine." I laughed, then wiggled my fingers at her. "Now go on, run back to your table before you get The Touch."

I turned my back to her. Tasha shot Kara a cold smile. "Go on, now," she said waving her away with the back of her hand.

"Whatever," Kara snapped, then strode out of the cafeteria.

I watched her retreat, my face stretching into a smile that felt just as icy as Tasha's.

When I turned back Tasha was gathering up her lunch.

"Where are you going?" I asked. "I barely got to talk with you."

"Oh, I'm sure you'll be fine with Ricky," she said, still not looking at me. She turned and walked out of the cafeteria.

"Tasha!" I said. I shrugged at Ricky, then followed Tasha. I grabbed her arm as she headed down the hall in long strides. "Please stop! Let me talk to you."

Tasha whipped around. I sucked in my breath at the anger I saw in her eyes. *She's jealous,* my brain finally provided. But Tasha being jealous of *me* was such a mind-blowing thing. A smaller, pettier part of my brain whispered, *She's jealous about Ricky—not you.* Either way, I had somehow hurt my best friend.

"It wasn't like that—me and Ricky hanging out, I mean. It just happened," I said.

Tasha took a deep breath, and some of the anger evaporated.

"It was because one of the kindergarteners—Piper—didn't have anyone at her birthday party. I called Ricky because he lives by there. Besides, with all of his brothers and sister, he could make it a real party for her."

Tasha stilled for a minute. "It just doesn't feel good, you know?" she said. "Being left out."

This time I was the one to raise an eyebrow. "I'm familiar with the feeling."

Tasha laughed. "Just don't leave me out, okay?"

I looped my arm in hers as we headed back to the cafet. "Tasha, you were there for me when literally no one else would even touch me. No way would I leave you out."

Tasha bent her head so it bumped mine. "You know what we haven't done in a long, long time?"

"*Yes!*" I squealed.

Tasha and I used to get together on Friday nights and binge watch the greatest television show in history—*Supernatural*. We watched it while eating egg salad with potato chips and drinking Dr. Pepper, and eventually falling asleep—Tasha on the couch, me on the loveseat. Maybe egg salad and chips sounds gross, but that is only because you haven't had Mr. Martins's egg salad. Dr. Martins, Tasha's mom, worked long hours, so Mr. Martins took care of all of the cooking in the house. That man was a genius in the kitchen, making his own mayonnaise and everything. There was a secret ingredient in the egg salad that I suspected was finely diced pickles. Technically speaking, I don't think Dr. or Mr. Martins knew that we ate the egg salad with a whole bag of Utz potato chips instead of on bread or over the spinach he served with it, but he never asked too many questions.

"I have to leave after lunch Friday for a dentist appointment, and then Dad's taking me to a matinee to see the new Marvel movie. Want to come over about seven? Maybe have a sleepover?" Tasha asked.

"Absolutely!" I said, squeezing her arm. "Wouldn't miss it."

Chapter Sixteen

Friday morning, Mom woke me up seven minutes before my alarm clock would've blared.

Everyone knows those last minutes of sleep are the absolute best. No one's bed is ever more comfortable than when there are just seven precious minutes left with it. Yet there was Mom, sitting on the edge of my bed.

"Pipi?" she whispered. "Are you awake?"

"No! No, I am not awake. You can clearly see that I am *not awake*. I'm in my bed, with my blankets up over my head, and there is drool trailing from my mouth across the pillow. Who could possibly think I was *awake*?" Of course, I didn't actually say this. My mouth was still too asleep to actually say anything except, "Imschleep."

Mom must've interpreted that as, *Please, continue to speak to me.*

"I feel like I've barely had the chance to talk with you these past few weeks. The gym business is growing so fast, and this baby news really threw me—and my stomach—for a loop. Eliza and Annie are going through some things. . . . Anyway, I just feel like you've been quite distant."

I rolled onto my back and rubbed my eyes open. "Yeah," I said. "This List thing. I've been busy."

"Is that what it is?" Mom asked. Her eyes scanned my face the way she sometimes would for a fever. Her hand even hovered near my forehead for a moment.

I pushed up onto my elbows. "Yeah, what else would it be?"

"Well, there was the nose thing and then I noticed you were spending so much time out of the house. When you are home, you're in here, making your birds." She gestured to the corner, where a cardinal I had crafted on Thursday morning was drying. I had gone to school with a smudge of red paint on my thigh, which Frau had pointed out and rolled her eyes in front of the whole class. Cardinal red paint. Did she really think *that* could be mistaken for period blood? Plus, it had been by my *knee*. For real. I shuddered, thinking about her smug smile as she had handed me the tissue and asked if I needed to be excused.

"So," Mom said, concluding what I guessed had been a rather lengthy talk that I had totally tuned out. "I just want to make sure you're okay."

"Uh," I said.

"That's what I mean!" Mom said. "It's like you barely even look at me or hear me. Are you feeling . . . left out?"

"You mean more than usual?" I joked.

Mom's mouth tightened into a white line. "What do you mean?"

"Nothing," I said. Or rather, yawned. "I'm just dealing with stuff the best I can."

"It can't be easy." Mom's hand stretched over her stomach. "I know how hard it was on you when Eliza was pregnant, all of the bullying you took at school. And now I'm pregnant again. I just don't want—"

"Wait!" My hand flew up in a stop signal. "You think I was bullied because of *Eliza*?"

"Well . . ."

"Mom!" I yelped. "Me being picked on had nothing to do with her or Annie."

"And now you're so distant . . ." Mom continued as if I hadn't spoken.

"Seriously?" I slammed my hand down to my side. "You think I was picked on because of Eliza? And now you think I'm trying to avoid you?" I shook my head. "Why does everything I do have to have something to do with you?"

I wiggled out from under my covers. "I can't believe this!" I said, still not entirely sure, to be honest, why I was so angry. I stood, shaking my head, trying to gather my cobwebby thoughts.

Mom stood, too, putting her hands on her hips. "I want to make sure you know this baby would never replace—"

"Mom!" I said. "Stop it. Do you really think I'm the kind of person who would resent a baby? A *baby*? Come on!"

"Well, no," Mom protested, "but—"

"*But?*" I questioned.

"But . . ."

A soft giggle leaked out from under the doorframe. Mom and I paused in unison as both of our eyes narrowed at the same time. I practically leaped toward my door, yanking it open. Annie fell forward onto the carpet, her hands still covering her giggling mouth. *"Butt,"* Annie the Spy erupted.

Mom wagged her finger at Annie. "What did we tell you about spying?"

"That I'm awesome at it," Annie said.

"No," Mom said. "That you should *not* spy on family members."

Annie shrugged. "I have to practice while I can."

"While you can?" I repeated.

Annie slowly put her finger up to her mouth. "Spies don't tell secrets."

I crossed my arms. "Isn't that *exactly* what spies do?"

Annie's forehead crinkled.

All three of us jumped as the alarm clock peeled. "Okay, okay!" Mom shooed Annie out of my room. "Time to scoot. All of us have to get ready for the day." Annie and I stuck out our tongues at the same time.

As she closed the door, Mom said, "I know you have your basketball game after school tonight, but maybe we could hang out afterward? Get some pizza, watch bad eighties movies?"

"Sounds great, Mom," I said. Man, I had totally forgotten about the basketball team and my role as manager. That explained the nagging forgetting-something feeling creeping under my skin. *Ugh,* I remembered. *Jackson Thorpe wants feedback on his poetry.* Ugh.

A few minutes later, I was brushing my hair in front of the bathroom mirror. Since we only had one bathroom for me, Annie, and Eliza to share, it got pretty hectic on days when we all had to be out the door at the same time.

Soon Eliza was in the doorway, wearing a bathrobe and yawning like she was woken up way too early, too. "Hey," she said. She must've been super drowsy because Eliza never voluntarily talked to me.

"Hey," I said back. "I'll be done in a sec."

Eliza shrugged. Also weird? She just stayed there, watching me. Not with a scowl or anything, simply like she didn't mind my presence.

Ever try to force the wrong sides of two magnets together? You might be able to get them to bump into each other, but the second you stop forcing them, they push off in different directions. That was me and Eliza. We weren't always like that, though. Before Eliza changed, we sort of got along. We snipped at and rolled our eyes at each other on the regular, but we also stayed up all night watching all of the Lord of the Rings movies, and sometimes when she had a nightmare, I'd wake up and she'd be curled on the floor beside my bed.

Then she found out that Annie was coming and she was

angry all the time. And that was during my fourth grade (on The List—PeePee-ing My Pants). The nurse had this big meeting with Mom and Dad and told them she thought I was regressing for attention. That between the fact that Eliza was having a baby *and* Mom and Dad were divorcing, I was peeing my pants. Like on purpose or something. I had to go to therapy and everything. No one believed me that it was a stuck zipper! Just a stuck zipper! Eliza was super mad that I was the one going to therapy. I remember her screaming at Mom, "Nothing is even happening to her and she still manages to make it all about herself!"

I put the hairbrush back in the drawer. Across the counter were dozens of makeup brushes and products—lipsticks, eyelash curlers, mascara, blush, eyeshadow. It was like Eliza used the entire shop before going to work. I got it—she had to showcase some of the products. But Eliza standing right there without a speck of makeup on was still stop-in-the-street-to-stare beautiful.

She saw me eyeing the products. "Annie told me something about your nose. About you not liking it?" Eliza picked up a pot of brownish makeup and swiped the brush through it. "I could contour it a little."

"Really?" I asked.

Eliza smiled. She swiped the brownish stuff down the sides of my cheeks and in two straight lines down the sides of my nose. In quick, swirling moves, she blended in the lines. Then she looked at me with narrowed eyes. "A little highlighter, I think."

She lifted a light pink tube and twisted it, then smeared some along the tops of my cheekbones. "Just where the light will hit it," she said softly. Looking at my cheeks and not my eyes, Eliza said, "Annie said she had a great time at the party with you."

I swallowed. "Yeah, she didn't play with the girl from school. But I introduced her to a kindergartener. They really hit it off."

Eliza nodded. "Annie came home with her phone number. We're going to meet in the park next week. Do you think . . . do you think Piper's family is going to be weird about it? About me? A lot of moms are."

I shook my head, then remembered that she was swiping my face with makeup. "No," I said, thinking about how joyful Piper's mom was to see her daughter and Annie play. "I'm sure they won't be."

"I owe you," Eliza said. She leaned back and studied my face, then filled in my eyebrows with a little pot of dark gel stuff. She smiled at me. "You've got great skin, Pipi. Stop by the shop sometime, and I'll give you a few freebies."

I turned toward the mirror, barely recognizing my own face. I mean, of course it was me. But I looked . . . pretty. I looked a little like my big sister. "Thanks," I whispered, but Eliza already had left the room.

Since it was Friday, Tasha was having lunch with the cross-country team; they usually met at the track and ate on the bleachers. Out of habit, I peeked into the cafeteria at our usual table as I walked by. Ricky was there, holding the book and looking toward the other entrance. I ducked my head and kept going. He was waiting for Tasha, not me.

I found my shadowy corner of the courtyard and sat down with a sigh to read Jackson's poetry. And then everything went fuzzy.

"Penelope? Are you awake?"

What was with people and that question today? I looked up and saw Ricky, nudging me with his foot. "I thought I saw you walk by the cafeteria earlier. Why didn't you come in to lunch?"

"Oh," I said, rubbing at my eyes. "Tasha has lunch with the cross-country team on Fridays."

"I know," Ricky said. "But you still eat lunch, don't you?" He gestured to my open lunch bag next to me.

I sat up—I had been curled on my side under the hedge. I gathered the plastic container with my half-eaten turkey sandwich inside and swiped crumbs from my lap. Ricky sat next to me. I took a deep breath. Better get this over with. "Ricky, I know you like Tasha."

"*Yeah*," he said slowly. "Don't you, too?"

"She's my best friend." I took a deep breath. "And it's really nice of you to sit with me, but you don't have to, okay? You don't have to sit with me because you feel bad for me."

Ricky didn't say anything for a long time. Then he said, "Don't be daft."

"What?"

"Don't be daft." He grinned. "I know all of this British slang I can't use now that Mr. Harper is on sabbatical. It's addictive." Ricky shrugged and sat cross-legged next to me in the shade. "So, what were you doing before you fell asleep?"

"Uh . . ." I looked down at my phone chock-full of Jackson poetry. "Oh, you know," I said. "Thinking about The List."

"The List? You're still doing that?"

"Yes!" I said, and it sounded prim even to my ears. "I finished kindergarten."

Ricky's laughter burst out of him.

"Okay, so maybe Piper went in an unexpected direction after my kindergarten interference, but I *did* give her the option of a life of popularity," I said, trying hard to keep my face smooth. "So that's off The List."

"Okay, fine," Ricky said after chuckling way too long. "What else?"

I rubbed my nose. "Well, it's not official yet, but on my birthday, I can get my nose pierced." I side-eyed Ricky. "Kind of take back what bothered me. You know, first grade. The nose picking."

Ricky nodded. "Are you going to do it? Get pierced, I mean."

I shrugged. "Doesn't matter. It's off The List. So now I need to think about second grade. The vomit-a-thon. Trigger of the Pipi Touch. I don't think I'm ever going to kick that."

Ricky put his chin on his knee, looking off like he was thinking. "And third grade was . . ."

"Basketball," I said.

Ricky crossed his arms. "You're the team manager, right?"

"Yeah," I said. "And I'm one of the trainers for the girls' team. So as soon as this season goes off flawlessly, *bam*. Off The List. No one can say I'm still a dolt about sports"—Ricky grinned at the slang; he was right, it was addictive—"if my mom owns the gym, I lead the training, *and* I'm the team manager."

"Do you like basketball, though? I mean, usually managers really like the sport."

"Basketball?" I said. "I hate it."

"But you're spending all this time—"

"Eyes on the prize, Ricky," I said. "Or at least, on The List." I looked down at my hands. *How am I going to lose The Touch?*

Ricky poked my side, his finger hitting a rib.

"Hey!" I said and threw a handful of grass at him.

He laughed. "Just trying to get the Pipi Touch."

I rolled my eyes and threw more grass at him.

Ricky grinned. "I'm serious. The last time I had the Pipi Touch was in fifth grade. Our lockers were next to each other, remember?" I nodded, and he continued, "Someone passed me The Touch and then we had our standardized tests. I couldn't pass it on to anyone for two and a half hours."

"The horror," I mumbled, and started packing up my bag.

He poked me again. "Guess what happened?"

"All your hair fell out?"

"I got a one hundred percent. Only kid in the grade to ace

205

standardized testing." He handed me an empty baggie that the wind had blown too far to reach. "I think it was The Touch. And I'm about to take an algebra test, so I need all the luck I can get."

I tried to smile, but it came out wonky, half my mouth going up and half down. "Thanks," I mumbled, not sure why my eyes were wet. It didn't mean anything. He was just being nice.

Ricky plucked a leaf off the hedge and twirled it between his fingers. "How do you decide when you've redeemed yourself?"

"Well," I said, folding my hands on my lap, "when I wake up in the middle of the night, I have this moment. This *what did I do?* moment where I think about all of the things I should've done differently throughout my entire life. Sometimes it happens in the shower, too."

I've spent way, way, way too much time under the shower spray, imagining a million different ways I could've prevented my humiliations while my skin pruned and the water chilled. "Like, I'll think about how if I had just kept my hands at my side like the photographer told us to for the first-grade picture, I never would've gotten the nose-picker reputation. And if I had taken my allergy medicine instead of hiding it in my breakfast banana, I never would've set off the puke parade. And if I had just kept that notebook secret, I could've played off like I hadn't been in love with Jackson—"

"What about seventh grade?" Ricky broke in. "Do you have a plan for that?"

Even though I already was in the shade, it felt like a cloud drifted over the sun. I felt cold. "I don't talk about seventh grade."

"Okay," Ricky said slowly, "but do you have a plan? It's about Frau, right?"

"I don't talk about seventh grade," I said again.

"But she's, like, the worst on The List, right?"

I nodded, not looking at him. "And Vile Kara Samson."

"Kara's up there with Frau?"

I nodded again. "That notebook," I reminded him. "And other stuff, too."

"But mostly the notebook?" Ricky asked. He shifted a little, staring hard at the leaf in his hand. "When do you know you've reached redemption?"

"When thinking about all my humiliations doesn't hurt."

The basketball scrimmages started at four thirty, right after school.

Coach had given me a case full of water bottles to fill up to have ready to give players as they left the court. And, I swear—it honestly took me a whole twenty minutes to fill them. I was not, of course, avoiding "The Orange Ball Is a Sphere of Sadness in Other Players' Grips" Jackson. How dare anyone suggest that.

The game didn't really count since it was just a scrimmage, which Sarah explained was more of a way to figure out how the team was doing before the season began. We played against Warrensburg Middle, which had been neck and neck with us the past three seasons, beating out Northbrook in the boys' division and coming in second in the girls'. Sarah said the only reason the Northbrook girls' team won the previous years was because of this incredible athlete, Ally, who owned the court. But she was in high school this year, so no one was really all that confident Northbrook could keep the record going.

The boys' team played first. Coach had all of the players in a huddle as I made my way toward them with the giant tray of water bottles. I put it down next to them and then headed over to the side table where I was supposed to track the score. Even though the manual of rules and scoring in basketball was as riveting as Jackson's poetry, I had memorized every bit of it. Redemption, baby. It was nearly mine.

The girls' team, already in uniform, filed in to watch the game from the bleachers just behind me. Vile Kara's upper lip curled in a sneer as she passed by. Sarah, just behind her, gave me a small wave.

Coach broke the huddle with less than a minute before the scrimmage began. Jackson glanced toward the kids filing into the gymnasium and then over at me. I tried to look busy with my official clipboard. I hadn't had the chance (ahem, endurance) to finish one poem, let alone try to derive a deeper meaning out of "the scoreboard glows with the red of winners' hearts."

No luck. Jackson trotted over to me. "Pip," he whispered. *Pip?* "So, what do you think?"

"Really good, Jackson Thorpe." *Brain!* He gives me a nickname, and my brain makes me say his first *and* last name. "Like, really, really good." I cinched my mouth, trying not to ask about the orange and maroon terry cloth headband he wore across his forehead. Northbrook colors were gold and navy. I also tried not to notice the five plastic bracelets on his wrist.

He clapped his hands together like he was giving himself a high five. "Did you learn a lot from it? I bet you learned a lot."

"Yeah, absolutely," I said, focusing on the clipboard, even though all I was doing was writing my name slowly across the top. I scanned the court as if tracking something, held up the clipboard, and sketched a tree in the corner of the paper.

"Cool!" He tugged on his socks, pushing the right sock up to its full height just under his knee and shoving the left sock down to mid-calf. I raised an eyebrow. "Oh!" he said, following my gaze to his socks. He shrugged. "My dads say I'm a weirdo for believing in good luck charms, but Dad gave me the bracelets and Pop gave me the headband. Every time I wear them, I win. And my socks were just like this when I nailed the three-pointer last season."

"I didn't know you were superstitious."

"What?" His bottom lip jutted out. "I just don't take

chances. Like, no shower on game day—you wash away the luck. Stuff like that."

Vile Kara called from the bleacher seat just behind us. "Good luck, Jackson!"

Jackson saluted her as Coach called his name and motioned for him to get to center court. Lowering his voice again, Jackson said, "I'll give you more poems later. I'm writing them all the time in my head." He smiled and I went blind for a second. So blind, in fact, that I didn't see that Jackson held his hand out for a fist bump.

I finally bumped it back and Jackson backward trotted a couple steps, still smiling, before joining the team on the court. *Jackson just fist bumped me.* My brain screamed the words. *Jackson just fist bumped me AND I'm in his secret club AND he sends me poetry AND he and Sarah are just friends.* I shook my head to dislodge the thoughts. I had to concentrate on my role of manager if I was ever going to get Third Grade Basketball Disaster off The List.

The referee stood in the middle of the court, with Jackson on one side and a player from Warrensburg on the other. The game was about to start, but people still streamed into the gym. The referee held the ball in both hands, about to throw it and start the game. (This was called a jump ball, according to my manual.)

Jackson got into position and a hush fell over the gym.

Just as the ref was about to blow his whistle and throw the

ball, Vile Kara half screamed, half whispered, "Oh, no! Jackson still has the Pipi Touch!" A little louder, she added, "I hope it's not bad luck."

And since it was so quiet, everyone heard her. A collective groan swept across the gymnasium. "Ooohhhh, the Pipi Touch!"

Jackson's mouth dropped open and he slowly turned toward me. The ref threw the ball. The Warrensburg player batted it toward his teammates. Before I could think, I was on my feet. I whipped around to Kara. Sarah, standing next to her, tugged on her jersey to get her to sit down again. Kara just met my eyes, a mean little smile on her face. She waved at me the same way Tasha had to her a few days earlier.

"Pipi!" Coach called and pointed to the court.

I turned back around, my face flaming, and sat down at the table. On the court, Jackson moved numbly. He rushed toward another player who didn't even have the ball, his right hand extended. Passing the Pipi Touch, I realized.

The other player dodged, practically doing a Matrix-style bend to avoid taking on The Touch and its bad luck. I stared down at the clipboard, my eyes stinging. And then I heard a *whoosh*.

The ball sailed through the net. The Warrensburg players cheered.

Jackson looked to the ball, over at me, and then down to his right hand. He dashed toward the ball and nabbed it. Not,

I realized when he just stood there, to throw the ball, but so someone would be close enough to pass The Touch. No one moved. No one wanted the bad-luck Pipi Touch. Even the Warrensburg players paused and looked at each other, trying to figure out what was going on.

Jackson groaned and threw the ball from across the court, not even glancing at the net.

The ball soared through the air and sank through the net.

The crowd gasped.

Jackson gasped. Again, he looked at the ball, at me, and then at his right hand.

"It's good luck!" I shouted, and then crammed my hands over my mouth. I hadn't meant to think out loud like that.

And then everyone erupted into cheers. Jackson blinded me with another grin and took off for the ball. Warrensburg had possession, but Jackson stole it on a dribble. No one was trying to avoid him now; the curse was broken.

Sort of. Because Jackson wouldn't let anyone near him or the ball. He was keeping the good-luck Touch. Again and again and again, he threw the ball and every single time, he scored.

"It's Pipi!" he shouted to his teammates. "The Touch is good luck!"

Suddenly, anytime a player was within three feet of me, they stretched out their sweaty, stinky arms and swatted at me. Then they went back to the court, tearing it up.

Even the other team tried to get the Pipi Touch. It was the

most intense scrimmage in the history of Northbrook Middle. (I mean, I'm guessing. It was the only one I had seen.)

At the end, we won, forty to twenty-two. Jackson sprinted over to me the second the alarm bell blared, fist out for another bump. Soon the rest of the team gathered around me, too, each of them asking for good-luck fist bumps. Then they lifted me up and carried me on their shoulders, cheering *Pipi! Pipi! Pipi!*

So, that last part didn't happen exactly, but the team *did* gather around me. Everyone wanted me to high five or fist bump them. *Me!*

The girls' team, prepping for their game, filed past us, each one touching my shoulder or my head. Everyone except Kara.

Guess who didn't score a single point?

Take that, Vile Kara Samson. As the girls' scrimmage ended, I shot her my sweetest smile, which was a little challenging since one of Jackson's teammates had reached out for a good-luck Touch and accidentally grabbed a piece of my hair.

The Touch wasn't a curse anymore. Now, it was a charm.

Sarah linked her arm through mine. Jackson put his arm around my shoulder. Sarah said, "Penelope, you *have* to go out for ice cream with us. It's our postgame tradition!"

"Yes!" Jackson said. "Maybe we'll have time to talk, too." He winked at me, and I knew it was because he was referring to his poetry, but I let myself pretend it was just because he was completely in love with me.

"Absolutely," I said. "Let's go!"

Chapter Seventeen

The ice cream shop was only a couple blocks from school. I texted Mom on the way.

Guess I'll eat this pizza and watch this movie by myself, she texted. I felt a twinge of guilt but only until she sent a smiley face a few seconds later.

Sarah wasn't kidding about everyone going for ice cream. It was like being in a tsunami of sweaty basketball players. "Pipi Touch saved us!" one of them said. I felt a half dozen or so pats or hair pulls as everyone wanted some of the Pipi Touch.

"Sarah!" Vile Kara Samson said when we got to the diner. She somehow had made it there first and was sitting in a booth. She patted the seat next to her.

"C'mon," Sarah said, pulling me toward her. Kara's face twisted in a grimace (but I'm pretty sure mine did, too). Jackson slid into the booth across from Kara. Quickly, I sat next to him and Sarah sat next to Kara.

I know it's not particularly nice or anything, but part of what made the evening even greater was seeing Kara's face contort like her ice cream was sour every time *she* was the one who felt left out. Like when Jackson texted me his poetry and I read it under the table. Maybe I even played it up a bit, going, *"Oooohhh!"* and pointing to stanzas even though my eyes skimmed right over them. Kara knew he was texting me stuff right in front of her, and *she* didn't know it was just poetry.

Plus, everyone else kept coming to the table to talk to Sarah and Jackson, and there I was, so they talked to me, too. Do you know how awesome it was to feel like people *saw* you? To not have their eyes slide right by where your body took up space? The thing was, I hadn't even really noticed that most people did that until they didn't. But having their eyes snag on mine, seeing their face warm with a smile, hearing people say my name—it was better than ice cream.

A couple of times my phone buzzed with texts from Tasha, too. *Where are you?* and then a few minutes later, *Hello?* But every time I looked at my phone, Jackson nudged me, thinking I was reading his poetry. I figured I'd answer her as soon as I got home. When I told her that I was having ice cream with Jackson and Sarah, *and* the entire basketball teams, she'd totally freak out.

I was just about to call Mom to ask her to pick me up when Jackson's dads came in and ordered huge platters of fries for everyone. A few people left as their parents arrived to take them home. Nearly everyone stopped by our table to say goodbye to Jackson, Sarah, and Kara. And me, too. They all tapped my shoulder or wanted a fist bump so they could leave with The Touch.

My lips twitched even though I was trying really hard to look nonchalant.

"This season is going to be epic!" Jackson said.

"Thanks to Pipi," Sarah added.

This was honestly the best day of my life. Another slash through The List. *Take that, third grade!*

It was nearly nine o'clock by the time I called Mom to come get me.

Jackson's dads sat in a booth nearby, but it felt really mature, especially considering by then most of the middle school basketball team had left and now all around us were high school kids. "Can you believe we're going to be like them next year?" I said.

Kara rolled her eyes. "It's not like they're so much different." But I noticed that she was smoothing her hair with her palms. "We should've changed first, like I said," she hissed to Sarah as a group of high schoolers sauntered by, giggling.

But Sarah was watching another table where five kids were sharing a plate of chicken wings and mozzarella sticks. Two of the girls got up and headed to the bathroom; both were laughing and leaning into each other as they went. One of them stopped suddenly beside our table. "Oh, hey!" she said and pointed to Sarah, Kara, and Jackson's clothes. "Are you guys on the basketball team?"

Kara straightened. "Yeah. You're Ally, right?" Ally, the superstar athlete from last year.

Ally nodded. "Going to keep my record going?"

"We're going to try," Sarah said. "Are you playing this year?"

Ally smiled. "Nah, I'm thinking about trying out for the musical." The other girl laughed, and it was, I'm not even kidding you, the most beautiful laugh I'd ever heard. "Whatever, Bhat," Ally said. "I could do it!"

Then I recognized the girl. Lilith Bhat; she was in theater club last year. She was so beautiful it made you smile to see her— thick, dark brown hair that shimmered even in the diner light, and a wide, bright smile. She was made to be on stage. Something had happened, though, and the play last year was canceled suddenly.

Turning back to us, Ally said, "I'm taking this year off sports."

Lilith pointed at me with one finger, the rest of her hand curled around a lip gloss tube. "Hey," she said, "you look super familiar. Do I know you?"

"I don't think so . . ." I trailed off. *Could this day get any better? High schoolers talking to me? Me!*

Sarah snapped her fingers. "I bet you're thinking of Penelope's sister, Eliza." She pointed to the lipstick tube in Lilith's outstretched hand. "She works at Glitter."

Lilith's smile stretched. "Yes! That's her. She's amazing!" Lilith nudged Ally. "Remember, I told you to go in there? Do something with your . . ." She pointed vaguely to Ally's entire face, prompting Ally to roll her eyes. "She made a special blend foundation for my skin tone."

"Let's start with the musical and work up to cosmetics." Ally laughed and pulled Lilith toward the bathroom.

"Let's not with the musical," Lilith said.

No one spoke for a moment after they left, but I felt Kara's eyes on me.

"Taking the year off?" Sarah said, her voice shocked. "But Ally was *amazing*."

"Guess she wasn't feeling it anymore," Jackson said. He stared hard at Sarah. "She was ready for a change. People don't have to do what they've always done just because it's what they've always done." He paused, repeating the sentence to himself, then furiously typing it into his phone.

"What?" Kara said, her eyes flicking between them and me. Her gaze landed longest on me. "Something is different about you," she finally said, and leaned back in the booth.

I touched my nose, thinking about Eliza's mini-makeover this morning. "I don't know what."

Sarah looked up then. "It's your eyebrows," she said and smiled. "They look a little different somehow?"

"Yeah," Kara said with a sneer. "Like there are two of them."

"*Oooh*." Jackson laughed. "I remember that! You only had one for about a year, right?" He laughed again.

Sarah rolled her eyes at them. "Well, they look really awesome now."

"Yeah, they grew back." I shrugged. "I don't want to talk about it."

"Kara's just upset because hers are so thin no one sees them," Sarah said.

"Sarah!" Two bright red circles bloomed on Kara's cheeks.

"I could talk to Eliza," I said super casually, wiping the corners of my mouth with a paper napkin. "Maybe she has one of the special blends, something that could work for your . . ." I motioned to her eyebrows.

The red spots on Kara's cheeks spread to cover her whole face. Looking down at her empty sundae bowl, she muttered, "Fine."

"Fine," I said.

Sarah nudged Kara, who rolled her eyes. "Thanks," she spit out like the word was rotten in her mouth.

Sarah got up to use the bathroom and Jackson went to talk with his dads a few minutes later.

Kara stared at me. I raised an eyebrow and smiled. Slowly, a smile spread across Kara's face, too. She leaned toward me across the tabletop. "You know this isn't real, right?" Kara said. "I mean, you sitting here acting like you're part of our group. But you're not. You are and always will be just a joke, Peepee McGee."

My mouth flopped open. My eyes filled, but I couldn't move.

"What's up?" Sarah asked as she got back to the booth. She glanced from me to Kara and back.

"I was just telling Pipi a joke," Kara said. She smiled sweetly at me.

Sarah's face darkened. "Not everyone gets your sense of humor, Kara," she said. Her eyes were wide as she turned to me. "But, Penelope, you know she's just joking, right?"

"Of course." I forced a smile.

Oh, Vile Kara Samson. You're going down.

After Mom brought me home, I could tell she wanted to hang out. Half the pizza was missing and there was a spoon in an empty pint of vanilla bean ice cream. Alec was asleep on the couch, curled up with his head on the armrest. "He fell asleep before she even remade the prom gown," Mom whined.

"It was a super long, super awesome day," I said. "I'm off to bed."

"Okay," she sighed and picked up another slice.

But when I got up to my room, I couldn't turn off my mind.

I went to my pile of paper scraps and started crafting, but I didn't have enough supplies to really make anything. Besides, I had started something in the art room and that was really the only thing I wanted to work on.

I lay back on my bed, thinking. Mean moments with Kara aside, the day was amazing. *Amazing.* Everyone wanted to be near me—even to touch me. I spent the whole evening with the three coolest people in the class. Everyone now thought of me as being *good luck* instead of a total virus. It was so much fun! *Was it, though?* I told my brain to knock off its questioning. Of course, it was fun. So. Much. Fun.

Which sort of made me think of P. Art Tee's and all the parents who kept saying, "Aren't you having *so much fun*?" to their kids over and over again. "Isn't this *so much fun*?"

And that, of course, made me think of Ricky and how we really *did* have so much fun playing Skee-Ball and dancing with Piper and being totally silly and not even caring one bit.

And thinking of Ricky made me think, of course, of Tasha.

Tasha.

Tasha, who had texted me twice.

Tasha, who was my best friend.

Tasha, who had invited me over to her house at seven o'clock for a sleepover and *Supernatural* and egg salad and potato chips.

I sucked in my breath, heart hammering, and checked my phone. It was after ten.

I called her with shaking fingers, my heart thudding that I was such a jerk, such a jerk, such a jerk. How could I forget our sleepover?

I was such a terrible friend!

The phone rang and rang. Finally, a super drowsy Tasha picked up, but she didn't say anything at all after "hello."

"I'm so sorry!" I blurted. "I'm so sorry! The basketball game went really awesome, and I somehow made The Touch good luck and then everyone wanted to be around me and they invited me to the diner for ice cream and then I told Kara I'd do her a favor and Jackson gave me fist bumps all night and then . . ."

"Then what, Penelope?" Tasha asked, her voice quiet over the phone.

"Then I . . ."

"You what?"

"I forgot—"

Click.

☑

Chapter Eighteen

Tasha ignored every one of my five thousand texts and calls on Sunday.

But I knew once I talked with her on Monday, she'd forgive me. I'd tell her how things just sort of exploded at the basketball game—with the Pipi Touch being a *good* thing now and another item off The List—and she'd understand.

Maybe I'd even tell her my plans for Kara.

But first, I had to make those plans a reality.

Sunday afternoon, I was helping out at Mom's gym. When things slowed down about three o'clock, I told Mom I was going to see Eliza, who was working next door. (Annie was spending the day mini-golfing with Dad.) Mom paused in the middle of entering new client profiles into the computer. "Eliza? Your sister, Eliza?"

I laughed. "Yeah. You've met her. Tall, pretty, a little bit angry."

Mom rolled her eyes but waved me toward the door. "Just . . . be nice. Eliza's been going through some stuff lately."

"What kind of stuff?" I asked.

"Things with Annie. She's getting to the age where she's asking a lot of questions." Mom stood and stretched. Her belly was just a smidgen rounder than it used to be, something I never would've noticed if I didn't know there was a baby bean growing in there.

The sky was a bright blue, with no clouds to temper the glare. It took a few moments for my eyes to adjust to the makeup shop interior. This one wasn't like the mall shop— it was bright and homey. The walls were painted white and twinkle lights shimmered around the ceiling. Instead of cold, dark countertops, antique-looking tables painted turquoise or purple displayed the cosmetics. The walls were covered in mirrors with different frames. The ceiling, I noticed, was the same bright blue as the sky outside.

Something twitched inside me as I looked around. The store had an appearance of Eliza's old bedroom. She had never gotten around to decorating my old room when she moved in just before Annie was born; it still was just brown walls, beige carpet. Annie's room, of course, was beautiful, with purple walls and paper lanterns hanging from the ceiling.

I hadn't been into Glitter since Eliza first started working there, when Annie was still in diapers. Then it had been a lot like the mall makeup shop, all smooth and cold. Eliza made this shop look like home. No wonder everyone called it her shop.

I heard laughter and spotted my sister in the back. She was wearing an apron, her bright blond hair catching the light, as she helped a customer pick out lipstick. The woman was old, maybe eighty or even ninety, with dark brown skin but hardly a wrinkle at all. She was wearing a soft purple pantsuit and was talking about getting ready for a dance she was going to that weekend.

Eliza caught my reflection in one of the mirrors and waved at me. I nodded back, then just browsed. The shop had a customization section with tiny blue glass bottles where people could blend their own moisturizers, cleansers, or foundation.

Eventually, the lady chose a mauve lipstick. Eliza wrapped up the cosmetic tube and walked the woman outside to the nursing home van waiting for her. As Eliza reentered the shop, I pocketed one of the bottles. It wasn't stealing, not really. The bottles were free—customers were just supposed to pay for the stuff in them. That's what I told myself, anyway. My heart freaked out, insisting that it was wrong.

"Pipi?" Eliza asked. "What are you doing here?"

I shrugged. "The other day, you said something about a makeover?"

"Really?" Eliza almost squealed. She grabbed my wrist and led me to one of the tables in the back of the shop. "Your timing is perfect; it's super slow in here today."

A half hour later, I had a bag full of samples of different products. I honestly wasn't sure I'd be able to figure out how to use any of them, but the *me* in the mirror looked a whole lot more like Eliza in all the best possible ways.

"How did you figure out how to do all of this?" I asked her.

"I've always loved makeup," Eliza said. "Don't you remember all the makeovers I used to give you?"

I glared at her. One of Eliza's "makeovers" ended with me having red lipstick that stretched out to my ears like a clown's mouth. She winked at me. "I've gotten a little better since then."

"I miss you," I blurted. It didn't make any sense; we lived in the same house. I saw her every day. But it had been so long since I had seen her like *this*—confident, easy, happy. I mean, obviously Annie made her happy. She was super in love with her. But in this shop, Eliza was herself.

Eliza's face stilled, like my words were settling across her. Her smile drifted away. "I do, too," she said, and I'm not sure if she meant that she missed me or if she also missed herself. She turned and cleaned up the makeup station, rubbing antiseptic wipes across the brushes she had been using. When she spoke, her voice was so low I could barely hear it. "I've been sort of, I don't know, invisible for the past few years. Everyone thinks they know me—teen mom, mess up, high school dropout."

"You didn't drop out!" I interrupted. Eliza had gotten her GED almost immediately after Annie was born; she started taking college classes before she would've graduated with her high school class.

"Yeah, I know that. You know that. But everyone else just assumes, you know?" She wiped at a smear on the mirror. "Poor

Eliza, so smart, so much potential, now just works at Glitter." I saw her reflection in the mirror as she cleaned it. Her mouth was set in familiar straight lines again. "Her own daughter doesn't even call her 'mom.'"

"No one says that," I whispered, even though it was a lie. Didn't I just overhear Vile Kara Samson blabbing the same nonsense? The bottle in my pocket suddenly felt hot against my thigh.

"It's okay," said Eliza, seeing right through me. "I know I'm smart." Her chin lifted a little. "Did you know Annie's pre-school asked to have her tested for giftedness? She's off-the-charts smart."

"Of course, she is," I said.

Eliza grinned. "Yeah, of course, she is." Her eyes stayed locked with mine. "I haven't always been the best mom. Or the best sister—"

"Eliza—"

She put up a hand, silencing me. "But, here? I'm really good at what I do. The classes I'm taking are a big help, too. I'm *good* at this job, at running this business." Her eyes met mine in the mirror. "I'm going to ask for a promotion, once my graduation is official at the end of this semester. The manager is rarely here, and the owners don't seem to care all that much. I think I could do it. I know I can do it."

"You're graduating this semester? Mom never told me," I said.

Eliza shrugged. "I didn't tell her. I doubled up classes this past year. I don't need a big party or anything like she'd plan. I just want to . . . want to kind of get me and Annie established, you know?"

I squinted at her. "What do you mean, established?"

Eliza threw away the paper towel she had been using to clean the mirror. "Never mind." The bell on the shop door rang and Eliza turned toward it. "I'll be right with you!" she called out.

"Thanks again," I said. "I'm just going to look around a little, okay?"

I stood in front of another section of the shop. Fingers darting out, I grabbed a tube of what I wanted, what would finally show Vile Kara what it was like to be me. Quickly, I went to the back of the shop, where a clerk smiled like we were old friends. "You're Eliza's sister, right?" she said. I just nodded. "I know she has some of this stuff at home, and just a smidgen goes a long, long way. Are you sure you don't want to check with her—"

I glanced behind me, where Eliza was now talking to the new customer. "No, I want this," I snapped. The clerk's forehead crinkled, but she stopped chitchatting and told me the total. "I don't need a bag," I said and shoved it in my pocket, where it fell with a subtle clink against the small blue bottle.

Eliza called out a goodbye and the door slammed shut behind me.

That night, instead of crafting a bird, I made a label. In small script, I wrote *Eliza's Eyebrow Serum* and affixed it to the little blue bottle. Then I filled it with the contents of the tube I had purchased and the eyebrow gel from my sample bag. My bedroom door was open, and I heard Annie and Eliza playing.

This was for them as much as it was for me, I told myself.

Monday morning, I made sure I was walking by Kara's locker. Word had continued to spread about the good-luck Pipi Touch, and dozens of people asked for fist bumps, saying things like, "Got a geo test this morning! Thanks, Pipi!"

Kara sneered as she opened her locker. "Enjoying yourself?"

I smiled at her. Really, though? The Touch thing was as annoying now as when people were actively trying *not* to touch me. Just then someone bopped me on the head. Annoying, yes, but also the opportunity I needed. I pretended it knocked me off balance and I fell forward, dumping my bag. As I reached for it, I sideswiped the little blue bottle, sending it scurrying toward Kara.

"Oh, no!" I said and started to gather up all my pens, pencils, and other stuff I had "accidentally" dumped. "Do you see it? A little blue bottle?" I asked. "Eliza made a special blend for my eyebrows yesterday and I dropped it."

With my head bent, my hair covered my eyes, but I saw Kara sidestep so the bottle was behind her foot. "What kind of blend?" she asked.

I pushed my hair back from my face and looked up at her. I had taken extra special care that morning, using all of the products Eliza had given me so that I looked polished. I even asked Eliza to help me with my eyebrows.

"Oh, it's just this eyebrow gel that she made especially for me." I stood, sighing. "But I guess she'll just have to make me more. Bummer." I started to walk away but then got stabbed by a sudden worry. Over my shoulder, I said, "It was super important to only put it on my eyebrows. Just my eyebrows. She said if it got in my eyes, it'd be incredibly bad."

"Whatever," Kara said. "Like I care."

I risked glancing back. Kara was bent over pushing something into her pocket.

Even though I knew I'd be late for homeroom, I sprinted across the school to Tasha's locker, hoping to clear this whole fight up. Her back was to me as I approached. Her head was thrown back in laughter at something one of her cross-country friends was saying.

"Tasha?" I said.

Her whole body stilled. She turned like she was made of glass. Her friends scurried away. I took a step back at the fury I saw in her eyes.

Wade ran down the hall beside us while Tasha and I stayed frozen in place. He shot out his hand and swatted my arm. Well, he tried to get my arm but ended up knocking the side of my face. "Yes! I got The Touch!"

Tasha's eyes widened and her mouth popped open.

"That's what I've wanted to explain to you," I said. "I'm so sorry about Friday night. I really am! But so much has happened. You wouldn't believe it!" I smiled and threw out my arms. "I changed almost everything. I'm almost done!"

Another kid—I think he was a *sixth grader*—jabbed me in the side. "Thanks, Peepee!"

"It's Pipi!" I snapped back, but he had already disappeared down the hall.

"Oh, yeah?" Tasha crossed her arms. "I thought it was Penelope." She turned her back to me and slammed shut her locker door. "I don't even know who you are anymore. Even worse?" Tasha tugged her backpack up her arm. "I don't think *you* know."

"That's not fair." I stepped forward and pressed my back against the locker beside her so I could see Tasha's face. "I told you from the beginning." I lowered my voice. "The List—it's working, Tasha. It's really working. On Friday, after the game—"

"You ditched me," Tasha finished.

"Look, I'm sorry about the egg salad and the TV show we've seen a million times, but something really big happened to me. Maybe you could be supportive? I mean, I'm finally doing everything you hounded me about for years." I didn't know where the words came from, but they tasted bitter. "What's with you? Why can't you be there for me? Be happy for me."

Tasha leaned closer to me. "I'm the *only* one who was there for you. Over and over and over again, *I* was the one who picked you up off the bathroom floor where you would've wallowed. Me."

"I know," I snapped. "But if you could just see, I'm so close—"

"If I could just see?" Tasha laughed, but it sounded like breaking glass. "That's rich, coming from you."

"What are you talking about?" The look she was giving me, it was so cold. It was a face I had seen before, but always directed at someone else. Someone like Vile Kara Samson.

I looked around. The halls were emptying, but more than a few kids were walking extra slowly down the hall, clearly listening to us. "Maybe we should talk later . . ."

"Why? Worried someone will see us? Or, rather, see you? Everything is always about *you,* Pipi. Everything. You're so worried all of the time about what other people think of you, yet you don't see yourself *at all.*"

"That's totally not fair!" I yelled.

"Friendships go both ways, Pipi!" Tasha's hands curled into fists and she slammed them down on her thighs. "Both ways. That means I'm there for you, but once in a while? You. Have. To. Be. There. For me!"

"I'm always there for you!" I bellowed back. *How could she say this? How could she* think *this?* "All I am is there for you. Waiting to cheer you on at your games. Waiting for when you can set aside time to sit with me. Waiting for you to grace me with your presence. Waiting for you to have time to answer my calls. I'm always waiting for you!"

"Is that what you really think?" Tasha shook her head. For a second, some of the anger seemed to seep out of her, being replaced with just sadness. "Yes, I have a life. Yes, I have other friends. But I always make time for you. And when I say I'm going to be there for you, I am. I always am. But, you? As soon as someone better comes along, you forget about me." She took a deep breath, closing her eyes. "Even when it hurts me, I'm there for you."

"When would it hurt you to be friends with me?" I asked. "Are you . . . are you talking about socially? Like, socially, it hurts you to be my friend?" I always knew it, always kind of felt it, but to actually confront not being cool enough to be Tasha Martins's friend? It sliced me up.

Tasha's chin lifted a half inch. "I don't just mean that, Pipi."

"Just?" I repeated.

"You're so ridiculous sometimes," Tasha whispered. "Only you could be so obtuse."

"Obtuse? What does that even mean?" I shook my head. When Tasha's super mad her vocabulary gets intense.

"It means you can't see anything beyond your own fat nose."

I gasped. "Low blow."

"Oh, don't be like that. I'm not talking about your literal

nose, but of course you'd think that." Her jaw was set in a line. "You have no idea what I've gone through this year. None! Did you know I'm not captain of the cross-country team anymore? I messed up some stats, keeping a runner out of an expo, and the team voted for someone else. Did you know I can't keep up with book club? They want to read a whole series that isn't on audio and Ricky isn't exactly up for reading to me twenty-four/seven."

"I'm sure he would," I butted in and rolled my eyes. "Ricky would do anything to spend more time with you."

Tasha paused. "You don't see *anything,* do you?" She rolled her eyes this time. "And, of course, my problems aren't real problems. Not compared to yours."

"I know I haven't been there for you recently. But if you'll give me a little time. Let me get through this List thing. I've got some things in motion and—"

"Know what?" she said with a fake smile. "Maybe this is a good thing. Maybe a little break is what we need."

"A break?" I said. "Like you're breaking up with me? Our friendship? Are you serious?"

"I'll see you around, Penelope." She turned away.

"Tasha!" I yelped. She paused. "This is going all wrong." Now it was my turn to take a deep breath. I clenched and unclenched my fists, searching for the right words. "Just listen, Tasha. Everything's all messed up right now. I'm just working on this List. And I knocked two more things off of it on Friday.

Two! I've only got a couple more, and I've got a plan for one of them. It's almost over!"

"And then what?"

"Then things will be back to normal. Egg salad, *Supernatural* normal."

"But wasn't the whole point to make things different?" Tasha shrugged without turning around. "Congratulations. Things are different now."

"Just need a little more time," I pleaded.

Tasha walked away. "I'm going to be late for homeroom."

I stood there, alone, as the bell rang again.

Chapter Nineteen

Frau Jacobs made me come back to homeroom during lunch to give her the ten minutes she said I "owed" her for being thirty seconds late to homeroom. I walked into the classroom and sat in a chair at the back. She spent the ten minutes flitting about the classroom, watering plants and taking an occasional bite from the tuna fish sandwich she had opened as I walked in.

"The thing about respect, Miss McGee," she said, "is that it's always earned. I earned your respect by walking through the doors. Showing up, being a teacher, that garners me respect. But you must earn your respect from me by behaving properly. That's in your actions and your choices. Too many of you girls just don't make good choices."

Maybe the fight with Tasha made my tongue loose and my defenses weak, because while I had walked into the classroom determined not to say a word to Frau Jacobs, I heard myself blurt out "Girls?"

"Yes, yes," Frau said and threw up her hands, still holding the sandwich. "I know I'm supposed to say 'girls and boys,' but it's only the girls I see pushing things too far. Trying to get away with inappropriate behavior." Her eyes mocking and wide, she looked around the room. "I mean, do you see any boys around here?"

I slouched in the seat, staring at the clock.

"If you'd just take personal responsibility, life would be so much easier. There are rules, Miss McGee." She waved her sandwich in my direction, hitting me with a whiff of tuna fish. "Rules and expectations."

She took a bite of the sandwich as she leaned against the edge of the desk, staring at me. Her voice dipped. "Expectations aren't hard to understand. We as young women, we should *expect* certain things to happen us. Certain changes. We should be prepared for them. To go on as if those changes haven't happened. To be all . . ." Frau Jacobs mimed being startled, her mouth flopping open and closed and hands (one still clutching the sandwich) waving in the air next to her face in mock horror.

It's me, I realized. *She's making fun of me. How I looked* that *day.* The day I never talk about.

I sucked in my breath. If shame were a liquid, my body was sucking it up, my fingertips straws, my veins open as it surged up my arms, over my shoulders and poured endlessly into my chest.

Her eyes narrowed as her smile stretched.

"When, really," she continued, "all fault lies on ourselves when we don't follow expectations. You've got to anticipate consequences." She took another bite of her sandwich, little flakes of tuna fish collecting at the corners of her mouth.

"How long until Mr. Harper is back?" I managed.

Frau Jacobs frowned at me. "Were you paying attention to anything I've said, Pipi McGee?"

The timer on her desk beeped, and she waved me toward the door.

Images flashed through my mind—memories I didn't want to have of the worst day of my life and of Frau Jacobs's smug smile through it all. I shook my head. I wouldn't think about seventh grade. Not ever.

I left the room on shaking legs.

I even made it down the hall to just outside the cafeteria. I could see Tasha sitting at a round table in the middle. She was laughing, and it was one of her laughs that fill up the entire room. I knew she wouldn't be at our usual spot, not after how we left things that morning, but I didn't think she'd be so happy about it. If I told her about what Frau Jacobs had said in the room, Tasha's face would twist in anger. She'd tell me that Frau Jacobs was awful, and she'd hold my hand while I cried.

Maybe I'd even tell her all of it, everything that had happened that day in seventh grade. I never had; she only knew the ending.

Everyone knew the ending. No one knew the whole story.

I stretched onto my tiptoes to see our usual table, sure it'd be empty. But instead Jackson sat perched on the edge, his mouth moving as he read a poem to himself. A second later, my phone pinged in my pocket. *Just wrote another one while I'm waiting here for you!* I scrolled down the message. The poem was long, long, long. I shuddered and put the phone back in my pocket. We were getting together after basketball practice for another poetry club meeting. Sarah had texted something about the open mic being a couple days away and needing to prepare.

I watched as Sarah took a seat across from Jackson, and soon Kara joined, too.

I looked back to Tasha, and she also was checking out our old table. She rolled her eyes and turned back to her cross-country team friends at their new table. Ricky, leaving the lunch line, paused halfway between Tasha's table and our usual spot. With another glance at Jackson, he pulled up a chair across from Tasha. Unlike times I had sat with the cross-country team, Ricky instantly was in the middle of their conversation.

Well, I had done it, huh? I had Jackson and Sarah as friends at last. And I had Kara right where I wanted her. *Yay, me.* I turned my back to the cafeteria and headed toward the bathroom, planning to take my usual spot in the third stall and cry until lunch was over.

But when I got to the bathroom, I suddenly remembered something else.

Kara. Didn't she go to the bathroom every single day just before lunch ended? Didn't she make everyone else leave so she could "do her business"?

Every single day.

You know what? I wasn't sad anymore. Something alto-gether different pulsed through me as a plan took shape. Kara was about to have a very bad afternoon.

Ten minutes until lunch was over. I got into position. Now, all I had to do was wait.

"What are you doing here?" Kara yanked open the bathroom stall and now stood in front of me, her lip curled up in its usual sneer. She jutted out her hip; a sliver of her stomach showed where her shirt rode up. Earlier she had been wearing a cardigan in homeroom. I guessed she figured she'd dodged Frau Jacobs's dress-coding and could wear the tight, short T-shirt.

"Going to the bathroom," I said, even though I had been doodling in a notebook.

"Oh, *gross*." Kara stretched out the word. "Are you writing Jackson's name in a notebook over and over again?"

My pencil point broke on the paper. "Haha," I said, my voice crisp. "Hilarious."

The stall door swung partly shut as Kara turned toward the mirrors and fluffed her hair. "That notebook was so pathetic," she said. I felt a mean twinge of satisfaction inside me as she ran a finger along her too-thin eyebrows. "It was *genius* of Ricky to show it to Jackson. I didn't think he had it in him." She laughed while I tried to make sense of her words.

"What? Ricky didn't give Jackson the notebook. You did.

You messed with me all year about him liking me."

Kara slowly turned around. A smile floated across her face as slow and satisfied as the one on Frau Jacobs's face earlier. She crossed her arms. *"No,"* she said, again stretching out the word. "I told you *someone* liked you. I never said it was Jackson. You made that leap all on your own."

"Then who liked me?"

"Ricky," she said with an isn't-it-obvious shrug. "Remember, his locker was on the other side of yours? He talked about you all the time." Her mouth popped open. "Wait! All this time, *still,* you thought it was *Jackson* I had been talking about?" She chuckled and turned back to her reflection. "Oh, that's priceless." She smeared on some lip gloss. "And it makes everything sort of make sense now. Why you thought you had a chance with him."

I stood up, the notebook falling to my feet. "It was *Ricky?*"

"Of course, it was Ricky. He's been in love with you for, like, *ever,* hasn't he? Even going to P. Art Tee's with you." She rolled her eyes. "But what a crap move on his part to out you to Jackson that way with the notebook."

She smiled at her reflection, then turned back to me and crossed her arms. "I had it all worked out—Ricky was going to tell you he liked you at your locker at the end of the day. I'd finally be done being his little messenger—"

"Wait! He told you to tell me all those things? About the dress and my hair and everything?"

241

Kara shook her head and rolled her eyes again. "Not *really*. I improvised. You know, as a joke. Just to see how badly you wanted someone to like you. I told him you were so pathetic, all I had to do was tell you someone would like you more if you cut off your hair and you would. He didn't believe me." She shrugged.

"How could you?"

Kara sighed. "I didn't do anything. You cut your own hair. Same thing with the dress."

Something must've twisted on my face, because Kara's eyes got super wide.

Her hands dropped to her sides. "It was a long time ago, Pipi. Let it go."

I stared at her, my heart hammering just as hard as when I was thinking about Frau Jacobs.

"Ricky wanted to tell you he liked you. I arranged it, told you that day was the day. All that. We were waiting by the lockers for you, and he started to chicken out. Then he said he remembered you had a notebook in your locker. He said he'd find a blank page and write the usual. You know, *Do you like me? Circle y or n.* I told him just write *y n* or else you'd probably circle *or.* You seem the type."

A low growl escaped me.

"*Touchy.* Anyway, he grabbed the notebook and when he flipped it open, there was Jackson's name written, like, a million times. He kept flipping—probably looking for a Ricky somewhere in there—but the last page was *Penelope Claire*

Thorpe." Kara made a gagging sound. "Of all the girls in our grade, why Ricky wastes any time thinking about *you,* I'll never understand."

"You like him," I said, thinking the words at the exact same time they left my mouth.

"Ricky?" Kara shuddered. "Ew. He's, like, in love with you. Always has been."

"But you tried. You tried to make him like you by making *me* look small and laughable over and over and over." Again, the words left my mouth at the same moment I had the thoughts. "Just hoping he'd stop liking me and notice you instead."

"You don't know what you're talking about," Kara said, her words clipped.

Still moving super stiff, she turned back to the mirror. She stared down at me in the reflection. I knew that was the closest thing to a confession I was going to get. My mind was soup.

"That's why you set me up like that, making me cut my hair. Why you made such a big deal about my eyebrow. Why you keep the Pipi Touch going. You like Ricky, and you can't stand that he likes me."

"Lik*ed* you," she clarified. Kara smiled again, and this one didn't look forced at all. "And that's what you really don't get, do you? I didn't set out to do anything to *you.* You were just there. I didn't spread the Pipi Touch because I don't like you. I did it because I don't *care* about you. Having everyone play this game *I* invented? It was fun." She shrugged. "That's why it was

243

so weird—Ricky liking you, I mean. I am the one who's interesting. Who actually does things."

"You can't stand that he likes me," I said again.

"If he had any feelings for you at all, why would he be the one who gave the notebook to Jackson? I wanted to shove it back into your locker. He was the one who called Jackson over and showed him the notebook. He told Jackson everything—the hair, the dress, everything." She turned to face me head-on. "He *laughed* while he did it, Pipi."

Then she was the one laughing. "Oh, poor Pipi. Are you going to cry?" She arched an eyebrow.

My breath left my mouth in a huff. I shook my head, ignoring the wetness around my eyes. *Focus, Pipi!* "It's the same now, isn't it?" I said.

"What are you talking about?" Kara's shoulders lifted and fell with another sigh.

"Except now it's not Ricky, right? It's Jackson. You spend all of your time trying to get Jackson to notice you, but he only likes Sarah. No one likes you, and you know it. No one likes you because if you're not being mean, you're boring."

Kara's nostrils flared and her jaw clenched. Something twisted behind her eyes. "Jackson doesn't like Sarah," she snapped.

"It's all jealousy, isn't it? That's why you won't let Sarah do anything without you. You know if you don't have her, you don't have anyone."

Kara shuddered, her fisted hands trembling. "You don't know anything, Pipi McGee. *I* protect Sarah. *I'm* the reason *she's* popular. If it weren't for me watching over her, everyone would know she's ga—" Whatever Kara was about to say was cut off as the bathroom door swung open. A sixth grader peeked in, saw Kara's scary statue face, turned on her heel, and left.

"Get out, Pipi. Forget I said anything," Kara said, "and get out. I actually have to use the bathroom." She grabbed my arm and led me out of the door.

"Wait," I said as the door fell back against my side. "Do you remember fourth grade? When my zipper got stuck?"

"Seriously, Pipi?" Kara rolled her eyes. "While this whole memory lane thing has been super fun, I actually need you to leave now."

"We were on a field trip, remember? Just the two of us in the museum library bathroom. And I begged you—*begged* you—to get the teacher?" I dug my heels in as she half pushed me out of the bathroom.

Kara sneered. "And then you peed your pants in front of everyone as you ran across the library screaming for help." She pushed me again. "It was hilarious."

"It was, wasn't it?" I said.

Kara rolled her eyes. Then she grabbed her stomach and grimaced. "Will you please *leave*?"

"One more question," I said as Kara groaned. "Would you do it again?"

She leaned in, her face a half inch from mine. "In a heart-beat," she said, and then shoved me out of the bathroom.

I smiled at her as sweetly as I could and let the door swing shut behind me. I waited just a moment to hear the click of the lock on a stall and then left, every roll of toilet paper and paper towel in my bag.

A few steps into the hall I paused. Quickly, I scribbled *Out of Order* on a Post-it and slapped it on the bathroom door.

All that shame that had poured in me earlier? Whoosh. Gone. Something bubbly and new filled me up instead, starting at my toes and bursting through me.

Revenge.

I swung by the bathroom again between classes, opening the door just a crack. "Hey! Hey!" Kara called out. "Who's there? Do you have any toilet paper? Hey!"

"I'm sorry, I can't hear you," I said back, disguising my voice.

"I'm stuck in here!" Kara yelled. "Bring me toilet paper! *Bring me toilet paper!*"

I opened the door just enough to let her voice leak into the hall as a group of girls walked by, then let the door swing shut again.

MINE. ALL MINE...

✔️ Chapter Twenty

What a day! Everyone whispering, the stories expanding and growing, taking flight and having *nothing to do with me*. Seriously, everyone was laughing at Vile Kara Samson, not me! And now for the cherry on top: my last class of the day was social studies with Kara.

I took my usual seat in the back and waited for her to enter, trying hard to cling to the glorious feeling of revenge and not the boiling unease of what she had revealed about Ricky and what she had been about to say about Sarah.

"Did you hear?" Becky Sprenkle asked as she took her seat. She wasn't technically talking to me, but around me. Everyone near us twisted toward her. "Kara Samson was stuck in the bathroom. No tp, no paper towels, nothing—and it was a, you know, number two situation."

Someone shrugged. "Eh, everyone poops."

"Yeah." Becky giggled. "But does everyone sit and scream for a half hour in an empty bathroom?"

Another kid snickered.

Becky sat back, clearly enjoying being the informant.

"That's why she's not here. Ms. Baqri was the one who found her," she said, naming the social studies teacher, who still hadn't entered the room even though the bell had rung. "I saw her running down the hall with a handful of toilet paper. She went into the bathroom and then dashed back out to get a janitor."

My heart thumped too fast in my chest. *What did you do?* my brain asked, as if it weren't responsible for the decision-making that led us to this point. *How much trouble are you in?*

Just then a shrill, *"Are you kidding me?"* sliced through the room.

In a whoosh, everyone in class scrambled to the door. Just outside it was Kara. In front of her stood Frau Jacobs. Holding a tape measure.

"Seriously?" Kara screamed. She threw her arms up in the air and slammed them down on her legs. "You're dress-coding me? *Now?*"

Frau Jacobs held up the tape measure. "Your shirt is three inches above your hip bone. Unacceptable. As the esteemed soprano Frau Greta Mila von Nickel would say, you're allowing others around you to give in to their inner swine-dog, a bit lost in translation there, but you get the idea, dearie."

"Did you just call me a pig-dog?" Kara growled. Kids huddled around the door on the other side of the hall, too.

"Your inner swine-dog, that which is base and inappropriate. But don't worry, dear. I have a suitable shirt for you right here." Frau Jacobs pulled the oversized white T-shirt with NORTHBROOK MIDDLE written across it in Sharpie from her shoulder bag.

PLEASE DON'T MAKE ME WEAR THE SHIRT OF SHAME.

NORTH BROOKE MIDDLE SCHOOL

"I am *not* wearing the shame shirt!" Kara stomped her foot. Frau Jacobs slipped it over Kara's head. It was so big that it draped over her arms, falling to Kara's knees and down to her wrists.

As Frau stepped back, Kara stomped again and something happened on her face that made Frau Jacobs tilt her head in one direction and then the other.

"What?" Kara stomped again. She turned toward the doorway where we all gathered.

In unison, we gasped.

Kara's eyebrows had shifted. There was a brown streak where the colored part of the gel had filled in her brows. But the actual eyebrow hair had shifted slightly to the sides when she stomped. The right eyebrow was sliding down the side of her face. The left dipped a little toward her nose.

All those revenge bubbles I had earlier? They burst in one explosion of contrition. *Oh, Pipi. What have you done?* My brain demanded to know. *It's your fault! You did this!* I slipped back into the crowd like a fish into an anemone.

Kara turned toward the other doorway.

Everyone gathered there gasped, too.

She turned back to Frau Jacobs. Ms. Baqri trotted down the hall toward us, one hand keeping her headscarf in place. She paused, too, and stared at Kara.

"WHAT?" Kara screamed.

Ms. Baqri put her hand on Kara's arm. "Perhaps we should go back to the bathroom, Kara."

By the end of the day, the whole school was buzzing about Kara being stranded in the bathroom, coming out without any eyebrows, and leaving early in the Shirt of Shame.

The nonstop whine of my brain—*What did you do, Pipi McGee?*—combatted with my inner pig-dog's occasional roar of *Vengeance is mine!* I swallowed down some panic at what repercussions I might be in for from Kara, along with something much bitterer that tasted a lot like guilt. *What did you do, Pipi McGee?* Standing there, Kara looked so utterly furious. But when that zapped away, what would she be left with (aside from no eyebrows)? And why would I want *anyone* to go to sleep at night, eyebrowless, with everyone's laughter ringing in her ears, even if that person was mostly responsible for the same thing having happened to me?

I was unloading my bag into my locker at the end of the day when I spotted Sarah. She marched up to me with her eyes narrowed. Quickly, I zipped up the bag before she could see the rolls of toilet paper stashed inside. "Kara just texted me.

She said you might've had something to do with the bathroom thing today?"

"Bathroom thing?" I echoed as I closed my locker door.

When I turned around, Jackson was trotting toward me from the other direction. "What bathroom thing? Or is it a girl thing? Never mind. Don't tell me." Jackson ruffled my hair like I was a dog. "I need an extra dose of luck," he said with a wink.

"Oh," Sarah said. "Just something with Kara."

"Yeah!" Jackson laughed. "I heard. Stuck in the bathroom. Classic."

Sarah's forehead wrinkled. "It's not funny, Jackson. She was really embarrassed." She turned to me. "She also said that you might've been the one to make her eyebrows fall off."

Even though my face felt like someone was hitting it with a hair dryer turned to high heat, I smiled. "How could I make her eyebrows fall off?" I slipped my arms through the backpack. "Maybe it was just a stress-related thing? When my mom's really stressed, she breaks out in hives."

Sarah shook her head. "I don't think that's it. She said she got a special blend of something from Glitter."

I crossed my arms, focusing on keeping my flaming face smooth. "I told her Eliza made me a special blend for my eyebrows, but I didn't give anything to her." I opened the front zippered pocket of my bag and pretended to root around.

I snapped my fingers, looking off into the distance. "You know, earlier today I tripped and the bottle rolled away. I couldn't find it, but it *was* right next to Kara's locker. I even asked her for help looking for it." I shrugged. "I guess she could've found it, but I told her it was a special blend for me. You don't think she would've kept it for herself, do you?"

Sarah's mouth opened and closed a couple of times. "Let's just forget about it," she finally said.

Jackson, still chuckling, shrugged. "Yeah, she'll get over it."

"Yeah," I said. "I mean, who hasn't lost an eyebrow or been embarrassed in a bathroom."

"Kara's not great at getting over stuff," Sarah said. "Listen, I'll see you guys tonight. Club meeting at the gym, right?" She bounced on her toes for a second. "Open mic is next week, so let's pick our poems. We can practice performing tonight."

She waved and headed toward her bus as if she hadn't just said something terrifying. "See you, Pipi," Jackson said and headed toward the doors.

"Jackson," I called and trailed after him. "Do you remember sixth grade—the, um . . ." My face was about to combust, but I spit out the words. "The notebook?"

"Oh, yeah." Jackson laughed. "That was so funny."

"Yeah." I forced a smile. "So funny. It must've really been hilarious when Kara gave you the notebook."

"Kara?" Jackson frowned. "Nah, that was Ricky."

I nodded. "Right. Must've remembered it wrong."

"You okay, Pipi?" Jackson asked.

"I'm fine," I said. "See you later."

"Yeah, cool." Jackson paused, scratched at the back of his head, and turned around. "You know it was just a joke, right? We didn't mean anything by it."

"Yep. That's what I'm good for, right?" I threw out my arms. "A joke."

About a half dozen kids ran by me, grabbing at my arms and hair for luck.

Jackson laughed. "So, we're cool?"

"Yeah, of course," I said, and pulled up the hood on my sweatshirt, blocking someone from grabbing at my hair. "Totally cool."

When the day was finally over, I slunk into Mom's gym, taking my spot behind the desk. I smooshed my face against the countertop and tried not to think. A pair of hairy, pasty legs in tube socks and a pair of dark, toned legs stood in front of me. They paused, so I rolled my eyes to look at them without lifting my head. Dad and Alec, fresh from the racquetball court.

"Everything okay there, Pipi?" Alec asked.

"Fine," I said, only it came out a little garbled since my face stayed smooshed against the countertop.

Dad leaned forward, resting his face on his palm. He smelled a little from the racquetball game. The light glinted off the little stud in his nose. I arched my eyebrow and touched it. "Yep, still rocking the hardware," he said and patted the back of my head. "What's going on, Pips?"

I sighed, my shoulders rising and falling. "Nothing. Everything is going exactly according to plan."

"Good. Good." Dad stood up.

"Should we call her mom?" Alec whispered.

"No, man. We're dads. We've got this." Dad poked my shoulder. "Does anything hurt?"

I shook my head.

Alec cleared his throat. "Did, um, someone say something . . ."

I shook my head.

"Just having a moment?" Dad asked.

I nodded. "Have you ever done something that felt good at the time, but then you felt guilty about it?"

Alec said, "Once I ate an entire bag of Tootsie Pops. Do you mean like that?"

"Kind of," I said. I squeezed my eyes shut. For some reason, Ricky bloomed behind them. "Or have you had someone you thought was on your side turn out to have hurt you?"

Dad patted my shoulder. "Everyone gives in to their swine-dog once in a while."

"Their what?" I sat upright, staring at him.

Dad grinned. "It's just something someone I went to high school with used to say. She liked this opera singer—wanted to be an opera singer herself. She got picked on a fair amount." Dad's face clouded for a second and he shook his head, like he was wiping something off a blackboard. "Anyway, she used to say the people giving her a hard time were just indulging their swinedog." He shrugged. "Guess it stuck with me."

I blinked, hard, staring at my dad. I tried to do some math. "Did you go to high school with Frau Jacobs?"

Dad's bottom lip popped out. He had pretty much blocked out most of high school. Loads of times people would come up to him and say how much they liked seeing his name in the paper, just like when he was the school paper reporter. Dad never remembered their names. He'd always say something like, "Oh, thanks . . . *you.*"

He nodded. "Yeah, I think that was her name. Angela Jacobs, though she went through this weird phase where she made us all call her Aahn-ka-la. She was always quoting an obscure German soprano."

"Greta Mila von Nickel," I said. "She was my Intro to Languages teacher. And now she's my homeroom teacher." I made a face.

"Be nice to her," Dad said. "She wasn't exactly treated well in school. I'm surprised she's a teacher, to be honest."

Alec drummed his fingers on the countertop. "I noticed that people sometimes stick with things that don't work, thinking that they can make them better long past when they should've moved on," he said. "I see that at work a lot. I'll advise my clients to give up on an investment, but they push through, expecting a payment that never measures up."

Both Dad and I looked at Alec. He cleared his throat. "I'm not doing the Dad thing where we say something vague, and it ends up being a metaphor. I'm just saying that literally some of my clients do that."

"Oh," I said.

"That was good stuff, nevertheless," Dad said.

To me, Alec added, "If you did something and you regret it, maybe undo it?"

"I can't," I said, slumping down again. "I think I made an unfixable problem."

"Oh," Alec said. He smiled. "My dad used to say that if you can't fix a problem, the problem is there to fix you."

Dad held out his fist above my head and they bumped. "You've got this down, Alec."

They both sat down next to me, one on each side, while I smooshed my face back into the countertop. We stayed like that for about five minutes, until I pushed back and breathed out. Finally, I grabbed my homework out of my backpack. Dad and Alec both kissed the top of my head and then left.

The doors to the gym opened and closed a bunch of times, but no one needed help, so I kept plugging away on my homework. Scheming hadn't exactly been great for keeping up my grades. I had just finished my algebra work when the doors opened with a *swoosh*. Annie skipped through holding hands with Piper.

"Hey!" I said, surprised. "What are you guys doing here?"

Piper grinned. "Being a unicorn." She held her pointer finger out on top of her head.

"I can't tell you what I am because it's a secret," Annie said, her face solemn.

"She's a spy," Piper whispered.

"*Shh!*" Annie said, but then whispered back, "Double agent, remember?"

"Right!" Piper said as she dropped Annie's hand to prance in a circle.

Coming in just behind them were Eliza and Piper's mom, both holding coffees. They were mid-laugh.

"Come on," Annie said. "Let's go back to the trampoline room."

"A whole room of trampolines?" asked Piper, her eyes perfect circles. "Like the walls and floors and the ceilings and the lights and the—"

"Just the floor." Annie sighed. "Just the floor."

"That's okay," Piper said. "But someday? My whole house is going to be a trampoline. I'm going to bounce all the time. Even on the toilet."

Annie stopped. "We're going to live together in our trampoline house." Piper nodded.

"I'll be just behind you all," Eliza said. "I want to talk to my sister quickly."

As Piper, her mom, and Annie rounded the corner, Eliza practically Piper-pranced over to the desk. "Can you believe it?" she said. "I think I have my first mom friend!"

"Told you Piper's mom was cool."

"So cool!" Eliza took a big breath. "And watching Annie play with a friend? I think I'm getting the hang of this. I think she's going to turn out okay."

I squeezed Eliza's arm. "Annie's perfect. You're doing a great job."

Eliza bit her lip and then nodded. "I think I am."

The girls' laughter drifted down the hall toward us.

Eliza's eyes filled for a moment. In a quiet voice, she said, "She called me mom. Annie, on the way here. She said, 'Hurry up, Mom,' when we stopped for coffee." I didn't know what to say, so I just nodded. Eliza smiled again and waved goodbye as she joined her daughter.

Before Jackson and Sarah arrived for poetry club, I remade my list from memory while again smooshing my face on the countertop. Someone tapped me on the shoulder in the middle of my musing.

Tasha! My brain supplied. But, instead of my former best friend, in front of me stood Annie.

"Piper and her mom are in the bathroom and my mom's on the phone," she said.

"Does Eliza know you're out here with me?"

Annie shrugged. "I think she'll figure it out." Annie scooted up to sit on the countertop as I resumed smooshed face. "You're melting."

"I'm just thinking."

"'Bout what?"

I shrugged.

"Is it The List thing?"

"How did you know about that?" I popped my head up so fast something creaked in my neck, feeling like a hot egg cracked on the inside.

Annie leaned in so her mouth was next to my ear. "*Spy.*" She looked around to make sure no one heard, then went back to her upright position. "Want to talk to me about it? I'm superior at puzzle-solving. It said so on a test. Superior. It means awesomely awesome."

"I know what superior means," I said. "You wouldn't get this."

Annie mouthed the word *superior* again.

Sighing, I sat up, too. "I thought this whole plan thing would be so simple."

"What did you do so far?"

I glanced at my niece. I was about to spill my guts to a person wearing corduroy overalls. This might be a new low. "For kinder-garten—when I made that bad self-portrait—I fixed Piper's. Got rid of the dinosaur and the unicorn horn."

"But she's going to be a unicorn when she's a grown-up," Annie pointed out. "So, that's not a great plan."

"It still counts," I insisted. I held up one finger. "I did my part to stop her from being labeled a weirdo."

Annie shrugged. "She likes being a weirdo. She has a song about it. *I am a weirdo. Weirdo, weirdo, weirdo. I am a weirdo and I love weird-ooooohs!*"

259

"Still counts," I said and held up a second finger. "First grade was the nose-picking thing."

Annie giggled. I ignored her. "I reclaimed my noble nose." I held up my other hand to stop her from interrupting. "Yes, I know that Dad ended up with the piercing, but it still counts. I don't hate my nose anymore."

Annie just blinked at me.

"And that, plus the second-grade vomit-a-thon, are both scratched off The List." I held up a third finger. "The Pipi Touch is a good thing now. People think I'm good luck. Isn't that awesome?"

Annie shrugged and held up her hands.

"Yeah. It is," I said. "The whole jabbing at me or grabbing strands of my hair is kind of annoying, but I'm not a virus anymore. People like being around me now. No one scrunches up their face and acts like simply being near me is going to make them sick."

Annie ran a little hand down the side of my head. "I like you."

"Thanks. But you've always liked me, so it doesn't count," I said. I held up a fourth finger. "Third grade, the wrong basket in basketball. I achieved total redemption by being absolutely amazing as a trainer and team manager." Annie clapped for me.

"What about fourth grade?" she asked. "You were a pants peer. Mom says it was because you were stressed and sad, and that if I'm ever stressed and sad, I should tell her and not becoming a pants peer like Aunt Pipi."

I huffed. "I am *not* a pants peer. I peed once. Once! And it wasn't because of stress. It was a snagged zipper and Vile Kara Samson's refusal to get me help."

Annie patted my head. "What did you do?"

I smiled. "I took care of that today."

Annie clapped again. "Tell me!"

"Well, I knew that Kara goes to the bathroom at the same time every day, so I . . ." I looked at Annie's clear hazel eyes, the excited just-waiting-to-cheer smile on her face, and suddenly my words burst inside me. "I . . . I . . ."

"Told her good job? For using the bathroom like a big girl?" Annie finished for me.

"Not exactly."

I tried to conjure up the satisfying revenge bubbles that had floated through me as the bathroom door swung shut earlier. But all that ended up happening was a burp. I kept thinking about Kara calling for help from the bathroom. About Sarah's wrinkled-up forehead as she said how embarrassed Kara was.

"Never mind," I said. "But it was taken care of. It all ended up just being a joke. Kara was upset, but she'll get over it."

"Like how you're getting over everything now?" Annie said.

"Right," I said, my face smooshing on the table again.

Annie held out one hand. "That's five things. What's next?"

"Fifth grade?" I said. "Well, Kara made me think Jackson loved me. That's what I thought anyway. But it kind of turns

261

out that she never actually said it was *Jackson* who liked me. She was being mean, trying to get me to do things, like cut my hair."

Annie grinned. "I love to cut hair."

"Yeah, well, I didn't," I said. "But it turns out that it wasn't really Kara who did the big mean thing—give Jackson a secret notebook. That was Ricky."

Everything was so messed up, and I had so much to sort through that I had been pushing Ricky to the back of my mind. Which had been working, until right then. *Stop thinking about Ricky,* I ordered my brain. *Do not think about how he liked you and you didn't even know it. Do not think about how he hurt you and never told you. Do not think about how he knew about The List and still didn't tell you. Don't think about how awesome he is at Skee-Ball and how he helped save Piper's birthday. Do not think about his dimple and how easy it is to talk to him, unlike, say, Jackson, who only talks about himself and shares really bad poetry and is in general much more boring than you thought he would be. Stop thinking about Ricky's dark eyes and do* not, *I repeat, do* not *wonder if part of Ricky still likes you. If maybe he always has liked you. Or did, because maybe you've really messed that up along with messing up your friendship with Tasha. Stop, Brain.* Stop.

"What was in the notebook?" Annie asked.

"Jackson's name."

Her forehead wrinkled. "Just his name?"

I nodded. "You'll understand when you're ol

Annie shook her head. "I have a noteboo

words over and over."

"Which words?" I asked.

"Cashew cheese."

We stared at each other for a second.

"Moving on. Back to The List," I said. "I got rid of sixth grade today."

"What'd you do?" Annie asked.

I didn't want to explain this one to Annie, either.

"Don't worry about it," I said.

"Why would I worry about it?" Annie said. "I'm four."

"I would rather not tell you."

Annie crossed her arms. "Is it inappropriate? MomMom has inappropriate words. When she uses them, she says sorry. She says if she can't say something to me, she probably shouldn't say it to anyone."

"It's not inappropriate words," I muttered.

Annie gasped. "Inappropriate dos?"

It took me a second to figure out what that meant. "Oh!" I said. "Like I *did* something inappropriate?"

Annie nodded, eyes wide.

"Let's just say that Kara's missing something."

"You're a *stealer*?" She gasped again.

"Not exactly." I leaned back, thinking about the little blue bottle and rubbing my eyebrows. "They'll grow back."

nie's eyes got huge. "You stole her eyebrowns? That's
..."

"I didn't *steal* her eyebrowns."

Annie shook her head. After a couple seconds she poked my side. "What's next?" She was holding up seven fingers. "Because the list on your corkboard has eight."

"I don't talk about seventh grade."

Annie kicked her foot back and forth a couple of times and then said, "I was scared to say something. And then the more I didn't say it, the bigger it got." Annie smiled. "And it's silly because the word is small." She leaned forward again and whispered in my ear: "*Mom*."

I smiled at her. "I like that word."

"So does my mom." Annie smiled at me. "First, I said it in my head a lot, and then I said it loud. And now I can say it all the time and it isn't scary."

We both turned at footsteps in the hallway. "Annie?" Eliza called.

"Coming . . . *Mom*!" Annie said with a told-you look on her face. "You should say it. What happened. You should say it, and then you can fix it."

"You know, you're pretty smart, kid."

She cupped my face in her hands. "*Superior*."

Chapter Twenty-One

I texted Sarah that I needed help working through an idea. *Can you come early to the gym?*

Her response was immediate. *Sure! I'll be there in five minutes.*

Once she walked in, with her bright, perfect smile and her happy-to-see-you wave, I realized I couldn't do this. How could I tell *Sarah,* of all people, my biggest, darkest shame?

But I couldn't tell Tasha; she was too angry with me. And I couldn't tell Ricky; he was too complicated. Jackson was out of the question.

I didn't have anyone else. And Sarah knew something about secrets.

I remembered Sarah standing in the gym bathroom while Kara berated her.

I remembered how she looked when she watched the spoken word poetry videos. How she said all she wanted was someone to hear her.

She would hear me. I knew that. She heard poetry—actual poetry—even in the drivel that Jackson was constantly writing.

Maybe if she heard me, she'd trust me enough with her secret.

Sarah needed someone, and maybe that person could be me?

She might even help me figure out a way to get back at Frau Jacobs without it feeling like my insides were boiling away when I thought of it later.

We went back to the little room we had met in before, but I didn't sit on the exercise ball and neither did she. Instead, we both sat in the middle of the room.

Deep breath. Okay.

"Can I tell you what happened to me in seventh grade?"

Sarah nodded. "But, if it helps, I know about the flagpole. Remember? I was there?"

I crossed my arms. Deep breath. Just thinking about it didn't mean it was happening, right? But my body reacted like it didn't know the difference. Let's get this over with. "But I need to tell someone *all* of it."

So, I told her, overexplaining every detail, even the ones that didn't matter, the ones that she already knew.

I told her how it had started in Frau Jacob's Intro to Languages, a required class for all seventh graders. We had spent the first third of the year learning Spanish, then a third focused on French, and finally the last part of the year we had learned German, but our teacher only wanted to be called Frau, not Señora or Madame. She taught the eighth graders

German, and she said it was better for us all to just get used to calling her Frau.

Because she had to teach the entire grade, Frau Jacobs's classes were double the usual size—fifty kids instead of twenty-five. "Remember the chairs in the mini-auditorium?" I asked Sarah. Fabric-covered, movie theater–style chairs set up in a horseshoe shape around the platform where Frau Jacobs had taught for the past fifty thousand years.

I sat beside Ricky for the first part of the year, and every time Frau Jacobs would spout off something about how boys shouldn't be distracted, *I'd* be distracted by the way he'd mutter under his breath about boys understanding that shoulders exist.

Frau also had this rule that if a kid was caught using a phone during class, the phone was locked in her desk drawer and the only way to get it back was to have your parents email and request it. The first ten minutes of class on the first day, both Becky and Wade had their phones out. But Frau Jacobs strode right past Wade and swept Becky's phone from her hand and locked it in the drawer.

"Notice a pattern?" I asked Sarah and then answered even as she nodded. "Frau Jacobs only targets girls. Ever."

I had known this from day one—Frau's anti-girl tendencies were legendary at Northbrook Middle, word of it trickling down to the intermediate school. But I didn't think *I'd* ever be one of her targets. She seemed to home in on the popular set.

Girls who could pull off fashionable clothes instead of my usual T-shirt and jeans combo.

"I was writing conjunctions of the verb *seguir,* when I felt it. An uncomfortable wet spot," I continued.

I had gotten my first period back in fifth grade, but it was never one of those every-four-weeks-for-three-to-five-days like health teachers acted was true for anyone. What really happened was I'd get my period for a couple hours. It'd go away for the rest of the day. The next day, it'd return and stay for a day or two. Then it would go away. Come back a day later. Stop by once in a while for another two days.

I got pretty used to figuring out the signs. But sometimes it just happened. Sometimes I thought things were done for the month. I'd go a solid week period-free, and then *bam.* Sitting in Intro to Languages on the worst-possible seating at school, wearing the white jeans I bought from Old Navy with my own money just three days earlier, conjugating the word for *continue,* when I had felt it.

I had raised my hand.

Frau Jacobs, who had been in the middle of instruction, raised an eyebrow. *"Si, señorita?"*

"I have to go to the bathroom." My face was flushing so hard Frau Jacobs looked half framed in red.

"En español, Pipi." She made my name sound more like Pepe.

"Permite me ir el bano," I stumbled, hoping I got the phrasing right. *"Por favor."*

Frau Jacobs crossed her arms. "No. We don't leave in the middle of class."

"I'm sorry, but—" The wet spot was definitely growing. As if trying to alert me that this was serious, a blasting sharp pain shot out across my lower back. I gasped, and Ricky shot a sideways look my way.

"Hand down," Frau Jacobs snapped, then turned her back to me and toward the class.

I lowered my hand. Maybe if I crossed my legs and tried not to think about it, it'd go away. I picked up my pencil, face still flaming, and tried to concentrate on conjugating.

The only thing was, I kept thinking of this super scary movie I once caught my dad watching when I got up in the middle of the night for a drink of water. The scene I walked into had this kid going up to an elevator. All of the sudden, rivers and rivers of blood poured out from the door and frame of the elevator, rushing down the hall and swooping over everyone. I was kind of convinced something similar might've just started down below.

I shifted in my seat, bending over my notebook and trying to make it not super obvious that I was peering down at my own crotch. My spine was all bones-don't-bend-that-way-Pipi. I shifted again, this time swiping my hand across the upholstery for moisture. Nothing. *Yet.* Another cramp rocked through me. I thrust my hand up in the air.

"*Senorita!*" Frau Jacobs exclaimed. "No. More. Interruptions."

"Por favor!" I said. "I really have to go to the bathroom."

Across the auditorium, a few kids snickered. A couple girls exchanged knowing looks. I wanted so badly for the ground to swallow my period-plagued body whole.

Frau Jacobs turned her back to me again and instead addressed the class. "What is the rule for going to the bathroom in my class?" she asked. "Hmm?"

No one raised their hand to answer, everyone either laughing under their breath or staring at me. "Well, I'll tell you," Frau Jacobs finally said in her fake sugary voice. "The rule is that we may use the bathroom *before* and *after* instructional time. Never *during.*"

My chest rose and fell as I tried to calm down. Option A: I could go to the bathroom now, even though it'd infuriate Frau, and everyone could think I either had diarrhea or know I got my period; option B: I could wait as blood leaked through my pants and onto the seat (*Would I have to clean up the seat? Would Mr. Russell, the janitor, have to do it?*) and I'd spend the rest of the day in ruined jeans. I kept my hand up. Frau Jacobs resolutely refused to face me. Her back stayed to me, even though I knew she knew my hand was up, since so many people were now whispering and pointing in my direction.

"To conjugate *seguir* in the subjunctive imperfect tense, you would say, '*yo . . .*'" Frau Jacobs singsonged the last word and waved her hand like a conductor, her cue that we were all supposed to join in as she finished with, "'*siguiera*.'" No one joined in.

I cleared my throat and said, "It's an emergency."

More people laughed.

"No, *señorita*," Frau Jacobs said. "It's an inconvenience. You are inconveniencing me and distracting everyone around you. Ricardo," she said Ricky's full name, rolling the *r*, "is here to learn. Aren't you, Ricardo?"

Ricky didn't move a muscle.

"Ricardo?" she said again. "*Respondeme*."

"She has to go to the bathroom," Ricky said instead. "I think that's probably pretty distracting to her learning."

Frau Jacob's mouth twisted. I pushed my hand straighter into the air even though my back cramped so hard it felt like my insides were ropes being braided together. She crossed her arms. I knew it then, from the look on her face, it didn't matter what I said or how often I asked. She was *never* going to let me use the bathroom, not with forty-nine students watching. This wasn't about me being a distraction anymore. It was about power. Standing in front of the room, she had all of it; I had none, and she wasn't going to let me—or anyone else—forget that fact.

Frau Jacob's eyes trailed up to the tip of my upstretched hand. Then she turned on her heel. Her back stayed to me the remainder of the class. A moment later, as the rest of the class rehearsed conjugating verbs into past imperfect, Ricky whispered in my ear. "Just go. I'll go with you. You get in trouble, I will, too."

I shook my head. I lowered my hand. "You don't understand."

"Look," Ricky whispered, "I *do*. I mean, we all had health class. It's not, like, your fault, okay? Just go."

But by then, I had felt it. "It's too late."

Fifteen minutes later the bell rang. Ricky lingered in his seat as everyone else trailed out. "Want me to . . ." he asked, his eyes lowered.

"Go," I said, the words too biting for the only person who had been nice to me. "Please," I added softly.

Ricky nodded, his lips pressed tightly together as he passed Frau Jacobs, who still had her back turned to me, though she now stood by the door. "Ricardo," she called out. Ricky paused but didn't turn. "I'll have a new seat assignment for you tomorrow. I don't think you and Miss McGee are a good pairing."

Ricky didn't move for another beat, and then he took quick strides from the room.

Slowly, Frau Jacobs turned back to me. Her eyes were wide in mock surprise and her arms crossed. "Well, now, for someone who *had* to go to the bathroom in such a hurry, you certainly are taking your time leaving, aren't you?"

Unable to meet her excited eyes, I stood from my seat.

My period hadn't just "arrived." It had descended like water from a slashed balloon. My upper thighs were sticky, even through my jeans. Tears streamed down my face, doing nothing at all to cool my cheeks as I turned to look at the upholstered seat. A blackish stain covered a grapefruit-sized spot in the middle of the cushion.

Frau Jacobs sucked in her breath, but before she could speak, I rushed past her into the hall.

I ran to the gym, figuring I could duck into the locker room and put on my gym clothes for the rest of the day. I made it, too, tossing my backpack on a shelf, swirling open my locker combo, and shrugging out of my tunic shirt, which, yeah, also was blood-smeared. I was just wearing a tank top and was unzipping my soiled formerly white jeans when it happened.

Fire alarm. (I'd later find out that some jerk pulled the fire alarm to get out of in-school suspension.)

The girls' gym coach rushed into the locker room. "Pipi!" she called and grabbed my arm. "We've got to go! This isn't a scheduled drill!"

"But I—"

"Safety first!" she yelled and ushered me outside, not listening to anything I said about choosing death by fire over going outside, as the halls opened and students poured out.

Did I mention? Anyone caught in the halls or locker room during fire drills instead of with their class had to stand by the flagpole in the middle of the courtyard. Every other class circled around the flagpole in straight lines like sunbeams, facing the flagpole. This was to give teachers the chance to spot missing students and to count them on their class lists.

The entire middle school faced me, my ruined pants on full display, thanks to my tiny tank top. Everyone laughing. Everyone pointing. Everyone so glad they weren't Pipi Period McGee.

Chapter Twenty-Two

Funny how reliving the memory felt like hours but really only a few minutes had passed. I wiped at my eyes and dragged in another deep breath. "It's silly, isn't it?" I said to Sarah. "To get that upset about it?"

Sarah shook her head. "No, Penelope. It's not silly at all. Why is something our bodies biologically *have* to do treated like an embarrassment? It's not right. I mean, we all know what happens; it's part of health class."

"That's what Ricky said," I muttered. Sarah raised an eyebrow. "That day, I mean. He reminded me that everyone had health class and knew what periods were."

Sarah nodded. "Ricky was right. What happened to you wasn't your fault. But how everyone reacted was *their* fault. It happened to you, and it was wrong. And it's the beginning of a really great poem—"

"Poem? No," I said, backing up a little. "It's not a poem. It's too hard to even tell you, let alone anyone else. I just needed to say it."

Sarah nodded, her eyes locking into mine. "I know what that's like. To have something you want to say, but you can't figure out how to do it." She squeezed my hand. "I'm really glad you trust me like this, because I need to trust someone, too."

I tried to keep my face smooth and my expression surprised. "Oh," I said, looking at my hands. "You have a secret?"

Sarah laughed. "Your innocent face is the worst ever. The absolute worst." I glanced up, relieved to see Sarah's smile. She fake punched my shoulder. "Kara told me she almost let it slip to you. You might even have guessed?" Sarah arched an eyebrow at me.

I shook my head, this time not faking the unsure face.

Her mouth wobbled a little and she took a deep breath. "That would've made it easier."

"It'll make you feel better," I said. "To say it, I mean."

Sarah nodded. "It's funny—I'm hesitating, but the whole thing, the whole reason Kara and I are fighting, is that I want it to *stop* being a secret. I want it to be something that's real, just something that *is*."

I didn't say anything, trying to put together the pieces she had spread out in front of me. What she said about needing to be heard, about being told to keep quiet, something that Kara thought she had to protect, something that Jackson—who never took anything (his own poetry aside) seriously—could be trusted with knowing.

"I . . . I know a lot of people assume that Jackson and me are sort of a couple. But we're just friends. And we'll always just be friends because the truth is . . ." Sarah paused, taking another breath. "I don't like boys. I . . . I'm gay, I guess. I mean," her shoulders squared and her chin lifted, "I'm gay."

"Oh." I had figured out her secret moments before she spoke it. What I hadn't yet figured out was how to respond.

Say something! my brain screamed. *Say something.* Tons of words swarmed down to my mouth, but none of them tasted right.

The strings of words crowding my mouth—words like: *My uncle is gay.* Or *Gay people are great!* Or *Oh, wow! Gay!*—were all just bad attempts at connecting.

Maybe I didn't have to say anything. Instead, I reached out and squeezed her hand. Sarah smiled, her shoulders drooping like she put down a heavy box. I smiled back at her.

"I'm glad you told me," I said.

"I'm glad I told you," she said, and then scooted to where her backpack was and pulled out a notebook. She held it up. "It does feel good to talk about it. I mean, I write about it in here. I think that's why poetry is so important to me; it's really helped me sort my thoughts."

"Does your family know?" I asked. I tried to imagine Mom, Dad, and Alec's reactions if I told them I was gay. I knew they'd hug me. I knew they'd tell me they loved me. I hoped it was the same for Sarah. Her mouth wobbled a little, and I guessed it hadn't happened like that.

"They're okay," she said. "Honestly, they're pretty cool about it. My dad especially. But I think my mom was more worried about Aunt Estelle finding out than anything. She's Kara's mom. She kind of is used to directing things, you know?"

I nodded, even though I didn't really.

"I know she knows—my mom told her, and then Kara did, too—but she never talks about it. No one ever talks about it. It's like they think it'll go away, or I'll outgrow it."

"Is that what your poem is going to be about?" I asked.

Sarah shook her head. "No, there's another idea I have, something really . . . I guess, important to me."

"Hey!" Jackson broke into the room with a literal bang as the door flew back on its hinges and hit the side of the wall. "You guys should've told me you could meet earlier! I have so much stuff. I'm going to read it all to you guys, okay, and then you can help me pick out which one to tell at the open mic."

Sarah smiled and raised an eyebrow. "We'll talk later," she said. To Jackson, she said, "We've still got plenty of time to prep for the open mic."

"I'm not so sure about this open mic thing," I muttered.

"Friday night, JV Bookstore in Collinsville," Sarah said. "You *have* to be there, Pipi! Promise me!"

Collinsville was the next town over, at least a half-hour drive from my house. Jackson nodded. "My pop is up for driving us. He loves the bookstore. Even promised not to listen to the open mic to respect my privacy, even though I've read him my poems about a dozen times."

Sarah and I exchanged a quick glance and then looked away.

"I'm not ready for that," I said.

"I'm not sure I am, either," Sarah responded. "But I hope I will be. I hope when I get there, I'll be able to share this poem I've been working on a really long time."

Jackson put down his notebook and looked up at her. "Let's hear it!"

Sarah shook her head. "I want to do it there. Share it there for the first time." She nudged me. "Maybe there's something you want to say?"

Quickly, I shook my head. "No, but I'll be there. For you guys. The thing is? I don't think I'm really a poet—"

I held up my hand as both Jackson and Sarah started to protest.

"Really, I don't." I lifted my chin. "But I am an artist. And I was thinking I'd be in the talent show, but for my artwork instead."

Jackson said, "You mean, like your portrait?"

I blinked at him. "My bacon portrait? The picture of me as bacon with boobs? The one I drew when I was five?" I blinked again. "No, Jackson. Not like that."

Sarah coughed, but it sounded a lot like a laugh. "What kind of art, Pipi?"

I stared down at my lap. "I make these birds? Out of papier-mâché?" Everything I said came out like a question. "Anyway, I was thinking about it. About maybe creating something, a display or something. It was just an idea."

Sarah smiled. "I think it's a good idea."

"Yeah," Jackson said, "birds. They, like, take flight. Take our imagination to flight. On . . . feathers. Feathers of flight." He snapped his fingers and then picked up his notebook to write a new poem.

When Mom and I got home from the gym that night, it was pretty late. She had stopped to pick up chicken salad and hoagie rolls from a deli. "Lazy dinner tonight. I am wiped out," she said. But when we opened the door, the amazing garlicky scent of Alec's homemade spaghetti sauce wafted toward us. We floated into the house like those cartoon animals that sail into a kitchen on scent alone.

"Hey," Alec said and came around the table, which was set with garlic bread, spaghetti, and salad. He kissed Mom. "Welcome home!"

"What's the occasion?" Mom asked.

Eliza came out from the kitchen with Annie just behind her, both of them bringing salad dressings. "Annie and I had a great day. Alec did, too. So, we made a feast!"

Mom and I looked at each other and just about ran to sit at the table. It was dark outside, the wind blowing, but the dining room was warm and bright. Everyone told stories about their day, and all four of us sucked in our breath when Annie casually called Eliza "Mom." ("Mom jumped higher than anyone on the trampoline! She even did a flip!")

Between the amazing food and the endless laughter around the table, I barely thought about Vile Kara Samson and her slippery eyebrows. At the end of the meal, Mom grabbed Eliza's hand and squeezed it. She and Alec exchanged the kind of smile that makes previous conversations transparent, and then she said, "We love you so much and are so proud of all you've accomplished."

Alec nodded and ruffled Annie's hair. "Aren't you proud of your mama, about to graduate at the top of her class?"

Eliza's hands flew to her mouth. "I didn't think you knew."

Mom wiped at the corner of her eyes. "You've done so much, love. I admire that you've wanted to do it on your own—from scholarships and student loans—"

"Mom," said Eliza, clenching her hands on her lap, "you've given us a place to live, rent-free, you've practically raised—"

Mom reached over and pressed her fingers to Eliza's mouth. "I've raised my daughter, who is raising her daughter. And we love you and would do it all again in a heartbeat. Please, let us in. Let us help you."

Alec got up and moved closer to Mom, putting his hand on her shoulder. Mom said, "Your dad and I saved for college tuition for you and Pipi. But since you did it all yourself, we invested your portion. Alec found some amazing stocks and we've had a bit of a return on it. We'd like you to have it as a nest egg. Something to help you feel more secure." She reached into her pocket and pulled out a check.

"Is this for an apartment? Do you need room for the baby?" Eliza asked, her voice soft and her face unreadable.

"No!" gasped Mom, shaking her head. "No, we'll figure that out. This is your home, always."

Mom held out the check again. After a long pause, Eliza took it. Her eyes widened at the number. "Are you sure about this? What about Pipi's college?"

"We have a separate account for Pipi," Mom said, and I quashed the part of me that had been worried for just a second. "This is yours."

"But I didn't . . . I don't . . ."

"It's yours," Mom said. Alec nodded.

The warmth at the table, the carb-loaded fullness in my belly, the radiance of Eliza's nearly forgotten smile—all of it filled me up so much that for a while, I forgot all about Kara Samson's slippery eyebrows or Frau Jacobs's smug pig-dog smile.

But Kara hadn't forgotten about me.

The next morning, Alec offered to drop me off at the primary school so I could sleep in instead of taking the bus to kindergarten volunteering. I felt a small pang of guilt at the idea of Ricky being the only teenager on the bus—I even pulled out my phone to text him—but then I remembered the notebook. *Ricky* had given it to Jackson. I still couldn't picture it; it was so much easier to hate Kara, who had never been nice to me, who didn't make me laugh, who hadn't been there when I needed someone.

I got to the school just in time to take everyone's lunch orders. About half of them still ordered croutons every day. "Penelope?" Ricky said from his spot in the coat closet, where he was helping the kids get out of their jackets. (This was a surprisingly difficult task. Somehow Narrator Boy ended up wearing his jacket again, only backward, after Ricky helped him slip one arm out.) "I missed you on the bus today."

"Yeah, I slept in," I said, keeping my eyes on my chart, counting up all of the lunches to make sure I had twenty-four to match the number of students.

"Is everything okay?"

"Yeah, of course." But even *I* could hear how cold my voice was. Only twenty-three. I looked around the room. Piper was missing.

"It's just . . ." Ricky helped Narrator Boy out of his jacket for a third time. ("And now my jacket is upside down. Look at that, upside down.")

"I'm trying to count, Ricky," I snapped, even though I had already finished. I went to mark Piper as absent, but then saw she wasn't on the attendance list anymore. In fact, her cubby in the cloak room didn't have her name or picture anymore.

"Miss Gonzalez," I called, "what happened to Piper?"

"Oh," Miss Gonzalez said. She had been passing around morning work coloring pages. "Piper's family decided she needed another year before pursuing kindergarten. They've pulled her out for the remainder of the school year and are going to re-enroll her next year. We all agree that she wasn't quite ready."

"Oh." My heart thumped. *Was this because I had pushed her so much?*

"Besides," Miss Gonzalez said, "they said she made a really great connection with another incoming kindergartener. So, we're going to give it another shot next year." And I couldn't even help it, I smiled at Ricky knowing he'd be smiling back, both of us thinking of Annie and Piper taking over kindergarten next year.

Ricky hung Narrator Boy's jacket on his hook and stood beside me. "Pipi, I talked with Tasha. She says you're almost done with The List thing?"

I nodded, the smile wiped from my face. "Tasha was talking about me?"

"Not about you," he said. "I just mentioned you, and she said you were kind of taking a break from each other until this List thing is done."

"Only one thing left," I said, still not looking at him. I concentrated on moving all of the lunch orders into the folder to send to the office.

"Only one . . . so you finished with sixth grade?" Ricky's hands were at his sides. I noticed they were shaking. We were standing so close—only a couple inches between our arms. I could feel his breath on my shoulder. It was a little shaky, too. Something dislodged in my chest.

"I know about the notebook. I mean, about you being the one who gave it to Jackson." Ricky swallowed, and I looked up at him. His dark eyes were serious and eyebrows peaked. "It was a long time ago, huh?"

His mouth tightened into a line. "I should've told you," he whispered. "I'm really sorry. I'm, like, *really* sorry, Pipi." He mopped a hand over his face, clutching a handful of hair behind his head. "I don't know what I was thinking then. I mean, I really thought you liked me, which was *so* daft. Kara kept saying stuff like, 'Look, she's wearing white. That's because I told her you like white.' And I didn't believe her. She said she was going to tell you I liked short hair. I didn't think you'd do it—honest, I didn't! I don't even know why I was talking to her."

He sucked in another breath, all of his words coming in too fast. "But it felt so good to have someone to talk to. And then Jackson started being my friend, too, since Kara always wanted to talk to me and he was always around her. So, when I found that notebook, when I saw what you wrote in it, I . . ." He scrunched his eyes shut. "I messed up."

"It was a long time ago," I said again.

"Not to you. Not to me." He pulled in another breath. "I'm sorry. I'm really sorry."

I nodded. "I know." I took a small step sideways and he winced. "I don't know what I'm feeling," I admitted. "I know

285

that's not really helpful. But I don't think I'm mad at you, Ricky."

"We're good?" Ricky asked.

I shook my head. "You lied to me. And then you let me be mad at Kara. You could've told me every single time I brought up The List. You could've—"

Ricky nodded. "I know. I should've told you everything. I messed up, bad. I was . . . I guess I was so . . ."

"Hurt?" I said.

"Yeah." He took another deep breath. "Did you hear Miss Gonzalez talking to the class after Piper said she didn't like anyone?"

I nodded. "She said, hurt people hurt people."

"It's not an excuse. It was wrong. And I wouldn't do it today. You know I wouldn't." Ricky's eyes met mine for a long time. Then he pulled a folded piece of paper out of his pocket and shoved it toward me. "Just take this."

"What is it?" I crossed my arms.

"Come on, Pipi." Ricky stretched out his arm with the paper toward me. With the other, he rubbed the back of his head again. "Please."

I searched his face. Usually, Ricky was calm, steady. This Ricky? He was stone soup, just like me.

"You weren't the only one who had a notebook," he said. "I've . . . I've held on to this for too long." He drew in another breath. "Like, literally. I started carrying it around in sixth

286

grade, and now it's two years later and I still had it on top of my dresser. Just in case."

I took the paper. He winced and then went into the classroom to help the kids with their morning work. The paper was wrinkled and folded five times to be in a pocket-sized square. I smoothed it out on my leg before lifting it up to read. In careful, just-learned cursive was:

> *I think you're smart, and you're pretty, too.*
> *I want to hold your hand and laugh when*
>   *you laugh.*
> *If I owned a band, they'd only play your*
>   *favorite song.*
> *I want you to be my girlfriend.*
> *But I'll always be your friend.*

I read it again and then again. Then I folded it carefully back up and slipped it into my pocket. It was the most beautiful poem I'd ever read.

"Are we good?" he whispered when I sat down next to him for the morning announcements a couple minutes later.

"We're good."

But I wasn't good a few hours later.

My first sense that anything was wrong happened at lunch when Ricky and I sat at our usual table. Sure, it was a little bit awkward around Ricky. We were both smiling way too much, but soon we were talking and it was normal.

Tasha wasn't there, of course, but her eyes met mine briefly from where she sat across the cafeteria when Vile Kara Samson got up from her table and stomped toward me. Tasha smiled and rolled her eyes, but it was quick as a flash and then she turned back to her new crew.

Kara stood in front of me with her arms crossed and a surprisingly wide smile on her face. I stared at her. Somehow her eyebrows were magnificent. I mean, they were entirely drawn-in—but they were perfectly shaped and dark. "Surprised?" she said and pointed to them. "I watched your sister's tutorial on YouTube."

"I don't know what you're talking about," I managed. My heart thumped.

"Oh, don't worry. I'm not mad." Kara smiled. "I'm inspired."

She leaned down so her elbows were on my table and lowered her voice. "You're going to regret messing with me, PeePee McGee. Although I have to admit, I didn't think you had it in you."

I spent the rest of the day on edge, wondering if Kara was about to enact her revenge for my revenge. *When did revenge end?* But it wasn't until a few hours later that I understood the depths of Kara's diabolical nature.

I walked into Mom's gym after school to see Mom, Eliza, Alec, and Dad behind the counter. They were deep in conversation, but when the door opened, Eliza jumped to her feet. Within seconds, she was standing in front of me, her face pure white in fury. *"What did you do, Pipi McGee?"*

"What? What are you talking about?" My heart suddenly grew feathers that beat against my rib cage.

Mom came around the corner, her fingers wrapping around Eliza's shoulder. "Let's not accuse anyone of anything. Let's talk."

Eliza turned and buried her face in Mom's shoulder like a little girl.

Dad, his reporter's notebook in hand, came around the corner. Looking down at his notes, he said, "So it looks like someone in your grade—Kara Samson—suffered some physical damage due to one of Eliza's products."

"No!" interrupted Eliza, her voice muffled by Mom's shoulder. "There's *no way* anything I made would've done that."

Dad nodded and continued, sounding like he was dictating an article instead of his usual dad talk. "She's claiming, or rather, her mother's claiming, that a special blend from Eliza caused her daughter's hair loss. She cannot provide any store receipt for purchase nor can she provide a date that she visited Glitter. But she says that about ten minutes after her daughter applied this special blend, her eyebrows fell off."

"Oh no," I whispered.

"Further," Dad continued, "she brought the bottle into Glitter. It includes a label titled *Eliza's Eyebrow Serum* and does, in fact, match the bottles that Eliza is known to use for her blends. The label, however, is unfamiliar." Dad looked up from his notes at that and stared at me. All of them stared at me.

Her hand still squeezing Eliza's shoulder and her voice sharp, Mom said, "It sure does look like your handiwork, Pipi. The handwriting, the special paper."

I couldn't speak. Any word that I wanted to make wouldn't find its way to my lips, not when this bird-heart was beating its wings so fast.

Eliza pushed back from Mom and turned to me. Her eyes were narrow and her face set in stone. "Glitter was going to promote me to manager once my graduation became official in December. Now they're going to fire me."

My head shook even though my mouth still wasn't working. "No," I said. "No, they can't do that. You had nothing to do with this!"

"But you did, huh?" Eliza said. Her chest rose a fraction, her breath coming out in a quick huff. "This isn't some game to me, Pipi. That place is part of me. I'm *good* at what I do. I work *hard*. And you took that from me. I'm happy there. I belong. And you *took that from me*. Do you know what that's like?"

I nodded. I did know. But nodding was exactly the wrong thing to do. Eliza rushed me, Mom and Dad both bellowing and pulling her back, but I didn't move. Eliza's face was an inch from mine. "How could you do this to me?"

"I didn't mean to," I murmured. "I didn't think it had anything to do with you. I wanted to get back at her. You were just there." The bird-heart tugged at a memory, pulling it out and swallowing it whole. That's what Kara had said. Getting me to do those things—nearly every humiliation from inventing the Pipi Touch to telling me to cut off my hair—none of them had been because she didn't like me. It was because she hadn't cared about me. And to get back at her, I used Eliza; I had been so set on revenge I didn't even care what that meant for my sister.

"I had this bottle from Glitter. I filled it with eyebrow gel . . . and some hair removal stuff."

Mom growled. Dad's eyes narrowed. Alec's head hung. Eliza shook her head. "I didn't give it to her! I swear, I didn't!" I forced the next words out. "I dropped it near her. She's the one who picked it up! *She,* she, kind of stole it from me!"

Eliza's mouth twisted and her eyes filled. "How could you, Pipi?"

Dad cleared his throat. "Chances of them winning a suit against Eliza are slim to none. Pipi admits that *she* made the concoction, even though she had claimed it was Eliza. Kara came about it through nefarious means."

I breathed out in relief, but then Dad cleared his throat again. "*But* Eliza's manager is under no obligation to keep her employed, particularly if a customer launches a complaint."

I closed my eyes. "I'll fix this. I promise."

"You better," Mom said, as Eliza turned back into her shoulder. "You better fix this right now."

Chapter Twenty-Three

With Mom at my side, I went to Glitter to talk with the manager. An older woman led Mom and me to a cold office in the back of the store. Every surface was shiny and dark without any pictures or papers or items that indicated anyone actually worked there. Eliza had complained loads of times that the office manager spent less and less time at the shop since she had been hired, that she was the one handling day-to-day operations. The manager, Ms. Williams, had the type of shiny blond hair that I had only ever seen on people leaving a salon. Her makeup was precise and her smile as cold as the office.

With Mom's nudging, I told her about adding the hair remover to the eyebrow gel and that Eliza had nothing to do with it. "I did this all on my own."

The woman leaned back in her chair. "Well, Eliza is somewhat responsible regardless."

"She isn't!" I insisted.

Ms. Williams continued as if I hadn't spoken. "The Samson family is threatening a lawsuit. As it is, I had to agree to rather costly products to appease them both."

"Wait," Mom interrupted. "They're threatening to sue for faulty products but were willing to take their pick of items you sell?"

Ms. Williams sighed out of her nose, nostrils flaring. "More than five hundred dollars' worth of products, which will be taken out of Eliza's paycheck."

"That isn't fair!" I protested.

Mom made an angry *tsk*-ing noise, then said, "Since my Eliza began working here, she has improved the quality and vision of this shop. Are any of your other employees requested as often? Do any of them bring in as many customers? Have any others thought of starting YouTube tutorials to help market the store online? Do any of them have customizable blends? She deserves your loyalty."

Ms. Williams crossed her arms. "Eliza is a grown woman. If she has a problem, she can discuss it with me herself."

A knock on the door interrupted us. Another employee poked her head in at Ms. Williams's crisp, "Yes?"

"We have a few customers asking for Eliza to tint their lip glosses," a timid-looking woman wearing one of the Glitter aprons said.

"Do it yourself!" Ms. Williams barked.

"Mine never turn out like Eliza's," the woman said.

Ms. Williams threw her arms in the air. "Figure it out!" She turned back to us. "And, needless to say, Eliza will *not* be getting the raise she demanded last week for completing her degree."

Mom closed her eyes and took a deep breath. "You're making a big mistake."

Another knock on the door. This time a different employee poked her head in. She blew the hair hanging in her face away with a *puff.* "I don't know where we keep the extra face swabs. Eliza keeps tabs on them."

Ms. Williams's teeth gnashed together in an audible grind. "The shop's not that big! Find it yourself."

Before the door even fully closed, a third employee wrapped her fingers around it and pushed it open. Ms. Williams barked, "Figure it out!" and the hand retreated.

Mom smirked at Ms. Williams. "You need Eliza. *She*'s the one who runs this place, and you know it."

Ms. Williams glared at Mom. "I believe we're here to discuss your other daughter's mistakes, although it seems both of them have a tendency to get themselves in trouble."

Mom's face flushed an angry red I had only seen once— back when I was four and decided to see what would happen if I filled the coffee maker with honey.

"What if I talk to Kara?" I asked Ms. Williams before Mom could erupt. "What if I get them to cool off?"

She crossed her arms. "Well, that *might* be a way to keep Eliza employed."

I called Kara before we got to the car, but it went to voicemail. I texted her. *Please call me back.* No response.

The drive home was short, only about five minutes, but it felt like a year or two of my life since Mom spent the entire time radiating joy-sucking rage, and I wasn't sure how much was directed my way and how much was for Ms. Williams. I risked a sideways glance. Her lips were moving as she silently relived conversations, only this time saying what she really wanted to have said.

Please, I texted again.

All night, I checked my phone for a response. At about seven o'clock, the message went from *delivered* to *read.* For a heart-stopping five seconds I saw the floating dots. But then, nothing.

Annie had a playdate at Piper's house. Then she and Eliza went out to dinner. They didn't come home until after eight.

"Eliza?" I knocked on the bathroom door with my knuckle as Eliza gave Annie a bath. The door opened a crack and I saw about two inches of Eliza's angry face. "I'll pay you back for the five hundred dollars. I promise! I already have about three hun-dred from birthdays and stuff. I'm really sorry," I blurted. "I'm going to fix this. I am! I swear it."

Eliza let the door open a little more. My sister, for a moment, looked so much older than her twenty years. "Is Kara Samson anything like her older brother, Max?"

I shook my head. "I don't know. But she's pretty awful."

"Then she probably deserves no eyebrows."

I smiled but somehow was kind of crying at the same time. Eliza looked so tired. Defeated. She shut the door.

The next morning, Kara stood by my locker. I rushed toward her, intending to throw myself at her feet if that's what it took to get her family to lay off Eliza. But first, of course, I had to dodge about six people who needed good-luck touches. One pinched my arm. "Ow!" I slapped at his hand.

The kid, someone who must've been in sixth grade, didn't even say sorry. He turned to a friend and cheered, "I got double luck!"

I gritted my teeth and rushed toward Kara.

Kara held up one slim hand as I blurted, "You have to back off Eliza! You have—"

"You are not going to tell me what *I* have to do, PeePee McGee." She crossed her arms and glared at me. Clearly, she was using some of her five-hundred-dollar makeup because she looked flawless.

"Your contouring is amazing," I snapped.

"Thank you," she snapped back. Then her face smoothed into another snake smile. "I think you *are* good luck. I never would've gotten this makeup without you."

I glared at her, huffing my anger out of my nose. I imagined it unraveling around her like a net, sweeping her up and hanging her upside down by her nonexistent eyebrows. But all it really did was make me sound like a bull.

"You know Eliza had nothing to do with what happened," I said.

She shrugged. "Fine. I'll tell Mom to lay off."

I reared back. "Fine."

"Great," Kara said.

I blinked at her. This had gone unexpectedly well. "So, cool. I'll see you later then."

"Not so fast," Kara said, each word pelting me. "The eyebrow gel. The toilet paper." She snake smiled again. "I'm impressed."

The worst thing to do was to smirk at this compliment. But I did. Because the truth was? Before everything went sideways? *She was absolutely right.* I didn't think I had it in me, either. Those revenge bubbles started to float around me again. And then Kara opened her mouth and popped them all.

"And it made me wonder, why the sudden revenge schemes? The popularity, the way you're so joiny-joiny with Sarah and Jackson." Kara smiled. "I'm not sure what you're doing, Pipi, but I do know we have a common enemy. Frau Jacobs."

"I don't know what you're—"

Kara laughed. "Poor Pipi. Such a newbie. So much to learn." She patted my shoulder. I dodged it and she rolled her eyes. "First rule of being a mean girl: have lots of sources. Loads of them. Ones that report back things they overhear." She leaned into the mirror I had hanging on my locker door. It was only then that I noticed it was open.

"Did you pick my lock?"

Kara ran her thumb against her lip, making sure her gloss was in line. "You haven't changed the lock since fifth grade."

She straightened back up. "Like I said, you've got lots to learn.

"Ricky and Tasha were talking in the cafeteria last week. Patricia was just behind them in the pizza line. She told me all about some list that you're making. About how now that *I* am off The List"—again she rolled her eyes—"all that's left is Frau Jacobs."

"I don't know what you're talking about," I stammered.

"Save it," Kara nearly growled. "Second rule of being a mean girl: always be ready to turn the tables. You might've gotten at me with the . . ." She vaguely gestured at her eyebrows. "But now *I'm* the one in charge."

"But you're wrong," I said. "I don't want to be a mean girl." I stepped back from her. "Who *wants* to be a mean girl?"

Kara sneered. "Someone who's tired of being overlooked. Someone who's done being laughed at. Someone *smart*." Kara stepped toward me, closing the distance I had created. "You need me. We both need to get back at Frau."

"Because she made you wear the shame shirt?"

She lifted her chin. "I had to wear that home. My brother saw me."

Something shifted across Kara's face, like a mask slipping to the side. She looked raw. I felt a rush of reluctant sympathy.

"Don't look at me like that," she snapped. I looked away. "Anyway," she continued, "if you want me to drop this thing with Eliza—if you want my mom to drop it—you have to help me. It's a win-win. We both get back at Frau Jacobs."

What choice did I have? I promised Eliza I'd do whatever it took. I swallowed. "Okay."

She smiled, showing teeth this time. "Great. Find out more about her. Then we'll figure out a plan."

"What do you mean find out more about her?"

"What makes her tick," Kara said. "Aside from harassing girls who don't wear clothes straight out of the Never-Gonna-Have-a-Date catalog. No offense."

I glanced down at my outfit—jeans and a hoodie. Kara continued, "What do you know about her?"

"Nothing," I said. "She's horrible. That's it."

Kara rolled her eyes. "We're going to need more than that."

"I mean," I said, thinking out loud, "I know she loves opera. She's always quoting that soprano singer, right? My dad said she even did in high school."

"Wait!" Kara put up a hand. "Your dad went to high school with her?"

"Yeah," I said. "He said . . ."

"What?" she snapped.

My face felt hot suddenly. "He said people gave her a hard time in school."

Kara bounced on her toes. "Great! This is just what we need. Inside information! I can work with that. I'll work that angle while you pump your dad for more details."

"What do you mean 'work that angle'?"

"So. Much. To. Learn," she said, rolling her eyes again. "And

299

I thought you had potential. Leave it to me. You find out more info."

"I don't know about this. It feels wrong," I whispered.

She shrugged. "Fine."

"Fine?" I echoed.

"Yeah, fine. Don't do anything that makes you uncomfortable," she said, and for a moment she sounded so much like Sarah that I almost smiled in relief. "We'll stick with the original plan—your sister gets fired, and I ruin your life."

"I'll do it," I muttered.

Kara held out her hand to shake. Taking a deep breath, I grabbed it. Before letting go, Kara added, "Oh, yeah. One more thing. I'm also going to need you to tell me what Sarah's hiding."

"What?" I said and yanked my hand back. Kara held on, her grip so tight my knuckles crunched.

"My cousin. She's planning something and hiding it from me. I want to know what." Kara squeezed harder. "I mean beyond the poetry club thing she's doing with you and Jackson. And the other thing." She stared at me and I cursed my inability to keep an innocent face. Kara's chin jerked upward, and I knew she was reading on my face that Sarah had confided in me "the other thing." Kara's jaw clenched. "She's planning something. I want to know what it is, and you're going to tell me."

I shook my head. "No, Sarah has nothing to do with this." I managed to yank my hand free.

"Neither does Eliza, right? Yet here we are." Kara smoothed

her hand on her pants leg. My hand had been sweaty, I guess. "Sarah's hiding something, and I want to know what it is by the end of the week." She wiggled her fingers at me in farewell and headed down the hall.

"Are you okay?" Ricky asked me in homeroom.

I didn't look at him, just kept my eyes on Frau Jacobs. She was marking attendance at the front of the room. Patricia slipped into the room as the final bell rang. "You're late, Patricia! Go to the office and get a slip."

"But the bell is still ringing!" she whined.

Frau Jacobs clasped her hands under her chin. "A lady must always make an entrance, as Greta Mila von Nickel was fond of saying. But in my class, that entrance better be on time. And, according to our handbook—a copy of which you may pick up in the office—that means *before* the final bell."

Ricky nudged me.

"Do you have a math quiz later or something?" I snapped.

"What are you talking about?" he asked.

"You touching me. Isn't it for luck?" I pushed the hoodie sleeves down over my hands and crossed my arms.

Ricky's forehead puckered. *"No,"* he said slowly. "I'm trying to get your attention. What's wrong with you today?"

"Sorry," I mumbled. I kept my eyes on Kara, who went up to Frau Jacobs and complimented her for wearing a pen hanging from a string around her neck ("So practical *and* a beautiful accessory!"). Soon Frau Jacobs was showing her how the pen could change ink colors. Kara winked at me from across the room.

"I have a lot to figure out," I managed.

"Were you ... I mean ... Tasha and I were talking, and were you behind the eyebrow thing with Kara Samson?" He half laughed as he said it, like the idea was ridiculous.

"Yeah, I know you and Tasha were talking." I couldn't seem to get the sneer out of my voice. "Maybe you guys could *stop* talking about me."

Ricky reared back as though I had hit him. "We're worried about you. That maybe you're taking this List thing too far. I mean, what's the point, really?"

The speaker in the middle of the room beeped and then Principal Hendricks's voice called attention for the Pledge and the morning announcements.

"Pipi?" Ricky prodded.

"You don't get it," I muttered over Principal Hendricks's voice.

"Don't forget to sign up now for this year's talent show! Only two weeks until the big day. And this year, our very own Northbrook Middle School staff is welcome to join in on showcasing their hidden talents!"

Ricky had never been picked on or left out. He had never been a walking embarrassment. He didn't understand.

"So, tell me," he said.

Tell him? Tell him what? That everything was out of control? That going from laughingstock to good luck charm still made my skin crawl? That becoming friends with Sarah meant losing Tasha? That I couldn't stop revenging The List now if I wanted to—it was out of my control? That I was now aligned with the one person who hurt me more than anyone? That I had spent so much time feeling sorry for myself or thinking about how to get back at everyone that I never realized how much I had? That I would never be sure if Ricky really liked me for who I was and not because he felt guilty for what he had done? That I had hurt the only friend who had always been there for me? That I was going to have to betray Sarah, even though she had only ever been kind to me?

"Penelope?" he whispered.

"It's all—"

"Do you have something to add, Miss McGee? Something more important than the morning announcements?" Frau Jacobs asked.

"Really," sighed Kara from across the room. "Sorry you have to deal with such rudeness every day, Frau Jacobs. I bet Greta Mila von Nickel would whip her into shape!"

Frau Jacobs turned to Kara. "You've heard of the great soprano Greta Mila von Nickel?" she asked as if she hadn't mentioned the singer moments earlier.

"Oh, who doesn't love some von Nickel?" Kara winked at me again.

Chapter Twenty-Four

All week, Kara made a point of laughing at every one of Frau Jacobs's awful jokes. She shook her head at Frau Jacobs whenever someone walked by in a skirt. "I just wish you got recognition for your hard work," I heard her whisper to Frau Jacobs one morning.

Thursday morning, I woke up to a text from Kara. *You have one more day for dirt on Sarah. Say hi to Eliza for me.*

But even if I wanted to, I couldn't say hi or anything else to Eliza. I hadn't seen her all week. Every day, she had picked up Annie from preschool and then they were gone until after dinner. Mom and Alec whispered about it a bunch of times, Mom's hand on her belly as they talked, but they stopped when I walked into the room.

"Does Eliza still have a job?" I asked Mom as we headed to the car. She was dropping me off at school and Annie at preschool.

"Yes," Mom said over her shoulder as she led Annie to the back. Her face was buried in Annie's bag, making sure she had an ice pack in her lunchbox. "The Samson family hasn't officially decided not to pursue any further action, but Eliza's manager said she can continue working until they make a final decision."

"Is Eliza okay?" I sank into the passenger-side seat.

Mom sighed, bending over Annie to check that the belt buckle was latched. "I think Eliza would be the one to ask."

As Mom closed the backseat door and made her way to the driver's seat, I twisted around to face Annie. "Is there anything going on, with you and your mom, I mean? Is she okay?"

Annie put a finger to her lips and whispered, "*Spy.*"

I dodged Kara in homeroom by coming in just before the bell. She was stationed by Frau Jacobs anyway, laughing at something the teacher had said.

At noon, I braced myself for the cafeteria.

A part of me hoped that Tasha would be back at our usual table. Tuesday night, I had my first postfight conversation with her when I saw her and Ricky at the park after school. Both of them had been laughing under a tree. The *Crow Reaper* book was unopened beside them. Ricky had called me over, and then, when I sat down, he claimed he had to get a drink from the water fountain. "I'm sorry," I told her. I ripped up fistfuls of grass. "I was being a terrible friend, way too caught up in my own plans and not at all considering yours and all you've been through."

Tasha nodded. "Yeah, you were." Then she sighed. "But we've been friends for a long, long time, and this is the first time you've been like this."

"Yeah," I said. "Usually, I'm too available."

Tasha snorted. "I'm still hurt. I'm not over it. But I will be." She leaned back on her elbows. Across the park, Ricky peeked up from the water fountain and then ducked his head again into the stream of water when he saw us glancing over. We both cracked up. "I get that you've got stuff to figure out. Once you do, we'll work through this. I do miss you, Penelope."

"Don't call me that," I whispered.

Tasha raised an eyebrow.

"It sounds odd coming from you," I had said. I wasn't sure what to do then—give her a hug or something?—but Annie had called me over to push her on the swings and had saved me a response.

But when I got to lunch, Tasha and Ricky were at their new table. Perched around our old table were Jackson and Sarah, no doubt talking about plans for the open mic night tomorrow. Quickly, I sidestepped into the hall before they saw me.

I turned on my heel and went to the art room instead. The art teacher agreed to let me eat lunch there so long as I was working on a project, even if it wasn't for a grade. Two days a week, I had study hall right after lunch, so I had a solid hour and a half to work on those days, too.

It was so nice not to think, not to avoid anyone, not to push anyone, not to miss anyone, not to do anything but mix flour and water until it was thin and soupy. To grab handfuls of the old newspapers in the back of the art supply room and rip them into shreds, taking those old stories, tearing them apart, and making something new. A couple of times I caught my dad's byline as I lay the strips of newsprint into the vat of papier-mâché glue. I layered and molded, layered and molded, not even thinking about what I was creating until the shape was unmistakable. Wings. Two wide, outstretched wings.

"Did you just come up with that?" the art teacher asked me. "In just the past few days?"

I nodded. "I've stayed after school a couple of times, too, but, yeah."

She smiled. "That means you've been working on it in your heart for a lot longer."

The wings were beautiful, even without paint, as lines and lines of other people's stories faded and converged.

I heard a low whistle Thursday morning as I sat back and stared at the wings. For a silly half second, I thought it was Ricky.

But when I turned around, it was Jackson.

"Those are so cool!" he said. "Good luck wings, huh?" And before I could stop him, he reached out to touch the tips. Still wet, they folded in. "Oh, man. I'm sorry," he said, flicking some of the glue off his fingers onto the tabletop.

"It's okay," I told him. "I can fix it." He read me more poetry as I tried. I mostly fixed the wings, but it wasn't quite the same. I'd have to make the wings bigger to make up for it.

After school, we met in our usual room at Mom's gym. Sarah had told her mom (and Kara) that she was going to my house after school on Friday but left out that Jackson's father was going to pick us up about five o'clock and drive us to Collinsville.

"Why don't you want your family to know?" I asked and hated myself for doing it. Anytime I talked with Sarah at all, I felt slimy, like I was digging for information I could pass along to Kara. Which I guess I was.

Sarah stared at her hands for a moment before answering. "My family isn't like yours, Penelope. We don't talk. We don't hang out together, except for me and Kara. And Kara and I have always been kind of a packaged deal. Our moms being twins, us being born within weeks of each other, we're always just 'the girls.' I, like, don't exist alone." She shrugged.

"So, this is something you're doing on your own?"

"Right," Sarah said. "They wouldn't like what I want to say. And they'd break it down."

"What do you want to say?" I asked, hating myself for digging.

Sarah shook her head. "I'm still working on it."

Jackson came in late to the gym, holding a stack of papers about six inches thick. "I printed off my poems so I could figure out which one to use on Friday." Sarah and I quickly picked up our notebooks and started scribbling in them. Jackson's face fell. "Oh, guess you guys are busy."

"Yeah, but I'm sure whatever you pick will be awesome," I said.

He sat down and started spreading the poems out in a fan

around himself. "Oh, forgot to mention, I signed us all up for the talent show."

"What?" I stammered while Sarah grinned.

Jackson rolled his eyes. "Don't sweat it, Pipi. You don't have to read any poetry. Just show off those good luck wings. Sarah and I will perform."

"Together?" Sarah asked, her grin wobbling a bit.

"Yeah, sure," Jackson said. "We'll take turns."

After Sarah and Jackson left, I walked to Dad's apartment to have dinner with him.

I braced myself on the stoop, pulling in a deep breath, saying a little prayer that Dad had a good news day and not the wallowing-in-pizza-boxes kind of day.

"Hey, Dad!" I chirped as I walked into the house. "I'm home!"

I stood frozen on the linoleum patch in the foyer. "Dad?" I whispered. Had I gone into the wrong apartment? No, that was definitely my picture hanging on the wall. (The first grade, nose-picking one. Thanks, Dad.) And that was Annie's artwork on the fridge. But the apartment was clean. Like *sparkling* clean, with even the gray throw blanket folded into thirds and hanging off the armrest of the slipcovered sofa.

There was the fake aloe plant on the scrubbed-clean table.

"Oh, hey, Pipi," said this person who resembled my dad except he was clean-shaven and wearing a nonwrinkled black button-down shirt.

"Are you wearing cologne?" I asked, sniffing the air.

Dad's cheeks flushed. "Ah, well, Alec recommended a fragrance." Dad's face was now so red the gold stud in his nose was probably melting from the heat. "I, uh, wanted to talk with you. I'm going on a date later."

"A date?" I leaned in and sniffed him again.

"Yeah," Dad said as he slung an arm around me. "I've been doing a lot of thinking—you know, spending time with Alec, seeing you branch out and join the basketball team—"

"I'm just the manager," I cut in, but Dad ignored me.

"—and watching Eliza spread her wings a bit. It's time for me to be part of the world." Dad said all of this with his chest puffed up and the arm not wrapped around me outstretched. It was the same way he talked me into things such as summer sleepaway camp. And that's how I knew he was trying to convince himself, not me.

"I'm proud of you, Dad." I kissed his cheek. "That's super brave."

Dad shrugged, but the side of his mouth twitched. "It's just the movies."

"Do I know her?"

Dad shook his head. "Someone from work." He took a big breath. "But, you know, I've been inspired. Finally went through some of the old boxes to clean out stuff. There are only a couple left."

"Let's get to them, then," I said. My belly was full of

emotional stone soup again, but I kept my voice cheery. It was weird, I know. Mom was remarried, for goodness' sake. It's not like I expected or even remotely wanted Dad and her to get back together. But there was something comfortable about Dad being single. About him just being there, being the same. So much was changing so fast—Mom and Alec's new baby, and now Dad dating. Where did I fit in? *Do they want me to fit in?* It was just a fleeting thought. Of course, they wanted me to fit in. They loved me, I never once ever doubted that. But the thought was sharp, slicing, all the same.

I focused on the boxes. Only four of them left. I pulled open the crisscrossed cardboard top while Dad debated which theater he should take his date to the one with the reclining chairs, where he risked falling asleep if the movie was boring, or the one with seats so uncomfortable there's no way he'd fall asleep.

"The recliner one, Dad," I told him, even though I had only been half listening. "It's the fancy theater. Aim to impress." Inside the box I'd just opened was a photo album. Mom had every album from our childhood in a bookcase, but this one was from Dad's high school and college days. I flipped through it, sinking onto the floor.

"Never, ever go the mustache route again," I warned Dad.

"Hey, I could curl the ends. Only sophomore who could. It was epic!" Dad plucked the book out of my hands, laughing at the picture. He headed over to the bookcase along the wall and slipped the album onto it. I checked the box for more junk. Inside were four yearbooks. His and Frau Jacobs's yearbooks. Kara's words came back to me, even though I didn't want them to. *Pump your dad for details.*

I flipped open the one from Dad's freshman year. Signatures curled around the pages. Most were pretty generic. *Never change!* and *Northbrook forever!* Things I bet I'd have in my yearbook next year. I searched for Frau Jacobs's signature on the first two signature-covered pages. Nothing.

I flipped to the alphabetical listing of students. Under *J* was unmistakably a fourteen-year-old Frau. She had an enormous smile on her face, which was framed with thick bangs. I opened the sophomore yearbook. There she was again. The smile was smaller now. I flipped through the rest of the sophomore section. Frau Jacobs was in the chorus, front and center. The photographer got the shot during a performance, probably the spring concert. Her mouth was wide open as she belted out a song. Around her, other kids grimaced or smirked.

I hadn't realized that Dad was behind me. "Shame what they did to that girl. Angela, I mean."

"What do you mean, 'what they did'?" I asked. Leaving the yearbook open to the concert page, I rooted through the box for the junior-year yearbook. Frau Jacobs wasn't smiling at all in this portrait. She wasn't in choir, either. I checked the last one. Frau Jacobs wasn't in the listings. "Did she move?"

Dad rubbed his chin. "I think she studied abroad that

year—in Germany, I believe." He grabbed the sophomore year-book and looked again at the concert picture. "Angela Jacobs loved opera. I mean, lived, breathed, and talked nonstop about opera, particularly one singer . . ."

"Greta Mila von Nickel," I whispered.

"Right!" Dad snapped his fingers. "That's all she talked about. And she sang. Nonstop singing."

"Was she good?" I asked.

Dad smiled. "She was amazing. Absolutely amazing." He sighed. "She was, well, I guess a lot of people thought she was annoying. More than a few people—girls especially—went out of their way to pick on her. Things like tipping her lunch tray onto her lap, coughing into their fists through her solos, stuff like that."

"Did she stop singing?" I asked.

Dad shook his head. "No. That didn't happen until . . ." He pulled the junior yearbook from the pile and flipped through it until he got to a section where everyone was in costume. "The Halloween party."

"You had Halloween parties? At school? In *high* school?"

"It was the early eighties. I'm old." Dad pointed to a picture of a kid wearing sweatpant cutoffs with frayed edges, a torn-up T-shirt, and a werewolf mask covering the top of his face. Under the mask was a fluffy mustache.

"*No!*" I gasped. "You didn't!"

"I did," said Dad, another half smile on his face. "I absolutely did. But none of our costumes could hold a candle to Angela Jacobs's." His smile evaporated.

He flipped another page and then handed the book to me, tapping a photograph in the upper right-hand side. It was a group of kids, all of them wearing costumes and most of them laughing. At the far edge was a girl wearing an enormous gown with a sweatshirt over it. Her hands were covering her face and she must've been rushing away, maybe even running, because her picture was mostly a blur.

"What happened?" I whispered.

Dad sat beside me. He closed the book. "I believe it was what's now referred to as a 'wardrobe malfunction.' We had a contest for best Halloween costume. Every person who showed up to school in a costume paraded across the stage. Of course, we showboated. I growled and . . ." He threw out his arms side to side like a wild animal. "You know, werewolf stuff."

I snickered. "Very scary."

"Anyway, so kids started going across the stage. And there was Angela Jacobs in the most elaborate gown I've ever seen. I didn't know it at the time, but later I realized she had dressed as Elektra, Agamemnon's daughter."

"Who?" I asked.

Dad blinked at me. "Do they teach you anything at school?"

I blinked back.

"It's based on the story of Agamemnon, who was murdered by his wife and her lover. His daughter, Elektra, was obsessed with revenge. But once she finally achieved it, she danced past the point of exhaustion and died. It is a gory story, worse than any horror movie I'd let you see. Of course, that's probably why Angela chose that particular character for her Halloween costume. She went on the stage and started singing. And it was just *wow.*" He shook his head.

"What?" I prompted. For a professional storyteller, he was having a hard time getting to the point.

"She got on the stage, right? And this costume, it was a huge skirt with a supertight bodice, you know, the corset type? With . . ." He motioned to his chest area in rounded motions. He paused, his ears turning red. "You've been to the Renaissance Faire, right?"

"Oh," I said and grimaced. "Frau Jacobs? She wore something . . ." I copied Dad's motions.

Now his whole face was red. "Yeah. From what I could make out, Angela made the dress herself but used fabric glue, I think, instead of stitching. Anyway, she went on stage and began belting out this incredible music like nothing I had ever heard before. It was astounding! She was in magnificent character. None of us knew what was happening, other than it was big. Quiet Angela just exploding . . . that was the wrong word . . . just *being.* Just being so big, so bold on stage. And then . . ."

"Then *what?*" I nudged his side with my knuckles.

"I don't know if I should be telling you this. It was a long time ago." Dad started gathering up the rest of the yearbooks, too.

"Dad, c'mon! What happened?" I tugged on his sleeve, pulling him back to sit down.

"So, again, I learned this later, when your mom and I actually went to the Met to see a performance. I didn't even know it was the same one until this one scene—Elektra is so consumed with revenge, that when she finally achieves it, she launches into this bizarre dance. The music, rising, rising, rising out of her like . . . like . . ."

"Revenge bubbles," I said.

"More like lava," Dad said. Then he took a deep breath. He was facing away from me, but his eyes slid toward mine. "We were only supposed to walk across the stage, right? But Angela Jacobs was *performing*. And no one made a move to stop her. Just as she reached the peak of the aria, the glue holding her dress together, I guess, gave up the ghost."

"Oh, no." I covered my mouth with my hands.

Dad nodded, head hanging. "Yeah. She didn't know, either. Kept on singing. No one knew what to do at first. What was exposed wasn't anything more than a bikini would've shown, but still, everyone froze. And then someone laughed." Dad took another deep breath. "Then a few more people. And soon, everyone was laughing."

I squeezed my eyes shut.

I knew what that felt like.

"She only realized when a teacher rushed the stage, giving her a sweatshirt to put on." He sighed again. "I gotta admit, Pip,

I was one of the kids who laughed at her. I wouldn't now, but then? Yeah, I did. I wasn't a terrible person then, but I didn't get it. Didn't realize how cruel it was. It wasn't even really about *her*, though maybe it was for some people. Maybe some of them were jealous of her talent or showmanship or whatnot. But for most of us? It was just funny."

Kara texted me as I headed home. *Update? Frau? Sarah?*

I didn't reply.

A minute later, just as I got to the front porch, she texted again. *Mom has a friend over. A lawyer. How's Eliza?*

Rage boiled through me. And then I heard Annie giggling as Alec chased her around the house. Mom laughed as she took a seat on the sofa, a book in one hand and a glass of iced tea in the other.

"When's my mom coming home?" Annie asked Alec. "I want to show her how fast I can run now!"

Alec swept her up onto a piggyback ride. "Any minute," he said. "Should we draw her a picture?"

"Yes!" Annie said. "Of our house!"

I closed my eyes, took a deep breath, and pulled out my phone. I called Kara, who answered on the second ring. "Didn't I tell you we had company?"

Eliza's car pulled into the driveway. *It's for her,* I reminded myself. I tried to tell myself that Frau Jacobs deserved whatever scheme Kara dreamed up. Hadn't she humiliated me? Not only that, but she seemingly relished doing it. And high school had been so long ago for her—about forty years. Honestly, I doubted it bothered her anymore.

"I talked with my dad. Frau Jacobs was picked on a lot in high school. Mostly for a show-type thing where she sang an aria on stage in front of the school. There was a . . . wardrobe malfunction."

"OMG," Kara said. "Like, she flashed the school?"

"Kind of," I said.

Kara's laughter was so loud it couldn't possibly be real.

"That's all I've got," I said.

"Oh, this is perfect, Pipi! *Perfect!*"

"What do you mean, perfect?" I asked.

"This is the in we need," Kara said. "Listen, I've learned from the best. My brother, Max, he's got a gift for finding out info on people and then using it to get back at his enemies."

"Is Frau Jacobs really an *enemy*?" I said. "I mean, does anyone really have enemies in real life?"

Kara sighed into the phone. "You're so clueless, PeePee McGee. Of course she's our enemy. She mocked you. She mocked *me*. She has to pay. That's the way it works. Someone hits you, you hit back harder."

"Look, I don't want to get caught up in some scheme," I said. "Are we good?"

Kara paused. "Oh, Pipi. You're in it. As of tomorrow, you and I are going to be Frau Jacobs's favorite students. Speaking of favorites, what have you got on Sarah?"

I turned as Eliza closed her car door. She waved as she passed me and, when she opened the front door, Annie flew out of the house and into her arms. She whispered something into the little girl's ear and then closed the door behind her.

"I don't know what Sarah's keeping a secret," I said. *Lie.* I squashed the thought, but it echoed through my mind. I *did* know something of what Sarah hoped to share at the open mic. It was about having something for herself, breaking from the mold she was born wearing and just being herself. I knew that. I *felt* that. Wasn't that exactly what I had been trying to do for myself ever since the beginning of the school year? *And aren't you about to take that from Sarah?* The same unwanted thought refused to budge.

Kara was silent. Then, from far away as if she were holding the phone away from her cheek, she shouted, "I'll be right there, Mom!" She breathed into the phone, letting me know she was back.

I glanced up again, spotting Annie running through the house, showing Eliza the drawing she had made. *I had to do this. For Eliza.* "Tomorrow night? We're going to be at the JV Bookstore. Eight o'clock. It's an open mic."

Kara gasped. "Seriously? She's, like, reciting a poem or something? In public?"

"Or something," I muttered. "I don't know. I just know that it *really, really* is important to her. Sarah wants to share something, and she knows the people there are understanding. *Then* I think she'll share it with everyone else, maybe even at the talent show. So, it's not like you won't find out soon. Promise me you won't—"

The phone beeped in my ear and I realized Kara had hung up.

Chapter Twenty-Five

Why are some days so fast you want to catch them by the tail and hang on to them? Friday morning, Mom woke me up six minutes before my alarm was set to go off. "I have to get to the gym early today. Be ready to go in fifteen."

"That's how long my shower takes," I whined into my pillow, though she had already left my room. I pulled on jeans and an old band T-shirt that used to belong to Dad, shoved my hair into a ponytail, and slouched downstairs to eat a granola bar for breakfast.

"Really extending yourself," Eliza murmured over the top of her coffee cup. Her hair was in swirls around a handkerchief headband, and her makeup was, of course, perfect, down to the bright red lipstick. I scowled at her as Mom pushed me toward the door. But I also was secretly pleased; this was the first she had talked to me since the eyebrow incident.

The school halls were empty as I trudged toward homeroom. With any luck, Frau Jacobs wouldn't be there yet and I could slump my head over the desk and sleep until school started. Not only was the light on in the room but also voices carried out into the hall.

Vile Kara Samson sat cross-legged on top of her desk, facing Frau Jacobs, who was so caught up in explaining something that her hands swirled through the air like tentacles.

"Pipi!" Kara called out as if we were friends. "Frau Jacobs was just telling me the most *fascinating* story. It's about Alexa—"

"Elektra," Frau Jacobs and I corrected at the same time. Frau Jacobs's eyebrows raised in my direction. Slightly behind her, Kara's hands jerked out in a go-with-it motion and her face turned fierce.

I swallowed a lump in my throat and muttered, "Yeah, I heard it's an opera or something."

"Only *the* best opera that's ever been created," Frau Jacobs said. "I've seen it performed a dozen times. Each time, it's more beautiful. A great regret of my life is that I wasn't alive while Greta Mila von Nickel sang on stage." Frau Jacobs's hands fluttered in the air again, and I knew the aria played in her mind.

"I wish I could see it, too," Kara said in a somber voice. "But we never go to the opera. I bet no one in the school has heard live opera music."

Something shuttered in Frau Jacobs's face. "Yes, well . . ." She sat behind her desk. "Maybe someday."

"It's just such a shame, you know. That no one can hear it," Kara said as the first bell rang and students began to wander into the classroom.

Frau Jacobs pulled up her email on her computer. "Please find your seat, Ms. Samson. School is about to begin."

After the morning announcements, everyone buzzed about what they'd do for the talent show. Only a few kids had signed up, but those who had talked about it nonstop. Okay, so maybe it was just Jackson who talked about it nonstop. I had never noticed how his voice carried over the entire room.

"Yeah, me and Sarah are going to perform," Jackson bellowed. "And Pipi will be there for good luck."

At that, a few kids batted at me for their good luck of the day. Other kids kept trying to touch them to steal the luck, leading to a lot of Matrix-like dodging, even though I was literally right there.

"Jackson, I thought we were keeping that quiet," Sarah said. A deep red blush spread across her face and her eyes were super shiny.

"Perform, huh?" Kara said as though she were surprised. "Perform what, exactly?"

"It's nothing, really. I'm probably not even going to do it." Sarah swallowed. "I'm sorry; I should've told you."

"Oh, hey, I'm sorry, Sarah," Jackson said. "I just got excited and—"

"Of course, you're going to do it," Kara said. She wrapped an arm around Sarah's shoulder. "And you'll tell me about it when you're ready."

When I was younger, Mom used to take me and Eliza camping a lot. We had inflatable mattresses that took forever to blow up, even with a pump, but when it was time to pack up the next morning, all we had to do was pull a plug and, *whoosh,* all the air left the mattress in five seconds. Hearing Kara say that to Sarah? It felt like I was the mattress and her words were the yanked-out plug. Every bit of guilt and worry about telling Kara about the open mic just *whooshed* away.

From the look on Sarah's face, they had the same effect on her. "Really? Wow, thank you so much," she said and leaned into her cousin for a hug.

Kara bent her face over Sarah's shoulder so she was facing me. Her snake smile spread slowly across her face.

And the worry and guilt pumped right back inside me, where it threatened to burst.

I headed to the art room again at lunch. The wings would be dry enough to paint now; Ms. Adams, the art teacher, had helped me hang them from a rolling platform so I could reach every bit of them. When I arrived in the room, the wings were in the middle of the room. A boy I recognized from when Jackson, Sarah, Kara, and I were at the diner the other week was standing in front of them. He had been at the table with the girls, Ally and Lilith, who had talked with us. He had thick, dark hair that fell in an old-fashioned swoop across his forehead. He ran an outstretched finger across the layering of papier-mâché feathers on the wings. I noticed his fingernails were painted black.

Awkwardness bricked me in by the door. Was he pointing out all of the things that I could've done better on the wings? Or even worse, was he about to *compliment* them? Not sure what to do, I placed my bag on one of the back workstations and, of course, toppled a can of pencils and pens, which smacked the countertop and then rolled off the edge, clattering in a staccato across the floor.

The boy turned toward me. He smiled, the corners of his gray eyes crinkling. "Hey," he said. "I'm here to help the back-stage crew with the talent show prep and stopped by to say hi to Ms. Adams. Is she here?"

I shook my head, for some reason unable to form words. I gathered up the pens and pencils in a pile and he bent to pick up the can.

"My name's Jason," he said and held out his hand. I grabbed to shake it, only too late realizing he was just handing me the can. I shook the can. I shook the can like it was his hand. Jason laughed.

"I'm Pipi," I managed, only I pronounced it wrong. Yep. Told the hot high school boy that my name was PeePee.

"What's that?" he said.

I managed to squeak out, "Pipi. I'm Pipi McGee."

"You wouldn't happen to know who made these wings, would you?" he asked.

"Me did. It was me," I babbled. "I made them."

He smiled again. "Wicked. Love the layering. I work more with sketching, but paper craft is awesome. I love that they have movement. Like, I don't know if they're about to sweep out or tuck back in. Was it tricky?"

I shoved the pens and pencils into the can. "A little," I said. Talk about me? I was ridiculous. Talk about one of my projects? Suddenly, my tongue worked and I could actually speak sentences again. "Newspaper's a good place to start. You just have to make sure the glue consistency is right. Perfectly smooth."

Soon I was showing him how I had crafted the wings, which were the length of my arms and layered to resemble feathers. "I thought I was going to paint them today, but now? I don't think they're big enough."

"Yeah," said Jason, stretching out the word. "Make them huge."

"I could show you how to mix up the plaster."

"Sweet," Jason said and pushed up his sleeves.

With both of us working, by the end of lunch period the wings almost touched the ground. Maybe I'd paint them Monday.

"Well, it was awesome meeting you, Pipi McGee, even though I totally missed the talent show crew." He glanced again at the wings, nodding to them with his chin. "It's kind of cool with just the plaster and the newspaper. All those stories running up and down the wings. How are you going to paint them?"

I shrugged. "I'm not sure yet."

"You'll think of something." He glanced around the empty art room. The hallways were buzzing as lunch ended and students headed to lockers or classrooms. He hesitated and then said, "You know it gets easier, right? I mean, high school isn't always *fun,* but it's not middle school."

For a second my eyes filled. "That obvious?" I said. "That I don't have friends, I mean."

He grinned. "We can sort of spot our own, I guess. I'll look for you next year. There's a group—a club—of us."

"I'd like that," I said, smiling for what felt like the first time in weeks.

"Cool," he said. "We watch out for each other. Everyone else, too." He squinted like he was picturing his words before he said them. "I guess technically Principal Hardy calls it an anti-bullying group, but really we're just looking for people who aren't jerks to other people."

"Oh," I said. *Whoosh.* Good feeling gone. "Not sure you'll want me around then."

Jason paused, waiting for me to continue.

I shrugged. "I tried to get back at some people. But, now? I'm doing the kind of stuff that they did." I worried he'd ask me what I'd done. I was even more worried that I'd tell him everything.

The bell rang.

Jason smiled. "So, stop. Stop being a jerk." He laughed, but his eyes got squinty again and I knew he wasn't thinking of me. "It's easier than you think."

I had just enough time after school to shower and put on clean clothes (I wasn't sure what people wore to open mic, but black seemed like the best option, so I put on a black dress and black chucks). When Sarah arrived, I made us sandwiches from the chicken salad Mom had bought earlier that week. I had been so caught up in crafting the wings at lunch that I barely ate. Plus, having a mouthful of chicken salad kept me from saying the wrong thing to Sarah. Things such as, "I accidentally-on-purpose told Kara about the open mic night and I'm scared she's going to show up, and not just because—and I don't know when this happened—you're literally my only friend right now, and I don't want to ruin this thing for you, even if I don't quite understand it."

But, of course, I didn't say any of that, just crammed the sandwich in my mouth.

Luckily, Sarah didn't seem to notice my stress eating. She nibbled at her fingernails as she thumbed through the poem she had on her phone. Her hair was in its usual pigtail braids and her face was shining. She was so excited she practically vibrated.

A few minutes later, Jackson's father picked us up in his minivan, and we were on our way. Jackson read snippets of different poems the whole drive, so no one noticed when I didn't speak, though Mr. Thorpe did make eye contact with me once in the rearview mirror. He winced as Jackson rhymed "realize it" with "Cheez-It."

"So, you guys are done with this poetry thing after this, right? All out of your systems, on to the next hobby?" he said kind of hopefully.

"Poetry is life, Pop," Jackson said. "Poetry . . . pop . . ." He went back to scribbling in his notebook.

Sarah sat next to me, thumbing down her poem with one hand and chewing on her nails with the other. Without thinking, I reached out and squeezed her arm. She flashed me a quick smile. "I'm being silly," she said. "It's just a poem, right? And maybe I won't even perform it."

I smiled back at her. "No, it's not silly at all."

She squeezed my hand. "I knew you'd understand, Pipi. I mean, I really admire you."

"Me?" I blinked. "Why?"

"I'm scared about how strangers—people I never have to see again if I don't want to—are going to think of me after I read this poem. But, you? I mean, even after what happened in seventh grade, you just came back to school. And earlier, after the . . ." Her pretty face twisted and she muffled a gag. "You know." She motioned throwing up with her hand. "You just kept right on going. I'd look over in the cafeteria and you'd be laughing so hard with Tasha. And I mean, Ricky. He's been in love with you forever."

I pulled back my arm. "What are you talking about?"

Sarah bit her lip. "I'm saying this all wrong, I think. I just mean, you're really brave. My mom calls it grit. She says I don't have enough of it, that it's why I shouldn't stand up to Kara—that I wouldn't be able to handle the fallout." Her voice dipped so only I could hear it. "Mom says the only people we can trust are family. Kara says to be quiet and just follow her lead."

"I know she's your cousin, but Kara can be really—"

"Awful. I know," Sarah said. "But it's just how her family is."

"Miss Gonzalez says hurt people hurt people," I said. I thought about Frau Jacobs. "Did . . . did something happen to Kara? I mean, to hurt her?"

She twisted her fingers, now that the fingernails were gnawed off. She smiled, but it wasn't a real Sarah smile. More like a smirk. "I used to wonder that, too." She shook her head. "But it's like there are two types of people in my family—bull-dozers and wallflowers."

"You're hardly a wallflower. Everyone knows you. Everyone likes you."

Sarah's response was so low I had to lean toward her to hear it. "They know me because Kara makes sure everyone knows us. They like me because I'm nicer than her. Without her? I'd be like . . . I'd be . . ."

She didn't have to finish. I knew what she was too polite to say. She'd be just like me.

"Kara's like her brother and her mom. They want to be in the middle of everything. If you're on their side, you can be there, too. If you're not? Then they'll knock you over so hard you can't get back up again. Mom says it's better to stay on their side. This thing tonight? The open mic? It's the first thing I've ever done without Kara weighing in on it. It's the first thing that's just mine. Kara would be furious if she found out."

I swallowed, the chicken salad sandwich threatening to come back up my throat. I didn't want to hear this. "Kara's practically your sister. I mean, she'd get over it, right? And it's not like you're doing anything *wrong*. You're just doing something without her. She couldn't be angry with you over that!"

"Have you met Kara? Of course, she'd be angry," Sarah said. "And any fight I have with her would also be between Aunt Estelle and Mom, too. You know, bulldozer/wallflower. I mean, even when it's pretty clear that what her kids did was wrong, Aunt Estelle still figures out how to make *them* the victims. That's what happened with Max."

"I remember hearing about how he got suspended—for the locker thing. Where he vandalized a boy's locker for being gay," I said. "Eliza told me he was mean to a lot of people."

"Aunt Estelle tried to justify that. Can you imagine?" Sarah's face flushed red. "Even knowing . . ."

"That's awful," I whispered back, feeling cold.

Sarah breathed out like she had been underwater.

"Sarah, I have to tell you something," I blurted. I had to let her know that Kara might show up to the open mic.

"I shouldn't have told you all of that," Sarah said at the same time. "It's family stuff, and I shouldn't have said it. Family comes first."

Eliza popped into my head. *Sarah's right,* I told myself. *Family comes first.* And if Sarah really believed that, she'd know that I *had* to tell Kara she'd be at the open mic night so I could protect my family. "Just remember," I whispered, "Kara is the one who is wrong here. Not you."

"Forget everything I said. I'm not making sense," Sarah continued. "I think I'm just so super nervous and it's blocking my filter or something."

"I won't tell anyone," I said. *Family comes first,* I repeated to myself again. But my stomach boiled. "I need to tell you—"

"Thanks." She breathed out in relief. "I knew I could trust you."

Just then Mr. Thorpe pulled into a parking spot. All around us, people were streaming into the bookstore for the open mic. I scanned them for Kara. I didn't see her anywhere.

What if Kara didn't show up? Then telling Sarah I had given Kara the heads-up about the open mic would solve nothing. It'd just ruin Sarah's night by making her worried. She probably wouldn't perform, she definitely would never trust me again, and what good would that do? *Except maybe get Eliza fired when Kara found out I double-crossed her,* my brain answered.

Honestly, the best thing to do was to stay quiet. *If* I spotted Kara, then I'd tell Sarah. Honestly, everything was going to be fine.

Chapter Twenty-Six

I had been in the JV Bookstore a few times—it was the kind of place where the workers noticed what kind of book you were reading and brought over a couple others that were just as great. It was in the arts district of the city, one of the old row houses lined up on a road with wide sidewalks and old-fashioned lamp-posts that were beginning to flicker to life. Inside, the store's decor was crisp and white with graphic artwork on the walls, dark wood beams across the ceiling, and an all-glass storefront.

That all-glass front was what I was counting on. I'd sit in the back of the room and watch the window. If Kara came toward the doors, I'd spot her and somehow signal to Sarah. But, honestly, I doubted she'd even show. I mean, I told her how important this was to Sarah. I was sure she'd be respectful.

But when we walked in, the shop owners directed us to the back of the bookstore, where there was a narrow staircase leading up to the attic space. Here the walls were faded red brick and the ceiling peaked with wooden planks and crisscrossing beams. There were a couple of windows and a skylight. Strings of yellow lights—the kind usually hanging over outdoor cafes—provided the only light aside from some shaded lamps plugged in at the corners. At the front of the room, there was a spotlight on a wooden stool and a microphone stand. All around it, seating formed a horseshoe. The seating varied; some looked like kitchen chairs, and others were cushioned benches. In one corner, there was an overstuffed, scratched-up leather loveseat.

People wandered around, finding seats. Most of them obviously knew each other from previous open mics—a few even said hello to Sarah or flashed her the thumbs-up. "I can't believe they remember me," she whispered. I squeezed her arm. Jackson moved up the small aisle in the middle, choosing a chair two rows back and motioning to us to sit beside him.

"Are you guys sure you don't want to sit in the back? So we can see everything?" I asked them.

"No, these seats are great!" Sarah chirped.

It'll be fine, my brain supplied. *Just pivot in your seat a little.*

Soft music started playing and I looked forward to see a white man, maybe in his mid-twenties, strumming an acoustic guitar. He was wearing jeans and a flannel shirt, his long hair pulled back at the base of his neck. After a few moments, a black girl moved forward to stand just beside him. She also was in her twenties, I guessed. She wore a magenta, form-fitting silk dress and matching lipstick, her polished look contrasting with the man's casual appearance. He smiled at her, and she smiled back, nodding softly as he strummed a melody I didn't recognize. Soon she was humming, and then singing harmony.

After a couple of minutes, he stood and bowed, and she did, too, as people snapped their fingers or clapped. Then they shook hands.

"Do you think they knew each other?" I asked Sarah.

She shook her head. "I told you, this place is magical."

As the chairs filled, I believed her. I had never seen so many different and diverse people in one space.

An old woman with long, gray hair and a flowing dress sat down behind us. Next to her was a younger woman who looked like any of the moms in the school pickup line at the end of the day, wearing what my mom called a "statement" necklace, a turtleneck, and slacks. A group of older teenagers showed up, and then a cluster of college-aged kids joined. An Indian couple took the bench in front of us, holding hands and whispering jokes into each other's ears. We were among the youngest, although the beautiful woman standing by the door greeting people had a small son with a mop of dark hair with her; he sat at her feet reading a book that seemed too thick for someone his size, while his mother's laughter filled the room. At the front of the room, another woman with long, wavy hair and a smile that made me smile back even though it wasn't directed to me set up a podium next to the stool. She hugged a blond teenager in a cheerleading uniform, who took a seat on the stool and began singing a solo of a popular song, somehow making it dreamy instead.

After a few minutes, the woman who had been greeting people at the door moved to stand in front of the microphone.

"Welcome to the JV Open Mic!" She introduced herself as a poet and professor at the local university, then laid out some rules for the event. Each speaker would have no more than ten minutes to perform and each audience member would allow that person to be heard. "Today we've had a request to skip the live stream and keep things a bit more intimate, so know that if you speak your truth, it stays in this room." Then she welcomed the other woman—the one with long hair and a wide smile—to the floor. The woman moved the stool to the side and stood, her back arched with a confidence that reminded me of Piper. She warmed us all with her smile.

I kind of understood what spoken word poetry was from Sarah and the videos she had shared with me, but being there, listening to this poet, was so different. The words seemed at times to begin at her toes, sprouting through her to blossom in front of us. She spoke about the power of names, the ones we are given and the ones we assume. I couldn't look away for a moment as she spoke about becoming herself, fully and truly, and when she talked about the sadness that colored her joy, I ached, feeling it in a way that words alone never had been able to do.

"Wow," I whispered to Sarah. "Is everyone like that?"

She smiled and shook her head. "No one is like that. But I think we all try to be."

A girl only a couple years older than us went next. Small and pale, she used a white cane as she strode purposefully forward and then lowered the microphone. The font on her printed pages was large and dark enough for me to see a couple rows back as she organized them on the podium. "I'm going to tell you about the time my family surprised us with a vacation," she said with a wide smile that quickly faded—although everyone else laughed—as she added, "to Cleveland. In the winter." Her poetry shifted from stand-up comedienne funny to achingly poignant and then back to humor.

"Wow," I whispered again to Sarah, who mouthed, *"Right?"*

Next a middle-aged white man took a seat on the stool. He held a lined piece of notebook paper in his hands and read in a soft, lilting voice a story about a dragon climbing up a mountain from a cave. The paper in his hands shook just a little, enough to show me his bravery. The applause when he finished was just as strong.

A tall black man wearing a hoodie from the local university smiled over his shoulder at the hostess as he walked up the aisle to perch on the edge of the stool. "I wrote this on the way here," he said, and then softly began a poem that quickly gathered steam until my heart pulsed with his words.

On and on people took the stage, being beckoned by the woman who had greeted most of the people at the door. She was as young or younger than most of the audience, but somehow felt like the mom, if that made any sense. Maybe it was the way she threw open her arms to welcome every speaker.

Jackson went next, with Sarah and I clapping so hard that my palms were red as he took the stage.

"Uh, I just started writing poetry," he said. The spotlight added a halo around his head and he grinned, flashing his dimple. I waited for the usual rush of heart fluttering that always hit me when Jackson smiled. Instead, I just felt happy—happy for my friend. *Guess we're not crushing on Jackson anymore,* my brain pondered. And then, in a totally uncalled-for move, it flashed a picture of Ricky in my mind. Not fair, Brain. Not fair.

Jackson gave his "sitting on a sphere of air" poem, which actually did sound a lot more philosophical when he wasn't literally sitting on a ball of air. When his ten minutes were up, the hostess walked to the stage while clapping. She beamed at him and told him she was so proud and so excited to see how he would continue to develop his ideas. Jackson grinned and bowed.

"Next up," she said after a few performers, some of whom took up the full ten minutes and some who only spoke for a minute, "is Harp, who's here with their partner Lila. Sometime soon Harp and I will convince Lila to share her story, but for now, join me in celebrating Harp!"

One half of the couple in front of us went up to the stage.

Harp smiled into the audience like a kid in front of birthday cake. They spoke about family and how it meant love and nothing else. All around me, people snapped instead of clapping so as not to interrupt their performance. While they spoke about falling in love, tears streamed down Lila's smiling face. A lump formed in my throat as I thought about my family and how lucky I was that love was just a given.

"Anyone else?" the woman asked when applause for Harp dampened. I glanced around, saw no one new, and nudged Sarah, who nodded and stood. Her face glowed. *She* glowed. Sarah had always, always been *the* pretty girl in our grade, but seeing her glide toward the front of the room, she seemed different. *This place is magic,* she had said when we arrived. She was right, and she was transformed. She wasn't pretty; she was powerful.

I bit my lip watching her take her seat on the stool. She held her phone in her hand but barely glanced at it. "So, this is the first time I've done this," she said. Most of the people snapped and her smile stretched. "But I feel like I've been writing this poem forever. Which I know, being that I'm thirteen, doesn't sound like a long time." Laughter trickled through the room. "I'm also super grateful for the spotlight because I can't see any of you right now." Now the laughter was even stronger.

"So, here's my poem. It's titled 'Confusion.'" She cleared her throat. After a big breath, she recited,

> *When I told them, they said,*
> *"Oh, you're just confused.*
> *You just need time."*
> *But I've been listening to the clock,*
> *I've watched its hands*
> *sweep across its blank face only to repeat*
> > *itself and*
> *I* am not confused.
> *Maybe others will say I don't know,*

That I'm too young to know my heart
or to understand how this works,
But I live in this body.
I feel this heart pump
And each pulse tells me that
I am not confused.

Sarah paused. A tear glinted on her cheek, even though her face still glowed. In front of me, Lila and Harp snapped, joining a chorus all around us. I glanced at Jackson and he was smiling so big, nodding with each word that Sarah spoke. I felt the same smile on my face. I realized I had always seen her as one half of the Sarah-Kara whole. But on her own, she didn't seem tiny and fragile. On her own, up there on the stage, she was powerful. She was strong. I wanted that bravery for myself. Sarah wasn't as polished or as powerful as the first speaker—yet. But she looked so at home, speaking her truth. She smiled and finished the poem.

I will make my words simple.
I will make them direct.
I will make them clear.
I will say that I know what I know
And I know that love is what matters.
This body, this heart, this girl
standing in front of you?
That is what matters.
And she's telling you her truth.
How could that ever
Be confusing?

For a moment no one spoke or moved. Sarah cleared her throat again, took another deep breath, and smiled out to us. I jumped to my feet, clapping so hard and smiling so much I thought both my face and hands would crack. I wished I could do one of those awesome whistles with two fingers, but luckily Jackson could, and did.

"So, yeah," Sarah said as audience members slowly settled back into their seats. "I've been here before and I just listened. And I caught a couple live streams, too. Really glad there wasn't one tonight," she said to more laughter. "My two best friends— they're here with me—know I'm gay." Something in my chest twisted, a knife slipping between my ribs, at Sarah calling me her best friend. *If she knew you risked this moment for her . . .*

Sarah continued, "My family knows, too, but ignores it. But I'm tired of ignoring who I am." Snaps broke out around the room. Sarah nodded. "I thought if I could be brave here in front of all of you, I could carry that with me, wherever I go." More snaps. She took a deep breath. "Next year, I'll be in high school, and we have to do a service project. I'm going to make a gay services alliance club." Sarah's chin lifted. "Maybe I'll be the only member, but I won't be alone."

Jackson whistled again and I jumped to my feet to clap for her. I was proud of my brave friend.

Sarah stood. The hostess gave her a huge hug and whispered something in her ear before announcing a small intermission before more performers would take the stage. As Sarah walked back to our seats, Harp and Lila stood, both clapping for her. She stood at the end of our row of chairs as Jackson hugged her and then me.

When my arms dropped, she moved to slide in front of me to her seat. Sarah's eyes widened and a small noise escaped her throat. And I knew before I even turned around what—or rather, who—she saw. I had been so caught up in Sarah's performance, so sure I was in the clear, I had forgotten to look for Kara.

"I'm so sorry, Sarah," I said, grabbing each of her arms in my hands. "I'm so sorry."

But Sarah didn't look at me. I'm not sure she even heard me, though Jackson did.

"What did you do, Pipi?" The disgust was plain in his voice.

Soon Kara was standing beside us. "Well," she said, "when Pipi gave me the heads-up that you'd be here, I never thought you'd be planning something like this. A club, really? That is so not going to happen. Everyone at school is going to *know*, Sarah! How could you be so selfish! People are going to *talk*."

Around us, the people attending the open mic quieted. The happy murmuring stopped, and the air suddenly felt thick.

Kara's mom sauntered down the aisle, her arms crossed. "It's time for us to leave. Come with me," she said to Kara. "You, too, Sarah. Let's go home."

Sarah shook her head. Jackson piped in, "My dad's going to give us a ride home."

Kara's mom lifted her chin. She acted like she didn't even see Jackson. "*Now,* Sarah." Again, Sarah shook her head. Estelle leaned in, her mouth an inch from Sarah's ear. "It's bad enough that you air your dirty laundry in public. Do *not* make a scene."

"Dirty laundry?" Harp said. "Are you serious?" Lila motioned for them to step back, but Harp stayed put.

Estelle acted like she didn't hear them.

"If you need a ride home, kid, we can help," Harp said to Sarah.

Estelle straightened. "My niece will be coming home with me."

"No," Sarah said. Her voice was quiet but firm. "I'm going home with Jackson. Please leave."

Kara sighed. "Are you serious?" Sarah stared down at her feet. I watched as a tear fell from her face and hit the floor.

After what felt like forever but was probably just a few seconds, Estelle turned and marched out of the room with Kara following. She held her cell phone to her ear.

"I'm so sorry!" I gushed to Sarah. "I didn't know what you were going to say! I didn't know for sure they'd be here."

Sarah's eyes narrowed. "I told you, though. I told you how much this"—she gestured around the room, now emptying of people—"meant to me. I *told* you."

"I had to," I said. "You don't understand, if I didn't do what she wanted—"

Sarah held up her hand. "It doesn't matter, Pipi. Whatever

your reason, it doesn't matter. You took this moment from me, and I can't get it back."

"But it's not like they didn't already know! I mean the only new thing is the club and—"

Sarah ran to the bathroom in the back of the room. The hostess watched her and then glanced at us. Quickly, she followed Sarah.

"You don't get it," Harp said. "The 'coming out,' it never stops. It's all the time. And it sounds like Sarah's family didn't take it the way they should've. This was a chance to feel loved. To feel supported."

"I didn't know," I said, but Harp and Lila turned away. I pivoted to Jackson, pulling on his arm. "Listen," I said, "if you understood—"

"Save it, Pipi," Jackson said.

We rode home in silence. Jackson's dad said, "So, uh . . . the spoken word didn't go well, I take it."

Jackson stared out the window but said, "Mostly, it was awesome."

Sarah didn't look at me. Her cheeks were wet.

☑️ Chapter Twenty-Seven

I spent the rest of the weekend holding Myrtle the Turtle and wishing I could papier-mâché myself a shell. Every couple of hours, I checked my phone to see if anyone texted me. No one did.

I texted Tasha late Sunday night. *How are you?*

Almost immediately, I saw the three dots.

I added: *I messed up.*

The dots disappeared.

I called Sarah over and over, without a single response. After dozens of apologies, I added: *I messed up, but the club is a great idea. It's a really great idea.*

I couldn't get Harp's words out of my mind. I had stolen this from Sarah. Even worse? I had used her the same way I had been willing to use Eliza to get back at Kara. Just like Kara, I manipulated people to get what I wanted.

On Monday, I waited for Sarah at her bus line. She paused when she saw me and then turned her back to walk away.

"Wait!" I rushed behind her. "Sarah, wait, okay? Let me explain!"

Someone tapped my shoulder from behind. Kara, of course.

"And just what would you explain?" She crossed her arms.

"I'm going to tell her the truth." I backed away from Kara. "That if I didn't tell you about the open mic, you'd get Eliza fired."

"Which I'll *still* do unless you keep your mouth shut," Kara snapped. She fluffed her hair. "Besides, what do you care? You've been friends with Sarah for, what? A month? She's *my* cousin."

"You know that makes it a thousand times worse, don't you?" I said. "She loves you; you hurt her for no reason."

Kara shrugged. "She shouldn't have kept secrets from me."

"Sarah should've been able to talk to you when *she* wanted to."

"And who's to blame for that?" Kara raised a painted-on eyebrow.

"Both of us," I said.

"Whatever." Kara rolled her eyes. "Of course, Aunt Belle said it's all *just fine*. That Sarah can be *whoever she is everywhere she is*." She crossed her arms again. "Can you believe she actually kicked Mom out of the house? Mom was trying to protect her, to let her know what had happened and how starting a club like that would mean *everyone* would know and it'd affect Sarah *forever,* even if it turns out that she's just conf—"

"She *isn't* confused! Didn't you listen to anything she said?"

Kara rolled her eyes. "Aunt Belle kicked me and my mom out! Her own sister and niece!"

After two days of nonstop worrying, my face felt like it was splintering at the sudden grin that popped up on it. "I would've liked to have seen that."

Kara glared at me. Her nostrils flared for a second, and then it was like her face shifted into a stony smile. She linked her arm into mine and squeezed it against her side as I tried to shimmy it free. "You spent this whole year trying to get revenge on Sarah, Jackson, and me. Congratulations, you succeeded." She shrugged. "Now, let's stop talking about Sarah and start thinking about Frau Jacobs."

"I'm done," I snapped. "I gave you what you wanted for both of them. What you do now is up to you." I yanked my arm out of hers.

Kara moved so she stood in front of me, blocking my escape. The fake sugary smile vanished, and her arms crossed. "You want out? Fine. But you've got to stay out. Stay away from Sarah. Stay away from Jackson. Do that, and I won't bring up Eliza again."

"They hate me now," I said.

"Great. Keep it that way." Her snake smile stretched. "Now, if you're not going to help me with Frau Jacobs, get out of my way."

"Can't you just stop all of this? I mean, enough people have been hurt. Let's just move on."

347

"Move on?" Kara cocked an eyebrow.

"Yeah," I said. "Move on."

"Yeah, why don't you do that, Pipi McGee?"

"I will," I said, more than a little surprised at Kara's warm smile. "Can you? I mean, let this go with Frau? With me? I'm sorry, okay, if that's what it takes. I'm sorry."

"*Aww*. Thanks." Kara smiled. "You know, seeing Sarah on stage on Friday? It was really empowering. It's a shame that the school took that away from Frau Jacobs so many years ago." She shrugged. "I'm going to make sure she gets the welcome back to the stage that she deserves."

I stood in the hall, letting streams of students pass by me and waiting until the last possible moment to go into home-room. Kara practically sprinted down the hall ahead of me.

When I finally got to the classroom, Kara stood by Frau Jacobs. She had one earbud in her ear. The other was in Frau Jacobs's ear. Both of them swayed to the music.

Sarah sat in her usual seat, smiling at something the girl beside her was saying. She looked totally normal, like nothing in the world was bothering her. Jackson glanced my way, scowled, and turned around. Despite Kara's sneers about everyone finding out about Sarah's poem, I hadn't heard any rumors or whispers about her. I knew no one from the bookstore would repeat it, and besides, no one from school aside from Jackson, Kara, and me had been there.

Principal Hendricks came over the intercom with the

morning announcements and again talked about the talent show. "Don't forget, students and staff, today is the last day to sign up for this Friday's talent show! Sign-up sheet is outside the office."

Kara nudged Frau Jacobs, who blushed and waved her hand like she was brushing away a gnat. But when I swung by the office at the end of the day (to make sure my name was still next to Jackson's and Sarah's), Frau Jacobs's name was on the talent show sheet.

After school, Mom told me the basketball team had decided to stick with weight training and wouldn't need me to lead spin classes for them anymore. Mom scheduled me to instead lead for the Fab Over Fifty spin class. I was so not into it that one of the women threw her towel at me. "We're old, not dead," she snapped.

The next day, I told Coach that I didn't want to be team manager anymore. She nodded. "I don't know what's going on with you and the team, but maybe that would be for the best." And that's how I knew everyone was talking about me.

I didn't tell Mom or Dad I had quit. Instead, I spent the time I was supposed to be at practices in the art room, working on the wings. I listened to that opera, *Elektra*. The first time, I watched it on YouTube, taking in the subtitles. Then I just listened to the soundtrack.

On Tuesday and Thursday, Sarah somehow managed to

be on the other side of the kindergarten classroom the entire time we volunteered. Jackson shot me a look every once in a while, something between disgust and pity. On Thursday, as we waited for the bus to take us back to the high school, I confronted Sarah and Jackson.

"Look," I said. "I'm going to back out of the talent show tomorrow, okay? You guys can perform, but I'm going to—"

"No," Sarah said, even though Jackson had started to nudge her in the side. She shook her head at him and then looked at me with eyes so cold I could've mistaken her for Kara. "We're doing the show together. All three of us." Not meeting my eyes, she added, "Bring the wings you're working on. Jackson says they're awesome."

"Are you okay, Sarah?" I asked. "I mean, I know you got in that fight, but I see you with Kara at lunch, and if you need to talk or—"

Sarah glared at me. "Kara and I are fine." She smiled, but again, she looked just like her cousin. "We're fine, too, Pipi. I *want* you on that stage with me."

"I don't have to be there," I said. "I could bring the wings and not be there." But Sarah was already turning away.

"Are you sure you want to do this?" I heard Jackson ask her.

Sarah nodded. "She deserves it."

She is such a better person than you, my brain whispered, which of course made me feel even worse.

Ricky still sat next to me on the bus, but we didn't talk. His arm pressed against mine and it was all I could do not to lean into it.

A few of the sixth and seventh graders must not have gotten the text that I was back to being a social pariah, because kids still purposefully swatted at me or tugged on a piece of hair in the hall for luck. But by the middle of the week, that had mostly petered out as well.

In fact, by Thursday afternoon no one would even look at me. I wasn't a laughingstock anymore. I was invisible.

I had gone straight to the art room during lunch every day that week. Every day, I thought I'd finally paint the wings. But every day, they seemed too small. I added more, making them stretch just a little bit farther until they were so big the art teacher had to help me hang them from a rolling wardrobe hanger since the stand I had been using wasn't strong enough to keep them upright.

But you know what? They were beautiful. They were so beautiful.

"Are they done?" I turned to see Jason, the high school boy, as he popped his head in the art room on Thursday afternoon. "A club we started at the high school is going to expand here next year, so we were meeting with Principal Hendricks. Thought I'd check on the wings."

I shook my head. "Not done. Still a work in progress."

We both stared at the wings. He smiled. "Maybe that's the point."

On Friday, the day of the talent show, I stood in front of them. They were slightly bigger still.

"Well, the talent show's about to begin," I told the wings. "You're not finished. You're all out of proportion. And you've got nothing attached to you. Are you ready?"

The wings didn't answer.

I was prepping to roll the wings down to the stage when Jackson and Sarah showed up in the art room.

"Hey!" I rushed toward them. "You're here!"

Jackson just nodded. "Yeah," he said. "Figured you could use some help getting the wings backstage."

I had wrapped the wings in black fabric to protect them from any dings along the way. And, yeah, to keep them a surprise when they were rolled out onstage during our performance. I had texted both Jackson and Sarah last night: *Want to meet to rehearse before the show?* All over school that week, I had spotted kids working on their performances together—and I'd seen Jackson and Sarah together, of course—but no one was talking to me. Sarah had replied: *We each get five minutes. You, me, Jackson. You explain the wings, we'll read our poems. No rehearsal needed.*

I texted back. *Are you reading the same poem, Sarah? I hope so.*

Neither of them had replied. I wanted to ask again now; the squeaking wheels of the cart were the only sound between us. Jackson's lips moved silently as he rehearsed his poem, but Sarah was completely stone-faced. I wimped out and didn't ask.

Once we got backstage, I checked out the schedule of performers posted on a corkboard beside the curtain. There were four acts before Frau Jacobs performed, and then Jackson, Sarah, and I were last. A kid in sixth grade juggled red bouncy balls. A seventh-grade girl twirled in a pink leotard and matching cowgirl hat. A trio of girls in my grade worked on their dance steps. A sixth-grade math teacher smiled to himself, his shoulders shaking in silent laughter, as he flipped through notes on index cards.

Sarah grabbed the other end of the wardrobe roller from Jackson. Without meeting my eyes, she said, "We're going to enter from stage right with the wings. You enter stage left." She motioned across the stage. "The theater teacher said it'll be more dramatic that way."

I squinted across the stage. The curtain was down, but I could hear kids filing in. "Shouldn't we stick together?"

Sarah cocked her head to the side. "Are you calling me a liar now?"

"What? No, I just—"

"Go, Pipi," Jackson said. "The theater teacher sent another

person over there, too. She said entering from different sides ups the tension or something."

I paused, scanning both of their faces. "Are we okay? I mean, we haven't talked."

The theater teacher, wearing a big headset and holding a clipboard, clapped her hands and called for everyone to get to their spots. Sarah nodded toward the other side of the stage. I grabbed for the wardrobe.

"No," Sarah said. "We'll bring the wings out."

I squinted at her. "But they're my part of the performance."

"It takes two people to push them, and you're the only one over there," Sarah said. "Would you just go?"

I darted across the stage. My hands were sweaty and my stomach squiggly at the idea of everyone staring at my wings, but mostly my heart just thumped with worry at Sarah's fierce expression. Would she ever forgive me? Would I ever be able to explain to her why I told Kara about the open mic? Would she believe me that I didn't have a choice? I gulped away the guilt that insisted I *had* a choice. I could've told Sarah the truth.

I stepped up to the edge of the stage and peeked behind the drawn curtain. Kara was in the audience, flitting from row to row, whispering and laughing like a toxic butterfly. After she left, whoever she was talking with turned and talked to the person next to them, always laughing. The hair on my arms stood up and I shivered. What was she up to?

One by one, eighth-grade kids—the ones Kara had just talked to—trickled from the side of the auditorium toward the stage. A few seconds later, they went back, laughing and whispering to the people around them.

I spotted Principal Hendricks enter the auditorium, ushering families to the front two rows. Mom and Dad hadn't told me they were going to be here! Alec spotted me peeking and waved. He winked and pointed to me, which I didn't understand until I felt a little poke on the back of my thigh that made me jump into the air and squeal. I turned around to see Annie standing just behind me.

"Hey," she said.

"What are you doing back here?" I whispered.

Her eyes slid from side to side, then she said, "Spying."

"Well, you better get back to your seat. The talent show's going to start soon."

"What's an applause?" she asked.

"It means clapping."

"They're all going to clap," she said. "Clap and clap and clap. But not for you."

"Geez, thanks, Annie. That's super helpful encouragement," I said, ushering her back to the sidelines.

She blinked at me solemnly. "They're going to applause and applause."

"Yeah, I get that," I said.

Annie narrowed her eyes. She squeezed my hand. "It's

okay to be nervous. That's what Mom said on the first day of preschool."

I gave her a quick hug. "Try not to pee," she said and darted back along the sidelines. I peeked one more time to make sure Annie made it back to Mom. Tasha and Ricky were sitting together toward the back of the auditorium, Tasha leaning forward to talk with someone in the row ahead of her. My heart flopped again at the sight of them. Almost like she heard it, Tasha looked up toward the stage. She whispered something in Ricky's ear, and the two of them tried to push their way out of the row of people finding their seats. The teacher at the end of the row gestured for them to get back, but it looked like Tasha was arguing with him.

"All right, crew!" called the theater teacher from the middle of the stage. "Remember your schedule and your time to go on stage. When you're on deck and standing on the sidelines, know if you can see the audience, they can see you."

A few seconds later, Principal Hendricks welcomed everyone to the show. The juggler took to the stage, only dropping one thing. Unfortunately, it was a plate. A janitor went across the stage with a wide broom to sweep up shards.

What are we even doing here? Brain demanded. *Jackson and Sarah hate us. Kara is definitely up to something.*

The juggler left the stage to a surge of applause and the trio of dancers made their way out. The cowgirl hat tap dancer took her spot on deck. The juggler passed by me, wiping the sweat from his forehead and laughing. "That was amazing!" he said.

Maybe this *would* be amazing. Maybe letting me continue being part of the show was Sarah and Jackson's way of forgiving me for the open mic catastrophe.

Maybe Kara's plan for Frau was as simple as she had said—to give her another chance to be on stage.

Maybe this whole thing with Sarah and Kara—maybe even with the eyebrow prank—had shown her a lesson. Maybe Kara was turning over a new leaf.

And maybe you're a peacock and this is Mars.

Remember how I said I wasn't nervous? That was a lie. I couldn't seem to figure out what to do with my arms and legs. I looked around; Sarah and Jackson had said another performer would be on this side of the stage. Someone stepped out from the sidelines. Frau Jacobs.

Her usual smug smile was wiped from her face, and she seemed smaller, younger than I had ever seen her. "Nervous, Miss McGee?"

"I guess I am," I said, nerves making me blubber. Maybe the nerves were behind not feeling the usual rush of hate that happened when I saw Frau Jacobs. Then again, I hadn't felt that at all since I found out about her own humiliation when she had been a girl. "I'm, um, supposed to say something when my group comes out. I have five minutes and I thought I'd just, you know, come up with stuff. But now I'm kind of blanking."

"You're unprepared?" Frau Jacobs raised an eyebrow. "I thought preparation was a lesson I taught you well."

Okay, yeah. Some of that shame was rushing right back to its familiar corners.

"I had an unfortunate experience on stage once," she said. "It took forty years to get over."

"This is the worst pep talk in the history of pep talks," I said.

Frau Jacobs blinked. "I wasn't giving a pep talk," she said.

"I know," I replied.

She tugged at the hem of her shirt. She was wearing a pink blouse that buttoned to the neck. When she shifted, I saw a darker splotch at her armpits. "I don't know what I'm doing here." Her face twisted, the smugness gone. Her hands drifted to just under her face and her chest rose and fell with quick breaths.

"It's okay to be nervous," I whispered.

Frau Jacobs shook her head. Her voice trembled as she said, "Can you believe I once wanted to be on stage all of the time? I was going to travel the world."

"Oh," I murmured.

"What's done is done. That doesn't matter," Frau Jacobs said as though I had asked what had happened. "I hadn't prepared. I hadn't been ready to deal with the consequences of that lack of preparation or presentation." She turned and looked at me full on. "I've dedicated my life to making sure no other girls are so unprepared. As female people, we have certain concerns, certain considerations that we must keep in mind. When we don't, when we're unprepared, the consequences can be . . . painful. Being here, doing this again, I thought it might be a chance at . . ."

Both of us turned toward the stage at the sound of clapping. Frau Jacobs was up next. She clutched her stomach.

Something inside me tore, the edges as tattered as the ripped newsprint I had used to craft the wings. She wanted to be out there; I could tell. I remembered how Sarah had looked in that halo of light when she was at spoken word. Some people are meant to be on stage, and Frau Jacobs might be among those people.

But some people—ahem, Kara—only wanted to bring other people down. I wasn't sure what she had planned for Frau in encouraging her to perform, but I knew it wasn't good.

Principal Hendricks's voice echoed across us. "Next up, welcome Frau Jacobs, who will be singing an aria from the opera *Elektra!*"

I touched Frau Jacobs's hand. "You don't have to go. I mean, I'm sure you could next year . . ."

A small smile on her face, Frau Jacobs said, "I don't just sit and stare into the darkness."

"Before I die, I want to live," I whispered back.

A smile lit up her eyes. "You know *Elektra*?"

I swallowed. "I watched it on YouTube a few weeks ago, with subtitles. I've been listening to it, too, while I work on my wings."

"Your wings?" she asked, but then the applause began.

Frau Jacobs squared her shoulders, tugged on her shirt hem again, and strode purposefully toward the spotlight as the applause continued.

Chapter Twenty-Eight

They're going to applause and applause.

Annie's words came back to me as I listened to the audience welcome Frau Jacobs. She centered herself in the spotlight, again tugging on her shirt hem, and pulled in such a deep breath that her shoulders fell back and her back arched. Her face set and her eyes closed for a moment as she prepared to begin her aria.

But the clapping didn't pause.

I peeked behind the curtain. Mom, Dad, and Alec twisted in their seats to look out across the student section. So did most of the teachers, many of whom were calling on students to stop clapping. Annie sat up straight, staring toward where I was hidden.

Principal Hendricks stepped onto stage, a wobbly smile on her face. Over the ongoing applause, she leaned into the microphone and said, "What a warm reception! Now, let's allow Frau Jacobs to perform."

A lot of kids did stop clapping then, but many didn't. And those who didn't only seemed to clap louder. At the center of them, of course, was Kara, who slammed her hands together with a huge snake smile on her face. Just like the adults who were twisting in their seats to see why people were still clapping, so did the students. Soon, with wicked smiles, they also were clapping again. Laughter rippled across the auditorium, some kids clapping their hands in circles for a "round" of applause.

They're going to applause and applause.

One minute ticked into two, into five, into ten. Still the kids clapped. Principal Hendricks again called for everyone to stop. She directed teachers to remove rowdy students. Some of the louder clappers were pulled from their seats and ordered into the hall by red-faced teachers. For a moment, it was silent.

Frau Jacobs began the opening of the aria. Her hands went to her sides, dipping and rising as she began the monologue, singing out what I knew was Elektra's brother's name. She pulled out the word, "*Orestes,*" rolling the *r*.

No one spoke or moved. Frau Jacobs was *good.* Who knew such beauty could bloom from one word? She continued the monologue, and soon her hands swept up over her head as her voice peaked and poured across the auditorium.

Everyone clapped again, their hands smashing together in applause. But again, it didn't stop. The clapping rose and fell, rose and fell, as sections of the auditorium were swept up in it. It seemed like everyone in the student section was laughing, knocking into each other. The applause drowned Frau Jacobs's powerful voice, seemed to crowd out the lyrics. Soon her voice dropped and she stood there alone in the spotlight, her eyes wide and confused.

She tried again, holding up a hand to stop Principal Hendricks from again coming onto stage. Her shoulders squared and her chest rose as another song took shape in her throat. But there it stayed. Another snippet of *Elektra* lyrics played in my mind, one where Elektra's sister laments being a caged bird on a perch.

I glanced out at my family. Mom's eyes were filled with tears, her hand holding Annie's. Dad held his head in his hands. Alec sat straight in his chair, the set of his jaw the only indication of his anger. But, the students? Most of them weren't even looking at Frau Jacobs, as if what they were doing had nothing to do with her. They were too busy egging each other on, clapping in each other's faces and seeing who could whistle loudest.

Frau Jacobs's arms fell to her sides. Her eyes slid across the auditorium. Then, in a rush, she turned and ran backstage.

Frau Jacobs rushed to the little bathroom near me. I heard her crying.

Congratulations. Isn't this what you wanted? And then, jerk that it was, Brain supplied a memory—one of me on the first day of school, saying that so long as Kara, Sarah, and Frau Jacobs were crying in a bathroom, my revenge would be complete.

Hurt people hurt people. But when does it stop?

Principal Hendricks again strode out to the microphone. Her anger was fierce. "What has gotten into you all today? I am ashamed of your behavior!" Her lecture continued, but I barely heard it.

Because I was next. And, peeking out into the auditorium, I saw one face. Kara's.

She was smiling back at me.

"Now," Principal Hendricks said as quiet fell across the auditorium finally. Several more students had been pulled out of the auditorium by teachers. "We're going to have one more go at showing true Northbrook Middle School pride. I refuse to take a moment to shine from the three students who are about to take the stage, and I expect—no, I *demand*—that you show them the respect they deserve."

She forced one of those plasticky, not-going-to-budge-no-matter-what smiles and looked over at Sarah and Jackson, and then at me. She leaned back into the microphone and continued. "Now presenting Penelope McGee, Jackson Thorpe, and Sarah Trickle."

Sarah darted forward from the offstage wing. A few people in the audience hooted. She slipped a piece of paper into Principal Hendricks's hand and then rushed back to the side with Jackson. Principal Hendricks unfolded the paper, cleared her throat, and said, "The trio would like me to say they've been working on projects that reflect their truth."

Yes! Sarah was going to read her poem! I stepped forward feeling lighter than I had all week.

From the other side of the stage, Jackson and Sarah emerged, pushing the wardrobe with the wings. The big black blanket, now bunched at the sides, still covered the wings. I glanced again out at my family. Annie waved. Eliza opened a door in the back and glided down the side of the auditorium. She picked up Annie and slid into the seat with her on her lap.

Jackson looked at me and then back over at Sarah. She motioned for me to go to the microphone.

I took a deep breath and stepped toward it.

For a moment, all I saw was the bright spotlight. But then I started to make out faces. Tasha leaned forward on her seat, sitting on her hands and sucking on her bottom lip the way she does when she's nervous. Ricky, beside her, crossed his arms. He nodded at me and I breathed out. *Flutter, flutter, flutter* went silly Heart. *Not the time,* Brain ordered, on my side for once.

"So, I'm, um, Pipi McGee." I swallowed. "And, uh, all year so far, Sarah and Jackson and I have been working on creating a club. A poetry club. But I'm not a poet." I took another breath. "I'm an artist."

Got anything? I asked Brain. Brain supplied cricket noises.

On the offstage wing, Principal Hendricks motioned for me to continue, the slip of paper from Sarah still in her hand.

"Like she said, these projects reflect our truth. Who we really are," I said. "I made these wings." I half turned to the side. Jackson raised an eyebrow to Sarah, who nodded, and then they began to tug at the blanket. I turned forward again. "I guess it's sort of a poem. They show who I am, someone who wants to be more than . . ." I thought I saw a movement on the blackened side of the stage from which I had emerged. ". . . a caged bird on a perch. These wings are *me*."

I heard the swoop as the fabric hit the stage floor. Then a gasping of breath. I closed my eyes, knowing what they were seeing. Wings, as long as me, stretching slightly upward, about to take flight. The newsprint layered over and over, shining like pearls due to the plaster.

And yet, I heard laughter. "I haven't finished them yet," I said, my eyes taking in faces, like Tasha's and Ricky's, with wide eyes and open mouths, and others, like Patricia's and Wade's, covering their mouths with their hands and giggling. "They're a work in progress," I said, remembering the conversation with Jason. "But all the blank space, it's kind of, I don't know, the point? It's ready for me with whatever I figure out about myself."

More laughter trickled throughout. Mom stood, her hands covering her mouth. Alec reached out toward her. Eliza winced. Dad closed his eyes.

I heard a clatter behind me. Slowly I turned around.

Jackson and Sarah weren't on stage any more. Just my wings.

Scrawled across them, covering nearly every blank space, were words. *LIAR* was the biggest, written in thick red paint across the top. But all around them were more words, in different handwriting: *Selfish. Ugly. Dork. Freak. Virus. Nose picker. PeePee. Pathetic. Gross.*

There were more, covering every inch of my delicate wings. The wings dented in at the sides with the force people must've used to write on them. All the work I had done to make them bigger and bigger was just to provide a better canvas for everyone to mock me. Everyone in the class must've written why they hated me on the wings. Was that why Ricky had nodded? Not to encourage me but because he was, once again, in on it? Is that why Tasha tried to leave, so she could be first in line to write on my wings?

My heart thudded. *Run,* Brain ordered me. *Run, run, runrunrunrun.* And I nearly did. I almost ran offstage. But there was Frau Jacobs, half-hidden by the shadow. I turned back to my beautiful wings. *LIAR* screamed back at me.

"Enough," I said. In my mind, I had shouted it, but it came out as a whisper.

Principal Hendricks stepped onto the stage, but I shook my head at her. "Enough!" This time, I *had* yelled.

I looked out over the audience. Ricky stood, gripping the back of the seat ahead of him, his face set in anger. Next to him, Tasha held her hands to her face, tears streaming down her cheeks. There's no way they knew about this.

"I went into eighth grade with a list. A list of things that I was going to do to make up for problems that I couldn't shake.

Ones that trailed me since kindergarten. Such as, you know, drawing myself as bacon."

Someone in the audience, probably Wade, screamed, "With boobs!"

"With boobs," I agreed, and more people laughed. Amazingly, I even smiled. "And I thought to make up for that one, I needed to save other kids from being weirdos, the way I had been. To be more like the cool kids, you know, like . . ." I caught a glimpse of Kara, her snake smile a little smaller now. "I don't have to say their names. You know who they are. But you know what? The weirdo kids are having a lot more fun." Someone hooted in the audience. It was Jason, the high school kid. He saluted me, and I smiled.

"I worked through this list I made, trying to get revenge or redemption or whatever. And it worked," I said. "Everything I wanted to happen, happened. I scratched every single thing off my list. But here I am." I laughed. "And none of you want to be me right now.

"*Hurt people hurt people.* That's something I learned this year. And I hurt a lot of people. But sometimes people don't hurt others because they've been hurt. Sometimes they hurt other people because they're mean. They're simply mean." I met Kara's eyes full on, even as she glared back at me. "But here's what I learned: it doesn't matter."

I pulled in a bigger breath, squaring my shoulders. I yelled. "*It doesn't matter.* Enough!

"Enough of my body being a virus or a good luck charm. Enough of shame shirts and covering it up when *someone else* has a problem. *Enough!* I won't feel shame when my body acts like a body.

"Enough of making my embarrassment your entertainment."

A couple kids clapped at that, the loudest coming from Jason and his group of friends. One, a girl with spiky dark hair, jumped to her feet and raised her fist. A handsome black boy—I recognized him as last year's class president—stood beside her.

Some people still smiled behind their hands or whispered to each other. Kara rolled her eyes to the people around her. It didn't matter.

Like Sarah had said earlier in the year, something about having space to be heard matters. I wasn't running from it. I owned it.

I glared right at Kara. "I figured something out this year: most of the stuff I carried, the humiliation—it wasn't even about me. It was about you." I pointed out to Kara and then the rest of the audience. "It didn't matter who I was, so long as I wasn't you."

I glanced back at my wings. You know what? They were *still* beautiful. "Enough," I said again, and this time it wasn't a yell. "These wings? I worked hard on them. They aren't attached to anything until I make them that way. They're a work in progress."

I walked quickly to my wings. I reached toward them, ready to shred them in half. To destroy them. But instead, I just ran my hands down the sides. "Enough."

As I turned to go offstage, Frau Jacobs emerged, freezing me in place. She strode quickly across the stage. "No more," she said, but I think I was the only one who heard.

Then her chin popped up, and she took the microphone from my hand. The way she stood, positioned in front of them, it was like the wings were hers.

No one moved.

A few kids started whispering, but then something else happened. Frau Jacobs began singing. I knew which aria it was—Elektra's sister's monologue about desiring freedom from revenge, to live. It washed out over everyone like magic.

I walked across the stage and headed down the stairs.

Mom met me there. She wrapped me in her arms and Dad patted my back. Alec smiled at me. I nodded at him.

When Mom finally let me go, I stepped back to see Tasha standing behind her. I moved toward her, and she grabbed my hand and squeezed. Ricky stood on the other side, his arm close to mine.

"I'm sorry," I said to them both.

"Shut up," they said in unison.

I squeezed Tasha's hand and let my head fall against Ricky's shoulder. We're all works in progress, I guess.

As I left the auditorium, Kara strode over to me. She crossed her arms.

"This isn't over, PeePee McGee," she hissed. "I'm calling my mother. Do you want to be the one to tell Eliza she's fired or should I?" She held her phone in her hand.

"Tell my mom what?" Annie had been standing just behind Kara, quiet as a . . . well, as a spy.

"Yes," said Eliza, sliding down the row of seats toward us. "Tell me what?"

Kara's face flamed. Her chin popped up in the air. "I'm getting you fired." Her voice wobbled. "From Glitter."

"You can't," Eliza said. Not in a scared way, either. Just matter-of-fact.

"What?" Kara snapped.

"You can't fire me from Glitter. I own it."

Kara and I both said "What?" this time. It echoed a little, which I was pretty sure was from Mom, Dad, and Alec, all of whom surrounded us.

Eliza smiled. "The money from Mom and Alec? I used it to buy out the shop. It's mine." She grinned at Annie. "It's ours."

"I want to rename it," Annie said.

"Whatever," Kara snapped. "Maybe I can't get Eliza fired, but the damage is already done. Threatening to destroy Eliza got you to turn on Sarah, and she's *never* going to stop hating you." She shrugged. "I still won." Kara whipped around, right into Sarah.

"You threatened Pipi? To get at me?" Sarah's face was white with shock.

Kara groaned and passed by her. Sarah stared at me. After a second or two, the hurt on her face dissolved. "I'm sure she didn't mean it the way you took it," she said. "I mean, in her heart, she probably just wanted to know so she could help me."

I didn't say anything to Sarah. We both knew that wasn't true.

Sarah's eyes stayed on the wings. "Enough," she said softly. Then she shook her head. "Forget that. I'm done apologizing for her."

I stepped closer to Sarah. "I'm sorry. I used you."

"Why didn't you tell me the truth?" Sarah said. "I mean, I thought we . . . I thought we were friends."

"I'm sorry," I mumbled.

Sarah nodded. She looked up at the wings. "Me too," she said.

I turned toward them, still encircled by a spotlight. "It's okay. They're still beautiful."

Sarah smiled, staring up at them. "Yeah, they are."

Jason and the other high school kids were by the back of the auditorium where Kara had tried to disappear. They were handing out fliers for something. I picked one off the ground. "JOIN THE RECKLESS CLUB" was printed across the top.

One of the high schoolers, the girl with spiky hair, leaned

into Kara as she passed and hissed like a cat. Kara jumped and backed up. "Stop scaring the newbies, Rex," the boy she stood next to said. He grinned, showing a deep dimple.

Rex smiled back, then met my eyes and nodded.

"Wait. We should talk about this," Dad said, drawing my attention back to my family. Dad whipped Annie up into the air, blowing on her belly and making her giggle. "Your mom, the businesswoman!"

Mom cried happy tears, hugging Eliza, and Alec shook her hand. "It has an apartment over it, too," Eliza said. "So, Annie and I . . ."

"I get a new room! And it has three windows!" Annie chirped.

"You knew about this?" Mom said.

"I know lots," Annie said. She turned back to her mom. "But about the name . . ."

Eliza took Annie from Dad's arms. She looked at me. "How about Wings?"

Chapter Twenty-Nine

I knew this year would be different.

I was heading into the second half of eighth grade older, wiser, and maybe even kinder.

After the talent show, everyone talked about the Work in Progress Wings for a few weeks. I even worked it out with Principal Hendricks to keep them in the lobby of the school with some paint pens so people could paint over the words if they wanted to. But, eventually, that meant people dented the edges or wrote mean stuff on them and otherwise acted like middle schoolers.

Frau Jacobs was the biggest change. Once Mr. Harper returned for the second half of the year, baking champion and new celebrity, she resigned. She joined a local theater company. Her first show was going to be this weekend. I saw a poster at the library—Frau Jacobs in a costume with shoulder cutouts! Ricky, Tasha, and I were going to go. Dad, too.

I wasn't the little lamb I had been at the beginning of the year. Only a few weeks had passed, and yet I felt pretty certain I'd never go back to my third stall bathroom office to wallow. I matured. I was even, right this moment, taking my first chemistry lab. I took my seat at the long black table and listened as the teacher gave instructions for the Bunsen burners in front of us. Was I being too poetic again to say I felt like I was ready to turn those old wings to ash? *Yes. That's Jackson Thorpe–level poetry.* Thanks, Brain. Keep it real.

I thought ahead to high school, just a few months down the line. I wouldn't be going to it scared or embarrassed. I already had the backing of Jason and the rest of the Reckless Club. I was a member of another club, too. Sarah decided not to wait until high school to start the gay alliance club. For a few weeks after she started the club and came out at school, loads of people whispered about it. Some were jerks. But her friends shut them down every time, especially Jackson.

Sarah, Jackson, and I met at the JV Bookstore once a month for open mic. We recently started to get coffee afterward. Sarah was meant to be on stage, but Jackson stopped performing. He was into parkour now.

As for Kara? I had no idea. And that felt pretty great, too. I did notice she sat with Wade at lunch now instead of Sarah.

Yep, this new year was different.

My life would no longer be marked by humiliations. Just works in progress.

I leaned forward to turn up my burner, one of my curls swinging forward.

Huh. It was almost like those wings really were burning. I smelled them singeing away.

"Look out!" Becky, my lab partner, yelped. I looked up to see Mr. Albert, my new chemistry lab teacher, hurdle the lab table like it was a pommel horse, slide across the top, whip up a fire extinguisher like Hawkeye would an arrow, and blast away. My face.

"Your hair was on fire!" Mr. Albert said. "Are you okay, Penelope?"

I wiped the foam from my face and let it splatter to the ground.

"It's Pipi," I said. "Pipi McGee."

ACKNOWLEDGMENTS

Mortifying middle school moments. We all have them.

Thank you to my friends and family for answering the call to share their humiliations, which included a lot of eyebrow losses, mistaken crushes, and digestive issues. This book benefited from every one of them, though I can't say poor Pipi herself did.

Nicole Resciniti, who championed Pipi from the moment I mentioned her—it's an honor to be your client and a blessing to be your friend. Julie Matysik, my amazing editor and treasured friend, I can't say enough how much I love working with you. Let's never stop! Running Press publicity manager Valerie Howlett, I'm so grateful for your drive, your insight, your incredible attention to detail, and, most importantly, your heart.

Thank you to the entire Running Press team, including cover and interior designer Frances Soo Ping Chow, project manager Amber Morris, copy editor Christina Palaia, director of marketing and publicity Jessica Schmidt, and publisher Kristin Kiser. Thank you to Billy Yong for creating such a spot-on Pipi and gorgeous cover.

Much love to Jon, Emma, and Ben, and my family and friends. I owe so many of you a slice of pie (which reminds me—Kari, there are a few more places in Texas to scout out).

Luke Shaw, thank you for sharing insight about dyslexia. Kirsten Shaw, thank you for being an inspiring teacher and an amazing friend who makes me laugh even when I'm trying hard to wallow.

To Jacqueline Welsh and Veda Leone, who welcomed me and my daughter to share a sacred space of storytelling, I'm forever grateful.

And, finally, to a certain middle school teacher who turned her back to a young girl in white jeans with her arm stretched in the air and panic in her eyes so you could finish a lesson uninterrupted. I'd like to say I forgive you. But I'm still working on it.

Also available from Beth Vrabel and Running Press Kids

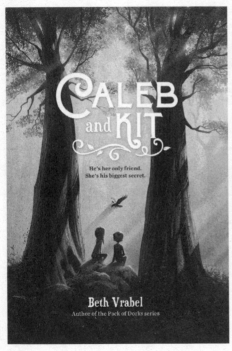

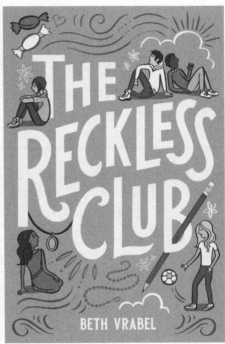

Available wherever books are sold!